Silent Samaritan

James Tucker

Copyright © James Tucker, 2012

Without limiting the rights under copyright reserved above, no part of this publication may be reproduced, stored in or introduced into a retrieval system, or transmitted, in any form, or by any means, (electronic, mechanical, photocopying, recording or otherwise) without the prior written permission of the copyright owner.

Publisher's Note:

This is a work of fiction. Names, characters, places, and incidents either are the product of the author's imagination or are used fictitiously, and any resemblance to actual persons, living or dead, events, or locales, is entirely coincidental.

ISBN-13: 978-1479162628
ISBN-10: 1479162620

For my wonderful family: Kim, Scott, Brad, Peter, Micaela and Kane

Contents

Chapter 1 1
Chapter 2 12
Chapter 3 33
Chapter 4 41
Chapter 5 53
Chapter 6 60
Chapter 7 69
Chapter 8 83
Chapter 9 96
Chapter 10 107
Chapter 11 125
Chapter 12 133
Chapter 13 143
Chapter 14 154
Chapter 15 166
Chapter 16 181
Chapter 17 186
Chapter 18 201
Chapter 19 209
Chapter 20 219
Chapter 21 225
Chapter 22 236
Chapter 23 250
Chapter 24 260

Chapter 25 271
Chapter 26 288
Chapter 27 297
Chapter 28 307
Chapter 29 326
Chapter 30 337
Chapter 31 351
Chapter 32 368
Chapter 33 376
Epilogue 388

1

"We better do a quick drive-by, make sure he's in place." Mike Dombroski twisted the key in the ignition and the Chevy groaned. A sharp jab to the knob on the radio and right away there was the familiar twang of a country-western guitar. "Enough with the Kenny Chesney for Chrissake. Gimme Toby Keith." He sounded pissed and smacked his hand on the dashboard right above the radio.

Manny Romero was staring straight ahead through the filthy windshield into the night, fingering his gold cross through the thin material of his dress shirt, the one with the flyaway collar and an unusual pattern that looked like scribbles. Looking left, he saw Mike staring at his chest and shaking his head. "What?" he said.

"Don't go getting all religious on me, altar boy." Mike crossed himself then gave Manny the finger. "You got a job to do." The Chevy started down the dark street.

"Screw you. The Lord is my shepherd. He guideth me."

"Sonny know you're a religious freak?" Mike chuckled.

"Watch it," Manny said, changing tone, sounding serious. When Mike let it drop he said, "So Sonny paid for all three?"

Mike glanced at Manny and nodded, one hand on the wheel, now leaning back, looking cool and relaxed. "Said the less we met the better." He was a cowboy, long hair over the collar of a short leather jacket the color of an old saddle. And he had a mustache, a thick one that curled around his lip and almost snuck into his mouth. The chicks loved the way it tickled. "Had me come out to this fancy gym that smelled too pretty to get a good workout, know what I mean? Sonny's on the StairMaster, towel around the neck, working the legs. He leans over and whispers: Charlie Hawk, Seymour Rosen, and Alec Fortune."

Manny turned his head sharply to look at Mike in the dark. "Alec Fortune?"

"You heard me, buddy boy."

"Oh my God, what'd you say?"

"I went, 'Alec Fortune, Jesus fuckin' Christ.'"

"What'd he say?"

"'Hey, watch your language.' Then he kept on climbing, made me stand there and watch him a couple minutes. Then he goes, 'You're not up to the job, I got a guy in Scranton who is.'"

Manny swiped his hand across his forehead. "So then what?"

"I said no problem. What the fuck you think I'm gonna say?"

"Jee-sus." Manny fingered the cross some more.

Mike said, "I sure as shit don't want Sonny pissed at me. Anyway, he points to this gym bag on the floor, goes, 'Hey, Eddie, you almost forgot your bag.' You know, loud, so everyone would hear. Then he winks." The Chevy rounded a corner as Mike was reaching into the backseat without looking, leaning back until his butt was six inches off the seat. He grabbed a light blue gym bag with a yellow Nike swoop and plunked it in his partner's lap.

Manny worked the zipper. It was stuffed with money, tight bricks of bills fastened together with yellow paper straps. He held a pack of crisp fifties in front of his face and riffled through them so he could take a whiff. "I love that smell," Manny said as he dropped five thousand bucks back in the bag and zipped it up.

They were three, four hundred yards from the building now, close enough to see two vehicles in the little parking lot. Mike hit the brakes hard. The gym bag slipped off Manny's lap and onto the floor. Before Manny knew it, Mike jerked the Chevy into a U-turn and was heading back to a lonely stretch of road protected by a grove of evergreens.

Manny said, "Oh, shit, now I can't go in there and just do it. Where the hell's my tie?" Now it was his turn to reach into the backseat. He snatched a hideous paisley tie from a heap of clothing, slipped it under his collar, and worked it back and forth until it lay flat. He sported a goatee connected to a thin mustache by two lines of whiskers that took so much time in the morning to shave he was thinking about getting rid of it. Working the thick fabric of the tie into a crooked knot, he glanced out the window. The wind was blowing cold October air, whistling right in his ear through the skinny gap where the window didn't fit right in the door. "My last goddamn winter in Pittsburgh. Next year this time? You'n me got a restaurant or a bar on one of them islands. 'Member I told you my idea? What do we got, I mean altogether, the both of us?"

He and Mike had been driving the Chevy, and bitching about it, for almost two years, ever since they took it off some punks on the Northside. It was one of those cars that would have looked better up on cinder blocks in front of a double-wide, but here it was, crappy enough not to draw a lick of attention in an industrial park northwest of the city. It was almost ten o'clock.

"Five hundred, give or take." Mike smoothed his shirt and looked down at a pair of hand-tooled boots he had picked up in New Mexico. He clicked on the dome light. "Don't get pissed, okay pardner?" he said, reaching down to wipe a smudge from the leather. Manny was fingering the cross, tracing up, down, back and forth. Over and over like he was polishing it with his finger. "Maybe you wait in the car, keep the engine going."

Manny whipped his head hard to the left. "Fuck you, Mike. Forget it. We're always down the middle, ever since the first job. The money too. It's my turn."

The dome light went dark. Mike looked straight at Manny. "You think fingering that thing makes it okay? That you can do whatever the fuck you want, and He's gonna look the other way?"

Manny waited a second or two before he said, "You ever *been* on a horse, cowboy?"

"How long you been holding onto that one?" Mike stared straight ahead out the front window into the darkness. His voice softened. "Look, we're pardners. You just seem real nervous. I ain't looking for a beef."

"You sure as hell don't get it. That's what confession's all about. He knows we make mistakes. All's you gotta do is tell the truth, the slate's wiped clean. I ain't looking for a beef either."

"Whoa. Back it up. You're telling me you confessed what we've been doing to a priest?" There was an edge to his voice.

Manny couldn't tell if Mike was pissed or scared. "Nah, don't worry 'bout it. Anyway, this ain't close to my first job and you know it. Besides, Charlie Hawk's no schoolteacher or Peace Corps guy. He's been arrested." Manny opened the glove box and removed a 9mm Smith & Wesson pistol with a stainless steel slide and barrel.

"For a DUI. He ain't exactly a rapist. Hey, you ever bother to shoot that thing?"

Manny popped the clip, turned it over in his fingers, double-checked to make sure it was loaded. Then he wiped it down with his tie and slipped it back in the grip of the gun. Smacking it home with the heel of his hand, he said, "Last week, up in the woods? I was hitting everything. Man, I'm gonna hate getting rid of it." The car was moving again. "Hey Mike, one thing I been thinking about. You ever wonder why Sonny hired us?" Manny leaned forward and slipped the gun into the small of his back.

"Not because we look like a couple smart guys who know how to get things done, like he said?"

"It wasn't no accident, was it? We're lightning rods. Sonny had to know it. Look how he works us. Nothing to connect us to him. Cash in a gym bag. Calling you Eddie. Never seen the inside of his office. Shit, if things get hot, he'll get us caught in two seconds and you know what a field day the press would have. When this's over we gotta disappear."

"You do make a tasty Cuban." Mike grinned. "So what else do you know how to cook?"

Manny smiled. "Partners?"

Mike eyed the Smith & Wesson. "Make sure you wipe it down after."

"Let me say it again. Fuck you."

■ ■ ■

Silent Samaritan

Hawk Inc. was located in the back of an industrial complex. It was an architectural yawn, one of those uninspired, rectangular buildings you drive past every day but couldn't pick out of a lineup. This was where Charlie Hawk barked out orders to half-a-dozen secretaries and ran his little empire of Cheap Charlie's. Eleven outlets altogether — another one about to open in New Kensington — that sold televisions and stereos all over Pittsburgh. Out front stood an old-fashioned street lamp with a cluster of white spherical globes that would have looked better in front of an ice cream parlor.

Two cars were parked in front of Hawk Inc.: a late-model Jaguar, dark blue, sexy in the dim light. And right next to it, a red Dodge pickup with the Ram insignia on the taillights. Mike pulled up next to the pickup. "Heavy-duty suspension," Mike said. "The dude means business. Maybe I *should* go in with you."

"Now you're being me." Manny forced a laugh. "If Charlie was s'pecting trouble the Ram would've been around back in the dark. Besides, *I* know what's gonna happen. They don't." He reached in the backseat and grabbed a wrinkled sport coat. "Hell, I can buy as much time as I want talking a little business. I don't do shit until I know the whereabouts of both of them." Now he was acting confident, moving more quickly. Hopping out of the car, he slipped into his jacket and headed around to the trunk where he grabbed a scuffed-up accordion briefcase. He heard Toby Keith coming out of the trunk, a little set of speakers installed back there, throbbing with bass. In the front seat he could follow the back of Mike's head bobbing to the beat. It looked like Mike was packing some chew into his mouth and leaning toward the door so he could stow the can in his pocket.

Manny closed the trunk quietly and marched right up to the front door. Placing his hand into the side pocket of his jacket, he reached for the door handle through the fabric to avoid leaving prints. Then he stepped into the lobby, a rectangular room with an empty desk where the receptionist sat during business hours. He could see a hallway leading to the back offices. There were two spiffy leather sofas and a cluster of leafy plants that made him wonder how much time it took to water those things every day. He counted six large windows and decided he'd have to wait to do it until they got back to Hawk's office.

"Sonny?" The voice came from somewhere in back. Charlie Hawk rounded the corner with a big smile on his face that vanished the second he saw Manny. Charlie was in his late fifties but in good shape, dressed in pleated khaki slacks and a yellow golf sweater over a white turtleneck. Manny could picture him doing the TV commercials as Cheap Charlie. For those he wore a hobo outfit with torn clothes and a little dirt smeared on his forehead. Charlie stopped abruptly, eight feet of space separating the two. "Where the hell's Sonny?" He looked out the glass door behind Manny. He could see the front end of the Chevy was missing the fender.

Manny stuck out his hand in a friendly sort of way. "Getting laid or something; you know Sonny. He asked me to stand in for him. I'm Manny." He held out the briefcase. "All set to go."

"Manny with no last name?" Charlie said, sounding irritated. If he noticed Manny's hand out there waiting for a shake he acted as if he didn't.

Manny kept his hand right where it was. "Romero, sorry. Manny Romero."

"So Sonny doesn't show up for this?" Charlie ran his hand through his white hair while he mulled things over.

"Hey, you look real uncomfortable. Maybe you have a phone. I could call Sonny."

"Hold on, hold on," Charlie said, still thinking.

"Look, Mr. Hawk, I noticed you got somebody here with you. Drives a heavy-duty Ram. Maybe some guy from the loading dock you said to stop by? You know, just in case, what with all the money you're gonna walk outta here with." Manny softened his voice, trying to sound sincere. "Get him out here, you'll feel better." He smiled then held up the briefcase and took a step toward Charlie.

Charlie held up his hand like a traffic cop. Manny did as he was told. By now his hand was down at his side. Charlie turned toward the doorway and raised his voice. "Hey, Johnny Ludd, c'mon out here."

Manny opened and closed his right hand and wiggled his fingers like an athlete staying loose. Now he was on automatic pilot, thinking so clearly and working Charlie so easily he was in total control even if Charlie was calling the shots.

And the Ram-tough guy was about to emerge from the shadows.

Johnny Ludd appeared. He was thick like a weight lifter, wearing a B.U.M. sweatshirt and loose workout pants with flames down the sides, his thighs so beefy he waddled. Before reaching Charlie he cocked his head to one side to crack his neck.

Manny couldn't decide if he looked stupid or bored. He said, "That's some heavy-duty suspension you got out there."

Charlie turned to Johnny Ludd and motioned with his head toward Manny.

As Johnny Ludd approached Manny he held his muscular arms out to the side like a scarecrow. Manny went right into the drill, dangling the briefcase from his open hand as he posed with his arms extended, allowing Johnny Ludd access to the inside of his sport coat. Starting with his shoulders, Johnny Ludd patted him down, sliding his hands from his chest to his side and finally down to his waist. To make it look good, he even squatted down and quickly touched each of Manny's ankles.

Manny said, "I didn't know better I'd say you were a cop."

Before Johnny Ludd could stand up he had to give himself a little push off the floor, creating some momentum. Now he went eye to eye with Manny and squinted. "I know you?"

Manny caught a whiff of onions. He squinted back, scrunching up his face, looking like he was racking his brain. "Maybe from Gold's Gym."

Johnny Ludd shook his head. "No, I seen you before, man. Ever been arrested?"

Manny turned toward Charlie and tried to look like he was insulted. "Hey, c'mon, Mr. Hawk. That's outta line. Sonny don't hire punks. Call him, you don't believe me."

Johnny Ludd scratched his cheek before he turned back to Charlie. "He don't have nothing."

Once again, Manny thrust out his hand and stepped toward Charlie and the two shook and smiled at each other. "You got the paperwork?" Manny asked.

The tension eased from Charlie's shoulders. He managed a thin smile. "In the conference room. C'mon."

Manny had a sudden thought: What if Charlie didn't want the weight lifter in on the deal? What if he headed in a different direction? How the hell would he get the two of them together again? Maybe this was his window of opportunity. He was certain. In that brief moment when Charlie Hawk and Johnny Ludd turned to lead Manny out of the lobby and away from all those windows, Manny slipped his hand behind his back, found the Smith & Wesson inside the back of his pants, and dropped the briefcase on the floor.

By the time Charlie and Johnny Ludd reacted to the noise and turned around, Manny was racking the slide and taking aim. "On your knees, the both of you," he said, his voice commanding. He moved the stocky barrel up and down, reinforcing the words.

Charlie instantly dropped to his knees and gave Johnny Ludd a look that screamed, *For Chrissake, do something!* Easing his way down to his knees, Johnny Ludd hissed something vile at Manny as he planted one of his thick arms on the floor so he wouldn't topple over.

Charlie said, "I thought you patted him down."

Manny laughed. "Checking the ankles made it look like you knew what the hell you're doing. But a gun fits pretty snug in the small of your back. Remember that. You hardly feel it but you gotta be goddamn careful when you pull your pants down to take a crap or you'll lose it down the toilet."

"Wait a second, please," Charlie said. "We have a deal. Sonny's buying me out. Do you understand *he* set the price? Christ, I'm moving to Florida in two weeks."

"All Sonny needed was a look at the books. You're too good of a businessman. And your boy here's a fuckin' coke dealer." Manny pivoted slightly and aimed at Johnny Ludd. "I ever been arrested. Fuck you."

Johnny Ludd's eyes went big and his mouth opened as if he was about to say something.

Manny squeezed off a round. The bullet caught Johnny Ludd above his left eye, snapping his huge head back. His brain box recoiled in slow motion as he slumped to one side and ended up on the floor.

Charlie's breath rushed from his lungs and he started babbling wildly, pleading with Manny — but calling him "Mr. Romero" — to let him go. "Tell Sonny he can have the business free if that's what he wants." He glanced sideways at Johnny Ludd, motionless, a ghastly expression on his face, one thick leg cocked awkwardly under the other. Then he looked up at Manny and did his best to make eye contact. He tried to slow his speech but it sounded as if he was on speed. "I'm begging you. Please, Mr. Romero." Manny leveled the gun. Time was running out. "C'mon, let's talk this out, I've got cash, yeah, twenty thousand in the back, maybe thirty, it's yours, every penny. Just call Sonny or something, I'll beg if that's what you want."

Manny jumped at the sound of gunfire. Charlie let out a little yelp as he whipped his head around to look behind him, his face scrunched up with fear.

Manny was knocked several steps backward and stumbled to keep his balance. He grabbed his chest. Already his white shirt was turning red.

Another person was in the room, a second bodybuilder, thick as Johnny Ludd, only his pants didn't have flames on them. But he had a gun.

Manny stared at his bloodied hand. He collapsed to his knees heavily and began squeezing off rounds, the first shot in the direction of the shooter, then one toward Charlie, who was up and making a dash for it.

That's the last thing that Manny Romero remembered.

2

"Carl, can I bug you?" Kensey Shaw caught the thin gold chain around her neck with her index finger and twisted it around. It was twenty of eleven. Her shift ended at midnight if everything stayed quiet. If disaster struck she would stay until the sun came up. Not that anyone ever saw a sunrise working in the Emergency Department because there weren't any windows.

Kensey stared at Carl Daley, the third-year resident in charge of the ED. He was asleep in a chair, tipped back and balanced perfectly, the toes of his sneakers touching the floor lightly. Kensey waited, studying the slow rhythm of his breathing.

University Medical Center was ranked eleventh in the country. In a nineteen-floor concrete-and-steel monstrosity in the heart of Oakland, the ED took up most of the first floor. Surprisingly, it was laid out quite logically. Twelve exam rooms and four trauma rooms surrounded a central bullpen where doctors and nurses hung out together to dictate their notes, answer phones or wolf down fast food. Each of the trauma rooms was outfitted as an operating room with an overhead light and enough equipment to handle any surgical emergency.

A scream came from room 4. Kensey pictured her patient sitting on the exam table, hand clamped over his ear, sweat and tears dripping from his face onto the floor. She had a good idea what to do for the kid, but she was a first-year resident and first-years went by the book. So she was waiting for Carl Daley to wake up.

"Carl?" Now she said it loud enough one of the nurses turned her head toward Kensey and giggled.

Carl wore a light blue scrub shirt over clean white pants and a black stethoscope draped around his neck. Every residency group had a Carl Daley, the one who had *chief resident* written all over him the first day of internship. He was forever quoting from *The New England Journal of Medicine* and refused to call for help in the middle of the night. Whether it was a breech baby about to pop out, a Swan-Ganz catheter that needed to be floated into the heart, or a foreign body that required retrieval from one of several orifices, Carl made it known he was the man.

Kensey had caught Carl's eye on day one. He liked the way she looked in scrubs, the way her top pulled away from her chest when she leaned over a patient to check for the spleen, showing off her bra. But the thing he couldn't get out of his mind was her mole. A tiny, chocolate dab of color on her right cheek, no more than an inch from her eye. It made her look like she was forever smiling. And it was heart-shaped. Guys went absolutely nuts over that little mole. Twice Kensey caught Carl staring at it, but that was as far as it went. Carl was gunning for chief resident, and he wasn't about to get bogged down with some cute intern, even one with a sexy mole that made it hard to fall asleep at night.

"You awake?"

"Kook or a car wreck?" He didn't bother to open his eyes. Kensey knew this was for effect.

The patients in the ED were divided into three groups: kooks, colds, and car wrecks. By eleven o'clock the colds and flus had been tucked into bed with their bottles of NyQuil. The kooks, on the other hand, didn't own watches, and car wrecks knew no time.

"I'm taking care of this guy, a teenager really, got some sort of bug stuck in his ear. It's in too far to grab with forceps."

"I was just about to enter REM sleep. My dream was loaded in the projector." Eyes closed, voice quiet.

A scream of agony came from room 4.

"That the bug?" Carl opened one eye.

Kensey nodded.

Carl closed his eye. "Tell you what. Let me present the case to you." His chair remained in balance. "First of all, don't call it a bug. You wanna sound smart? If it's big enough to bring a teenager to that," he motioned with his head toward room 4, "it's a cockroach." Another scream. "An American cockroach, to be specific. Nothing else does that. Mean little fuckers, get right up next to the eardrum and buzz like a sonofabitch. They say you make a friend for life when you take a roach out of a drunk's ear."

A cry of "Hey, doctor," came from room 4.

Kensey looked that way, pulling at her gold chain. "I want to know—"

Carl opened an eye. "I'm right, he's drunk," he said, cutting her off.

Kensey nodded.

Carl noticed several nurses listening to what he was saying. He turned up the volume just enough to make sure they could hear everything. "Since he's a teenager, and not some homeless wino, my diagnosis is he's a frat boy. Lemme guess, DU?"

"Phi Sigma Kappa." Kensey didn't want to get into it with Carl — but thought he was being a smart aleck — so she said, "He's in a lot of pain."

"PSK. Know what that stands for? Pledges Sucking Kegs. A fine establishment where lonely roaches and virgin drunks hook up for the night. Kid slips into a stupor and the roach finds a cozy home."

Now it was obvious Carl was enjoying himself. She waited six, seven beats. When it was clear he was done with his speech, she said, "You want to take a look?"

Carl brought the chair to all four legs. He leaned toward Kensey and lowered his voice. "I don't. And forget about looking up ear roaches in any of these." Carl waved his hand over several fat medical texts scattered on the desk in front of them. The kid screamed again. Carl winced. "Jesus Christ," he said and shot a glance in the direction of room 4. "And don't you dare call ENT on my watch." Carl crossed his arms in front of his chest. "Okay, I'm gonna tell you the most important thing you're gonna learn this entire year. Do the exact opposite what they taught you in medical school. Forget all the textbook crap. Listen to your patient, Kensey. Figure out what he needs and do it for him. Try thinking outside the box." Carl tipped his chair back and closed his eyes.

Kensey bounded out of the bullpen in search of supplies.

Inside room 4 an eighteen-year-old freshman sat on the exam table, his legs dangling off the side. He was wearing an unbuttoned designer dress shirt over a Green Day T-shirt, cargo pants, and a pair of black dress shoes. One hand was cupped over his ear, the other balled up so tight his knuckles were purple. His hair went in six different directions and both eyes were tightly shut. Whenever he wasn't whining about how much pain he was in, he was sobbing. The room smelled like a beer-and-vomit casserole was percolating in the oven.

He spotted Kensey standing in the doorway, in blue scrubs and red clogs, tucking her hair behind one ear. Mustering whatever strength and dignity that remained, he said, "Gimme something to knock me out, please."

He watched Kensey pull up a stool and spin the seat around and around to make it taller. As she sat down he spotted the mole and for about a second it took his mind off the pain until …

The roach started doing the cucaracha against his eardrum, making him scream and wince until a glob of drool dripped out of his mouth and crawled down his chin.

Kensey placed a little tube of Super Glue and a single wooden toothpick on a small metal Mayo stand next to where the kid was sitting. "I need you to calm down so I can help you."

The boy pulled away from Kensey. "What's that?" His voice trembled.

Kensey kept her voice a soft whisper. "Hold still so I can see exactly where the roach is."

"A roach? You didn't say anything about a roach." His voice shot up two octaves.

"Hold still."

"I'm gonna puke." He turned his head and vomited off the other side of the table onto the floor. Using his unbuttoned shirtsleeve, he wiped his mouth.

Kensey donned surgical gloves. "It's touching your eardrum." Slowly but firmly she peeled the boy's stubborn hand from his ear. It was bright red and hot to the touch. Every so often a hideous buzz came from the canal.

"I wish I never went to that stupid party." The boy clamped his hand over his ear.

"Listen to me, Joshua, this is going to take a little willpower." Just as she was placing his hand in his lap it shot back up. "That's it." Kensey stood up. "Enough is enough. You've got a choice, young man. Either hold still or go back to the frat house and puke your guts out the rest of the night."

"Okay, okay. I'll try."

Joshua lowered his hand to his lap, clenched his jaw and bared his teeth. Kensey thought about offering him a bullet to bite on. Maybe he would laugh. Instead she put a glistening drop of Super Glue on the end of the toothpick, tugged on his ear to straighten the canal so she could visualize the rear end of the very angry roach, and carefully applied the sticky part to it. Holding the toothpick in place long enough for the glue to start to set, she removed her hand. Now a sliver of wood two inches long stuck straight out of his ear. "Do *not* touch your ear or you'll jam that roach right into your brain."

"Okay, okay," he said quickly. "Do my parents have to find out about this?"

Kensey chuckled. "I'll put down you had an allergic reaction."

The kid forced a smile.

Carl poked his head into the room and pointed at Kensey. "Couple of gunshots coming, less than two minutes. Cut the roach motel loose." Carl disappeared.

"What?" the kid said, reaching for his ear.

"No!" Kensey caught Joshua's hand in midair and forced it back into his lap. She took hold of the toothpick and carefully worked it back and forth, easing it out of the canal, towing the roach until it was free, its black legs running wildly through the air.

In several seconds the kid experienced instant and complete relief. He shook his head back and forth and smiled at the sight of the roach. "Cool. Can I have it?"

Kensey handed it to him and headed into the hallway just as the automatic doors slid open and two stretchers raced inside with paramedics and cops hustling along. Nurses were holding IV bags aloft and a paramedic was bagging one of the two patients with a plastic Ambu bag. A paramedic spotted Carl and called out, "Both took a bullet in the chest. This one here was bubbling mucus out of his mouth, had to tube him. Least the other one's breathing on his own."

Sirens were wailing outside. People were coming through the automatic doors two and three at a time, a couple of female officers in uniform, then macho cops with boots and motorcycle helmets. There was a lot of whispering going on. No one seemed to know exactly what had happened. An older nurse in a crisp white uniform and little folded nurse's cap positioned herself between the crowd and the stretchers, ready to do battle with anyone who tried to get too close.

Carl approached the stretcher with the patient who was intubated and snapped on a pair of blue surgical gloves. The paramedic yanked the stretcher to a quick stop. A white sheet covered the unconscious patient. Briefly, the paramedic lifted it. The man was wearing a yellow sweater and white turtleneck. Now they were stained red and had been scissored right up the middle to expose the man's chest, sticky with dried blood. A bloody square of gauze had been secured to the right side of his chest with long strips of white tape. Someone in the crowd was whispering something about his heart. Carl ignored the comment. Using a penlight he opened the man's eyelids and shined the light.

"Name's Charles Hawk," the paramedic read from a clipboard. "No other clinical."

Carl said, "Pupils react. Get him into Trauma One." To a nearby nurse: "I want X-ray up here STAT. Get a chest tube ready." He spoke confidently.

A guy in the crowd said, "All right," and gave a little fist pump as though the way Carl barked out orders meant he was going to save him. The cops in uniform stared the guy down until he shut his mouth.

Carl placed his hand on one of the side rails and gave the stretcher a shove. Three nurses and a couple of paramedics guided Charlie Hawk away.

Kensey couldn't figure out what to do with her hands. Two gunshots and two doctors. Carl never called for help. The math was easy. She tried to cross her arms in front of her but that didn't feel right. Her neck began to itch. She had to go to the bathroom. And there were so many people watching.

Turning his attention to the other stretcher waiting a few feet away, Carl said something to the other paramedic. The paramedic checked his clipboard and answered, "One-forty over eighty-five." Only the patient's head was visible, the rest of his body swathed in a white sheet. The paramedic lifted the sheet by a corner so that the non-medical onlookers were blocked out. But Kensey got an eyeful. The man's dress shirt, stiff with dried blood, had been torn apart and was hanging away from his body. On the left side of his chest was a bloody wad of gauze loosely held with adhesive tape. A gold cross dangled from a chain around his neck and rested on the stretcher. Kensey knew this one was hers. Carl would keep the intubated victim for himself. Thank God this man was breathing. He looked to be in his late thirties, had a thick sweater of black hair on his chest, and a mustache-goatee combination that gave him a south-of-the-border appearance. Maybe he was Mexican. His eyes were closed. Carl turned his head to look at the paramedic. "Name?"

"Emanuel Romero."

Someone in the crowd called out, "Manny."

Carl didn't look up, but he was grateful. First names were important when you were addressing a patient who might not be fully alert. People responded better to their nicknames. "Manny, can you hear me? Hey, Manny," Carl said in the same big voice he used to communicate with deaf people.

Manny opened his eyes a crack. "Yeah." His voice was thick.

"You gonna stay with me?"

"Yeah."

There was a murmur of relief from the crowd that now numbered more than a dozen. They were pulling for some good news, every one of them, and it was great to know Manny was going to make it.

"Take him to Trauma Two," Carl said. The stretcher started moving. Carl found Kensey standing off to the side. "Listen up, you baby sit this guy. Get a chest X-ray, make sure he doesn't have a pneumothorax. And watch his BP."

Kensey stepped around several nurses who were waiting for something to do. Briefly, she touched the tubular railing on the side of the moving stretcher, accepting responsibility for Manny Romero, his scuffed brown shoes sticking out from under the white sheet. Nodding her head, acknowledging she could handle the responsibility, Kensey stood still and stared as the stretcher made a couple of turns and rolled straight into the trauma room.

Now Joshua was cruising through the crowd. He was in no hurry to step back into the night, evidently needing a better story to tell back at the frat house so he wouldn't have to answer too many questions about his ear. He gave Kensey a little wave. She didn't see him.

"You gonna stay with me?" Carl said, this time to Kensey, loud enough to embarrass her and snap her into action.

A glaze of sweat shone on her forehead. "I'm on it," she said and turned toward the room with a large numeral 2 on the wall next to it. The white curtain that was supposed to offer privacy was pushed all the way over to one side. One of the cops was saying something about the other two dying. Carl strode into Trauma One and was already barking out commands.

Everyone in Trauma Two was wearing gloves. It took four people, two nurses, the paramedic, and Kensey, to heave Manny Romero from the stretcher to the skinny black examination table. As the paramedic was packing his equipment he waited to give report. The bags of intravenous fluids, one for each arm, were hung from portable metal poles. "Hey, Doc," the paramedic said. "Bilateral breath sounds. Belly's soft. Pupils brisk. Pulse one-fifty, BP one-forty over eighty-five. I got him to talk on the way over. Anything else?"

Things were happening quickly. An attractive nurse with a bouncy ponytail removed the white sheet from Manny's body. A second later a tall male nurse with a shaved head and thick arms wrapped with tattoos stripped him of his socks and shoes. His pants were unbuckled, pulled off, and tossed on the floor. His boxers and torn shirt were cut apart with heavy shears. Now Manny Romero was naked.

Kensey thanked the paramedic without looking at him. Her eyes never left Manny. "Is that X-ray coming?" she said to no one in particular and the answer, "On its way," floated through the crowd.

In the hallway the crowd was growing. Men in bad sports jackets and wide ties were streaming in and being brought up to speed by the uniformed cops who had been there from the beginning. They moved out of the way as the paramedic pushed the empty stretcher toward the door. One of the uniformed cops touched the paramedic on the shoulder and said, "He gonna make it?" and the paramedic quickly shot back with a thumbs-up.

Most of the crowd had migrated toward Trauma Two. Kensey glanced out and noticed the audience, quiet now, attentive, waiting for more news.

Kensey began her exam. "Mr. Romero," she said, imitating Carl's loud voice.

"You don't have to yell it," he said with a hint of a Spanish accent. "And it's Manny."

"Okay, Manny." Kensey peeled away the gauze to reveal a finger-sized hole in Manny's chest two inches left of the sternum. It was caked with dried blood like a little volcano, now dormant, with no active bleeding.

Several of the officers in the front row took deep breaths and swallowed hard.

Kensey listened to his chest, first one side, then the other, back and forth.

"Both lungs seem to be working. Does it hurt when you breathe?"

"A little."

Gently she palpated around the wound, but Manny groaned and she stopped. "You're lucky. You look pretty good."

Manny managed a smile. "For a guy with a bullet."

The nurse with the ponytail placed a tourniquet on Manny's forearm. "How many units of blood you want crossed?"

"Three. No, get four."

Manny coughed. His hand grasped at his chest and he moaned loudly. In the length of time it took Kensey to answer the nurse, something was different. It was the way Manny was breathing. Kensey listened to his chest again. He was working harder, like he'd just run up a couple flights of stairs. But his lips were pink and his eyes were opened and staring at her.

A wall-mounted monitor showed continuous readouts of respiratory pattern and EKG. Every minute or so the blood pressure was taken by an automatic cuff and the numbers were displayed on the monitor. The nurse with the ponytail called out, "BP's one-twenty over seventy-five. Pulse one-ten."

"That's odd," Kensey said to the nurse, then turning to Manny asked, "You okay?" Without waiting for a response her stethoscope was back on his chest. Again she listened to one side, then the other. "Where's that chest X-ray?" she called out and wondered if her voice sounded anxious.

The male nurse was hanging another bag of IV solution. He answered, "They're having trouble in Trauma One. Hanging another bag of Ringer's, Kensey."

Manny spoke quietly, his voice coming through dry lips: "I'm okay, Doc. Just a jolt of pain."

"Run it in wide open," Kensey said. To the female nurse she added: "Take the BP again, please." The nurse hit a button on the monitor and the cuff inflated.

"Hey, Doc, come closer so's you'n me can talk," Manny said. His voice was hard to hear with all the chatter in the room. "What's your name?"

"One-twenty over seventy," the nurse said.

Kensey bent down, bringing her ear close to Manny's mouth. "Dr. Shaw."

"Siddown, Doc, will ya? Ain't nothing for you to do." He turned his head away from Kensey and said to the male nurse, "Give us a minute, will ya?"

Kensey checked the monitor. The EKG was ticking along at 118 beats per minute. The up-and-down sine wave that represented his breathing was consistently thirty to thirty-five breaths per minute. He was stable. The male nurse shrugged and headed out of the room; the nurse with the ponytail hurried after him. Kensey and Manny were alone.

The cluster of onlookers had become more diverse. A man in a nice-looking suit had joined the attentive crowd. One other person had slipped into the Emergency Department without anybody noticing. He was a cowboy wearing a short leather jacket and fancy boots. Leaning up against the wall a dozen feet behind the uniforms, parked between an old man with no teeth and the shadowy corner where the Coke machine met the wall, he brushed the palm of his hand down his thick mustache, then sunk it into the side pocket of his jacket and fished out a can of Skoal. His vantage was off to the side, giving him a pretty good view of Kensey and the upper half of Manny's body. He slipped a pinch between his cheek and gum, his dark eyes never drifting from Manny. Even when the male nurse with the tattoos walked by with an unlit cigarette in his hand and he was close enough to say, "Hey, buddy, how's he doing?" he kept his gaze steady and his mouth shut.

Kensey slid a metal stool close to the exam table and sat down. The automatic blood pressure cuff made a noise when it inflated and a series of numbers appeared on the monitor. "Your blood pressure's down a little."

"I can't feel my feet so good."

Kensey reached down and gently placed her hand over the top of his foot. It was cold. "Can you wiggle your toes?"

"It don't matter. This is God's work." He took a couple of breaths. "I ain't fighting it."

"You're gonna make it. I promise." Kensey looked up at the monitor. The blood pressure was 102 over 56. She found his wrist and took his pulse.

"I tell you something, Doc, you keep it to yourself?"

Kensey looked him in the eye. "Doctors aren't allowed to reveal anything their patients tell them."

Manny wriggled his hand out of hers and patted Kensey's slender wrist. "Don't do that no more." He winced in pain, showing his clenched teeth. "You a Samaritan?"

"You mean like a Good Samaritan?"

He nodded. "Luke ten. Read it last Sunday. You think you could do me a favor?" He left his hand on her wrist, his fingers gently curling around.

"Sure, what do you want?"

Manny swallowed and exhaled loudly. "I gotta confess some stuff."

"There's a priest on call—"

"I've done some bad shit." He gently tugged on her arm so she would know he was serious.

Kensey leaned closer. She whispered, "You want a priest? They could call him, be here in no time."

"That's just it. No time. Getting really," Manny grabbed a quick breath, "weak." His grip tightened slightly. "Three people."

He was breathing harder now. The skin over his collarbone retracted each time he sucked a breath. Kensey reached for her stethoscope. Manny pulled her arm toward him.

"You're not listening. I said three people. Not counting tonight."

"Three people what?"

"I killed three people." Manny reacted to a jolt of pain.

"What?" Her voice was a sharp whisper. Abruptly, Kensey pulled her hand away from him. She placed the stethoscope on his right chest and listened as Manny sucked a couple breaths.

"Got paid a lot of money," he said. His hand went to his neck, his fingers working the chain, sliding back and forth. "My cross, where's it at?"

Kensey let the stethoscope dangle from her ears. She located the cross for him, behind his ear, and helped him slip the chain around his head. She placed it in his hand and he clutched it tightly.

"The favor," he said, the words coming between breaths.

"What do you want me to do?" She sounded frightened, as if the favor would be something she wouldn't want to do.

"St. John's, over on the Northside. Father Flaherty."

"You want me to see if we can reach him?"

His hand found her wrist. "I don't want to go to hell, Doc. It's dark down there." He started to cry. He brought the cross to his lips and kissed it. "Confess my sins to him ... you know ... after."

The male nurse walked back in the room. "What the hell. BP's sixty over thirty."

"Oh my God," Kensey said, looking up at the monitor. "Get me a big needle."

"Fourteen gauge?" The nurse spoke quickly as he pulled open a glass door on a cabinet.

"Yes, anything," she said, panic in her voice as she hopped off the stool. For no more than a second her head turned and dared a look out the doorway. The cops and men wearing ties stood there, hands at their sides, staring at her.

Now the nurse was tearing open a small cardboard box and producing a large bore needle. Kensey was leaning over Manny, moving her stethoscope back and forth.

"Breath sounds are diminished on the left. It's a tension pneumo," Kensey said. "Where's that needle?"

Kensey put out her gloved hand, palm up, and the nurse handed her a two-and-a- half-inch-long needle. Working quickly now, she started at the top of his chest and counted down with her fingers until she found the third rib. She inserted the needle, sliding it over the top edge of the rib to minimize bleeding, driving it down to the hilt.

Kensey put her ear to the end of the needle. She shook her head. "There's no air coming out."

The male nurse said, "What's that mean?"

"It's not a tension pneumothorax."

The nurse with the ponytail hurried into the room, took one look at the monitor, and said, "You want me to get Carl?"

"BP's holding," the male nurse said without a trace of emotion.

Meanwhile, Manny was watching the whole procedure with detached curiosity. Kensey was back with the stethoscope, left side, right side.

"Hey, Doc, listen to me, I'm feeling okay, maybe even better. I don't want you to do no more. No needles. Forget that thing in your ears. I said, take a chair."

Kensey withdrew the needle.

Manny coughed. Moving his head back and forth so he could look at both of the nurses, he said, "I want to talk with the doc. Alone. So get outta here."

"Maybe just wait outside for a minute," Kensey said. "I think we're okay."

The male nurse frowned. He made an adjustment to one of the IV bags.

"I'll holler if there's a change."

The nurses left the room and headed off to the side of the onlookers. Kensey sat on the stool.

"Doc, I just need to know you'll see my priest."

"Why don't you want me to help you?"

"Please, do what I say. No more nothing, 'kay? The world's better without me."

"St. John's?"

"Yeah, up on the hill. One more thing." He was grunting with each breath. "Alec Fortune and Seymour Rosen." He pulled in a shallow mouthful of air and eyed Kensey. She was sitting absolutely still, holding onto every word. "You're a pretty girl, you know that?" He took a breath. "Write it down." Another breath. "You'll forget." Three breaths. "Alec Fortune, Seymour Rosen." As Kensey pulled out a pen and began scribbling, Manny continued, "They're next." Three more breaths. "Tell 'em Sonny…" A breath. "…ordered it… " Two more breaths. "They better watch their backs."

Kensey looked out the door at the uniformed officers. "Let me get one of the cops."

"No." Manny reached out and grabbed her wrist hard. "No cops, goddamnit."

She didn't pull away. "But if a crime's about to be committed—"

Manny lifted his head. For a moment he seemed energized and his fingers dug into her skin until it hurt. "You hear what I said? Listen to me. You go to the cops you'll get killed. Shot. Stabbed. Smothered. It don't matter which way, it'll happen."

"Okay, I won't."

"No, swear. Swear on your mother's grave."

"I do. I do."

"All right." He released his grip. "The two I jus' tol' you about. *Just* warn 'em, they're smart enough to know what to do." He took a couple of painful inspirations. "I don't feel so good." He looked at Kensey's face. "Pretty girl." He smiled, then his eyes closed and his head drifted to one side as his hand slid off its perch on his chest and the cross slipped from his fingers.

Kensey looked up at the monitor. "Oh my God. He's gonna code." She placed her finger on Manny's wrist.

The male nurse hurried back into the room.

Kensey said, "BPs forty over twenty, pulse is thready. Get Carl."

The male nurse stayed calm. "He's coming. He just called off the code in Trauma One."

A piercing alarm sounded on one of the monitors.

"Oh, shit," Kensey said and called out: "Cardiac arrest!"

The male nurse took three steps to the doorway of the room and hollered, "Code in Trauma Two, code in Trauma Two."

Kensey whipped her head back and forth. "No, wait, he said he didn't want us to—"

Everything happened in a blur. Once the code was called everyone went all out. It couldn't be put back in the bottle. Nurses and respiratory therapists came dashing into the room. The cops and the men in ties and jackets got the hell out of the way.

A respiratory therapist slapped a bag and mask on Manny and pumped oxygen into his lungs.

Reluctantly and helplessly, Kensey began chest compressions.

The cowboy was leaning against the wall. He kept watching Manny and Kensey. Down by his side he held a white Styrofoam cup. Every once in a while he brought it up to his mouth and spit in it.

Carl ran into the room. "What the hell—"

Between compressions Kensey said, "All of a sudden his breathing got worse. His BP bottomed out and his pulse dropped."

Carl turned toward the light box where X-rays were supposed to be displayed. It was empty. He spoke right at the light box like it was an orderly who didn't speak English. "Where the *hell* is the chest film?" Carl snapped his stethoscope on and listened to Manny's chest.

"The tech was tied up with you," Kensey said, still working the chest. "Just listen to me for a second. He told me he didn't want us to keep trying. He was ready to die."

Carl stopped what he was doing long enough to look Kensey in the eye. "And was he in a state of mind where he could make a rational decision about his life, Doctor?"

"I thought so."

"Then why the hell are you doing CPR?"

"I don't know."

"So you babysat this guy and watched him crash." Then to the male nurse: "Take over for her." To another nurse: "Let's get some syringes drawn up. I'll take epi first."

The male nurse didn't look at Kensey as he stepped in and began chest compressions.

"No," Kensey said, protesting. "After I tapped his chest he wouldn't let me do anything else."

"Okay people," Carl was saying as if Kensey weren't in the room. "We're not losing this guy, goddamnit." To the male nurse, quieter: "Work the chest harder."

As people moved in around the table — three nurses, two respiratory therapists, the X-ray tech and Carl — Kensey was squeezed away from her patient. The male nurse was strong, leaning over Manny, using both hands, one on top of the other, taking advantage of his size to compress the chest. Each time he leaned into it, Manny's arms flailed about lifelessly.

Kensey spotted something on the floor and bent over to pick it up.

Carl surveyed the room. "Where the hell is Kensey?"

She stood up with Manny's cross in her hand. "He dropped his cross." Her voice was so quiet no one heard what she said.

"You ever have a patient who's going downhill, get the senior. You hear me? You don't have the authority to stop treatment."

A nurse called out: "I can't get a BP."

Carl was still looking at Kensey. "Unless there's another roach to remove, why don't you call it a night." To the male nurse: "Harder, goddamnit. He's not perfusing." Carl ran his gloved hands through his hair. He checked the monitors. "Stop for a second." The male nurse took his hands from Manny's chest. Carl stared at the EKG tracing. It showed tiny blips that barely registered. "Go … GO," he urged to the male nurse and chest compressions resumed. To the respiratory therapist: "Bag him faster."

Kensey wandered out of the room. She was crying. The crowd parted. Cops in uniform averted their eyes. At the doorway she turned around and watched the medical drama. It was a scene out of the television program *ER*, everyone huddled around the patient, valiantly trying to save his life. Carl caught Kensey's eye as he said, "Let me do that." He was speaking to the male nurse. He looked away from Kensey and began pounding on Manny's chest.

Kensey heard Carl scream, "Shit."

She wiped her eyes and headed down the hallway toward the doctors' lounge.

3

"Dr. Shaw?"

The sliding glass doors that would release Kensey from the Emergency Department into a night of clean air and quiet streets had already opened. A refreshing coolness swept in and blew her hair. In no time she had changed into travel clothes: stonewashed jeans and a yellow rugby shirt, New Balance running shoes, a backpack slung over one shoulder, and a wet ball of Kleenex in her hand. "Can I help you?" Her voice was a weary monotone.

"I'm Frank Hennessey. I'd like to sit down with you, get your take on the situation." He held out a white business card.

On any other day she would have been happy to give Frank Hennessey a second look. Short-cropped hair combed to one side, tight sideburns, and a great jaw. He looked athletic and crisp, like a successful attorney, in his tailored brown suit, powder-blue shirt, and red tie Windsored tightly at the neck. Kensey scanned the card. "You're a cop."

"Three people were killed tonight." He turned and looked back toward Trauma Two. "So far."

"Carl Daley? He's my senior, taking care of Mr. Romero. Probably should talk with him." Kensey turned into the breeze.

"Mr. Romero," Detective Hennessey said, drawing out the syllables as if committing the name to memory.

Kensey thought it was odd the cop didn't know his name already, but figured it was a way to get her talking, ease her into making a statement. "Manny Romero." Not saying more than she had to.

"Won't take a couple minutes. You look like someone who could use a Coke." Detective Hennessey smiled and held out his hand in the direction of the red-and-white vending machine. Kensey noticed his eyes. They were friendly. When he spoke they crinkled at the corners. She nodded and they walked away from the sliding doors, past Trauma One where Charlie Hawk's body was swathed in a white sheet from head to toe. Already it was being transferred to a black gurney by two orderlies. Kensey kept a step or two ahead, hurrying along to get whatever the detective wanted over with, Hennessey hanging back, acting nice and relaxed.

The cowboy noticed them approaching and turned away toward the toothless old man. He moved his head up and down and did something with his hand so it looked like he was saying something.

"So," Detective Hennessey said, filling in the silence as he dug in his pocket for change, "you an ER physician?"

"No, internal medicine. We just rotate through here."

"I came in late, tell me what happened."

Kensey thought to herself that he had to know what had happened if he was a cop. Any one of the officers could have told him about the shoot-out. Detective Hennessey suspected something. And if a cop suspected something and was coming to Kensey with questions, it had to be about the whispering she had done with Manny. Everyone had to know about it. For God's sake, she had an audience of twelve.

Nearby was a small waiting room that was empty this late at night. Red leatherette chairs and angular sofas ran the perimeter, an assortment picked out of a catalogue by someone who never intended to sit on them. On the floor was a scattering of Styrofoam cups and an old diaper rolled into a smelly ball. Kensey chose a chair with pen marks all over the cushion. Her backpack was stowed at her feet. His business card was in her hand, her fingernail catching the corner and flicking it to make a sound. Detective Hennessey popped his Coke and waited for Kensey to do the same. As she took a sip she made the mistake of turning her head and gazing toward Trauma Two. The detective studied the movements of her facial muscles like a poker player searching for a tell. Now his eyes were serious.

All Kensey could see of the entire room was Manny's left arm, dangling off the examination table, bouncing around in time to the chest compressions. Kensey wondered how much time had gone by. At least fifteen minutes of CPR, maybe more. Some of the senior residents would have called it off by now. But not Carl. He'd already lost one patient tonight and Kensey knew this wasn't going to be over any time soon.

Pulling her eyes from Manny's arm was impossible. It seemed to have no life of its own, flopping about like it was artificial, constructed of rubber. His wish to be allowed to die was being ignored well past the time when his life had left him.

The cowboy had moved. He was stationed outside the waiting room, leaning against the wall so neither Kensey nor Detective Hennessey could know he was there, his head turned so he could watch Manny's arm at the same time he was getting every word that went back and forth.

Kensey was an easy read for Detective Hennessey. Tears were creeping down her cheeks. "Dr. Shaw?" He waited for Kensey to look at him. "So, how long ago did Mr. Romero arrive?"

Kensey lifted the red can to her mouth but did not take a sip. She consulted the business card. "Detective—"

"Would you be comfortable calling me Frank?"

"I guess."

He could tell by the way she said it she wasn't going to be taking him up on his offer.

"Thirty-five, forty minutes ago." She looked at her watch. "I don't know."

"It's hard to keep track. How many times was he shot?"

"Once." Kensey tapped the left side of her chest. "Right about here."

"Was he awake when you examined him?"

"Yes."

Frank looked out toward Trauma Two. "He tell you what happened?"

"Not really."

Frank returned his gaze to Kensey. "I couldn't help notice you pulled up a chair."

"Listen, Detective, we didn't talk about the shooting, if that's what you want to know."

Frank took a sip of Coke. He looked back at Trauma Two. Kensey couldn't help but follow his lead and steal a glance. They sat in silence, Frank sipping his Coke, Kensey holding hers in her lap, Manny's arm flopping around.

Finally Kensey said, "He wanted to know if he was going to die."

"I know this is awful talking about it."

Kensey noticed the way he said that, softly, as if he really did know how awful it was.

Frank said, "So ... what'd you say?"

"'No way, you're gonna be just fine.' What're you supposed to say?" Kensey took a swig of Coke to wash the words from her mouth. She raised her eyebrows, letting Frank know she'd said what she thought best at the time even if it seemed stupid right now.

"That's the right thing to say. Seemed like it went on longer than that, your conversation. There were some, I don't know, thoughtful pauses."

"He asked about his heart." Kensey looked Frank as straight in the eye as she could, not wanting him to sense she was being anything but truthful.

"You think the bullet got his heart?"

She shook her head. "Probably close. He wouldn't have made it here with a bullet in it."

"I saw you put a needle in his chest. Why was that?"

"I thought maybe he had a tension pneumothorax."

"English, please." Frank sounded confused.

"It's when your lung collapses and free air gets in the chest when you breathe. The air can't get out so pressure builds up and the heart and lungs get squished. You can relieve the pressure with a needle."

"And?"

"Didn't work. He kept getting weaker, blood pressure dropping. Probably was bleeding inside."

"Looked like he felt comfortable with you. Putting his hand on yours. You seemed very compassionate."

"Maybe a better doctor would have done less handholding." As soon as the words were out of her mouth she regretted saying it and made a face.

That got Frank to pause for a second. "Four people were involved in the shoot- out. Two were found dead at the scene.

Mr. Hawk in Trauma One? Never regained consciousness. We don't have a clue what happened. I was hoping," he paused for a second, letting what he said sink in, "Mr. Romero might have said something that would shed some light."

It was impossible to put Manny out of her mind. Kensey turned her head and glanced toward Trauma Two. His arm was bouncing around, then it slowed, swinging back and forth gently in a decreasing pendulum until it hung absolutely still, his stubby fingers pointing straight down toward the hell where Manny was sure to go.

"I told you. He didn't." Kensey snatched her backpack from the floor and took a final swig of Coke.

"Sorry. Just grasping at straws. Hey," he said gently, as if a thought popped into his head just that moment, "I noticed a couple of times Mr. Romero pulled you away from using your stethoscope."

"I don't think he knew what he was doing. His blood pressure was dropping, he may have been a little delirious."

"I guess so. One more question, then I'll let you go."

Kensey wondered about the scrap of paper in her pocket. The names were already burned into her memory. Seymour Rosen. Alec Fortune. Who the hell were they? Was there any way the detective saw her writing them down?

"Dr. Shaw?" Frank waited for Kensey to look at him. "I couldn't help overhear something you said during the code. You said something about him being ready to die."

The cowboy wasn't even looking in the direction of Trauma Two anymore. He was staring at the floor, his ear inches from the doorway to the waiting room, holding his breath as Kensey started to speak.

"I don't know why. Maybe a religious thing."

Frank bent his head forward and scratched his neck, giving himself a chance to put his thoughts together. "Couple times in my career I was face-to-face with a guy who was shot up pretty good. Never once seen one of 'em ready to die."

Kensey wiped her eyes with the back of her hand, the can of Coke still in her grasp. "This was my first time."

Her voice was so lonely Frank wanted to put his arm around her. "Twenty years from now you'll remember Manny Romero like it was today. Heck, I can name every one of mine."

Kensey nodded a thank-you.

"Funny thing, though. Twice I was with someone thought he was gonna die – guys I didn't know from Adam – and I heard some pretty intimate stuff. Stuff I didn't want to hear. 'I was screwing my secretary but tell my wife I love her.' That sort of thing." He stopped speaking, sipped his Coke, and waited.

Kensey waited too, until it was painfully obvious that Frank was going to sit there forever. She said, "He didn't do anything like that."

Frank glanced sideways as if something in Trauma Two caught his eye.

Kensey grabbed her backpack, tossed the Coke in the trash, and hurried out of the waiting room, bumping right into the cowboy with the thick mustache and pinch of Skoal in his mouth. "Excuse me."

He mumbled something and there was that awkward moment when she went left to get around him at the same instant he went right. Each reversed direction to go the other way. It looked like a square dance, one of those quirky situations when one of them was supposed to say, 'Want to dance?' and the other would laugh and that would be that. But the cowboy didn't smile. He used the interlude to memorize Kensey's face, studying her eyes and the heart-shaped mole on her cheek, drilling into her hard enough to frighten her and make her turn her head and hurry away. For a second she thought about going back to Hennessey, but she didn't. As she hit the sliding glass doors she glanced around to make sure the cowboy wasn't following her.

4

Ten minutes after leaving the ED Kensey was in her used Honda, forest green, 86,000 miles, and running as smooth as it did the day she bought it from her cousin before starting at Cornell Medical. She zipped across the 40th Street Bridge. Traffic was nonexistent. Then south on Route 28, the towering U.S. Steel building off in the distance, past the Heinz factory where they cooked up everything but ketchup, and finally turning right onto East Ohio Street. Kensey wound her way behind Allegheny General Hospital, the despised rival of University Medical Center, and climbed the steep hill in search of Hemlock Street. Tidy row homes shared the neighborhood with family restaurants. American-made cars were wedged bumper-to-bumper on narrow streets. A white patio table waited for daylight on the sidewalk, secured to a downspout with a length of serious-looking chain. An occasional kitchen chair stood guard in the street holding someone's parking space. Working people lived on the Northside, people who used to work the mills. Now they were in heavy construction. Some drove long haul. Good people. Solid. The kind of neighbors you wanted to live next to. But make no mistake about it. That chair said *this parking space is mine, even if I'm working the late shift and won't be needing it for the next eight hours.*

Hemlock Street took some time to find. No one to ask directions. Forget about streetlights. Kensey finally stumbled on it after driving by twice. A church was tucked into the middle of the block, an alley on one side, a miniscule parking lot on the other. This was a building fifty years past its prime, constructed of heavy stone blocks with two white wooden pillars in front.

Now it was undergoing a major refurbishing. A large Dumpster sat heavily in the parking lot. Sheets of plywood covered the outside windows. A lone concrete cross was planted in a bare patch of dirt on one side of the front steps, a nasty tangle of bushes adorned the other.

There was no sign out front, but Kensey bet this was St. John's. She took a parking space at the far end of the block. Before leaving the safety of her car she scanned the street up and down two times. Hemlock Street was a ghost town.

Kensey trudged up the narrow front steps and tried the heavy wooden door. This was a horrible task she was about to do. The image of Manny's arm flailing about popped into her brain. Should she have gone to Carl for help *before* Manny's heart arrested? She played it over in her mind, reciting Carl's admonition to figure out what the patient needed. What Manny needed was to die. And he had good reason for his decision. But the guilt she felt was choking her.

As the hour was late she prayed the church would be locked up tight. She wanted to go home and take a shower and wash Manny Romero away. She promised herself she would come back first thing in the morning....

But the door pulled opened with a creak. Kensey stepped inside the dark vestibule and waited for her eyes to adjust.

St. John's was filled with a dusty silence. Each step Kensey took on the old wooden floor left footprints in the sawdust and squeaked out a high-pitched whisper as she passed bins of waste, more sheets of plywood, and tidy stacks of two-by-fours.

Now she entered the nave. It was simple: a long rectangular room with three heavy stone pillars standing tall on each side. Modest in size, no more than one hundred fifty people could squeeze into the congregation at one time. The pews were draped in heavy plastic. Light came from a series of wall-mounted iron sconces. Sheets of plywood were tacked to the concrete walls where the stained-glass windows had been removed.

Kensey ventured halfway down the center aisle before spotting an old woman in heavy black clothing by a table of glowing votive candles in the front of the church. She was completely absorbed in her work, totally unaware she had an audience. She was blowing out a match after lighting one of the candles. Then she did a curious thing. Placing her hand out with her palm facing down, she held it a foot or so above the candle she had just lit. Slowly, her hand descended toward the tiny flame, closer and closer until it was no more than four or five inches above the burning wick. She held her hand in place briefly as if it were cold and needed to be warmed.

A familiar feeling crept over Kensey, one she remembered from a childhood that began outside Boston. Her father wasn't a religious man, never permitting a prayer before dinner, and he managed to sleep late every Sunday. But her mother made certain her only child attended church regularly, always in her best dress, the same one every Sunday. On her seventh birthday she went to confession for the first time.

She remembered what it was like to approach the confessional. It was as if she couldn't get comfortable. Her bladder would do dipsy-doodles while the sweat glands under her dress pumped away. Her fingers pulled at her hair, her dress, anything. It was hard to whisper aloud the things she had done or said. And even harder to admit some of the things she was thinking about. But the priest always absolved her. Three Hail Marys and it was over.

"Hello," the old woman said softly, turning from the candles.

"Hello," Kensey said back. "This is St. John's, isn't it?"

"Yes, it is. I thought I heard someone. Thank you for being patient. I know I'm too slow," the old woman was saying as she stood with one hand on the table. Kensey noticed how small and bent over she was. "And I apologize for this terrible mess. Tell me what you think of it."

Kensey scanned the room. Scaffolding had been constructed along one wall. It was draped in giant sheets of clear plastic. Most of the pulpit, the altar, and the great chandelier had been mummified in white cloth. There was very little to see. "It looks like they're doing a wonderful job."

"It's a labor of love. Some of our parishioners donate their time, mostly on the weekends. How does the stone look to you? They started it this week."

Kensey glanced at the walls through the clear plastic and recognized that some of the stone did look cleaner. "It's beautiful."

The old woman smiled. "Sandblasting. It's so noisy, makes it hard for me to get around."

"I was looking for Father Flaherty."

"My child, Father may have gone to bed. Are you in trouble?"

"I can come back."

A deep voice came from the back of the church. "Can I help you? I'm Father Flaherty."

"Oh, Father," the old woman said, "I didn't hear you."

Father Flaherty thanked the old woman, calling her Sister, then encouraged her to get some sleep. She nodded, said she had one or two last candles to light, and turned back to her work. The priest was dressed in black, attaching his collar as he strolled down the aisle. A patina of white dust covered his jacket.

"Should have brought proper work clothes," he said, brushing off his arms and chest. "I don't believe I recognize you."

"I'm Kensey Shaw," she said, her voice hushed.

The priest shook her hand. "How can I help you?"

"Father, one of my patients died in the Emergency Department at University Medical Center. Before he passed he asked me …" Kensey's voice drifted off. She took a deep breath and tried again. "He asked me to … oh, Father." She began to cry as the memory of Manny's lifeless arm flooded into her head. "I've been holding it in for the last hour." Her hands shot up to her face and covered her eyes.

"Come here." Father Flaherty took a generous step closer and wrapped his arms around Kensey, pulling her in.

He smelled of fresh sawdust. Right then and there Kensey decided she would stand there all night if he'd let her. She opened her eyes, her wet cheek tight against Father's jacket, and watched the old nun working.

"I'm here because," her whispers became lost amid her tears, "I promised I'd make a confession."

The priest reassuringly rubbed Kensey's back. "Of course," he said quietly. "Do you think you're ready?"

Kensey pulled away and nodded as she rooted for a Kleenex in her pocket.

Father Flaherty placed his hand on Kensey's back and gently guided her down the aisle, around a workbench, over several ladders, and to the doors of the confessional. The confessional was a simple affair, side-by-side wooden doors, louvered on the bottom, both doors showing cracks and gaps where slats were missing. White light came through the louvers and cut a series of bright lines onto the dusty floor.

"I haven't been in one of these in years."

"For some that's the most difficult confession." Next to the confessional were two handsome wooden doors in plastic wrap, leaning against the wall. "I hope you don't mind the clutter."

Father Flaherty opened the door for her. Kensey stepped inside. It was a mess. A large white bucket squatted in the middle of the floor. It was caked with thick white plaster and a crusty spackling tool was balanced on top. Smears of dried spackle dotted the dingy walls, and there was a hole—a big one—gaping at the bottom of the back wall of the cramped room. Kensey could peer through the hole into darkness and make out some debris scattered about on the wide planks of an unfinished wooden floor.

Father Flaherty closed the door quietly. Kensey slid the plastic bucket out of the way with her foot and knelt down on the padded rest. She could hear the squeak of the other door open, then close. A decorative metal screen separated the two sides and she could see Father Flaherty's profile as he took his seat, positioned his head close to the screen, and patiently waited for her to speak first.

A part of her yearned to say, *Forgive me Father, for I have sinned*, and then launch into how she got caught up in Manny's story and let his life slip away. Instead she said, "Father, Manny Romero died this evening and asked that I come to speak with you."

"Manny Romero." Father Flaherty sighed and stared directly at the screen that separated him from Kensey. "My Lord. I've known Manny since he was a boy. A fine man. He'd come here after work and pick up a paintbrush and work past midnight."

"This is so difficult. He told me some things he wanted you to know."

"Oh? This is not your confession?"

"No, Father. I'm confessing for him."

Kensey heard a soft creak inside the church and imagined the old nun taking the priest's advice and heading home.

"What happened to him?"

"He was involved in a shoot-out. Shot in his chest. Several others died as well."

"His life was full of danger. But it was the path he chose."

Kensey thought she heard the old nun saying hello just as she had to Kensey. There was no conversation that followed. Maybe she was a lonely woman who talked to herself.

"This has been a horrible night. Manny spoke privately to me, told me he was ready to die. Father, I would never speak ill of the dead."

Creak. Creak. Creak. The sound of footsteps on the old church floor was getting louder.

Kensey continued. "He wanted to confess killing people for money."

■ ■ ■

The first thing Mike Dombroski spotted when he entered the dimly-lit church was the old nun. She seemed to be caressing one of the small white candles, her bony fingers starting at the base and sliding up to find the wick and stand it tall. Her head remained absolutely motionless as she worked, her fingers skimming the surface of the table until they found the box of matches. Striking a match on the side of the box, she held it aloft with one hand while her other waited at the candle. Finally, she brought the match to the top of the candle and held it in place for several seconds. Before the flame reached her fingers she brought the match to her lips and blew softly.

Mike was a patient observer. He waited in the back of the church, safely ensconced at the edge of a deep shadow, directly behind the last pew. He turned his head toward the confessional doors. The soft murmur of voices snuck out and echoed its way back to him. He caught a deep male voice say the word *Manny*, but otherwise the sounds were a blur to his ears. He was wearing a pair of leather gloves, tight ones that had taken time to wiggle into.

The old nun was turning away from the table and reaching out until her fingers found the plastic-wrapped end of each pew as she made her way up the aisle toward Mike.

She was in no hurry, slowly getting closer to Mike. Now the old nun was four pews away, staring right past him, acknowledging his presence in no way. Not making a sound, he leaned forward, abandoning the safety of the shadow, letting his face catch the light. With a single nod of his head Mike offered the most perfunctory of greetings. The old nun did not return the gesture. Her hand glanced on the back of each pew, making the plastic crackle. As her hand came to rest on the second-to-last pew she stopped walking. Now lifting her head slightly, as if looking up to the heavens, the old nun sniffed the air lightly.

"Hello?" she said.

Mike said nothing. He remained absolutely motionless.

She sniffed the air again, then continued up the aisle and walked into the darkness.

Mike entered the aisle and moved toward the confessional. The floor creaked under his weight. His hand slipped under his leather jacket and withdrew a 45 caliber Beretta Storm, nine rounds in the clip. As he approached the confessional he racked the slide and the distinct metallic click bounced and rattled in the church for several seconds.

■ ■ ■

Kensey was trying to recall the exact words Manny had used when she heard the metallic sound. At first she had no idea what it was. It was oddly out of place so late at night. Remembering the volunteer workers, she imagined one of them arriving after putting in an eight-hour shift at the factory. Any second now she expected to hear the whir of a table saw.

"Father, he didn't want anyone to know. He made me swear not to go to the police. He told me he and his partner had been hired to kill three people."

Father Flaherty said, "The three who died tonight?"

■ ■ ■

Silent Samaritan

Mike took an aggressive stance outside the confessional, one leg slightly in front of the other, arms outstretched, two-handed grip on the weapon, aiming at the door on the left, the one Father Flaherty had entered. He listened carefully, heard Kensey speak softly about the shootings and his partner. She didn't mention him by name. But she was talking about him. Then she dropped the bombshell.

■ ■ ■

Kensey was saying, "... he and his partner had been hired to kill three people." That's when something drew her eyes to the bottom of the door where several of the slats were missing. A fancy cowboy boot was no more than three feet from the door. Someone was listening to everything she was saying. Kensey's pupils dilated. Her mouth opened and her breathing quickened. Her words drifted off into silence. She leaned over and could make out another boot and a pair of blue jeans, one leg in front of the other as if bracing himself. Placing her hand on the filthy floor, she lowered herself to get a better look out the slats. The man was wearing a leather jacket. He had a thick mustache. Right away she was certain this was the man who had bumped into her in the hospital.

He was leveling a black handgun at the confessional.

Kensey opened her mouth wide to scream. ...

The gun was incredibly loud — *Bam! Bam! Bam!* — echoing off the stone walls.

■ ■ ■

Mike fired in rapid succession into the first door, the bullets ripping three splintery holes through the thin wood in an equilateral triangular pattern, one high, two low, about six inches apart. He pivoted and squeezed off three more rounds into the other door. The pattern was the same. In ten seconds it was over. Mike stayed in position while his heart thumped wildly in his chest, listening for sounds of life behind the doors. He reached for the first doorknob.

Behind him a woman screamed. Instinctively he ducked behind the first pew and readied his weapon.

It was the old nun in the back of the church crying out, calling Father Flaherty's name. Mike watched her standing behind the last pew, looking everywhere and nowhere. He stood up and ignored her cries. Turning his back to the old nun, he snatched the knob on the left and jerked the door open. The priest spilled out onto the floor in a bloody heap. One side of his face was shrouded with pink ooze from a hole above his ear.

The old nun would not stop. Now she was getting hoarse, bleating out Father's name over and over.

Mike shot a bullet straight up in the air. "Shut up, you old prune." This silenced the nun, who turned and hid behind a heavy column.

Stuffing the gun under his leather jacket and into the shoulder harness, Mike was moving quickly now, grabbing the other door and yanking it open. The cubicle was empty. No blood, just the bucket of dried plaster and three quarter-sized holes in the back wall. When he saw the gaping opening in the wall he curled his upper lip and hollered, "Shit."

It was too small for him to squeeze through. Taking one quick step forward, he raised his right foot and grunted loudly as he thrust it out so the sole of his cowboy boot smacked the upper margin of the existing hole. His foot ripped through the old plaster and kept on going into the darkness beyond the confessional.

5

Kensey was trembling in the darkness on the other side of the wall. She was in a storage room with a slatted floor that smelled like an attic. For the moment the church was quiet. She was breathing through cupped hands, standing butt-flush against some old pipes, as far from the opening she had just crawled through as the room would allow. Already she was looking around for something to use as a weapon. Piles of smelly carpet and an old toilet were stashed next to her. The light from the confessional cast a feeble glow through the hole.

Any second he would be coming through the wall. There were five bullet holes in the wall, each glowing with a dot of light, two on the right, three on the left. She ran the numbers. There had been one more gunshot than there were bullet holes. Now a woman's voice was calling out Father Flaherty's name. She sounded desperate.

Kensey guessed who the cowboy was. One other thought crossed her mind: If she hadn't gotten warm and toasty with Manny Romero and he hadn't died, none of this would be happening.

As her eyes adjusted, different objects were coming into focus. On the far side of the room Kensey could make out the top three slats of a wooden ladder. It ran straight down the wall rather than leaning against it at an angle, disappearing through a skinny hole cut in the floor. There didn't seem to be another way out.

Her mind was playing wicked games inside her head. She imagined the man with the gun punching through the wall and grabbing her by the neck. In one quick move he would drag her through the hole, stripping off her clothes in the process. Then he would kill her.

Kensey shuddered. She bent down and felt around. Some books. A length of lumber, a two-by-four, three feet long. She grabbed it and instantly felt a stab of pain in her palm. Yanking her hand away and bringing it to her mouth, she could taste blood.

Moments later she was ready for a second try. Now she groped in the darkness more carefully.

A single gunshot rang out and some more yelling, this time from the man. Then the world became silent.

Locating the board a second time, Kensey discovered two long nails protruding several inches from one end. One of the nails stuck straight out, the other exited at a crooked angle, hinting that someone had bent it while prying the board loose.

The cowboy hollered, 'Shit.'

The other end of the board was free of nails. Kensey grabbed it with both hands, hoisted it above her head, and sidled up to the wall like a cat waiting for a mouse. Any second now he would poke his head through the hole looking for her and —

There was a loud crash of plasterboard and his leg burst through the wall. At first Kensey jumped. Before he could pull it back she took a single quick step forward and slammed the board into the man's thigh, grunting like a tennis player smashing a crosscourt drive.

A piercing scream came from the other side of the wall. The cowboy began cursing and tried to yank his leg back through the hole, but it was trapped. The nails had sunk deeply into the fleshy muscle of his thigh and were digging into his bone. The combination of a straight nail and a crooked one teamed up to create a claw that latched tight and refused to let go. The more he pulled his leg the more the daggers stabbed his femur.

Kensey watched in horror, close enough to touch the man's leg, her hands clamped over her mouth to keep from screaming.

His gun went off and a bullet hole appeared in the wall, letting another dot of white light into the darkness. Kensey dropped flat to the floor, kicking up clouds of dust, her head inches from the cowboy boot. Then another blast from the gun and another bullet hole and finally the harmless click of an empty gun being fired in desperation.

The man began pounding on the wall with his fist, creating little puffs of dust from the bullet holes. He was enraged, screaming that he had a knife and was going to cut her throat and watch her bleed to death.

Kensey pushed up and moved toward the ladder, sliding her feet along the old wooden floor, careful not to fall down the hole. She grabbed the ladder and gave it a shake. It was attached to the wall and descended into a blackness that revealed nothing about itself.

Now the man had stopped banging and had slipped his arm through the hole where his leg was entrapped. He was working the two-by-four back and forth and screaming what he was gonna do when he got her.

Kensey's decision became easier. She gave the ladder another shake, this time a hard one, and when the ladder held firm she started down. The slats were rough-cut and narrow. She held on tight and descended into the darkness, six, eight, ten steps.

The room she entered was cool. Rats scurried and scratched about noisily when Kensey's foot hit the dirt floor and the stench of their urine was overpowering. It was hard to take in a full breath without gagging.

The room was a long rectangle, the same as the one above but with dozens of boxes lined up along one wall and metal shelves along another. On the far wall, just above eye level, was a little push-out window no more than ten inches in height. If she stood on her tiptoes she could make out the light of a faraway porch lamp.

An empty wooden table had been pushed up against the wall right below the window. At the other end of the room was a door with three slit windows. Immediately she bolted for it and grabbed the knob, twisting it back and forth until her hands hurt. The door would not budge.

"Shit," she whispered and headed back toward the window.

The man with the gun was banging around upstairs. Every one of his footsteps could be heard on the floorboards. Kensey gazed up. Dust was falling from the ceiling. It wouldn't take him long to spot the ladder.

She hopped up on the table. It swayed under her weight and she grasped the windowsill to keep her balance. The window had a metal latch at the bottom. It required a quarter-clockwise turn to unlock it, then a sharp push. The window swung open. Fresh air blew into the room. Shimmying through the narrow opening was Kensey's best bet. Placing her hands on the concrete sill she ...

A tiny light shone down from above. Kensey froze. It reminded her of the beam from the penlight she used to check patients' pupils. The man had found the ladder and was checking it out. He shook it and placed his foot on the first step.

"Just so you know," his voice filtered down to the subterranean room, "I'm gonna kill you slowly. I'm gonna make it hurt."

Kensey looked through the narrow opening. He was coming down the ladder and she'd never make it out in time. Quietly, Kensey hopped off the table and hid behind a wall of boxes, flattening herself on the dirt floor and willing herself not to move even if a rat scooted up her leg.

The boxes weren't stacked neatly. Through a sliver of space she could see the dark silhouette of the man coming down the ladder. The flashlight was in his mouth, the beam bouncing around the room as he turned his head this way and that. By the time his foot touched the floor he'd spotted the open window. "Goddamn," he said, and by the acid in his voice it was clear to Kensey the man with the gun thought she had escaped through it.

He switched the flashlight to his hand. Scanning the room, he noticed the door and soon was turning the knob. Although Kensey couldn't see much of him as he moved toward the other end of the room, she could hear the syncopated cadence of someone with a limp. He too couldn't budge the door, but with the help of his little penlight located a bolt that slid up into the jamb and unlocked it. In a matter of seconds the door was wide open, a great rush of air hit the dank room, and the man disappeared outside.

Kensey was too frightened to move. Silently she counted to a hundred. One Mississippi, two Mississippi, three Mississippi, four Mississippi, five Mississi —

He was back. He strode to the table and groaned in pain as he hoisted himself up on it and shined his flashlight on the windowsill for several seconds, then turned around and drew his gun. Slowly and methodically he worked his little flashlight around the room, starting near the ladder.

"No time for hide-and-seek. That old bitch's probably called nine-one-one." Opting for a one-handed grip so he could shine the light, he took aim in the direction of the boxes in the rear corner. He squeezed the trigger and a deafening blast hit Kensey's ears hard. She closed her eyes and for a moment everything seemed bright. "Very clever, climbing up on the table and opening the window. You almost got me."

He aimed several feet to the right of the first shot and squeezed the trigger two times. The bullets ripped through the boxes and smashed loudly into the cinder-block wall. "When I got outside I said, 'You blew it, asshole, she's gone.'" He grunted loudly. "Shit, my fuckin' leg. Goddamn you." After several noisy breaths he said, "But I noticed outside that window, all these broken bottles and shit. If you belly-crawled through it—" Pivoting several degrees clockwise, the cowboy aimed his gun one box over and kept pulling the trigger until it clicked harmlessly. He popped the clip and dug in his pocket for another. "— you'd be cut up to pieces, bleeding all over the place like a stuck pig. But there's no blood." He slipped the new clip in the grip and rammed it into place. "I figured maybe you changed your mind." He aimed one box to the right and squeezed the trigger twice.

By now Kensey's ears were ringing so loudly she couldn't hear what he was saying.

"You ain't so smart, bitch. You made another mistake." He aimed the weapon at the column of boxes next to Kensey and squeezed the trigger three times. "You left a handprint on the windowsill. If you wiggled through that little space you would've cleaned it off nice." He pivoted and squeezed the trigger. The bullet tore through the box and over Kensey's shoulder and into the cinder-block wall behind her.

About that same time Kensey heard the sirens. The man with the gun heard them too. He glanced out the window and jumped off the table. "My fuckin' leg," he hissed, then emptied his gun into the boxes and kept on clicking the trigger as he hobbled to the door and into the night.

As much as Kensey wanted to find the police and tell them everything that had happened, what Manny said to her in the hospital came back: "You go to the cops you'll get killed." Something about the way he said it. Not that it was a threat. It was a warning, Manny being a Samaritan.

The sirens were louder now. Kensey slowly pushed herself to a standing position. Silently, she thanked God for protecting her. She looked around the narrow room, knowing she would never be back. Pulling the ball of Kleenex from her pocket, she wiped her handprints from the little window and tore out of the room.

6

Kensey rented a small house in Highland Park, an older enclave in Pittsburgh with homes that ran the gamut from splendid old mansions to modest two-bedroom duplexes on lots you could spit across.

For the last half hour she had driven like a maniac all over the city, chaotically racing around blocks two and three times, making crazy U-turns, and scooting down a one-way street the wrong way. No one was following her. When she finally turned onto Bryant Street she rolled her little Honda to a quiet stop half a block from her house.

When she rented the house four months ago, her landlord bragged that the two-story white clapboard was purchased right out of the Sears catalogue sometime in the 1950s. It had arrived from the factory on a flatbed, everything down to the nuts and bolts included. The house was typical Sears: rugged, like one of its hammers. Front door, side door, front hall, living room, dining room, kitchen, full bath, and two tiny bedrooms. Nothing fancy. Nice, affordable homes for those tired GIs coming home from World War II. "Christ," her landlord mentioned when he was giving her the walk-through, "a tree fell on it once and didn't even chip the paint."

Kensey shut off the engine, scrunched down in the seat and spied on her own front yard. It was nearly three AM, but Kensey was wired. From time to time cars drove by. Even a white police cruiser with a rack of lights wandered down the quiet street but didn't seem to notice anyone sitting in the Honda.

After about forty-five minutes Kensey was beginning to wonder if she was wasting her time. The cowboy with the mustache kept jumping into her head. There was no way he could have overheard Manny Romero ask her to go to his priest and offer confession. Manny had made sure of that. But he could have listened to what she had said to Detective Hennessey, figured out it was a bunch of lies and decided to take care of her. And while he was hanging out in the Emergency Department he could have sidled up to one of the nurses and asked the name of the doctor in Trauma Two.

Thankfully, she had an unlisted phone number. Like many women who lived alone, Kensey didn't want some creep from the hospital bugging her at night. And the hospital would never give out her address. So there was no realistic way the man with the mustache could find her. She was being paranoid and scolded herself as she reached for the ignition.

A pair of headlights appeared in the rearview mirror. The car crept up Bryant, inching its way down the block as if the driver was searching for house numbers. He didn't notice Kensey. But as he coasted by she got a gander of his thick mustache. Definitely the guy, driving a pathetic Chevy two-door missing a taillight. It stopped briefly right in front of her place, the guy's head turning to see where she lived, taking it all in for half a minute, then moving again, slowly down the block and around the corner.

One Mississippi, two Mississippi, three Mississippi, four Mississippi. Not till she hit a hundred did she allow her fingers anywhere near the key in the ignition.

■ ■ ■

"My God, Kensey, you okay?" Susanne Smerdell already had her arm around Kensey, the two standing just inside the front door, Kensey looking numb. Before throwing the door closed, Susanne dared a quick look out at the street.

Not a soul was out for a walk this time of night.

"What happened?" Susanne's voice was shrill, her hand trembling as if she'd developed an acute case of Parkinson's. Susanne's thicket of red wavy hair usually sat on her head like a coonskin cap. Now it was all over the place and Susanne didn't waste time taming it with her hand. Her arm clutching Kensey's shoulders, the two moved into the living room like mourners at a funeral, then huddled together on the sofa.

Susanne's world was filled with hand-me-downs. Nothing matched but she had one of everything: a three-cushion sofa, comfy easy chair, coffee table, end tables, and lamps to spare. The only thing new in the living room was the little Sony television, a graduation present from her parents the day she left for Pittsburgh. Decked out in white sweat socks and a three-quarter, flannel nightgown, Susanne now felt the chill of the night and crossed her arms under her breasts. She was twenty-six, the same age as Kensey.

Kensey was a mess. It looked as if someone had given her a shampoo with dirt. Thick streaks of grime covered her cheeks like war paint. Her yellow rugby shirt was torn in several places. And Susanne was eyeing the bloody cuff of one of the sleeves. Kensey started to cry, sobbing, covering her face with her hands.

Susanne was from Georgia, a fellow intern with a sweet southern accent. Waiting out the silence, Susanne picked slivers of wood from her hair. Finally she said in the softest voice, "You were raped, weren't you?"

With a quick shake of her head, Kensey said, "No, no, nothing like that," and for the next ten minutes recounted the entire story. When she got to the part about the cowboy showing up at her house she said, "So I came here."

"What about the cops?"

"I wanted to." Kensey's hand massaged her wrist where Manny had squeezed it. "I kept hearing his voice telling me I'd be killed if I went to the cops. He made me swear."

"The cowboy?"

"No, the guy who got shot."

"You want a drink? I got Southern Comfort."

"He knows who I am, Susanne. How can I go home?" She threw her arms out in front of her as if giving up. "I don't know what to do."

"I'm getting you some Southern Comfort." Susanne started to push up from the sofa.

"No. Please." Kensey placed her hand on Susanne's arm. "I need to think."

Easing back into the cushion, Susanne said, "Long as you want, you stay here. I'll sleep on the couch."

"He knows I work at the hospital. I can't even go there."

"Maybe take some time off, go see your mom."

"Soon as I come back he'll be waiting. It doesn't matter how long I'm gone."

"Then you're going to the cops. Period," Susanne said.

"They can't protect me twenty-four-seven for the rest of my life." Kensey glared at Susanne. "Don't suggest it again."

Susanne scrutinized Kensey. "All right, you're my best friend and you came to me, so you're gonna listen." Her voice had some authority to it.

"Then you better put on some coffee."

"Good idea." Susanne padded the several steps behind the sofa toward the little kitchen.

Kensey nodded. "I'm listening." She slipped off her shoes and sat cross-legged, her back toward the kitchen.

After plugging in the Mr. Coffee, Susanne turned her head toward Kensey while she counted scoops. "You're basing everything on a sound bite from a *hit* man."

Kensey shook her head. "I don't think I'll ever be able to explain it, but he had a...quality."

Susanne was reaching into a cupboard for two mugs. "A quality?" she said and immediately dropped a mug into the sink, which broke. "Look what you made me do, talking crazy like that."

Kensey pushed up from the sofa and took a step toward the kitchen.

"I got it." Susanne was looking at her. "It's not your fault." As she picked up the pieces of the mug and deposited them in the trash, Kensey eased back onto the sofa, her eyes settling on the silent Sony.

Her voice quiet, as if Susanne were still in the room, Kensey said, "When he was talking to me he put his hand on my wrist." She placed one hand on her own wrist. A moment later she was examining the palm of her hand where the nail had entered. It was filthy. In the middle was a tiny hole no more than an eighth of an inch across, the sides sealed up nicely like a little smile.

Susanne appeared at the door to the kitchen, leaning forward, one hand on each side of the jamb. "This the first one you ever lost?"

Kensey nodded.

"Maybe that has something to do with it."

"Detective Hennessey said I'd remember his name twenty years from now."

"The one with the nice eyes?"

"I didn't say he had nice eyes, I said kind eyes."

"What do you think about him?"

Kensey whipped her head around and shot her a look. "Who? Detective Hennessey? He's a cop working a case. Forget I said anything about his eyes."

"Kensey," Susanne paused.

"What?"

"I meant do you think you can trust him."

"He's a cop. I don't know."

"When you were telling me the story and you got to the part with the detective? You didn't notice but some of the tension in your shoulders eased until you got to the part about the cowboy."

Kensey shrugged her shoulders as if testing them out.

"Kensey, I'm not making it up."

"You're reading something that wasn't there."

Susanne was back in the kitchen opening a bag of cookies. "So ... you're on a first-name basis with the murderer. And he's got a quality Detective Hennessey doesn't have. Yet talking about Hennessey relaxes you—"

"Stop." Kensey reached forward and picked up the remote control from a wooden side table. As she fingered the power button the television came to life. Susanne came back into the room with a plate of cookies. A single tear was running down Kensey's cheek, crossing stripes of grease and picking up color. "I trust you more than anyone in this city. So don't get that goddamn, sarcastic edge to your voice. Please."

Holding out the plate, Susanne said, "Milanos. Your favorite." Her voice was tiny. She sat down next to Kensey.

"Just so you know, Manny spoke from the heart. He was scared to death he was going to hell and was confessing his sins. We connected." She grabbed three cookies and nibbled one as Susanne slipped her arm around her shoulders.

They munched cookies while they watched the end of an infomercial for a squeegee that cleaned tile floors. Suddenly Susanne hopped off the couch. "The coffee."

Now there was a talking head in front of an active newsroom. The coffee would have to wait. Susanne joined Kensey on the sofa. Silently, the two stared at the TV. "A shoot-out took place earlier tonight at an industrial complex in O'Hara Township. Two victims were found shot to death at the headquarters of Cheap Charlie's. Their names have not been released by police. Two others were taken to University Medical Center with gunshot wounds. One of them, Charles Hawk, fifty-seven, of Fox Chapel, was pronounced dead in the Emergency Department."

"Shit, gimme that," Kensey said, leaning forward to snatch the remote control from the side table.

"A second victim—"

"I'm not listening to this." Her voice was loud. Taking aim with the remote control she fumbled to find the button.

"—Manny Romero, a member of—"

The picture went black.

"What'd you do that for?" Susanne asked gently. "Maybe they'll have something about the church."

"Manny's arm was just bouncing around as they pounded on his chest. When they finally stopped it just sort of..." Kensey hesitated before she said, "...hung there. I kept wondering if I did the right thing."

"If Manny wanted you to warn these future victims, why would he care if you went to the police?"

"When I was sitting in my car I had a lot of time to think about that. He's got a shred of moral fiber left—"

"Bullshit," Susanne interrupted.

Kensey held her hand in the air and raised her voice. "And," she paused to make certain Susanne was listening, "suspects Sonny'll be watching me. If I go to the cops they'll kill me."

"If Hennessey's a problem for you, find out who the captain is. He'll know what to do."

"Manny was protecting me. I know it doesn't make sense, but that's what he was trying to do."

"Maybe the priest was just wounded. Let me turn on the TV."

"I don't want to know."

"So what happens now?"

"I could take a shower here. You and I are the same size. You know that green sweater I told you I like?"

"That creep had no trouble hanging around the ED without anyone getting suspicious, getting a good look at you and finding out where you live." Susanne went over to the front window and pulled back the drape. "Jesus Christ. He's out there somewhere."

"Don't worry. I doubled back and made a bunch of loops. He didn't follow me."

"That's not what I'm talking about. You got lucky at the church. But you can't beat this guy. He's gonna try again." Susanne sat back down. She said nothing until Kensey took a sip of coffee and looked at her with wet eyes.

"Is that what you think?"

"If you don't go to the cops first thing in the morning, I will."

7

The Zone 5 squad room in East Liberty was hopping. Kensey paused in the doorway to survey the space. Her hair wet from the shower, she smelled better, though it felt strange wearing Susanne's clothes. Several times she caught herself staring at anything reflective to check out the look: a green turtleneck sweater over gray slacks. Typical Susanne.

Set on a busy one-way street, the police station was a hulking, three-story, concrete building built when central air-conditioning was too extravagant for cops and no one gave a dang about the people they arrested. Now half the windows sported heavy-duty air conditioners. Conveniently, the station was across from a McDonald's. Nearly every uniform walked through the front door toting a little white bag of food.

On one side of the room a dozen heavy wooden desks were lined up, each with two chairs in front. Long wooden benches aligned against the opposite wall looked like church pews and several vending machines sat shoulder to shoulder near the front door. In the rear of the room was a metal door that saw constant in-and-out traffic. Kensey wondered if it was hiding the cells. Halfway back, between two sets of desks, was a wide wooden staircase that went up to the second floor. Change of shift was in full swing and it was noisy. Two uniformed officers were wrestling some punks with sideways hats and pants down to their pubes into chairs and handcuffing them to the armrests.

A couple of cute coeds in blue vests with the Pitt logo in yellow script were huddled on one of the benches. One of them was crying, leaning against her friend.

Two benches away were two women with big hair and tiny patent-leather bags they wore over their shoulders on long spaghetti straps. One was reapplying bright purple lipstick, the other sported torpedo breasts that strained to break free of their lacy constraints and fly across the room.

A chubby female officer with short, squat legs and a nightstick bouncing off her hip was waddling toward the front door. Kensey approached her and said, "Excuse me, is the captain here?"

"Cap'n Adkins?"

"I guess."

The female officer turned and scanned the room. "Back there, black man in the tweed suit."

There was a cluster of men standing in a little circle in the back. Kensey mumbled a thank-you to the officer, then tiptoed into the room. She took a seat on the bench where the women with the big hair were sitting, keeping an eye on Captain Adkins. Someone walked by with an Egg McMuffin half-wrapped in thin paper to keep his fingers clean while he ate it.

Captain Adkins was a big man, broad-shouldered with a way of standing that made Kensey think jock. Probably football, maybe baseball. He was smiling, coming across like a friendly guy wearing a pair of reddish-brown tortoiseshell glasses that made him look studious at the same time.

"These dancer benches."

Kensey heard the voice but let it slip right through her brain.

"Ex*cuse* me."

This time it registered. Kensey turned and realized she was being addressed. "I'm sorry, were you talking to me?"

"Yeah, honey," the one with the torpedo breasts said. "You a dancer?" She had a look about her that was all business, muscular arms sticking out of little hot pink sleeves. But the way she said *dancer* made Kensey look down at the gray slacks she was wearing.

Sitting in the noisy squad room, Kensey shook her head and said, "No."

"Then you belong on that bench," the woman with the purple lipstick said, tilting her head toward the two coeds. "That's the I'm-waiting-for-my-daddy-to-bail-me-out bench. Them two's from Sewickley. Heard one of the cops talking about 'em." She turned her head toward the coeds. "Isn't that right, girls?" She used a high-pitched voice. Then to Kensey: "One of 'em's Muffy, the other Logan. They scared of us."

Kensey started to get up.

"No, no, no," torpedo breasts said. "Stay." She scooted over toward Kensey and leaned forward slightly as she spoke. "Oooooo, is that thing real?" She tapped a long sparkly fingernail on her own cheek.

"What?" Kensey leaned forward so she could see the woman's cheek.

"What *is* that, a tattoo?"

"No, just a mole." Kensey smiled. "I was born with it."

"Gotta get me one a' those." She turned to her friend and said, "Lipstick red, only bigger. Maybe with an arrow through it. Everyone's got something on the ankle. Guys like that sorta shit where they don't 'spect it." She turned back toward Kensey. "Oh, I'm Sapphire. This here's B.J."

"I'm Kensey."

"Kensey? Maybe you know Muffy over there. What the hell kind of a name's Kensey?"

"Short for McKenzie."

"La - di - da. What're you, a college girl?"

"I'm a doctor."

"Where?" Sapphire asked. "Over at Mercy?"

"University Medical."

"Hey," Sapphire said, giving B.J. a quick flash of her eyes, "B.J. here got herself a shot of penicillin there last month." Turning back to B.J., she asked, "What was that doctor's name?"

"He was cu-ute. Hey, what're you in for anyway, girl?"

"I'm just here to report a crime. Waiting for Captain Adkins."

"Well, go talk to the man."

Kensey looked over her shoulder toward Adkins, who was still chatting it up in back.

"He just shooting the shit with his posse," Sapphire said.

"But he s'posed to be on the clock," B.J. added.

Softly Kensey said, "I don't know."

"Get going, girl. Me'n B.J.'ll keep your seat warm."

Kensey looked at Adkins then back at Sapphire.

Sapphire stood. "Don't worry, I'll call him over for you."

"No, don't do that." Kensey stood and headed toward the little huddle of men, past uniformed officers sitting at desks, talking on the phone, typing reports, drinking coffee, and eating McDonald's. There were five people in the conversation: Captain Adkins, facing toward Kensey, smiling and laughing. Two young uniformed cops, one on each side of the Captain, hanging on to every word their boss said. A tall man with his back turned toward Kensey, wearing a tattered barn jacket with an upturned leather collar and faded jeans. And finally, an overweight man with thin, greasy hair and a bad sport coat.

Now the guy in the barn jacket seemed to have the floor. He was excited, using his hands as he spoke, telling a good one because when he reached the punch line everyone laughed and Captain Adkins even high-fived him.

Kensey glanced back at the front door and gave serious consideration to leaving until she spotted Sapphire standing next to the dancer bench, making little shooing motions with her hands. She called out, "You go, girl."

Kensey took one more step toward the boys' club when the guy in the barn jacket turned away from the others to cough. He was quite handsome in a rugged Marlboro Man sort of way, clean-shaven, long hair and a strong chin and —

Kensey stopped walking. People were going around her on both sides but she just stood there, unable to will her legs to move. By the time she realized what she was witnessing, her heart was off and running. Lowering her head and moving sideways between two desks so she could lean against the wall, Kensey took a breather. Images of last night seized her brain and she wanted to run as far away from this place as possible.

It was something about his posture, the way he stood with one leg in front of the other that was making her crazy. Her heart was ticking along wildly and she wasn't even moving.

She knew this guy.

Now Captain Adkins was taking his two index fingers and placing them side-by-side just below his nostrils. He stroked them away from each other, outlining his lips until they were halfway around his mouth. He repeated this a second time, pointed to the man in the barn jacket and all five of them shared a hearty laugh. The man in the barn jacket was going along with the joke, laughing as hard as anybody. Finally he held up his hands palms out, as if to say Okay, enough with the joshing.

Kensey was lost in a flashback of every goddamn thing that had happened in the church with the cowboy. The gun he had and the way he was standing outside the confessional before he opened fire. "Oh my God." She heard the words and didn't realize she had said them.

At this moment she was gaping at the guy who had shot the priest. He was no more than twenty-five feet away, laughing it up with the Captain, slapping high-fives. So what if he shaved his mustache. It was the same guy.

Now he turned around a second time to cough. He looked straight at Kensey but was so cool about it she couldn't tell if he recognized her because he went right back toward the captain. And that's when Kensey noticed that he had a badge on his belt.

All she had to do was walk to the front door and keep on going. She begged herself not to panic. Just turn and walk. ...

"Saved one last night, Mike. Catch you later," Captain Adkins said loudly, as if he was jubilant about a basketball game his team had won. Again he stroked above his upper lip and laughed and the five men went in separate directions.

Mike. Now he had a name.

Kensey lowered her head and made the turn toward the door. Somewhere in her peripheral vision Sapphire and B.J. were standing and calling out her name and pointing in the direction of Captain Adkins as he went over to a coffeepot and poured himself a cupful.

Kensey stopped walking and stared at the floor in front of her feet. Every time she heard Sapphire or B.J. call out her name she cringed. Avoid eye contact, she told herself. Maybe her new best friends would get bored and go back to tormenting the coeds.

But Mike knew. As if he had nothing better to do, he moseyed over to a secretary at a desk nearby and picked up the sports section. He turned the page and shot a casual glance at Kensey, keeping her on the radar, a paralyzed wallflower waiting to be plucked. Now Sapphire and B.J. were on their way toward the back of the room, torpedo breasts and purple lipstick attracting attention, guys unable to keep their eyes on their computer screens. Sapphire having trouble with a long feathery scarf dragging on the floor, yanked it up toward her neck and trailed it in the air dramatically.

One of the uniformed officers was coming over to the two girls, pointing in the direction of the benches. But Sapphire would have no part of that, saying loudly that she had to go pee and trusting her momentum to propel her toward Kensey.

Mike watched the whole scene unfolding. Absently his fingers went up to his face and stroked the naked skin where his mustache used to be.

The uniformed officer was saying that Sapphire could use the bathroom but B.J. had to return to the bench. Then Sapphire was saying that B.J. had to pee too, louder now so everyone in the squad room knew what was happening, the uniformed officer doing his best to corral the two ladies, but Sapphire getting him tangled up in her scarf and turning his face a nice shade of red.

The punks were taking it all in. One of them started rolling his chair toward the front door as if he intended to make a run for it.

In the commotion, Mike dropped the newspaper on the desk and was coming toward Kensey. He was favoring his right leg, hobbling like Chester Goode on *Gunsmoke*, but moving fast enough that Kensey had to make a decision. She knew she could outrun him easily but chose to walk toward the front door rather than make a break for it and have one of the uniforms think she was a prisoner escaping.

"Let's get control, people." Captain Adkins was yelling now, moving toward the center of the room. He was standing hands akimbo, shaking his head.

Every officer in the room jumped into action. Two uniforms immediately took up positions at the front door, black nightsticks in hand, challenging anyone in the room to get by them. Kensey stopped in mid-stride. No more than six steps away, Mike was coming toward her, one hand on his thigh. The front door was out. If she was quick about it she could do an end run around the crippled cowboy and head to the back of the building, but that would mean skimming by the Sapphire-B.J. imbroglio and who knew where the back door was. Then there were the stairs.

Kensey darted up the wooden stairs two at a time, disappearing before Mike grabbed the railing. About the time her foot touched the wide floorboards of the second floor it hit her: Getting stuck upstairs couldn't possibly be as negotiable as hunting down a back door. She faced a long, empty hallway lined with closed doors. The walls were institutional off-white. Endless banks of fluorescent lights dotted the ceiling. Every door had a frosted pane of glass with a hand-lettered name on it in black paint. The first one belonged to Captain Adkins. Kensey didn't bother and dashed right by the next three.

Halfway down, the hallway crisscrossed a similar-looking one at right angles. This one was also empty. Kensey's first instinct was to go right. But looking like a running back tripping up a defensive end, she faked right then moved left, sprinting down a hallway that looked exactly the same as the one she'd just abandoned.

Her timing was impeccable.

Mike pulled himself to the top step using the handrail. He was treated to a decidedly empty hallway. Not wasting a second, he gave a quick two-knuckled knock and opened one door after another, poking his head in each office for a split second before moving onto the next one. He was methodical yet cool. Whenever he encountered someone in one of the offices he mumbled, "You seen the captain?" After that he would apologize for bothering them and head to the next one.

Kensey was trying doors as well. The situation forced her to be a bit more selective. She found a door marked *Maintenance*. It was locked. Then failed again with one marked *Storage*. There was a solitary window at the end of the hallway. The building was fifty years old and the windows had never been modernized. It wasn't locked but layers of paint sealed it shut. Kensey worked at it for several seconds, turning red in the face and letting out a grunt before noticing she was standing between the doors to the bathrooms. Men's on the left, women's on the right. Once again instinct sent her toward the women's room. After giving the door a gentle shove she turned, dashed across the hallway and ran straight into the men's room.

Mike had worked his way to the crossroads of the hallways and stopped so he could massage his right thigh while he caught his breath, his head sweeping left and right. He was sweating now, his face glistening under the harsh lights. Time was running out. By now the melee downstairs had certainly been quelled. If he chose the wrong hallway he would hand Kensey the opportunity to double back and stroll out the front door.

A soft sound came from his left. Immediately he recognized it: the heavy thud of a wooden door closing against the jamb. A little smile made him look giddy. His prey was hiding in the bathroom. Ignoring the police-issue weapon in his shoulder holster, his hand slipped behind his back and returned with his Beretta, the same one he had used in the church. He plunged his hand into one of the big patch pockets of his barn jacket for a four-inch silencer. It threaded quickly onto the short barrel. Mike dropped his hand to his side and took casual strides down the hallway. If anyone saw him he looked like a guy on his way to take a leak.

■ ■ ■

The bathroom had little black-and-white tiles on the floor, circa the fifties, with bigger ones, the same colors, on the walls. Here and there tiles were broken or missing. On one wall were two stalls and two tall urinals with white cakes that looked like hockey pucks. Across the room she saw two sinks with a single mirror in between them. On the far wall directly opposite the door was the lone window. At first Kensey ignored it. Instinct told her to get in one of the stalls, stand on the toilet seat and crouch down, leaving the door ajar to avert suspicion. After opening the door to one of the stalls and eyeing the filth someone forgot to flush, she looked back at the window. On the dusty sill was a two-foot length of lumber. It wasn't heavy enough to make much of a weapon. But it meant something important: the window lifted easily. With almost no effort she had it all the way to the top. When it refused to stay open Kensey wedged the wood into the sash channel to hold it. This being the backside of the building, she looked out at a vacant gas station with weeds growing out of cracks in the asphalt. Not a soul in sight.

Kensey leaned out. She estimated she was fifteen to twenty feet from the ground. Directly below the bathroom window was one of the window air conditioners sticking out almost two feet. She glanced over her shoulder at the bathroom door, then at the stalls and made a decision.

■ ■ ■

Mike pushed the bathroom door open and slipped inside. It looked empty. He eased the door closed behind him so it wouldn't make a sound. The metal doors to both stalls were partially open. No shoes under the doors. Tiled floor, tiled walls, two stalls, two sinks, a window and a mirror. He'd seen enough movies to guess what she had done. He tugged at his sweaty shirt. Silently he moved to the first stall, the Beretta out in front, safety off, finger on the trigger. One shot was all it would take, right in the head so she wouldn't be able to scream. The gun was a throwaway, something he'd slipped in his pocket when he busted a dope dealer three years ago. All he had to do was wipe it down, toss it in the trash, and head over to Mickey D's for some breakfast, maybe bring the

Captain a McMuffin and hash browns when he came back. He opened the door to the first stall. Nothing. Taking a deep breath, he glanced back at the bathroom door, making sure no secretary was standing there watching him. He gave the door on the second stall a quick shove, whispered, "Jesus fuckin' Christ," and limped off to the men's room.

■ ■ ■

Kensey hopped up on the sill, swung her legs outside, and ducked her head under the window. Looking like she was sitting on the edge of a swimming pool, dangling her feet in the water, she was thinking about how to turn around without falling. Gripping the sill tightly, she flipped over onto her belly so that her legs were out in the cold morning air while her head was still inside the bathroom, eyes on the door, praying it wouldn't open. She slid further outside, Susanne's green sweater riding up until her body was all the way out the window, smack-dab against the concrete, her hands technically still inside the room, white-knuckling the lip of the sill. She peeked down. Where the hell was the air conditioner? She couldn't see it. It had to be six or eight feet below her feet but it was absolutely impossible to locate. Her grip slipped and she dug with the toes of her shoes to keep from falling.

 The door opened. Mike took a quick step inside, saw the way Kensey was struggling with her grip and limped toward her, not bothering to check out the rest of the room. He figured if some other guy was there Kensey wouldn't be going out the window. He took an aggressive step toward the window, breathing like an asthmatic, then assumed a shooter's stance, one leg in front of the other, and brought the silenced weapon up with a two-handed grip.

Kensey screamed and let go. The sleeve of Susanne's sweater tore as it scraped across the rough concrete. Her hands flailed out to the side and accidentally dislodged the piece of lumber. As she dropped out of sight the window slammed shut. What happened next would always be a blur to Kensey. After a brief encounter with the air conditioner, she tumbled to the ground, ending up on her side, sore but uninjured.

Mike was at the window, hoisting it up so that it banged at the top, thrusting his head and torso outside. Using his shoulders to keep it open, he aimed the Beretta. This was always a difficult shot, shooting down at a moving target. Kensey was rolling onto her knees, scrambling. He squeezed off a round that made a muffled popping sound. Several feet away from her torso the ground puckered and sent up a spray of dirt. Now she was up on her feet and making a run for it, the corner of the building less than fifteen feet away.

Mike had time for two more shots. Kensey never broke stride as she rounded the building.

Before reaching her Honda, she had one last surprise. Sapphire and B.J. were strutting down the sidewalk, arms swinging, feathery scarves fluttering as if they were going to pick up a john right in front of the precinct. When they recognized Kensey they gave her a big howdoyado, telling her Captain Adkins got so pissed at the little incident they caused he told them to get the hell out of there.

Kensey stopped running and tried to catch her breath. "Hey," she said to the ladies in between mouthfuls of air, "Captain Adkins, does he have a nickname or anything?"

Sapphire and B.J. looked at each other. Sapphire leaned to the side so her shoulder touched B.J.'s like she was wobbly from a couple beers. She said, "Ballbuster's all we call him."

"Ever hear anyone call him Sonny?"

"Sonny," Sapphire said and convulsed with laughter. She threw her long scarf around her neck and put her hand on B.J.'s shoulder. "Listen to this," she said, face-to-face with B.J. "Sonny Adkins. Sounds like a guy runs a strip club or something." B.J. was laughing it up. Sapphire tapped B.J.'s shoulder so she would hear the next part. "Ladies and gentlemen," Sapphire said in a deep announcer's voice, "Sonny Adkins is proud to present Sapphire in her Pittsburgh debut." They laughed again, but by the time they turned back toward Kensey, she was halfway down the block.

■ ■ ■

Mike was sitting on one of the commodes, his gun balanced on the little shelf made by his blue jeans pushed down to his ankles. He was peeling off a white square of sticky gauze on his thigh where the nails had pierced, the two holes plainly visible in the bad light. One was a simple puncture wound, the lips puckered up in a pouty pose. The other was different. Nearly an inch long and ragged, the soft tissue looked like mismatching puzzle pieces shoved together.

His hand slipped into a side pocket and located his cell phone. One push of a speed-dial button and he was talking quietly into it. "Hey, it's Eddie. The stuff on TV? That's only the half of it. I'm on my cell."

8

Kensey tore through the Emergency Department, avoiding all eye contact and headed straight for the little white refrigerator in the med room where the nurses escaped from the doctors when things got crazy. Already Kensey had finger-combed her hair and brushed herself off. This was a no-food-allowed refrigerator, vaccines only. As she began rummaging through the tiny boxes, a skinny woman in a starched white outfit sidled up to Kensey.

"Been trying to reach you all morning," she said. Her name was Helen and she'd been working in the Emergency Department more than thirty years. "Taggert wants you at Morning Report."

"Morning Report?" Kensey snatched a box from the refrigerator and pushed the door closed. "I'm not on inpatient." Her face sagged.

"He came down himself, wanted to know when you went on duty."

"Eleven o'clock."

"That's what I told him, eleven o'clock. And he said, track you down for Morning Report. Been calling your house."

"Is Carl around?"

"He and Taggert went up together."

"I was just here to … Actually, I do need to talk with him."

"Carl?"

"No, Dr. Taggert. My mother's in the ICU back home, maybe a stroke. I was going to see if he could get someone to cover for me."

Kensey opened the box, took out a small glass vial, and snapped off the little plastic cover.

"What's that for?" Helen asked.

Kensey opened her hand and showed Helen the wound. "There's a nail sticking out of the railing on my front porch. Never saw it before last night. Who knows when I had my last tetanus shot."

Helen wore half-glasses on a silver chair around her neck. Slipping them on, she took hold of Kensey's hand to examine the cut. "That looks deep. You want one of the surgeons to look at it, maybe clean it out?"

"No, no. It hardly hurts."

Helen shook her head. "That must've been some nail."

"I can't do this." Kensey handed her the little box.

Helen worked quickly, drawing up a half milliliter of tetanus toxoid into a syringe at the same time Kensey forced the sleeve on the green sweater all the way up so it looked like a tourniquet. "This won't hurt a bit," Helen said with a smile as she plunged the needle into Kensey's upper arm and forced the vaccine into her deltoid muscle. "You better put yourself on some antibiotics."

"I took some Keflex." Kensey checked out a wall clock. "Morning Report's almost over," she said and hurried out of the ED.

■ ■ ■

Morning report was Francis Taggert's baby. He was chairman of medicine, a pit bull of a man, and supremely self-confident. He had one or two favorites in every residency group; the others were grunts who put in their three years, then got the hell out of his hospital. Monday through Friday, at precisely seven-thirty AM, Taggert strode into the conference room and said good morning to a dozen or more internal medicine residents who would then present every admission from the last twenty-four hours. The room had a long walnut table that would be piled with charts and notes and cups of bad coffee. No beepers were allowed. A single senior resident was excused from Morning Report to run the hospital. Taggert never took a chair, opting to pace around the room or half-sit on the corner of the table. One by one the residents would take his or her turn at the front of the room and present the medical history of the patient, pertinent physical findings, laboratory and radiologic information, and finally — the moment Taggert waited for — the diagnosis and plan. A simple problem such as cellulitis could take as little as two or three minutes to discuss. But Taggert could ramble on endlessly about complicated cases. If he detected weakness in the presentation or faulty analysis or, worse, a glaring error of omission, he could skewer a resident and enjoy making a show of it.

No matter how well the patient was managed and presented, Taggert would ask one stinger of a question. Always. In the end he made it clear he was smarter than anyone in the room.

Kensey snuck into the conference room at six minutes after nine. Carl was front and center, freshly showered. Instead of his ever-present blue scrub shirt he was showing off a powder blue shirt with a button down collar and a striking silk rep tie. Already he was pretending he was chief resident. Looking quite irritated when the door opened, he ran his hand down his tie to smooth it and stopped speaking long enough for everyone in the room to turn and stare at her. Taggert, with his bald head and ramrod posture, said nothing but pulled up the sleeve on his three-quarter-length white coat and checked his watch. He then nodded to Carl to continue.

That's when Kensey was certain that Taggert knew everything that had happened to Manny Romero. Ordinarily, being late to Morning Report got you a sarcastic comment from Taggert. "Next time we'll schedule around you," was one of his favorites. But Taggert was already focusing his attention on Carl, his back to Kensey. Everyone in the room knew that being ignored by the boss was an order of magnitude worse than a comment. Her fellow residents felt her pain and watched her slip into a chair next to Susanne.

"Don't ask," Kensey whispered. Susanne's eyes went wide as she scanned her up and down. "I'll replace them. They do Romero yet?"

Susanne shook her head.

"To continue," Carl said, bringing all eyes back to him, "Mr. Hawk had a single entrance wound, below the right nipple. His initial BP was seventy over twenty, he was intubated when he arrived. We ran Ringer's lactate in two sites. No breath sounds on the right. Couldn't really hear the heart. Pupils reacted bilaterally. I put a fourteen-gauge needle in the right side thinking maybe a tension pneumo and got blood. Chest X-ray showed a complete white-out. We put in a call for a thoracic surgeon, then I popped in a chest tube and got about four hundred cc's of blood before he arrested. We completed three rounds of drugs, shocked him times two, never got the heart back. That's when I called it off. He was pronounced dead at..." Carl ruffled through some papers.

Taggert, who had been sitting on the corner of the table, stood and waited. He never proceeded until the entire case had been presented.

"Eleven fifty-seven."

"Tough case."

Carl nodded and began gathering his papers.

"One question."

Carl smiled. Another chance to shine. He held his ragged sheaf of papers at his waist and waited for it to come.

"What color was the blood?"

"It was dark."

Kensey was next. Manny Romero was coming right after the stinger.

"So what's the source of the bleeding?"

Carl answered quickly. "Dark blood is venous blood. The bullet probably caught a vein in the posterior chest."

"No way could he compromise his cardiac function with venous bleeding. The pressure would have stanched the bleeding. I'll bet the bullet caught a branch of the pulmonary artery. Check out the post and let me know. Okay, thank you." Carl took his usual seat in the front of the room, near the corner of the table where Taggert perched himself.

Taggert stood and addressed the room. "Not a typical Morning-Report patient but a no-win situation you'll be faced with at one time or another. This was the more difficult of the two cases. No matter what anyone did, Mr.—" Taggert quickly consulted his little index card "—Hawk was going to die. It was handled well, Carl, very well. Dr. Shaw. You're up."

Kensey's hands were shaking. She pushed out of her chair and took the first step toward the front of the room.

Taggert read from the index card. "Let's see here. Detective Emanuel Romero arrived in the ED at the same time Mr. Hawk did."

Kensey froze. Everything suddenly seemed worse, as if doing the bidding of a hit man was not as sleazy as helping a crooked cop. A flood of memories caused the downy hairs on the back of her neck to stand straighter than she was. She could see herself sitting tight with Manny, his hand on her wrist. He was talking with her, begging her to be a Good Samaritan. She got caught up in the moment. Then she remembered: his cross was in her pocket.

"Kensey, you okay?" Taggert had taken off his glasses and was cleaning them with a small chamois.

Kensey continued to the front of the conference room. Her eyes sought Susanne's and got a wink of encouragement. Kensey began: "Mr. Romero ... excuse me, Detective Romero ... was brought to the ED with a gunshot wound..." "Kensey's voice tapered off. She nodded and the best she could manage was a hoarse whisper. After an audible breath she said, "I'm sorry, could I get some water?"

Susanne was right on it, bringing her own bottle of water. Under her breath Susanne said, "Be cool."

Kensey took several gulps. She was beginning to sweat. Her shirt was itchy and she pulled at it. "Detective Ro—" She coughed.

"Dr. Shaw." Taggert thrust his arm out in a showy way so his sleeve pulled up and exposed his watch. He made certain everyone knew he was checking the time.

"I'm sorry, sir. Long night."

Turning to Carl he said, "Can I impose on you to present him?"

Carl's hands were on the armrests of his chair, ready to launch him into action.

"Absolutely not." Kensey shot a look Carl's way that warned him to stay put. "Detective Romero had a single gunshot wound to the left side of his chest." She spoke quickly, trying to develop some momentum. "When he arrived in the Emergency Department his blood pressure was stable and initial exam showed—"

"The blood pressure was stable?" Taggert cocked his head to one side.

"Yes, sir."

"What does that mean to you, Dr. Shaw, *stable blood pressure*?"

The answer was too obvious. "It was in the normal range?"

Taggert shifted in his seat and exchanged glances with Carl Daley. Kensey had stumbled and he was going to enjoy watching her get a skinned knee or two. "What exactly was Detective Romero's blood pressure?"

"I don't have the number in my head."

He stood and addressed the entire group of residents as if an important take-home message was about to be delivered. "Can a *single* blood pressure reading be stable?" Now his back was toward Kensey.

She answered, "I thought so."

"No." He spun around and raised his chin imperiously before continuing. "It takes a minimum of two readings, Dr. Shaw, to show the blood pressure is stable over some period of time. Continue."

"I should have known that. The patient's blood pressure on arrival was normal. Both pupils reacted briskly, heart sounds were normal, breath sounds equal bilaterally. He was conversant. There were two IV's running with Ringer's lactate. He was stable for eight minutes or so. Then he became weaker."

"Did you test his muscular strength, Doctor?"

"No." Kensey drew out the word, buying time for her brain to figure out why the heck she should have tested a trauma patient's strength.

"Then you have no idea if he became weaker. Be more specific."

Her lower lip quivered. She was going to be damned if she was going to let Taggert make her cry.

"His blood pressure dropped and his breathing became labored."

"Good. Chest X-ray?"

"The portable machine was tied up in the other trauma room."

Taggert glanced at Carl, who was leaning back in his chair, rotating back and forth, the tip of his index finger touching the middle of his neck just below the jaw line so he looked quite pensive. "Sometimes, Dr. Shaw, we actually have to put our stethoscope in our ears."

"I did."

Taggert smiled. "Brave. Go on." He eased himself onto the corner of the table.

Kensey took a deep breath while the corners of her mouth curled up in a plastic smile. "I listened to his chest and the breath sounds were more difficult to hear on the left side. I made a presumptive diagnosis of tension pneumothorax. I placed a fourteen- gauge needle into the second rib space but there was no audible rush of air."

"And the patient did not improve."

"That's correct."

"What did you do next?"

"Mr. — I mean Detective Romero started to talk with me. He was quite lucid. He said he knew he was going to die and confided in me that he wanted nothing further to be done medically."

Again Taggert stood. This silenced Kensey and Taggert let her stand there in front of the room, not knowing what to do with her hands. Finally he said, "So you sat there?"

"He asked me to keep him company. We prayed together."

"And that's when Carl joined you?"

"It was a few minutes later. When Mr. Romero worsened." Kensey paused. "I called a code and we were beginning CPR—"

"Let me get this straight. You were requested by the patient — who you determined to be quite lucid—" Taggert waited for Kensey to nod before continuing, "— not to intervene further and yet you began CPR."

"Things happened quickly. I got caught up in the moment when I was talking with him. His request for no further therapy seemed perfectly rational. His decision did not seem to be influenced by extreme pain or medication. He understood the gravity of the situation and made his request more than once." She paused to wipe her eyes. "But when those alarms went off and he arrested I couldn't just sit there and watch his life slip away. Everyone came running into the room. I had to do something. But I was torn between honoring his request and trying to save his life."

"Is that it?"

"No, sir. It was wrong of me to make a decision of such gravity without input from more experienced medical personnel. I feel terrible about it."

Taggert paced the room as he organized his thoughts. "The issue of 'do not resuscitate' in the Emergency Department on the mere say so of a patient is risky business at best. I agree with you: An intern should never contemplate making someone DNR without consultation with a more senior physician. However, I respect and appreciate your honesty. Watching the life force leave a fellow being is one of the most difficult things we are asked to do. Fortunately, in the end, you resisted this urge." Taggert looked around the room, making brief eye contact with each member of his house staff. Back to Kensey he said, "And then what?"

"Carl came into the room and pretty much took over."

"And you assisted in the resuscitative effort?"

"Actually, no." Kensey glanced at Carl. At this moment Carl shifted from his comfortable position to lean over the table in order to read some notes he had brought with him. He looked quite busy. "Carl felt more comfortable running the code by himself. I know it went on for several minutes, but I do not know how many rounds of drugs he tried and I don't know the exact time of death. I was speaking with a police detective when he expired."

Now it was Taggert's turn. Kensey expected a stinger, something about the anatomy of the bullet's track, or the appropriate first drug to use, or even the type of documentation she wrote in the chart explaining the patient's request to be left to die. She shifted from one foot to the other, tugged on her sweater, then tucked a stubborn strand of hair behind her ear.

Taggert shot Carl a look. Carl was leaning forward in his chair, his head cocked to one side, a sneaky little smile on his lips. Every resident in the room could see he was salivating, a sprinter in the blocks ready to explode. Briefly, he looked at Kensey but refused to make eye contact. It disappointed Kensey, who was expecting — hoping, really — for Carl to give her a little nod of support.

"Why don't you sit down, Kensey."

"Thank you, sir." No stinger. A deep breath. Kensey grabbed the bottle of water, slunk to her chair, and took a slug of water.

"Carl, finish this up for us, will you?"

Kensey clutched the water bottle in one hand.

Carl moved slowly, playing it like he was reluctant to jump on the Taggert bandwagon, but he took his position in front of the room and took a deep breath that he blew out of pursed lips, as if he was saying, Wow, what a case. "The detective's BP was falling rapidly despite two IV's wide open. We had chest compressions going and were bagging him with one-hundred-percent oxygen. I hit him with some epi, then atropine. Nothing. We were drawing up some calcium when I noticed the QRS complexes on the EKG monitor had markedly decreased amplitude. Seeing where the entrance wound was, I figured maybe the bullet grazed his heart and he tamponaded."

Taggert looked at Kensey. Her fellow residents were kind enough to busy themselves, reading charts or jotting notes in their PDAs.

Taggert said, "Dr. Smerdell, educate me about cardiac tamponade."

Susanne looked up at Taggert. "It's when the pericardial sac fills with blood so tightly that there's no room for the heart to beat."

"How much blood does it take?"

"A couple hundred cc's?"

Taggert shook his head. "The pericardial sac is a bag barely big enough to fit the heart inside. It's non-elastic so it only takes only about sixty cc's to cause big-time trouble. Two ounces." Turning to Carl, he continued: "So, without an echocardiogram to seal the diagnosis, what did you do?"

Kensey placed her hand on her forehead and shielded her eyes from the overhead lights.

"I took a spinal needle—"

Taggert cut him off, saying to the residents seated around the table, "All right, people, pay attention. This is important."

The room rumbled with the sound of a dozen hands digging into backpacks for pieces of paper and pens. Kensey sat up straight and glanced over at Susanne, then around the room. Finally she focused on Taggert as he nodded at Carl to continue and her throat tightened.

"I took one of the EKG leads from Detective Romero's chest and wrapped it round the spinal needle. I attached a fifty-cc syringe to the needle and entered just below the sternum."

"What about chest compressions, Carl?"

"I ordered them stopped."

To the room Taggert said, "I know stopping compressions makes your sphincters tighten when you're faced with a patient like this. But you must do this, otherwise you don't know where the needle is going." With a smile he nodded at Carl.

"I pulled back on the syringe and angled the needle toward the heart."

"Kensey, why did Carl wrap the EKG lead around the spinal needle?"

Kensey, knowing the answer but worrying what this was leading to, said, "Uh… if there wasn't any blood in the pericardial space you'd want to know the moment the needle touched the heart. The EKG jumps on the monitor so you don't pierce it by mistake."

"Carl?"

"I got back blood."

"How much?"

"Fifty-three cc's."

Taggert looked around the room and caught a nod or two from the Carl Daleys of tomorrow. "So what happened?"

"It was unbelievable. BP came back, the detective opened his eyes, and asked if he was dead."

"Terrific job, Carl."

Taggert turned toward Kensey and took a moment to study her face. He watched her swallow and blink away a tear. "Detective Romero is up on the seventh floor with a chest tube in place. He's on my private service, Dr. Shaw, but I'm turning him over to you. Why don't you give me a call after you see him."

9

As soon as the elevator door opened on seven, Kensey spotted a uniformed cop sitting fifty feet away on an uncomfortable chair in the hallway. He was leaning forward, elbows on knees as if he was on the can trying to go, reading a tightly folded copy of the *Post-Gazette*. Getting closer, she could see the handle of his black service revolver poking out of a holster on his hip.

From time to time city cops appeared on chairs in the hallways. Usually they were assigned when a prisoner from a local facility was hospitalized.

This one had a marine haircut, shaved shiny on the sides, an oval patch of buzz cut on top. From a distance he looked young enough to be a Boy Scout. Kensey figured he needed to shave maybe once a week. She couldn't remember if he was one of the cops talking with Captain Adkins.

Approaching him, stethoscope dangling from her hand, she said, "I'm Dr. Shaw," then studied his face to see if he reacted to her name.

Right there was the headline in the paper, huge letters snatched from the 20/60 column of the Snellen eye chart: Three Shot Dead In O'Hara. Kensey wondered why it couldn't have been four.

The cop looked up, his eyes pausing on her breasts before making it all the way to her face. "You his doc?"

Kensey nodded.

"They said you'd be coming. Go ahead. He's asleep last time I checked." With the back of his hand he gave the newspaper a little tap and smiled, like it was something big to be camped outside Manny Romero's door at the same time he was reading about him.

Kensey slipped into the room and silently let the door close behind her. It was an old-fashioned hospital room, bed on one side, wall-mounted TV on the other, and a single straight-back chair with a blue vinyl seat next to the bed. No artwork. White walls that needed a coat of paint three years ago.

Daylight spilled through a window with a nice view of the Cathedral of Learning. The television was going in the background, quietly, a morning talk-show audience laughing it up.

Manny was in the bed, head turned away from Kensey, eyes closed, in need of a shave, asleep. He was covered with a thin, white sheet pulled up nearly to his neck. From where Kensey was standing there were some red marks on his neck. They looked like scratches. A plump IV bag ran clear fluid though pencil-thin tubing that disappeared under the sheet on the right side of the bed. Snaking out from the left side was a much thicker tube that ended in a thin, rectangular box — the Pleur-evac — hanging from the foot of the bed. Partly filled with water, the Pleur-evac bubbled away merrily while keeping constant suction on the tube that burrowed into Manny's chest so his collapsed lung would reinflate.

Kensey lingered several feet from the bed, observing Manny's relaxed breathing. She had a clear image of Manny whispering "You a Samaritan?" Then everything went fast-forward: the cardiac arrest, his arm bouncing around, smacking Mike with the board, escaping from the police station.

A small monitor on the bedside table displayed a typical up-and-down EKG pattern peacefully floating by. The automatic blood-pressure cuff inflated. BP: 126 over 78.

Two steps closer and Kensey was examining Manny's neck. Both sides had vertical scratch marks that looked as if he'd been in a fight with a cat. These were new, and Kensey leaned in for a closer inspection, trying to imagine what had happened in the Emergency Department that might have caused them.

Manny turned his head and cracked an eye open.

"Oh, sorry." Right away Kensey stood straight up and took a quick step backwards away from the bed.

He peered at her sleepily as if he had a hangover. Pulling the sheet down several inches, his fingers explored the soft skin around his neck, sliding around it on one side, then the other. His thick tongue flicked out of his mouth and licked his lips, then went into a smacking sound inside his mouth. "I need some mouthwash," he said.

"I can have one of the nurses get you some."

"You ain't a nurse?"

Venturing a step closer, Kensey shook her head. "No."

Manny spotted her taking a deep breath and blowing it out through pursed lips. He coughed and his face twisted up in pain. His hairy arm came all the way out of the sheets and clutched his chest. "Jesus Christ, that hurts."

"I can order some pain medication for you."

Manny squinted at Kensey. "You some kind of doctor?"

Kensey didn't answer right away. She studied his eyes, saw the way he stared at her, then checked out what was on the TV, then back at her again. She hadn't breathed since Manny asked the question.

"You heard me, didn't you?"

Kensey let out her breath. "I'm Dr. Shaw, one of the residents. I'll be taking care of you, Detective," she said and took another step forward. "I reviewed your chart—"

"So, Doc, when am I getting out of here?"

"I don't know. Three, four days. Maybe longer. We've got to get your chest tube out."

"That long? Look, I gotta get outta here like two hours ago." He started to push himself up in the bed, winced, and flopped down on his pillow. From somewhere deep in his chest he groaned.

"You were shot last night. The bullet's still in you." She waited for his reaction, seeing if he was playing with her.

"You think you forget catching a bullet?"

"You have a collapsed lung. We've got to make sure it opens up and stays open."

"What about my heart, it get hit?" He was looking around the room now, finding someplace safe to set his eyes.

"The bullet nicked it, caused some bleeding. It was touch-and-go. Once the blood was drained from the sac that surrounds it, you got better. You ought to be just fine." Kensey took another step closer. She was feeling okay explaining things to him, as if the Samaritan conversation had never happened.

"You mean good as new?"

"I think so," she said brightly.

He looked out the window at some sparrows flying by. "Who do I thank for that?"

"Well ... actually it was Dr. Daley. He's the senior who was in charge of—"

"You know, it's funny," he said, turning his head to look at Kensey. "This Dr. Daley, if he woulda asked me last night 'You want your life saved?' I woulda said 'No fuckin' way.' Now, look out that window." Manny rotated his head. "Look at that sky, those birds going by. I wanna kiss him." He dug around his neck again, then turned back toward her. "Don't know what happened to my cross, though."

"Do you remember anything that happened last night?"

Manny looked over at the door before answering. "Hey, there a uniform outside?"

"Excuse me?"

"A cop. Is there a cop out in the hall reading the sports page, looking like he'd rather be anywhere else?"

"Yes, there is." Kensey sounded surprised.

"Do me a favor, Doc. Go ask him why he's here."

"Why he's here?"

"You hard of hearing or what? Why he's here. It's a simple question. Ask him, will ya."

Kensey turned toward the door.

"Yo, Doc, hold up a second," he said, raising his voice, waiting for Kensey to stop walking and turn around. "Ask him like *you* want to know, not like I told you to ask. You know, curious. You think you can handle that?"

Kensey opened the door and leaned out, feet and rear end still in the room. Several seconds later she was back. "He says it's routine any time an officer gets shot."

"Oh yeah?" Manny took a deep breath and let it out in a whoosh. He smiled and showed off a nice set of teeth. "Only thing I 'member is the bullet hitting me." He had some life to his voice. "Hurt like hell. Yeah, it felt like my chest was on fire."

"That's all you remember?"

"I in an ambulance or something when I got here?"

"Yes," she said and felt comfortable enough to sit in the nearby chair. "You had a cardiac arrest in the Emergency Department. You nearly died."

Manny was staring at the television now, looking pleased. The talk show was over. A news anchor with big white teeth was beginning a morning update. "So what's your name again?" Manny said, not looking at her but acting interested in the television.

"Dr. Shaw."

"Do me a favor, Doc, turn this thing up." Working slowly, as if everything hurt, Manny reached behind his head and bunched up his pillow to prop up his head.

Kensey located the remote control buried under the sheets and pressed a button.

The anchor was in mid-sentence. "—in O'Hara Township last night three people were killed in a late-night shoot-out with police." A head shot of Manny in uniform appeared on a screen behind the reporter. "Detective Emanuel Romero was shot in the chest and is in stable condition at University Medical Center. Charles Hawk of Fox Chapel died in the Emergency Department at UMC. Also dead are Martin Eggers of Munhall and John Ludwikowski of Etna."

Kensey watched Manny's fingers go back to his neck and grab at the unshaven skin.

"That Johnny Ludd's a fuckin' coke dealer," Manny said to Kensey with his eyes still on the TV.

The anchor went on: "Mr. Ludwikowski had been released from the State Correctional Institution in Rockview fourteen months ago for dealing cocaine."

"See?" Manny turned to Kensey. He seemed delighted with himself. "Guy's a dirtball, got what he deserved."

Kensey studied Manny as he went back to the television. Now they were going to a commercial.

Kensey stood and approached the bed. "Detective, I'm going to examine you now." She placed the stethoscope in her ears and carefully pulled back the sheet. The chest tube emerged from the left side of Manny's chest. The area around the tube had been shaved down to a prickly stubble. First Kensey listened to his heart, then went back and forth listening to both sides of his lungs. "Detective, your lungs sound pretty good. I can hear you breathing on both sides. That means your lung is opening up. We may be able to turn off the bubbles pretty soon."

He looked at her. "Today?"

"I doubt it. I'll stop by later and check on you."

Before Kensey could turn toward the door Manny's left hand shot out from under the sheets and grabbed her wrist and pulled her hard toward the bed. She was bent over awkwardly as if she might tumble into bed with him, her face a foot from Manny's, close enough to smell the stench of his breath.

"You're hurting me, Detective."

"I may not 'member much from last night, but I sure as shit 'member my Good Samaritan."

"Let go of me." Kensey tried to pull her slender wrist from his mitt but he was too strong. Now she snapped her head toward the doorway and opened her mouth to say something.

Manny pressed his thumb into Kensey's wrist and she let out a little yelp. "Don't even think about it, Doc." He eased up on his grip. "So far's I know you didn't say nothing to the cops. The place woulda been crawling with 'em by now. Now siddown and be a good girl. You'n me gotta talk." He released her arm.

While she lowered herself into the chair Kensey was rubbing her wrist the same way they do on television as soon as a tight pair of handcuffs is removed.

"It woulda been better for both of us I died last night. But God was watching over me."

"Listen to me, Detective." Kensey rubbed her wrist.

Manny chuckled. "I like the way you held your breath, seeing if I remembered you. That felt good, huh?"

"Not as good as it did when you found out the uniform was here to protect you, not guard you."

"Listen up. Three years ago I busted Johnny Ludd. Sent his ass away. Once that gets out the whole thing with you'n me in the ER never happened." His voice became low and ominous. "I told you what would happen you go to the cops. Deal's the same. I got a partner out there. One call's all it takes."

"You mean Mike?"

"Hey." He sounded pissed. Right away his hand shot up to his neck, his fingers leaving red marks, they were digging around so hard. "I didn't tell you his name. How the hell…" His voice drifted away as he thought about it.

Kensey knew to keep quiet, let him do the talking. She could walk right out of the room. He couldn't stop her. But she'd be in the hallway, wondering what Manny's next move would be. She had to stay and deal with him.

"So what'd you do, meet him in the ER? He come up to you and give you that look he does, ask what's going on?"

Kensey held her gaze, her hands in her lap, trying not to twitch.

"One phone call's all it takes." His eyes drifted over to the phone on the bedside table, pulling Kensey's along for the ride. "And you don't make it to your car. I sent that coke dealer away. Far as anyone knows, Johnny Ludd's back dealing and I was busting him a second time. This was an undercover operation that went bad. That's all. Things you heard last night were bullshit, crazy talk from a guy doped-up on whatever shit you squirted in me." He stopped speaking and was breathing hard.

Now it was Kensey's turn. "Last night I went to a friend's house. I wrote the whole thing down. Your name. Sonny's. Seymour Rosen and Alec Fortune. The only thing you didn't give me was Mike's name. Now I've got that too. If anything happens to me, my friend'll release everything. And don't think my friend would be foolish enough to go to the cops. I know they're dirty. You story goes right to KDKA. It won't take them more than an hour to put it together."

"I know a bluff when I hear one." Manny shook his head.

Kensey glanced over at the EKG tracing, the screen now crowded with complexes, flying by faster than she could count. She had Manny scared. "I was afraid I wouldn't remember anything in the morning. I wrote everything down."

"You tell anyone else?"

"Your friend Mike followed me last night, did his best to kill me. So we'd better come to some sort of understanding pretty quick."

"Hold it a second. You go to the cops? I told you not to." Manny tried to sit up but it hurt too much and he dropped his head back on his pillow. "You don't mean nothing to him. Why the hell'd he try to kill you?"

"Why don't you ask him? Make sure he knows I know his name."

The EKG was packed, one complex riding piggyback on another. His fingers shot up to his neck and dug into his skin. Manny was breathing hard. "Shit, where the fuck's that cross?"

The news anchor was back. "In other news," he was saying, "a shooting at St. John's Church on the Northside left Father James Flaherty dead late last night. We'll have more at noon."

Manny's head made a hard turn to the television. "What was that? Jesus Christ. Did he say Father was killed?"

"I'm sorry," she said.

"Mike? Was it Mike?"

Kensey nodded.

"Turn that thing the fuck off," Manny said loud enough that he looked at the door as if he expected the uniformed officer to push it open and ask if everything was all right. Then he twisted his head to look out the window.

Kensey silenced the television. She spoke gently. "Mike must've followed me to the church. He snuck up on the confessional, heard what you told me to tell Father Flaherty."

Manny put a finger in each ear and closed his eyes tight.

Kensey stopped speaking. When Manny opened his eyes and lowered his hands she said, "Father Flaherty said nice things about you."

With his eyes on the ceiling he said, "Like what?"

"You were a good man. That you were helping out with the renovations."

"I want to be alone," Manny said, still not looking at Kensey. He knew she was getting out of the chair the way her slacks and sweater made a little swishing noise as fabric rubbed against fabric. "Don't forget, one call's all it takes. Don't think I won't do it."

Kensey reached into the pocket of her gray slacks and fished out Manny's cross. She laid it on his chest and silently walked toward the door.

"You'll forget those names I told you, huh?" Manny said. "You'n me, we have a deal." He kissed his cross.

Kensey started to pull the door open.

"Hey, Doc."

Her hand on the doorknob, she eyed him.

He was holding the cross by the chain, dangling it down like a tiny fish still on the line. "Thanks."

10

Helen was on Kensey the second she hit the ED, trailing her right into the bullpen like she was going to goose her, then rolling up a chair to sit next to her. Glasses down on her nose, acting midway between concerned and irritated, Helen said, "You're late, you know, and Carl's in a snit. I've been paging you since Morning Report was over."

Kensey had already changed into light blue scrubs. "I'm not late. I don't start for—" Kensey checked her watch — "eighteen minutes. I was taking a nap."

"That's what Susanne said you were doing. I called her. Then I tried you in the on-call room."

"I wasn't in the usual on-call room. I went into one of the ob-gyn rooms so no one would call me."

"What if someone needed to reach you in an emergency?"

"They would have had to call Carl. Why's he in a snit anyway?"

"He's upset about you going to see your mom in the ICU. Someone's got to cover your shift."

Kensey's hand went to her hair and brushed it back. "I talked with the doctor, looks like she's doing better. I probably won't have to go. So tell Carl he doesn't have to be in a snit."

"Well, that's good," Helen said, then quickly added, "I mean about your mom. Anyway, I know you're not on for fifteen minutes—"

Kensey checked her watch. "Seventeen."

"Seventeen. But we're backed up, already. Dr. Taggert called down and was talking with Carl and said he didn't think you'd mind sewing someone up."

At that moment, as if it had been planned and rehearsed several times, Carl Daley breezed by in his chief resident costume, giving the counter a little tap. "Call me if anyone wants to go DNR," and kept on going.

"Carl," Kensey called out, her tone different than she'd ever used with him before.

What he saw when he swung around with that smug little smile on his face was Helen snapping her head to look at Kensey. Kensey's eyes were waiting for him, her jaw out defiantly. Not for an instant did his posture change. Three steps and he was back at the counter that separated him from Kensey. "Hey, it's just a joke, lighten up."

"I know you're gonna have fun with this, Carl. But I've got way too much on my plate to deal with your bullshit. You need to back off right now." Eyeballs still on Carl, her words came out crisp when she said, "What about that chart, Helen?" and held her hand out.

Helen handed off a metal chart. "Room Two." Then she scurried away in the direction of the med room.

Carl was staying put, his cheeks matching one of the red power stripes in his tie, mouth open like he was just about to come back with something but couldn't locate the words.

"And while we're at it, Carl, would you mind terribly not peeping down my shirt every time I lean over to check someone's spleen."

Now Carl looked like he didn't know how to walk away. He just stood there like a buck private getting dressed down by his sergeant.

"I'll call you if anyone goes DNR, Carl. Bye."

Clumsily, Carl spun around and bumped into a nervous candy striper who stumbled out of the way while she was apologizing. Carl took just six strides to reach one of the trauma rooms and vanished behind the curtain without looking back.

After a glance at the patient's name on the chart, Kensey dragged herself toward the exam room. She pulled back the drape and stood in the doorway taking in a middle-aged black man with white hair in blue work clothes. His baseball cap was in his hand and he was watching a little wall-mounted television, the sound down low. He looked up at Kensey. "Good idea, these TVs. Better picture than I get at home." He grinned.

"Mr. Moore, I'm Dr. Shaw. Where did you get cut?"

"Construction project. I was listening to a joke and not paying attention."

"What part of your body?" She was all business.

Mr. Moore burst out laughing. "My arm here," he said and pulled up his sleeve to show his forearm wrapped in white gauze. He started to unravel the gauze, winding the material around his other hand, the two of them watching it change from white to pink to bright red. When it was off Kensey could see a three-inch laceration running from his wrist toward his elbow, the lips of the wound open with a slip of red muscle showing.

Kensey thought he looked like Morgan Freeman. "How'd that happen?"

"Like I tol' you, listening to a joke, the one about the horse and the chicken and the chicken is under the horse and looks up—"

"Sir," she said, pausing long enough to see the smile melt from his face. "What cut you?"

"I know 'sir' is a sign of respect and everything, but sometimes, Doc, the word cuts right to the bone. Not like an X-Acto knife. No, ma'am, *that's* what cut me. Looks somethin' like a box cutter. Had my foot up on a trash bin, fixing a new blade and I started laughing and my foot slipped and—" He held out his arm to show the laceration as if it was the punch line. "Looks like you'n me're having some kind of bad day."

Kensey took a step closer to Mr. Moore. "And it's not even lunchtime."

Helen stuck her head into the room. "Need anything, Doctor?"

"Can you get me a laceration kit, three mls of Xylocaine and some 4-0 suture?" Then to Mr. Moore she said, "Sir," this time allowing her facial muscles to curl up into a smile, "Do you know when you had your last tetanus shot?"

Mr. Moore frowned and shook his head. "I'd remember if I had one of them. Damn things hurt."

Helen left as Kensey slipped on a pair of surgical gloves.

"You know 'bout mine. Why don't you tell me 'bout yours?"

"My what?" Kensey began to examine his forearm. She palpated the wound.

"Your day. Might pass the time."

"Too many people to please and not enough hours in the day to do it." She focused on Mr. Moore's arm, asking him if this hurt or that hurt and he was going "Nope" and "Yep" as she worked her way around the wound. He was paying pretty close attention until he heard something on the TV that made him turn his head.

Helen was back before Kensey completed her exam, wielding two syringes. She unbuttoned Mr. Moore's other sleeve and pushed it up and gave the tetanus injection. Then she opened the tray that contained forceps, scissors, gauze, and a needle holder. She placed the other syringe on the side of the tray. "Call if you need me," she said and left the room.

Kensey cleaned the wound with Betadine, painting it in a spiral until she had sterilized several inches around the edges.

"You hear about that shooting up in O'Hara?" Mr. Moore said, his eyes tight on the television.

"Why don't you tell me the joke now."

"Now you want to hear it. Just a sec," he said absently.

Kensey readied the syringe of Xylocaine, flicking the side and watching the bubbles rise to the top. "This may sting a little," she said and squirted a drop into the air before injecting the anesthetic into the margins of the wound. Mr. Moore groaned as he felt the burn. Kensey came back with, "How 'bout that joke, Mr. Moore."

"He gave me one heck of a good deal on a RCA color TV last Christmas. The big one, you know, thirty-six inches, remote control," he said, eyes on the TV. A skinny reporter in a blue blazer was standing in front of a Cheap Charlie's speaking into a microphone. "You about done?" he said as Kensey pushed the plunger.

Kensey finished injecting the Xylocaine then compressed the wound with a sterile square of gauze and massaged it.

"Don't go rushing now, it don't feel numb."

"That's why I'm rubbing it, to spread the medicine around. It takes a few minutes."

"You mind turning up the sound?"

Kensey looked at the television, the reporter still in front of Cheap Charlie's. "I'd rather hear the joke."

"Now that I think about it, it's not the kind of joke a fella tells a lady, if you know what I mean." He moved his head toward the television. "How about it?"

Kensey stepped to the television and worked the volume control. Just then the camera shifted to one side, bringing a middle-aged woman who had been standing right next to the reporter into view. She was crying, her face puffy and red. The reporter said something about her being an employee of Cheap Charlie's, then asked how well she had known Charlie Hawk. "For more than ten years I worked for him. He was the most wonderful boss and I just don't—" she wiped her eye "—understand why someone would shoot someone as nice as him."

Not looking at Kensey, Mr. Moore went, "You know what I heard? Some guys from the loading dock done it. Betcha they were stealing them nice RCAs and selling 'em on the side and Cheap Charlie called the cops and one thing led to another." He was shaking his head.

The woman being interviewed was crying on camera, saying Charlie had lost his wife a year ago and was thinking of retiring to Florida.

Then they went to commercial.

Mr. Moore looked at Kensey standing by the television, her jaw open, tears running down her face. "You okay, Doc? Maybe you know him or something?"

Kensey shook him off and readied the suture in the needle holder. "No, I never met him. I think maybe you should tell me that joke anyway."

■ ■ ■

Ten after seven — her shift ending at seven — and she was in her Honda speeding away from Oakland, back in Susanne's sweater and slacks. She was heading to East Liberty, past an auto dealership on the right and the big church on the left, looking for an old, six-story brick building outfitted with tinted windows and glass front doors that were supposed to look robotic. Whatever that meant.

It was a cinch to find. She spotted the front doors from the car, the glass being etched to look like a schematic for the head of a robot. Kensey parked near a small sign that proclaimed *Rosen Robotics*. Next to the front door was a wall-mounted phone in a metal box with a directory above it. Kensey snatched the phone from the cradle, then punched three numbers without checking the directory. Everything on the other side of the door was dark. The phone rang. She waited. Ten, fifteen seconds. Nothing.

Except for the top floor, the building was pitch-black. ... No. A light went on, then off, on one of the lower floors. She gave the front door a tug. It opened and right inside was the elevator.

On the sixth floor the foyer was quiet. There was an empty reception desk and several chairs. Half the ceiling lights were dark. A narrow hallway veered off behind the desk and Kensey ventured down it. From her first step it was obvious that all the offices were empty except for one at the end. Yellow light spilled into the hallway.

If she stopped and held her breath she could pick up the soft buzz from the fluorescent lights, maybe the sound of a car driving down the street, but that was it. Each of the offices had a name on the wall along with the person's title. Closest to the reception desk was the sales manager, then the general manager, the executive vice president, and finally the assistant to Mr. Rosen. Doors were wide open, computers and desks shown in dark silhouette.

Seymour Rosen's office was last and by far the biggest. Every light was on. "Mr. Rosen?" Kensey stepped into the room.

No answer.

In front of the three large windows on the far wall, Kensey admired a U-shaped wooden and metal desk stacked with computers and various electronics. Two green wingback chairs faced away from Kensey toward the desk. Toward the middle of the room was a colorful Oriental rug with a leather sofa and two matching easy chairs arranged around a square coffee table. Leaning against the coffee table was a smart-looking leather briefcase with straps. A thin stream of blue smoke wisped away from a long cigar in an ashtray. There were two doors on opposite walls, the one closer to Kensey opened and served as a private passageway to Mr. Rosen's assistant. The other door was closed. Backed into a corner near one of the windows stood a pair of robots that looked like a couple of trash cans with arms and eyes.

Still hanging back by the doorway, Kensey checked her watch and was ready to retreat into the hallway when she heard the ding of the elevator arriving and a man's voice saying, "You're sure no one's here?" The voice was gruff and demanding.

Another man's voice, this one higher-pitched, said, "Yes, same as the floors we just checked. Just take what you want —"

"Who said anything about taking?"

Kensey dashed across Rosen's office and slipped through the door to his assistant's office. Now she had a view of the hallway if she looked to the right as well as a partial view of Rosen's office.

"Look. Look in the offices. Everyone's gone. I'm just here by myself."

The two were heading this way, their voices louder. They passed in front of the assistant's office: A man in a suit being followed closely by someone with a limp, carrying a black handgun, jabbing it into the other man's ribs to hurry him along. They turned into Mr. Rosen's office.

She heard Mike Dombroski say, "This's yours, huh. You don't have to share it or nothing?"

"No."

"The people downstairs in those cubicles know how big it is?"

"Of course."

"All right Seymour, take a load off," and Kensey saw Rosen cross over to the sofa and sink about four inches into the soft leather. She watched Mike scan the room, checking out the desk and the briefcase secured with the straps and finally the cigar. He looked back at Rosen. "'I'll be right down'?" Mike put his foot on the arm of one of the easy chairs and leaned against his knee. He was wearing a cowboy shirt with fancy black stitching and black jeans. He swiped his hand across his brow. Kensey noticed he was wearing brown leather gloves.

"Like I told you downstairs," Rosen started and stopped to clear his throat. "I thought you were one of my assistants."

"You don't say, 'Who is it?' someone calls up on the intercom?"

"No. If one of my employees needs to get back in, they know I stay late."

"Busy guy like you, Seymour, with what you got going on right now? I can't hardly believe you wouldn't want to know who the hell it is before you go all the way down the fuckin' elevator."

Rosen looked directly at Mike. "Sometimes the last thing you want to hear at the end of the day is a song and dance why someone forgot their key. And if I had asked, what would you have said?"

"Pittsburgh Police, Detective Dombroski. I need to have a word with you."

The phone rang.

"That someone at the front door?"

"No, it's my private line."

"How do you know?"

"The ring's different."

Kensey could see Rosen and Mike with their heads turned toward the desk.

When the phone stopped ringing she heard Mike say, "Nice-looking cigar. What is it?"

"Cohiba."

"*Co - hi - ba.* Wouldn't mind me one a them."

"Over on the desk, there's a—"

"I ain't blind." Mike walked out of view in the direction of the desk while he said, "Tell me you're too smart to do something stupid ... like run." From the sofa Rosen was following everything Mike was doing. When Mike returned to the sofa he was drawing on a lighted cigar, then holding it at arm's length to admire it as he exhaled. "That's good. What you call this is an end-of-the-day smoke."

"I like them," Rosen said in a small voice.

Mike stuck the cigar between his teeth. He limped around the easy chairs and bent down to pick up a corner of the Oriental rug, feeling it between his fingers as if he were a dealer about to make an offer.

Seeing Mike do this seemed to calm Rosen down. Eventually he took a deep breath and leaned back. "It's fake."

"Oh yeah? How do you tell, in case I ever wanna get one?" Starting at one end of the rug, Mike took measured strides straight across. For a moment he disappeared from Kensey's view.

"The price. This one cost a thousand bucks. You buy a good one—"

"Will you shut the fuck up." He saw Rosen's head recoil as if he'd just fired a shotgun. "You got your end-of-the-day Cohiba going, your fancy little briefcase waiting right here." Mike stopped speaking for several seconds. "The desk chair's tucked in for the night. Your desk all nice and neat."

"So? What's the point of all this?"

"You better hope we don't hear a goddamn different ring in the next ten minutes."

"I'm alone. I swear."

"You're packed up, ready to go home. But you run down the hall and ride the elevator to the lobby knowing you're gonna have to come all the way back for your shit. Now why's that?"

"I was just finishing up when you called."

"You didn't let me say hello. Just 'be right down.'" Mike pointed the Beretta at Rosen. "Forget it. What're you, anyway, six feet?" Mike came back into view, sitting on the arm of the chair. He massaged his thigh.

"Five-eleven."

Mike lifted one side of the square coffee table and slid it off the rug. Then he pulled the chairs away. He leveled the weapon on Rosen. "Okay, here's how it goes, Seymour. Push the couch back and lie down on the carpet."

"What? Why?" Rosen's voice was squeaky. He didn't budge, his eyes flitting about the room.

"Cause I need some answers and I don't think we have a lot of time 'cause you're expecting someone. Now get going."

"What are you gonna do to me?"

Kensey could see Rosen breathing fast and the ceiling lights reflecting off his sweaty forehead. He loosened his tie and scooted forward in his seat so his weight was mostly on his feet but he didn't go any further.

"On the rug, man, or I gotta put one in your kneecap." Mike racked the slide and Rosen sucked in a mouthful of air. Slowly he slid off the couch. "Now push it back off the rug."

Rosen turned around and gave the sofa a heave.

"Now onto the floor."

Rosen got down on his knees, his jacket hanging down, head hung low, his styled hair mussed and tears dripping off his face onto the rug. Mike stood next to him and took his boot and placed it on Rosen's side and gave him a little shove so he toppled over onto his back.

"I bet you got a fancy cell phone." Mike held out his hand and wiggled his fingers to get Rosen to hurry up and get his phone.

Rosen's hand slipped into his jacket and pulled out a slender phone. Handing it to Mike he said, "Go ahead, keep it."

"What a guy. All right, move up a little so your head's on the floor," Mike was saying as he gave Rosen little kicks to speed him up. "Now shimmy your ass over to the side. That's it. More. ... Stop." Rosen was now positioned at one side of the carpet, his head on the hardwood floor. With a nod of satisfaction, Mike said, "Keep your hand down at your side, grab the fringe and roll over."

Rosen's hand grabbed the white fringe and he rolled over, dragging the carpet behind him. Mike stood next to Rosen on the hardwood and used his foot to push Rosen over a second and then a third time until he was rolled up tightly with his head sticking out.

"I can't breathe." Rosen started wiggling and banging his head off the floor.

Mike set the Beretta on the rug right below Rosen's chin, aimed so if he looked down all he could see was the business end of the barrel. "You don't know Sonny, do you?" Mike was saying.

Rosen stopped flailing. "Who?"

"Sonny's interested in this little transaction you're doing tomorrow."

"Is that what this is about? He wants in? 'Cause if he wants in, no problem."

"What's *in*?" Mike asked, standing over Rosen, talking with some authority.

Rosen licked his lips before he spoke. "Uh, I don't know how technical you want me to get."

Mike kicked the carpet where Kensey imagined Rosen's lower ribs were. "Jesus Christ. Just tell me what the fuck's going on."

"Okay." Rosen spoke quickly, trying to sound earnest. "I started this company a decade ago. We went public four years ago and tomorrow we're announcing we're being bought by a bigger company. That's all. The stock's gonna jump, sixty, seventy percent. Maybe more. If your friend wants in I can arrange it."

"Nah, that's okay."

"Listen to me, you better not hurt me, otherwise this deal doesn't happen. I own fifty-one percent of the stock. If your friend knows about the deal he can't be stupid enough not to know— "

"Shut up," Mike said and gave the carpet another kick. He stood there watching Rosen for several seconds, one foot on the carpet like it was a log in the woods.

"I'm claustrophobic. I can't even have an MRI."

Mike squatted down. "Listen to me. We got a little business, you'n me, then I unroll you and we all go home. You don't cooperate ..." Mike extended his index finger and pointed his thumb at the ceiling. Placing the tip of his finger against Rosen's temple, he said, "Bang."

Rosen was nodding his head like crazy. "Okay, anything you want. Just tell me what to do."

"What's the name of the company buying you?"

"It's called ERT. It stands for—"

"I don't give a rat's ass what it stands for. Who's the president?"

"Charles Akelrod."

"What's Charlie's number?"

"What do you want with him?"

"You're gonna call him, tell him the deal's off, you're not for sale."

Rosen craned his neck to look at Mike. "Are you crazy?" The gun slipped off the rug and banged onto the floor.

Mike squatted down, picked up the gun and pressed it against Rosen's temple. "One. Two. Three."

"Okay, okay. It's area code two-one-two—" Rosen hesitated and rolled his eyes up in his head and thought for a second, then recited the seven numbers. "Look, Mister, he's not at work. You want to reach him, call him at home."

Mike punched nine numbers into the phone. "You're gonna get his machine. Gimme what you're gonna say."

"I don't want to do the deal."

"No," Mike said, getting pissed off. "I want *exactly* what you're gonna say. 'Hello Charles, this is your ol' buddy Seymour.' That sorta shit."

Rosen nodded. "Chaz — that's what everyone calls him — it's me, Seymour. I'm not going to do the deal." He paused for a second. "That okay?"

Mike leaned real close to Rosen. "Listen to me, you little asswipe, make it sound real, for Chrissake. Last chance."

Rosen was breathing hard, like a kid about to get a whipping from a bully. "Chaz, Sy here. Listen, we got problems on our end. The numbers don't crunch the same way they did when we talked. It's not going to happen. Give me a call."

"And the Academy Award goes to …"

"Your friend shorted the stock, didn't he?"

"What're you talking about?"

"He wants the stock to go down. Your friend Sonny borrowed shares of stock in my company. If the deal falls through the share price plummets and he makes a killing."

"You get one shot at this thing, don't fuck it up." Mike hit the last number, listened for several seconds, then put the phone to Rosen's ear.

"Hey Chaz, it's Sy. Listen, I got some bad news. We've been going over the numbers tonight and they just don't work. I don't think this is going to happen. We gotta talk." Rosen nodded to Mike, who listened for several seconds, then hung up the phone. "Was that okay?"

"You're no John Wayne."

"All right, a deal's a deal. Get me outta here."

"So you can call Chaz back and get the deal back on?"

Rosen said, "I have to wait until the deal falls apart?" He started wiggling and banging his head on the floor. "Jesus Christ! Help! Someone call the cops."

Mike was right in his face. "Sy, listen to me. I *am* a cop." He brought out his shield and showed it to Rosen.

Rosen was stunned into silence. "Goddamnit, why'd you tell me that?"

"So you'd shut up."

"You let me see your face. You tell me you're a cop. You're gonna shoot me." Rosen started to cry.

"I ain't gonna shoot anybody. Jesus Christ." Mike placed the Beretta on the floor next to one of the easy chairs and went over to the big desk and swiped the plastic trash bag from the waste can. "Get blood all over the place. I might leave a footprint."

Rosen was craning his neck to watch every move Mike made. Now he was coming toward him with the white bag held open. In one swift move Mike slipped it over Rosen's head and pulled it down snug. Flipping his head back and forth only sped up his breathing. He opened his mouth wide and sucked the white plastic into his mouth so Mike could see the outline of his lips and teeth. His tongue shot out as if he was trying to puncture the bag with it.

The whole thing took a minute. Rosen's head flopped to one side. The tension in the bag where it puckered into his mouth released and he stopped moving.

Mike used his foot to unroll the carpet. Rosen was lying on his back, head turned to the side, as if he'd fallen asleep fully clothed. Mike replaced the trash bag, stubbed out the cigar, slid the coffee table and chairs and sofa back in place, and squatted down next to Rosen. He took two deep breaths the way a free diver would before going under, then hoisted Rosen over his shoulder, turned off the lights, and headed toward the elevator.

Kensey could hear the sound of the elevator door open and close. She scanned the room then began to count. One Mississippi. Two Mississippi. Three Mississippi. She couldn't wait. Before she hit fifteen Mississippi she bolted through the door and into Rosen's office, squatting down near the easy chair and touching her hand here and there until she found it. Never in her life had she handled a gun. It was heavier than Kensey expected, more than a pound. And the grip was surprisingly rough.

"Goddamnit."

Kensey jumped.

It was Mike's voice coming from the hallway and now she could hear footsteps coming fast. There was no time to make it back to the assistant's office. She headed for the second door, the one on the opposite wall, Beretta in hand. Praying it would be unlocked, she grabbed the knob and hopped inside Rosen's private bathroom and closed the door almost all the way —

The lights went on in the office. Again Kensey's vantage was through the narrow crack but she got a good look at Mike, still wearing gloves. Rosen's body was nowhere in sight. Moving purposefully toward the leather sofa and kneeling down, he reached under the sofa and patted the carpet. He went over to the desk, back to the sofa, and finally to the easy chair, lifting it up and glancing underneath. He scratched his head, then did a quick 360.

Mike walked over to the door to the assistant's office and pushed it open, but his heart wasn't in it and he barely glanced inside. Now he headed across the room toward the bathroom. Kensey took two little steps back and to the side. If he did the same with this door he wouldn't see her. In case he flipped on the light and stepped inside, she brought the gun up with two hands, right hand around the grip, finger on the trigger, left hand wrapped around her wrist for strength. Just like she had seen on TV.

The door opened. Mike said, "Oh, forget it," and Kensey could hear him walking away. The lights went out and everything was quiet.

One Mississippi. Two Mississippi. Three Mississippi. All the way to a thousand.

11

Frank Hennessey stepped through the automatic doors into the Emergency Department a few minutes after nine, smoothing his short hair as he peeled off wire-rim aviators. He was in a blue suit with a white shirt, no tie, and was wearing brown wingtips. While his eyes adjusted he folded up his aviators and tucked them in an inside pocket. Down by his side he held a little white bag, the kind bakeries use. Finally one of the nurses recognized him and came over and asked if she could help him with something. He asked if Dr. Shaw had arrived and the nurse pointed toward the bullpen. He headed over to Kensey, in blue scrubs, her back toward him, head cocked to one side so her short hair hung down in an arc. She was writing a note.

"Dr. Shaw?" He made it sound like a question. She frowned when she turned to see who it was.

"Detective, what can I do for you?" She gave it a formal tone.

He smiled in a friendly way, his eyes crinkling at the corners. "Can I steal you for five minutes?"

She made a point of turning to look at seven metal charts stacked up on the counter. Then she stood and scanned the various rooms around the bullpen. All the curtains were closed.

Nurses raced about and someone out of sight was screaming. Kensey said, "He fell off a ladder and broke his arm. A piece of bone is sticking through the skin. We're swamped."

Frank looked around too and nodded in agreement. "Looks like it. Maybe you could come down to the precinct when you get off."

She considered this briefly and said, "Five minutes."

"Is there someplace private?"

Kensey stood, turned away from Frank, and said, "Anyone needs me I'm going to be in the lounge with Detective Hennessey." One of the nurses looked up and nodded. She walked out of the bullpen and led him down a short hallway past the Coke machine to a door marked *Private*.

The lounge was nothing more than a small locker room that neglected to get the once-over when the rest of the ED did. Metal shelves with a sloppy assortment of blue scrubs took up one wall, the others were lined with metal lockers like the ones you see in high schools. A couple of horrible easy chairs with the fabric worn smooth sat opposite one another and had been pushed close enough together so someone could stretch out and take a nap. A greasy white wrapper from a sandwich was on the floor and the smell of onions hung in the air like a nasal fog.

"Okay, what's up?" she said before the door had closed, then stood hands on hips while she faced him.

Frank dragged one of the easy chairs backwards to make some legroom. "You don't trust me, do you?"

"I'm just busy."

"You made sure all the nurses knew where you were going to be."

"It's an Emergency Department. There might be an emergency."

Letting it go, Frank held up the bag. "With your schedule you probably don't have time for breakfast. They had blueberry and cranberry."

"I don't like cranberry."

Frank pulled out the cranberry muffin and handed Kensey the bag. Watching her peer inside he said, "There's milk in there too." He sat down and peeled the paper from his muffin.

Kensey looked at Frank before pulling out an oversized blueberry muffin. She said, "Thanks," in a way that sounded more polite than grateful and eased into the other chair. Breaking off a little piece of the top, she popped it into her mouth.

"I stopped by last night around seven. Must've just missed you."

"Detective, I don't have a lot of time."

"I spent some time with Detective Romero. Said he dodged a bullet." Frank smiled. "Metaphorically, I guess."

Kensey pulled off another piece of muffin and opened the milk carton. "You know I can't discuss him from a medical perspective. Not unless he gives me permission."

"That's okay," Frank said. "You remember the other night, you and me sitting in the lounge? I swear we saw him die. How the hell'd he pull through?"

"I'm sure he told you he's doing just fine."

"I hope so. Look, Dr. Shaw, the reason I'm here ... I was worried about you." He sat back and took a small bite, catching some crumbs in the palm of his hand and cupping it under his chin while he chewed.

"You don't have to worry about me. I feel perfectly safe."

"Safe?" Frank stopped chewing and sat up. "I meant I'm worried about how you're handling the situation, you know, leaving for the night thinking you lost him."

"Oh," Kensey said, surprised at her mistake. "Sorry."

"It must have been quite a shock the next morning."

She forced a smile. "I blew the diagnosis. I'll spend the next three years living it down."

After considering her answer, he said, "Why'd you assume I was worried about your safety?"

Kensey kept quiet while her mind raced. "You know, what with the cop outside his room, I guess it makes me scared there could be trouble."

"So you don't feel any personal danger."

"No, should I?" Then she shook her head and took a bite and followed it with a slug of milk, trying to look casual.

"You and I know you didn't blow the case."

Kensey pulled the carton from her mouth. She watched him take a bite of his muffin, licking a crumb from his lip, looking at her. "Don't offer an opinion when you don't know what happened."

"I know you're a good doctor. With all the craziness going on you took the time to listen to him."

"I really don't want to discuss that with you."

"Did he tell you why he wanted to die?"

Kensey sat forward. "He didn't *want* to die. He believed he was *going* to die and said he was ready for it. There's a difference. Do you want me to explain it?"

"I could write a book, I know so much about Manny Romero. The guy's a scrapper. Always has been. If he's ready to die he's got a reason."

"Then go upstairs and ask him. I told you that night and I'm telling you now, Detective, he didn't confide in me."

Frank studied her closely, taking in the way she was breathing, the lines in her forehead, and which way her eyes went when she was done speaking. "I did. Last night, when I couldn't find you. He told me exactly what went down at Cheap Charlie's." He stopped talking and worked on his muffin.

"What happened that night?" She regretted the question as soon as the words hit the air.

"He'd been following this cocaine dealer, Johnny Ludwikowski. Followed him right up into O'Hara to that Cheap Charlie's, surprised the three of them doing a drug deal or something. Said before he knew what the hell happened someone was shooting at him. Never got off a shot. Next thing he's in the ED talking with you."

Kensey opened her mouth to drink some milk, not saying a word.

"He told me he busted Johnny Ludwikowski three years ago. Made me go look it up."

"Is it true?" Kensey asked.

"Testified at his trial. Is that sort of what you heard?"

"Like I *told* you the other night, he didn't say."

"Cause there're problems with the story."

Kensey felt her eyes getting dry; she was holding them open so long. Somewhere in her neck she could feel each thump of her heart. She asked herself what she would say if she really had no idea what actually happened. "Like what?"

"The three who died were killed with the same gun. They never found it."

"Was there someone else there?"

"Just what I asked. Manny's partner, Mike Dombroski? Maybe you saw him, dresses like a cowboy, keeps a pinch of chew in his mouth?" He waited for Kensey to shake her head. "Anyway, said he was just about to walk through the door when all hell broke loose and chased the shooter out the back, but had to let him go so he could call it in, save his buddy's life."

"So what's the problem?"

"Gun they found underneath Detective Romero? A Walther. I asked him about it, said how do you like it." Frank paused, giving Kensey time to digest. "He said he liked it real nice. I said I was thinking of getting me one and asked which model he had and he said it was the PPK."

Kensey shook her head, letting him know she didn't understand.

"It's a famous model, the one James Bond uses. Walther PPK."

"Why are you telling me this?"

"The gun we found wasn't the PPK. It was the P990. One thing cops know is their guns."

"I have a doctor-patient relationship with Detective Romero. That's all. I don't care about guns. And since when do cops talk about what they're investigating?"

"Kensey," he said, calling her by her first name, saying it gently the way Susanne would. "You may be in danger. Sometimes knowing secrets is more dangerous than anything else in the world."

"And you're here to assure me I can trust you."

"Manny threatened you, didn't he?"

"Absolutely not."

"Maybe he mumbled something he shouldn't have, then threatened you. Or is it something else?" Kensey's hands were shaking and Frank noticed. "I know I'm upsetting you. That's not why I came."

"That's exactly why you came and insisted we talk privately, so you could interrogate me."

"You're wrong."

"And you've been straight with me?"

"Absolutely," Frank said, looking surprised.

"That night we talked in the waiting room and they were still working on him, I called him Mr. Romero and you didn't correct me. I remember you sat there for a second not saying a word and I couldn't figure out why. Then *you* called him Mr. Romero — not Detective Romero — so I wouldn't know he was a cop."

"I saw something in your eyes. You were scared. I figured if you knew he was a cop you might be afraid to talk with me."

"So if what you're saying about him is true and he threatened me, how the hell do I know who you are?"

"I was at the church, Kensey. I know what happened."

She hesitated briefly, eyes drifting down to her muffin in her lap before saying, "What church?"

"Over on the Northside. The one Detective Romero belongs to. I saw that priest's body. A bullet to the head. I squeezed through the hole in the confessional and down that wooden ladder. There was a splotch of blood on the right side of every rung. There was more blood in the basement behind some boxes."

Kensey folded her right hand over the top of the milk carton.

"Show me your hand, Kensey."

Her hand stayed where it was. "What do you want from me?"

"Tell me who was shooting at you."

"I was at a friend's. You want proof?"

"There was a nun there, Sister Mary Francis. I spoke with her."

Kensey looked away.

"The sister described you. I know you were there. If I wanted to give you a hard time I'd take you down to the precinct and run your fingerprints. Maybe your blood type. Tell me what the hell is going on so I can help you."

Now she looked back. "No way did any nun describe me because I wasn't there. You want me to start trusting you? Put me in one of your lineups and let her pick me out. Then I'll start trusting you. I feel safer when you're not around."

Three steps and she was out the door.

12

"Do me a favor, make sure the door's closed all the way."

Kensey was in the middle of examining Manny's chest when he said this, as her stethoscope touched down over his heart. The adhesive tape securing the chest tube was pink instead of white. Foamy fluid moved back and forth in the clear tubing whenever he breathed. She crossed the room, pushing the door closed until it clicked.

Manny pushed himself up on one elbow and worked the remote control. The TV slowly came on, Manny playing with the volume so the cop in the hallway would hear it if he had his ear to the door. Frank Furillo was looking disappointed with one of his cops on *Hill Street Blues*. "Case anyone's listening," he said, tracking Kensey as she crossed back toward him, wearing wrinkled scrubs but looking fresh and pretty to him. He nodded toward a straight-back chair next to the bed. She sat down. "You know what it's called we have?" he said. "Détente." He pronounced it perfectly and caught Kensey off guard because she wrinkled up her forehead. "I got a nuclear bomb. You got a nuclear bomb. So long as you don't go to the cops and you forget about those names I told you, we're okay. You go to the cops, Mike'll know and—" Manny put his hands together, then pulled them apart in opposite directions and made a noise in the back of his throat that sounded like an explosion.

"You spoke to Mike?"

"Had to get our stories straight. Thank God for Johnny Ludd, you know? He made it easy. So while I was on the horn with Mike—"

"He knows I wrote it all down? Names, everything. Anything happens to me it goes public."

"Like I said, we got us a détente. Mike's aware your friend's keeping it. Everything's cool. Sleep at your house, take a walk. You don't gotta be scared or nothing. Now don't get me wrong — and I didn't say nothing to Mike 'bout it — 'tween you'n me, I ain't so sure you wrote any a' this shit down." Kensey leaned forward and opened her mouth to say something. He held out his hand to stop her before she had the chance. "Save it, Doc. I know what you're gonna say. Besides, long as I'm in here I gotta trust you like you gotta trust me."

"I can't stop the police from talking to me."

"Hennessey, I bet. What'd you say to him?"

"Nothing. And if I were going to the cops it wouldn't be him. For all I know he's one of you."

"Hennessey? Ain't one a' us."

Kensey studied Manny's face after what he said. Manny gave away nothing so she popped her stethoscope on and resumed her exam. "You sound good. Your air leak's really slowed. Pretty soon I'm going to clamp off your chest tube and see if any air reaccumulates." Her fingers palpated his thick abdomen.

"There ain't no hurry, Doc."

"I thought you wanted to get out of here."

"I pretty much 'spect a bullet when I get outta here, what with blabbing to you and all. So there's no rush."

"Really?" Kensey said softly and stopped her exam.

"When you're in this deep you don't walk away. It's usually a six-foot ziplock. My best bet is bolt outta here and keep going 'til I hit Mexico, then figure a way to get to Cuba. Got a cousin there. Hey, you want a piece of fruit or something before it goes bad? My captain sent it."

Kensey glanced over at a huge basket of fruit on the windowsill with an American-flag ribbon tied to the handle in a big bow. It was brimming with shiny apples and pears. She walked across the room and selected a pear.

"Gonna open a restaurant. You ever have a Cuban sandwich?"

Kensey shook her head.

"Sometime I gotta tell you about 'em." Two of the cops on *Hill Street* were wrestling an angry scofflaw to the floor. Manny noticed the television and pointed a finger at it. "Always liked cop shows. Still do. Betcha won't believe this. I hate the dirty cops. I mean I really want 'em to get shot." He looked at Kensey, knowing she would be looking at him.

She was.

He grinned. "I don't understand it neither. Probably need a shrink to explain it." They stared at the television together, watching a swarm of uniforms bring the situation under control. "You know how you tell the dirty ones on a show?"

"How?"

"It depends when you find out they're dirty. You find out at the beginning of the show, the cop's usually pretty nasty looking. Long hair, needs a shave. If you don't find out till the last minute it's some real nice-looking guy who's the last one you'd ever suspect. Oh yeah, it's always a guy and he's Italian or Irish, never black." His fingers found his cross and his eyes stayed on the television. He said, "I don't even know how the whole thing started."

"What thing?" Kensey said. She took a bite of the pear and had to hurry over to the sink and grab a paper towel to wipe the juice from her chin.

"Guy I was telling you about?"

"You mean Sonny."

"Guy I was telling you about," he said firmly, shooting a look toward the door and slowly shaking his head back and forth. Now softer: "What the hell? No names." His chest heaved twice, then he sighed. "Anyway, me'n Mike just happened to meet this guy in a bar one night two, three years ago."

Kensey sat down and listened.

"So he buys us a couple brews and we're talking like you do in a bar and he says, 'Hey, you guys look like you know how to get things done.' Just like that. I don't know what the hell he means but it sounds like some sort a' compliment. He ordered another round for us, then he goes, 'Hey, you think sometime you could look the other way?'" Manny sort of frowned and rolled his eyes like he was confused by what he'd just said. "I didn't know what the fuck he meant. And Mike was like, 'Whoa, whaddaya mean?' The next thing I know we're sitting in a corner booth, got nice steaks in front a' us and I'm telling myself, Hell, if I'm only looking the other way I'm not really doing nothing."

"Like what?"

"Maybe a delivery of something that might be ... private. I mean, I'm not making excuses or nothing. What I did was wrong and I knew it. But he's so goddamn good at making you go along with what he wants. I still can't believe it. You know what I mean?"

Kensey nodded. "I guess. When did things change?"

"You figured it out. 'Bout a year'n a half ago, me'n Mike, we're getting a couple thou a month for doing nothing. Cash. I mean everything's cool. Mike's got himself a nice set of wheels. Until one day our friend says there's this guy was hurting his business and could we take care of him. Right away I said, 'What the fuck? Who do you think we are?' and he told me exactly who we were: his boys." Manny's fingers were all over his cross, rolling it around, giving it a kiss when he wasn't talking. "Mike did the first one. I started puking and he had to do the second one too. I did the third. We go back and forth now. There been seven."

"What I don't get, Detective—"

"Hey Doc, how 'bout Manny?"

Kensey took a deep breath. "Manny, what I don't get is if you're so religious—"

He nodded quickly as if he were expecting the question. "Yeah, yeah, I know. It's like this, Doc — hey, should I call you Doc or's Kensey okay?"

"You might as well call me Kensey."

"Nice name. Your birth name or some kinda nickname?"

"It's short for McKenzie."

"Anyway, the religion thing. It's like I tol' Mike more times'n I can count, you come clean, God forgives. He knows we're flawed."

"It seems like you were taking advantage of His generosity."

Manny rubbed his stubbly face. "When you're in deep, drowning — and I mean drowning with lead weights hanging off your feet — you just want to grab onto something. Anything. All my life I wore one a' these," he said and held up his cross by the chain. "Went to church. But these last few years? I really stepped it up. Otherwise what'd I have?"

Kensey paused, thinking this was a difficult admission for him. *Hill Street* was over and before the commercial there was a newsbreak. The lead story was about Seymour Rosen disappearing during the night.

The two of them focused on the television, abandoning their conversation while they listened to a reporter positioned outside Rosen's building talking about the big deal that was supposed to happen today and speculating about whether the buyout would still happen.

Kensey was thinking that the press didn't know about the phone call Rosen made before Mike killed him. "Maybe I should have warned him."

Manny looked at her, studying her face before answering. "It just said they don't know where he is."

They turned their attention back to the television, the reporter saying the buyout was officially supposed to happen at noon and to stay tuned for further details. When he was finished Kensey had her hand over her mouth, breathing through her fingers.

Finally she said, "What does he do with the bodies?"

"You called him, didn't you?"

Shaking her head, she said, "No, I was too scared."

Manny rolled up on an elbow and worked the remote control to make the TV louder. "Mike tells me he shows up at Rosen's building after hours knowing Rosen works later'n anybody. He calls up on the intercom and Rosen goes 'Be right down,' like he's 'specting somebody. Doesn't ask who it is or nothing. Now Mike remembers Rosen unlocking the front door and pretty quick Mike's got a gun on him and they're checking round to make sure no one's working late. Thing is, Mike forgot to have Rosen lock the door."

"Why're you telling me all this?"

"Reason is, Mike lost his gun, a Beretta forty-five — that's all he uses. Berettas. Looked all over the damn place for it. Don't matter much 'cause it was a throwaway. And Mike wears gloves. Pretty careful guy. But he called me this morning and said maybe you were there and picked it up or something."

"Why'd he think that?"

"Been anyone else there they woulda called the cops by now."

"I already told you. I *should* have picked up the phone."

"Don't get no ideas about being a hero. Please. You'n me, we're on the same side. But Mike is one ugly human being."

"With you telling me all this, I feel like you did when that guy asked you to look the other way. I'm being sucked in a little at a time."

"Un-uh. There's a big difference. You don't have a choice. I did." He looked away.

"You're scaring me."

"No. I just don't want nothing to happen to you. I feel responsible for you."

"The daughter you never had?"

"The sister who didn't make it on the boat ride from Cuba. That's a story I never told nobody. Maybe sometime I'll tell you."

"Sonny," Kensey said, pausing a beat before she continued. "Is he a cop?"

"The answer don't matter so why get into it. You go to the cops our little détente won't mean much. I gotta take a nap."

Just like that, the conversation was over. Kensey turned and headed toward the door.

"Yo," Manny said as her fingers touched the knob. Kensey looked at him. "On the side there's a little safety. You push it so you see the red dot. Then it's good to go. Knowing Mike he racked the slide to scare Rosen. You don't have to cock it or nothing."

■ ■ ■

Kensey pulled up to her house just as the sky was getting dark. She let the motor run, the car still in drive, her foot lightly on the brake, and waited.

Four months living on Bryant Street and she never noticed so many good hiding places. But she couldn't take one more day of, "That looks just like one of Susanne's sweaters." So before the light was gone she removed the key from the ignition and headed up the walk.

Inside the front hall she deposited her backpack on the floor as her hand flicked on as many lights as possible without venturing ten feet from the front door. She waited at the bottom of the stairs, staring up into the shadows of the second floor, silently holding her breath and listening for sounds she never heard in her house. This took almost a minute. When the air in her lungs started to burn then burst forth in a loud rush, she fetched her backpack and rummaged through it until her fingers wrapped around the textured grip of Mike Dombroski's gun. The word *Beretta* was stamped on the black barrel. Remembering Manny's words, she found the safety and slid it up so she could see the red dot. After that she mounted the steps.

The bathroom was at the top of the stairs. Holding the gun out in front with two hands, she stepped onto the tiled floor. The shower curtain was dark blue and Kensey squared off in front of it. When her arms got so heavy she couldn't take it anymore, she released the gun with one hand, grabbed hold of the curtain in the middle, and yanked it clean off the rod.

The shower was vacant.

After that she proceeded to her bedroom, her hand reaching into the darkened room to find the switch for the overhead light. Her bed was unmade. Kensey knelt down and peeked underneath. She saw two suitcases and an empty plate.

Moving across the room, she approached her closet that had twin doors that swung away from each other. Daring to take one hand from the grip, she opened one door, then the other. It was packed with long dresses and skirts and jackets. She looked down at her huge assortment of shoes, slippers, flip-flops, and boots.

One of the boots was standing sideways. Kensey hadn't worn boots since she'd been in Pittsburgh.

Then something moved in the closet. One of her dresses shivered. Maybe.

Taking a quick step back, she used a loud voice. "I've got a gun. Come out slowly." She tried to swallow and some spittle leaked out the corner of her mouth. "I mean it. I'll shoot you."

Nothing.

Her heart was beating so hard in her neck she couldn't tell what the clothes in her closet were doing. "I'm counting to five, then I shoot. One Mississippi. Two Mississippi. Three Mississippi." Her breathing was coming in fits, loud enough if any sound came from the closet, no way could she hear it. Her voice rising, she said, "Four Mississippi." Waiting a second, she screamed at the closet, "Come out now, goddamnit. Five —"

Bang. The gun in her hand went off. Bang. Bang.

Three shots were fired and there was smoke in the room and some of her dresses were swinging back and forth as if they were in a gentle breeze drying on the line.

Lowering the Beretta to her side, Kensey took an aggressive step forward and started grabbing blouses and dresses and pants and throwing them over her shoulder until her room looked like the aftermath of a hurricane. She didn't stop until the closet was empty. Slumping down to the floor, she stared at the little constellation of holes in the back wall of her closet and began to cry.

13

"May I help you?" the stunning receptionist said, lifting lashed-up eyes from her word processor. She was on the twenty-third floor of a downtown building, dressed in something from Saks, working in a foyer decorated with showy sconces, perched behind a big curved desk that was surrounded by a low black granite wall, giving her some privacy. Behind her, the word *Fortune* was emblazoned in thick brass letters a foot tall, except the *o* had been replaced with a shiny gold coin. She had nice skin and a white smile that she used when she looked up.

"I was wondering if I could see Mr. Fortune."

The receptionist eyed the young woman in dark slacks and hunter green jacket, no makeup or jewelry. Frowning as she consulted a day planner, the receptionist said, "May I tell Mr. Fortune what this is in regard to?"

"I don't mean to be difficult but I need to speak with him alone. It's a private matter."

Shaking her pretty head as her finger slid down the day planner, she said, "He is absolutely booked solid. I'm sorry."

"I wouldn't waste Mr. Fortune's time if this weren't important. Please."

"And you are?"

"Kensey Shaw."

Picking up her telephone, she tapped two numbers, waited several seconds, and said in a hushed tone, "Mr. Fortune, I know I'm to hold all calls but a—" she looked up at Kensey as she continued— "Kelly Shaw is here to see you. I told her—" Now she stopped speaking, listened for several seconds, and put on a pouty face. Kensey took this as a hint it didn't look good. Then the secretary pulled the phone from her ear, cupped her hand over the mouthpiece, and said, "How *does* Mr. Fortune know you?"

"He doesn't. Tell him it's important."

The receptionist repeated exactly what Kensey had said into the phone, listened again, and hung up. "Mr. Fortune said he's very busy today and wondered if you could leave a brief note along with your number. He'd be happy to get back to you." She placed a piece of Fortune letterhead on the little ledge atop the granite wall along with a pen.

Kensey placed her hands on the polished stone and leaned over. "Call him back. Right now. Tell him I need two minutes and I'm not leaving."

"I may have to call security." Then keeping one eye on Kensey, she dialed the phone a second time, spoke softly enough that Kensey could not hear what she was saying, listened and hung up. Raising one perfect eyebrow, she pushed back from the desk. "If you'll follow me, Ms. Shaw."

Kensey was led down a short hallway with thick black carpet and walls adorned with black-and-white lithographs. Alec Fortune's receptionist opened a heavy wooden door that rose to the ceiling. She held out a hand, hostess-style, ushering Kensey into an office.

"He'll be with you shortly," she told Kensey. With a parting smile, the receptionist closed the door silently and Kensey was alone.

The office was huge. An enormous cherry desk with inlays of different colored wood was perfectly centered before a picture window with a view inside PNC Park. Kensey could spot third base and most of the pitcher's mound but at ten in the morning there was nothing going on. The desk held tidy stacks of papers and the computer was showing a screen saver with the Fortune logo floating lazily about while the gold coin sparkled. Behind the desk, under the window, was a matching credenza. An ice bucket and top-shelf liquor waited on a silver tray. In the middle of the room chairs and sofas had been arranged around a wrought-iron coffee table with a thick glass top. But it was the artwork on one of the walls that tugged at her. Three paintings were hung, each with its own ceiling spotlight and ornate frame thick with layers of gold paint. Kensey strolled over and examined them. Two by Cézanne, the one in the middle a Picasso.

"My decorator insisted I buy them so I could impress people. Did I waste my money?"

Kensey whipped around to see a man in his mid-thirties on the other side of the room. Dark tailored suit. White shirt. Stunning tie. Handsome, Kensey thought, but not in a Ralph Lauren pretty-boy way. He looked like a guy who could mix it up if he had to.

"The yellow in the Cézanne on the left matches the yellow in the Picasso. And of course, the green in the other Cézanne would match that in the Picasso as well. As my art broker put it,—the colors draw your eyes from one work to the other.'" He rolled his eyes. "I know it's a load of crap. Sorta like buying one of those ninety-nine-dollar landscapes just because it's the same length as the sofa."

"Mr. Fortune?" She waited for a nod and a smile. "I'm Kensey Shaw. Thanks for meeting with me."

"You told Suzanne it was important. I hope you're not an art snob."

"It is, Mr. Fortune. Important, I mean. But I must ask a favor before I tell you."

"Ms. Shaw," he said, getting serious right away. "I left my board meeting for this. If you have something to say, you need to get on with it."

"What I'm about to tell you is confidential."

He cocked his head slightly to one side as he moved to the leather sofa and stood behind it. "If you're expecting me to play cross-my-heart-and-hope-to-die, no thank you."

A door opened, a different door than Kensey had entered, one that blended into the paneled walls so well Kensey hadn't noticed it. A young man in a suit stepped inside. "Sorry, Mr. Fortune, we're ready for that vote. Some of the guys have to catch a plane."

Alec glanced at his watch. He turned toward the young man and said, "I'll be a minute."

Without another word the young man nodded and departed, silently pulling the door closed.

Kensey took a chair, her knees together, a hand on each one.

"Would you care to sit down?" Alec smiled. He remained behind the sofa.

"I'm an intern at University Medical Center."

"I had my knee done there last year. Were you one of the doctors who took care of me?"

"I've only been there four months." Now she crossed her legs. "Sir, did you hear about the shooting at Cheap Charlie's the other night?"

"Of course." Kensey picked up on a change in his voice, the way people talk when they're in the clinic and about to get test results back. "Several people died."

"Three."

"Okay, three."

"I took care of the police officer who was shot."

"I read he made it, didn't he?"

"Yes. But he was pretty sick when he arrived. Got shot in the chest, could barely breathe. He told me some things. People sometimes say stuff when they think they're going to die. He said he'd been hired to kill some people."

Alec's face twitched. It was almost imperceptible but Kensey spotted it, his right cheek tightening for an instant. Silently, he came around the sofa and sat down. He crossed his legs and picked a piece of lint from the fabric, balled it up between his thumb and forefinger, and let it slip to the floor. He had a look on his face that made Kensey think he was going to get sick. "This has something to do with me."

"Two more were supposed to be killed." Kensey listened to him breathe. "He told me you were one of them."

"What?" he said softly. Then he thought about what he had heard and asked, "Why me?"

"I don't know. I think maybe for business reasons."

"Business reasons." He rubbed the side of his face. "What the hell does that mean, business reasons? Is he some kind of disgruntled employee?"

"No, he's working for someone else."

"This is a cop we're talking about."

"An undercover detective."

Alec was breathing harder now, his hand coming to his mouth and wiping away a patina of perspiration. "What's his name?"

"Manny Romero."

"Okay, so this Romero guy that you're taking care of in the hospital is out to kill me." He watched Kensey nod, then pushed himself out of the deep leather cushion and headed over to the bar. "Drink?"

"Just a Coke."

"I need a little more than that." Alec used his hand to scoop several cubes into two crystal glasses. He fixed Kensey her drink, then poured two inches of Ketel One for himself, splashing another inch into the glass before leaving the bar. On his way back to the sofa he handed Kensey her drink, filled his mouth with vodka, and sat down, balancing the glass on his knee. "So it's business as usual until he gets out of the hospital. Then I start ducking?"

"It's not this guy. Not anymore. He's worried about his own safety."

He brought the glass to his lips. "Bottom line, who the hell're we talking about?" He took a hit of the vodka.

"I'm pretty sure it's his partner."

"Pretty sure. Give me a percent of certainty."

"I don't know. There could be somebody else I don't know about."

"What's his name? The partner."

"Mike Dombroski."

"How do I know this Manny Romero's not just blowing smoke?"

"You ever hear of Seymour Rosen?"

"The robotics guy? Who hasn't?"

"He was the other one."

"They said he disappeared." His voice sounded small.

"He's dead. And it happened the night before the biggest deal of his life."

"The cop tell you all that?"

"Something like that."

"So who's behind this thing?"

The door opened and the young man in the suit popped his head in. "Mr. Fortune?"

Alec looked at him and spoke in an even voice. "Tell the guys to forget it, Drake, something's come up. Thank them."

"You want to give me your proxy?"

"No," Alec said. "I'll call each of them next week." Alec turned away from the young man and when he heard the quiet sound of the door closing he said to Kensey, "Two years ago, maybe longer, I had a death threat. It totally freaked me out. I couldn't sleep. Lost nine pounds. In the span of a week I got six e-mails filled with the most vile—" He shook his head back and forth, looking for the right word. "— shit. Said he was gonna kill me and I better not go to the cops."

"So what happened?"

"I went to the cops. They traced it to some Internet café on the Southside. Then they stopped. Probably some employee who got fired. It makes you see how vulnerable you are. I mean, if someone really wanted to kill me... Anyway, this one's simple. For God's sake, we know who it is. We just call the authorities." He pushed up and headed over to his desk, reaching for the phone.

"No," Kensey said, loud enough to make Alec whip around toward her. "You can't. Manny's partner Mike, he's a cop too. He'll know if you call the police. They'll kill me."

"Is it just the two of them?"

"There's another cop investigating the shooting. He knows something's going on. He's asking me all sorts of questions."

"If he knows something's going on, talk to him."

"I don't know if I can trust him."

"You believe that? You keep your mouth shut they won't touch you?"

Kensey sipped her Coke. She had a clear picture of Manny lying in bed talking to her. "Yeah, I do."

"What's this Romero's motivation for keeping you alive?"

"I told him I wrote down every name he gave me. Anything happens to me, it gets released."

Slowly, Alec smiled. "Smart." Alec went behind his desk and unlocked one of the drawers. He pulled out a pistol, matte black, and returned to the sofa. "This is a Glock. They told me it was easy to shoot," he said, carefully placing it on the coffee table. "From now on it goes with me. Got it after those e-mails started, went to a range and learned how to use it." He looked at Kensey staring at the gun. "Don't tell me you're not frightened."

"Not as much now. I know a lot can upset this deal I made with Manny, especially if something happens to him."

"Manny." Alec let the word roll around in his mouth. "You're on a first-name basis with this guy?"

Kensey's eyes opened wide. "It doesn't mean anything. He's my patient."

"You ever shoot a gun?"

"A BB gun at Coke cans when I was a kid."

"I'm gonna buy you a gun and get you lessons at the range."

"Let me think about it."

"Do you know who hired these guys?"

"Someone named Sonny."

"Sonny who?"

Kensey shrugged her shoulders. "And don't ask me to find out."

"Sonny," Alec said to himself softly, trying to jog a memory. "Sonny." He shook his head, then said, "Suppose we go to the *Post-Gazette*. Christ, I'll hold a press conference right here if it would help. We'll name names. Trust me, it'll be the biggest news story in the country. And then I'll foot the bill for you to vanish as long as you like. You don't even have to tell me where you're going."

"Let me think about it. I have a question for you. The first killings were connected with a retail chain. Then a takeover of a high-tech company. Maybe there's a pattern. What sort of business do you run?"

"My father started the company thirty years ago. Fortune Accounting. A little nothing over on Liberty Avenue. The name was catchy so he did all right. He did the books for all sorts of businesses, made a comfortable living. Once in a while the businesses failed and he offered to take some of them over, fix up what was wrong. First a paper-products company. Some convenience stores. You heard of Perfect Cleaners? That's us. About a dozen of them. We should be called Hodgepodge Inc."

"And where do you come in?"

"After college I came to work for my dad. About seven years ago I took over. Dad's got all these hobbies, likes to travel, play golf. But every single day right before lunch he calls and we talk. I don't make a move without him."

"Can you think of any reason why someone would want to kill you?"

Alex put his hand over his mouth and kept it there for several seconds while he thought. Then he said, "No," in a voice so small Kensey could barely hear him.

"You're lucky to be able to work with your dad." She looked at her watch. "Please be careful." She stood.

Alec pushed himself up. "Kensey, I appreciate the risk you took for me."

"I had the responsibility for two people." She moved toward the door. "One of them is dead."

"You can't walk out of here like that. Wait." He saw her stop and turn back toward him. "You were thrown into this. How could you have known when he was going to be killed?"

"I spoke with him on the phone." Her hand went into her bag and dug around. "I could have told him to get the hell outta there. I thought the only way I could do it was in person." She pulled out a Kleenex and dabbed her eyes.

"I am so overwhelmed by what you did today."

"I guess I better go."

When she reached the door he said, "What if I asked you to dinner?"

"It wouldn't work."

"Sushi. You like sushi?"

"I'm an intern, you've got Picassos."

"Picasso," he said, enunciating the last syllable carefully. "Jimmy's World of Art only had one."

"You know what I mean."

For a second he thought she was going to giggle. She didn't.

"That's why we should get to know each other. Compare notes."

"I've got so much on my mind right now I don't think I'd make very good company. I'll let you know if I hear anything." Kensey opened the door. "Good-bye," she said and stepped onto the thick black carpet leading to the elevator.

14

Riding down from twenty-three Kensey was alone in the elevator. Thinking about the way Alec had said he only had one Picasso made her smile — maybe for the first time since Manny Romero rolled into the ED. She pictured Alec sitting at his desk in shirtsleeves, PNC Park behind him in the distance, working his Glock, snapping the clip into the grip, then slipping it into a shoulder holster and putting his jacket on over it. And everything he said made sense. Her détente with Manny was a flimsy house of cards. Should she take him up on his offer? Go public and vanish? How long would she have to go away? It would be like the witness-protection program. Lonely. Always waiting for something to happen.

The doors opened and she stepped into the packed lobby. Smartly dressed men and women crowded toward the elevator, others dashed back and forth. With a flood of daylight coming through the front wall of glass, she was squinting.

Now she headed toward the revolving doors, past little clusters of people standing and chatting, catching snippets of private conversations about luncheons and meetings. Rimming one wall were long couches, people scattered about reading papers and typing on laptops. Over by a grove of potted trees a man was buried deep inside his

Wall Street Journal, the paper opened wide like a curtain. A gentleman in a business suit crunched an apple as he hurried to catch the next elevator. Pushing through the glass doors, a chubby deliveryman was moving a dolly loaded with boxes while a fat woman, carrying a white bakery box by the strings, bumped into Kensey. She mumbled, "Excuse me," but never slowed down. Right away a security guard approached the man with the dolly and told him he needed to use the service elevator. The man with the *Wall Street Journal* turned a page and shook the paper to straighten it, and in the far reaches of her peripheral vision, Kensey spotted something. Slowing her gait, she waited for him to give himself away.

The deliveryman wheeled the loaded dolly past her. He was bitching about the goddamn bullshit but doing it in a quiet voice. Two young women with long hair and too much makeup were on a collision course with Kensey and had to separate to go around her, not skipping a single beat of their conversation.

Kensey never saw them. She was stalking the man reading the paper.

He turned the page again, this time taking an easy glance out toward the street, maybe a glimpse across the lobby. At that moment Kensey got a look at his face.

■ ■ ■

"How the fuck you think it looks you not coming to see me?" Manny was pushed up on one elbow, working the remote control for the TV. The white sheet was up around his neck, the Pleur-evac bubbling away at the foot of the bed.

"Nice to see you too." Mike was standing just this side of the door in a worn leather jacket with the collar up. He started across the room, his right leg swinging out to the side with each step as Regis Philbin roared on in that big voice of his, Manny adjusting the volume control to make it even louder.

Manny dropped the remote control over the side of the bed so it dangled from its thick wire. Grunting as he eased back into the pillow he said, "Where the hell's your 'stache?"

Mike touched his upper lip. A stiff crop of bristles was growing in. "I thought I needed a new look."

"She knows who you are."

"I didn't know when I shaved, asshole."

"So where you been since we talked the morning after?"

"Covering your ass, man. You owe me plenty," Mike paused, then sounded sarcastic, "pardner." He spun the stiff chair next to the bed around so he could climb into it like he would a saddle and leaned his chest against the back.

"Fuck you," Manny said. "What's with your leg?"

"Got banged up the other night."

"Jesus Christ, you're a sweatball." Manny eyed him up and down.

Mike glared at him for several seconds. "Listen to me, Manny," he said. "If I didn't follow that doc after you died, see what she was up to?" Mike gave a quick nod towards the door. "The Boy Scout out there woulda been guarding you 'stead of protecting you." Mike caught Manny opening his mouth like he was going to start talking and cut him off with: "The next day? Right after I got off the phone with you, *she* shows up at the station. I'm bullshitting with the captain, telling him how we almost lost you and there she is. Christ, I chased her out that bathroom on the second floor, you know, the one looks out over the lot."

Hand over hand, Manny retrieved the remote and pushed the volume to the max. With a little nod toward the door he said, "The Boy Scout's got big ears." Manny adjusted the sheets and Mike got an eyeful of the bandages and chest tube.

"Whoa, what is that thing?" Mike said, his eyes following the chest tube all the way down to the Pleur-evac. He stood up and limped into the bathroom.

"Why'm *I* calling you to get our stories straight? Jesus Christ, I'm the one with the goddamn chest tube."

Mike spit some brown tobacco juice in the sink. Coming back to the chair, he backhanded his lips dry. "You hadn't opened your goddamn trap—"

"Look, Kensey ain't gonna talk."

Their voices were louder now, things heating up, Manny settling his eyes on the television, Mike looking down at the floor.

Suddenly Mike lowered his voice to a whisper. All he said was, "Kensey?"

"You know her name. Stay the hell away from her."

"Her badge said *Mc*Kenzie. Now you're telling me, stay away from her, she's cool. You got a hard-on for her or what?"

"Like I tol' you on the phone, something happens to her, everything goes public."

"Which leads to the next question. Where the hell's that list of names? It's gotta be one a' her friends."

"Why're you bustin' my balls?"

Mike looked over at the fruit basket on the windowsill. "Maybe you look into it next time she stops by to take your pulse."

Manny said, "We're so fuckin' lucky it was Johnny Ludd."

Mike scratched his head. His tone softened. "Yeah. And we're totally cool with the captain."

"Christ, *he* was over here the next day, smiling at me like I made him look good. He says to me, 'Hey, where's Mike?' I had to lie and tell him you just left."

Mike paused, waiting to see if Manny had more to say. He leaned in close and spoke quietly. "What'd you tell him?"

"Like we agreed, Johnny Ludd was dealing again so we followed him."

"He buy it?"

"Two seconds later this cute girl with tits out to here comes in to take a chest X-ray and he winks at me and that was it. He left."

"That it? Nothing else?"

"If I say 'that's it,' that means nothing else happened." Manny sounded pissed. "Christ almighty, he was here maybe three minutes. Brought that fruit basket." Their eyes looked at the basket, a couple of red apples and an orange on top. "You want something?"

"That's okay. This détente thing you said on the phone, what the fuck is that?"

"Look it up. By the way, couldn't you tell which side the priest was in?"

"I knew where he was. She was telling him the truth, the whole truth and nothing but the truth. What the hell was I s'posed to do?"

"He's a priest, Mike. Telling him something is as safe as thinking it."

"Not as safe as my way. And if I'd killed the doc too… " Mike made a fist.

Manny rolled on his side so he could look at Mike without turning his head. "I swear, you touch her—"

"You do have a thing for her."

"You outta your fuckin' mind?" Manny slammed his fist against the side rail of the bed.

All of a sudden Mike grabbed his bad leg. "Shit!"

"The hell was that?" Manny said, leaning over the side of the bed to get a look at Mike's leg sticking straight out as if he was in the middle of a routine on the pommel horse.

"Fuck. That hurts." Mike clenched his jaw and scrunched his face so it looked like a walnut shell.

"What is that?"

"I don't know." He was breathing hard, waiting for the pain to subside. "Some sort of charley horse." Slowly he was able to lower his leg.

"That was no charley horse."

"Forget it." Mike leaned back and massaged his leg. "Just give me a second." He turned around and looked at the door, letting Manny know there was more business. Quietly he said, "So I talked to Sonny."

"I figured that's why you showed up." Manny eased himself back on the pillow.

"He called me, asked how you're doing." Mike twisted in the chair to check out the TV.

"*He* called you?"

"Yeah, he called me."

"You told him I was okay, huh? Gonna be back on the job good as new."

"I didn't know the 'good as new' part," he said, not looking at Manny but trying to focus on what Regis was saying.

"So long as he don't know nothn' about the other stuff. Right?"

Mike looked like he was paying full attention to the TV. John Travolta was strolling onto the set, waving to the audience, then kissing Kelly Ripa before he sat down on one of those really tall chairs. "Hey, look at that, Chili Palmer." Mike limped over to the fruit basket.

"Anything but the pears."

Mike grabbed the orange. "Love that guy." He dug his thumb into the skin and peeled it. Concentrating on what Travolta was saying, he ripped sections of the orange off and popped them into his mouth. "You know what movie I really liked him in?"

Manny's head was turning back and forth from the TV to Mike. His face was sweaty. Finally he said, "You fuckin' told him, didn't you?"

"What was that, the one with Samuel L.? Not *Pulp Fiction*. The one he's the interrogator?"

Manny used the remote control to change the channel, this time the shopping network; a pretty lady showing off dangly earrings. "Look at me," Manny said, not in the cool Chili Palmer way but pissed off like he could explode any minute.

Slowly, Mike turned his head. His fingers went up to stroke the bristles he was hoping would grow back into a mustache. "*Basic,*" he said.

"Basic?"

"Yeah, the movie. *Basic.*"

"I'm in this fuckin' hospital with a tube shoved in my chest and I'm trying to find out what the hell's going on—"

"Yeah, Manny, I told him. I told him you spazzed out before the job and then spilled your guts to the doc."

"Why the fuck did you tell him?"

"We ain't the only people he talks to. Sonny'll find out — maybe he already knows — and then I'm into him for lying."

Manny raised his arm and pointed at the door. "Get out."

"Sonny wanted to know if you told her his name."

"You didn't tell him 'no' did you?"

"I said I'd find out. You tell her?" Mike changed his tone and was bearing down like he was interrogating a witness.

Manny turned his head so he was staring at the ceiling. "I can hear him telling you to take me out the second I get outta here." Manny rolled his eyes toward Mike. "You'n me, we go way back before Sonny."

"You tell the girl or not?"

"Once you told him all the other shit, you shoulda said 'yes' and his name's on the list. You tell him 'no,' one of his goons takes Kensey out. Then your name gets released."

"Shit."

Manny said, "His name's on the list, right after yours. You got it? Now no one gets killed."

"Let me give you a piece of friendly advice, pardner. You want to get off Sonny's shit list, find out who's got that piece of paper." Mike grabbed his leg a second time before pushing out of the chair and shuffling toward the door.

■ ■ ■

"Why the hell are you spying on me?" Kensey was standing in front of the man with the *Wall Street Journal,* her arms crossed tightly across her chest.

Frank Hennessey lowered the paper and began to fold it. He looked good in a suit, trim enough to leave the jacket buttoned even when he was sitting down. "Two reasons, Dr. Shaw," he said. He finished folding the paper and set it on the bench next to him. "The more I learn about Manny Romero, the more I think you can help with my investigation. He's deeply religious, goes to confession at least once a week. I believe he confided something to you in the Emergency Department that took you to the church where Father Flaherty was murdered."

"I wasn't there. Unless you came down here to tell me that nun is ready to pick me out of a lineup, I've got to get back to the hospital."

"The nun is blind."

"So the last time we talked you lied to me. Again."

"She described you, your voice, the way you talk. I could arrange for the three of us to get together, see if she remembers you."

"You said you had two reasons."

"You have a minute for a cup of coffee?"

"Why is it always food with you?"

"There's a Starbucks around the corner. I need some."

Kensey checked her watch and they started walking.

On the street Frank said, "When I first joined the force there was a bank robbery. I interviewed everybody. The tellers, the manager, all of the customers. And even though everybody said the robbers were wearing masks, I kept coming back to one of the tellers." There was quite a bit of traffic, the street loaded with cars and buses, the sidewalk packed with people. It didn't slow Frank down. "She kept saying the same thing everybody else did. She had no idea who they were. Never got a look at their faces." They were at the Starbucks now, pushing through the door and getting in line. "Smells good in here."

Kensey took a whiff. "Go on."

"Anyway, I just didn't feel like I was finished with her. Don't ask me why, something in my gut. I kept coming back, talking to her. Trying to jog her memory."

They reached the front of the line and ordered, Frank the coffee of the day, Kensey the French roast. She pulled out her wallet. Frank waved her off.

They weaved their way around little round tables to one by the window, away from the lazy coffee sippers and hyper laptoppers. Frank finished his story. "One night, something clicks and the teller recognizes one of the guys sitting at the bar she goes to. It turns out they were both regulars. Apparently when he was cleaning out her drawer he threatened her. She remembered his voice." Frank sipped his coffee.

"So what else are your instincts telling you?"

He looked around to make sure no one was showing any interest in their conversation. "Not everything's instinct. I know some things. Detective Romero was into something bad. If it was coke, maybe he wanted it for himself. Manny shot those three people and made up an extra person who ran out the back. His partner did a switcheroo with the guns."

"How do you know that?"

"Manny was lying on the Walther, claimed he never got off a shot."

"Not the James Bond model."

Frank smiled. "Right. You were paying attention."

"Always. That's how I caught you with the *Mr.* Romero trick." Kensey sipped her French roast.

"Touché." He knew Kensey would smile and enjoyed it when it happened. "Here's the problem. Manny says when he busted in on the drug deal they were standing in the lobby and all of a sudden one of 'em is shooting. But the angles of the bullet entries are all wrong. Johnny Ludwikowski was shot in the head from above, like he was on the floor and the shooter was standing. Charlie Hawk was just the opposite, the bullet coming from below. No way was there a fifth person opening up fire and gunning everyone down."

"So if you know all that why do you need me?"

"I have a medical question. Remember I told you about the blood we found on the ladder in the church?"

Kensey nodded.

"AB positive." Frank watched Kensey pull her breath. "How common is that?"

"Not very."

"What, maybe two, three percent of people have that type?"

"Something like that."

"So what are you?"

Kensey placed her Styrofoam cup on the table. "Why don't you tell me, Detective."

"You donated blood last August."

"You know what, Detective, screw you. Every time you start out like a friend. *Let me buy you a Coke. How about a muffin? Let's grab some coffee.* Then you chat me up, let me in on a secret or two and try to scam me to see what I know."

"You're way off base."

"But even if I knew something —" now she got loud — "which I don't." Then quieter: "How're you gonna protect me mouthing off about a cop?"

Frank said, "Well…"

"Wait, I'll tell you. You're going to assign cops to protect me. But I don't know if I can trust them. Maybe they're dirty. And even if they're not, a month from now they'll be reassigned and I'm on my own."

"It's simple," Frank said in a soft voice. "I would protect you. As long as it takes."

"Who knows who the dirty cops are?"

"Unless they make a mistake, you can't tell." He sipped his coffee. "God, you're making it hard. I'm trying to do the right thing."

"You know how to tell a dirty cop on television?"

"On television?"

"It depends when you find out he's dirty. If you find out at the beginning of the show, he's some awful brute. But if it's not till the very end, he's a good-looking guy in a nice suit, the kind of cop who becomes your friend." Her eyes rolled down, checking out his suit and the tan button-down shirt.

Frank stood, abandoning his cup on the table. "If I wanted, I could've subpoenaed you two days ago, have your blood drawn and do a DNA analysis. Put you in the church the night Father Flaherty was killed." He started to walk away.

"No, you couldn't," Kensey said in a voice loud enough to turn heads. "There's something called *probable cause* and you don't have it. When I watch those cop shows I pay attention."

He didn't turn back to see the smile on Kensey's face.

15

Before she had a chance to ask how he was feeling, Manny said, "Tell me what happened to Father Flaherty."

Kensey closed the door. "I already did."

But his head was waving back and forth and he said, "No, every detail, don't skip nothing." Then he looked at her and said, "Hey, you're wearing regular clothes. You went home."

"You're supposed to tell me about Cuban sandwiches."

His fingers located his gold cross. "Please." He used the remote to silence the TV. The room was quiet except for the occasional bubbling of the Pleur-evac.

"You sure you don't want to keep that on? He's still out there."

"Not for this. Just talk quiet." He kissed the cross.

She draped her stethoscope around her neck and took a seat next to the bed, the same one Mike had been in.

Manny closed his eyes. In one hand he clutched his cross. His other white-knuckled the side rail as if his bed were about to be launched out the window. For the next several minutes she went through the story the long way: how the church looked, the plywood covering the stained glass, the blind nun lighting candles. How she cried on Father's dusty shoulder and what Father said before they went into the confessional.

She spared no memories. The stance Mike took. How he held the gun. "Three shots to Father's side, three to mine."

Manny was crying, tears disappearing into his unkempt beard like dust swept under a carpet. But he listened to every word. Once, when he winced in pain, Kensey stopped speaking until he begged her to go on.

The only time he smiled was when she described how she crawled through the hole in the confessional. He said that was next on the list to be fixed.

Finally, when she finished speaking and he'd heard about the ladder and the window in the basement, Manny opened his eyes and said, "Father didn't know about me. None of the stuff I told you. I always wanted to tell him. I just couldn't disappoint him."

"You could confess now. I could call a priest."

He shook his head and lifted his hospital gown. "I can't trust somebody I don't know. You better get started, Kensey, or you're gonna be late for your shift."

"Not until I hear about those sandwiches."

This made Manny smile. Pushing up on an elbow, he said, "First thing you do you get a loaf of Cuban bread. It's like French bread, only better. Then you put on ham and pork, some pickles and Swiss cheese, maybe some mustard."

"Sounds good."

"Wait," he was grinning at her. "You grill it on one of those cast-iron fry pans and put a heavy-duty bacon press on top to flatten it down." He licked his lips. "I gotta make you one someday."

Kensey examined him, said he sounded fine when she listened to his chest. Reaching into a side pocket, she retrieved a small metal clamp. "I'm going to clamp your chest tube."

"What?"

"I'll clamp it off for eight hours, get another chest X-ray and we'll see if any free air's accumulated."

While Kensey closed the clamp on the chest tubing, Manny said, "Don't hurry on my account."

"Maybe I'll stop by later." She moved toward the door.

"Come every day, okay?" he said as she neared the door. "Please."

She looked back at him. "Maybe I've got time for a pear."

■ ■ ■

The box was waiting for Kensey in the bullpen where she usually sat. It was a long, narrow one, glossy white and tied up with red ribbon with her name on a little pink card. Helen placed it on the desk without the slightest bit of fanfare and walked away. Everyone else snooped and there was quite a bit of speculation about who sent it. The nurses were waiting for Kensey to arrive so they could watch her open it and see the reaction on her face.

A unit clerk in her fifties announced that's why these sorts of boxes were delivered at work. For the *awwww* factor.

One of the nurses said she got a dozen roses from her boyfriend in a box just like that the day after he slept with her roommate. She picked it up and sniffed the side of the box but couldn't be sure if there were roses inside. Carl Daley happened by and saw the box and couldn't resist groaning how he wasn't going to get any work out of Kensey if she had goo-goo eyes during her shift.

Just then Kensey arrived with the smell of pear on her fingers. Carl went into a girlie voice and gushed that there was a package for her and hurry up, open it. Everyone laughed. By the time she stowed her backpack and walked into the bullpen he was gone, busying himself in one of the exam rooms and making small talk with a patient.

Someone told Kensey there was a card and to read it first. Kensey opened the card and when everyone went, "Who's it from? Who's it from?" she had to admit she had no idea. A phone number was written on the card that she didn't recognize. She made a production of sliding the bow off and pulling the top part away from the bottom.

No roses. Four cold packs around a little plastic box. One of the nurses said, "I bet it's a corsage." Kensey opened the box. There were no flowers inside. Just a tight roll of white rice wrapped around a sliver of raw yellowtail tuna. After a private smile and dispersion of the disappointed crowd, she popped it into her mouth and picked up the phone.

"Hey, you have a private patient, requested you by name," Helen said, breezing into the bullpen with a chart. "Pulled me aside, said to tell you it was William Bonney. Gave me a nice little wink." Then holding out the chart she said, "Room Two."

Kensey hung up the phone. "William Bonney?"

"You know him?"

"Maybe."

"He knows you."

"What's his chief complaint?" Kensey's eyes were on the chart.

"Something to do with a limp."

Kensey glanced about the ED. Just after ten am, and the colds and flus were wandering in. A woman on a stretcher rolled by, being pushed by an orderly in white scrubs. Nurses were moving in and out of the various rooms. A security guard in a dark blue uniform was speaking with two old women. It looked like he was giving directions because he was pointing and moving his hand back and forth and the two women were nodding. Kensey watched as the two women took off down the hall and the security guard leaned back against the wall, looking like he meant to stay put.

"You mind coming with me, Helen?"

Helen raised her eyebrows. "Whatever you want."

The two headed out of the bullpen, Kensey leading the way. The curtain was closed and in one brisk move, Kensey whisked it open. Mike Dombroski was sitting on the exam table, right leg down while the other was up on the table in a casual way. He was facing away from them reading a poster about the dangers of chewing tobacco, his leather jacket bulging behind his left shoulder.

Kensey wondered how deliberate his clothing was. It looked like the same outfit he had worn at the church, down to the tight jeans and fancy boots with pointy toes. "Mr. Bonney," she said. She and Helen hung back in the threshold.

He swung around. "Hey, Doc," he said in the friendliest way, then turned back to the poster. "Chewing— it's as bad as smoking it?"

"Yep," Kensey said. Under his jacket Mike was wearing a green cowboy shirt with snap-down flaps on the pockets. Parts of it were darker in color. At first she thought he must have spilled something on it. Then she realized he was sweating right through the fabric.

Mike glanced at the poster, then back toward Kensey. "You can't get lung cancer, tell me that."

"You can get cancer of the mouth. They dismantle your face when they cut it out so when you drink beer it'll leak out and ruin your jacket. What can I do for you?" Helen followed Kensey a step into the room.

"I got an infection or something with my leg." He pointed to his right thigh. "Been squeezing it but nothing comes out. Hurts like a sonofabitch."

Kensey quickly scanned the denim. "Tell me a little about what happened." No hole. He must have more than one pair.

Pivoting slightly so that he was looking at Helen he asked, "What's your name?"

"Helen."

"Tell you what, Helen, I'm real comfortable with the doc here. She patched up a friend of mine the other day, did a real nice job. But I probably gotta drop trou before this is over and I'd rather not show my BVDs to everybody. You don't mind pulling the curtain closed. The doc'll call you we need something."

"Oh, okay," Helen said, her voice rising, glancing Kensey's way before stepping back into the hallway. She pulled the curtain closed while saying, "Holler if you need me."

Mike smiled, showed some teeth, and waved. "We sure will, Helen, thanks." He waited several seconds before saying, "That's better. So how're you doing, Doc?" He smiled in a friendly way as if they were acquaintances who hadn't seen each other in a while.

"Billy the Kid? Is that who you think you are?"

"How the hell do you know that?"

"We watched two things on TV when I was a kid. The BoSox and westerns. You didn't really sign in as Bonney, did you?"

"Nah — I figured if I don't have an insurance card they might want to see an ID. I shoulda had a fake one. Hey, I'll bet you a six-pack the last thing you did before opening the curtain is make sure the security guard ain't on coffee break."

"Bonney was shot to death when he was twenty."

"Yeah," Mike said and sounded sad. "I've been to his grave."

"I hate westerns. So tell me about your leg."

"Get right into it, huh? Okay, I had an accident three days ago, got a nail stuck in my right leg."

"How did that happen?"

"Maybe it's infected or something. It's making me sweat."

Kensey placed the chart next to the sink and snapped on a pair of gloves. "I guess you better drop trou."

Mike hopped off the table and undid his big belt buckle that looked like it belonged in a rodeo. He pushed his jeans below his knees, then tried to catch Kensey's eye. The underwear was no accident. Tight red briefs that looked like a fancy jockstrap. Mike checked out his bulge and winked in Kensey's direction.

From six feet away she was inspecting his thigh. There were two red marks crusted with blood, and the skin was pink around them, extending out about an inch. "Sit on the table, please."

Mike eased his ass back on the table with his legs over the side. "Security guards don't carry."

Kensey rolled a metal stool over and sat down in front of him. Eyeing the puncture wound and the jagged cut, she said, "How did you get this again?"

He gave her a look, letting her know that he would play the game if that's what she wanted. "I was doing some work in the basement. I've got one of them old houses and I slipped on a banana peel and fell on this two-by-four with a couple of nails sticking out."

"I see," Kensey said.

"Good thing the asshole who left the board was long gone or who knows what might've happened."

"Does this hurt?" Kensey asked as her gloved fingers ran the margins of the wounds.

"Ahhh, shit, shit, shit." Mike said as his thigh went into spasm so that his leg kicked out and caught Kensey in the shin with the point of his boot.

She reached down to rub her leg.

Mike's thigh was rigid, the skin taut. His quadriceps bulged as if he were attempting leg lifts beyond his capability. Each time he sucked in a gulp of air he made a noise that sounded like a wheeze. "Goddamn, will you do something?"

Kensey had never seen such a dramatic response, an order of magnitude beyond the deep tendon reflex in the leg when it was tapped with a rubber hammer. Over the next sixty seconds the muscles slowly relaxed.

Mike was out of breath, his chest heaving to show off his ribs as he sucked air. "It's been doing that since yesterday," he said between breaths. "I never felt anything like it." He tugged at his shirt to separate it from his skin.

Sliding several feet to her left, Kensey poised her hand above Mike's thigh, her index finger sticking out and curled down. When it was obvious she was going to tap him with it, Mike's hand shot out and guarded his thigh. "Whoa, what the hell you think you're doing?"

"How many times has this happened?"

"So it means something?"

"Maybe. Let me try it again."

"Do it again and I'll fuckin' break your neck." He glanced at the curtain. "I don't care who's out there. It hurts worse'n getting kicked in the nuts." He leaned down and hissed, "And it's all your goddamn fault."

"That you slipped on a banana and fell on a two-by-four?"

"Don't get smart with me."

"You had any fever?"

"I can't stop sweating. I got a headache out to here and my heart feels like it's gonna jump out of my chest."

Kensey placed her hand on his wrist and felt for his pulse. "You ever have trouble with your heart before?"

"No, why?"

"It's racing." She looked at Mike. "Lie down." Kensey waited for Mike but he didn't budge. "If you want my help, lie down."

"I wanna know about this agreement you got. What'd he call it? Day something."

"Détente."

"How the hell you spell *détente*?"

Kensey pushed back on her stool. "If you've got something to say, say it. Otherwise lie down on your back."

Mike collected his thoughts all the while glaring at Kensey. "My buddy's got lots to say about you."

"Who, Manny?"

"Not Manny." He sounded pissed, as if she knew damn well who he was talking about but was jerking him around.

Kensey folded her gloved hands in her lap, crossed her legs, and fought the urge to speak. He looked so different without the mustache. He wasn't her type of guy, but she knew he was a guy who could pick out a woman at a bar and take her home to bed.

He glanced over at the curtain before continuing. "So you got a list or something. I wanna know more about it."

"Listen to me, go talk to Manny if you want information."

"You diss me one more time and I might forget about the fuckin' day-tant. I want to know where the list is and I wanna know now."

"In the safest hands. Anything happens to me it goes to the *Post-Gazette*, all the news stations. Trust me, you'll fry in the electric chair. Let me tell you why. Your blood is all over that nail. It puts you at the crime scene. That's the first thing on the list." She shot a little Mona Lisa smile at Mike.

"What's that for?"

"I cut my hand on the same nail before you did. You got some of me circulating in you. Now lie down."

"How do I know the person holding it ain't gonna do something stupid?"

"Like release it by mistake?"

"Something like that."

"Part of détente is trust. I trust you to keep your weapon in your pants and you trust me, blood brother."

Mike swung his legs onto the table and lied down. "Did Manny tell you the name of our boss?"

Kensey gave him a hard stare. "Captain Adkins? I figured out who he was before you shot at me in the men's room."

Mike's upper lip curled. "You know what the fuck I mean. Not the captain."

Kensey cocked her head to the side. "You don't trust Manny, do you?"

"I didn't say that."

"Sure you did. You said, 'Did Manny tell you the name of our boss?'"

"So?"

Kensey raised her eyebrows. "You visited him, didn't you?" Mike nodded. "Was it the first thing you asked him?"

"You got a point?"

"He wouldn't tell you 'no' even if it was true."

"And why's that?"

"That list is keeping both of you alive as much as it is me. So Manny must've said 'yes' and you're dumb enough to think he's lying."

"What the fuck, the two of you. You don't know what you're talking about."

"I know you're in the doghouse."

Mike sat up. "Trust me, the man ain't happy."

Kensey went back to the night in the ED when everything started. "That night Manny got shot, you bumped into me when I walked out of the waiting room. You were eavesdropping, weren't you?"

"Good thing I was."

"Was your boss in the ED that night?"

"So you have no idea, do you?" He grinned and wanted her to feel as if he had the upper hand.

"Maybe it's Manny who shouldn't be trusting *you*."

"I ain't the one flapping my tongue to some pretty doctor."

"The only way your boss knows is if you told him."

"Last time. Did Manny tell you the man's name?"

"And be grateful that he did."

Mike said, "Now gimme some medicine."

"I need to examine you."

Mike lied down on his back, folding his hands under his neck and shutting his eyes. He looked like someone waiting for a massage. Kensey stood and listened to his heart and lungs, then pressed around on his abdomen, finally sliding her hands under the waistband of the red underwear to feel for enlarged lymph nodes in his groin.

Mike said, "While you're there I'll take a happy ending."

Kensey smiled, a fake one with too many teeth. "That's funny, I'll have to tell the rest of the staff." While the smile lingered on her lips she smacked the exam table with her open hand.

Mike startled. His head came off the table and he used his arms to push partway up. But Kensey was focused on Mike's legs. If it weren't for his blue jeans tethering his ankles together the right leg would have kicked her in the face.

"*Fuuuuuck*," Mike said, his face twisted into an agonizing scowl. His fingers clutched at the sides of the exam table, his knuckles blanched white.

"Okay, pull your pants up." Snapping her gloves off, she stood by the sink and studied him.

For more than a minute he refused to budge. It was as if the spasm in his leg was torturing him to the point of helplessness. Gradually his muscles relaxed. His respirations eased. Sweat continued to drip from his face, soaking his hair and matting it to his scalp. When he finally was able to turn his head in Kensey's direction there was fury in his eyes. He worked himself into a sitting position and slid off the table. With effort he hoisted his pants and fumbled with the buckle. "You shouldn't have done that."

"Sit down," Kensey said. "I'm concerned about your leg."

"So gimme something for it."

"You see the way your leg goes into spasm? I'm not sure why it's doing that."

He drummed his fingers on the table. "Hey, Doc, let's not get all worked up about this. Gimme a pill, I ain't too crazy about shots."

"I can't treat you when I'm not sure what you have. We need to get an X-ray, maybe have a surgeon debride the wound."

"No X-ray. No other docs. Gimme whatever I need and I'm outta here. No stalling."

"Wait here, there's something I need to look up." Kensey opened and closed the curtain as she left.

Mike quickly shuffled over to the flimsy curtain and tried to track her. She was hustling into the bullpen and he lost sight of her. The seconds ticked by. People in different colored scrubs walked back and forth. A man on crutches hobbled by. Two nursing students in tight little uniforms stopped right in front of Mike and paused. One whispered something in the other's ear and they giggled. He was getting nervous. This was taking too long. He imagined her dialing 911. Reaching up under his jacket, Mike slipped out a pistol, another Beretta, another throwaway, this one a 38 caliber Cheetah. At the same time he found a silencer in a side pocket and screwed it onto the short barrel of the gun. A fake cough camouflaged the sound of the first bullet being racked into the chamber.

When Kensey opened the curtain, Mike had tucked the gun inside his jacket. She was carrying a thick text that was opened and she was studying the page.

"This's a book on infectious diseases. Right here it talks about the different types of—" she said without looking up.

Mike was fixing the curtain so no one could peek in through the side. He limped toward Kensey and interrupted her. He whispered, "Put the goddamn book down." There was acid in his voice.

Kensey lifted her eyes from the thick text. Mike slipped the weapon from under his jacket and quickly pressed it to her skin above the V-neck of her scrubs. Instinctively she backed up. Mike followed her step for step, grinding it in hard enough to make it hurt.

"Where's my other gun?" he whispered. "It cost me three fuckin' grand to get this one rigged for a silencer."

Kensey was mouth breathing, making a noise each time the air moved into her lungs.

"If you drop the book and make a noise I'll kill you. Do you understand? No one'll hear the shot. Time Helen finds you, I'm in my car."

Kensey held her head rigidly as if she was wearing a collar for a sprained neck. "Okay, what do you want?"

"It took you an awful long time to find that book. You make any phone calls?"

Kensey shook her head. "I was looking something up."

He eased up on the gun, taking it away from her skin. "See what you made me do? Now you got a hickey. I don't want to put any more marks on you so don't move. If a uniform opens that curtain both of yunz are dead. Now we're gonna go over to the counter and you're gonna gimme a script. Then I'm gonna walk out of here and you're not gonna say a thing."

"Listen to me. I think you're really sick. You need to be admitted to the hospital. Get a second opinion if you don't believe me. You're going to die."

"Funny." Mike ground the silencer into her chest until she pleaded with him to stop. "In one minute I walk outta here. You decide if you want to be bleeding."

Silently Kensey moved to the counter next to the sink and scribbled out a prescription.

Mike read the script. "Penicillin, huh?" Slipping the gun into the small of his back, he nodded in the direction of his chart. "Don't write nothing in there 'bout what happened. I mean it. And I don't care what anyone tells you, you open your mouth one time there aren't enough cops in this city to keep you alive." Then he touched his index finger to his forehead and moved it several inches toward Kensey in a little salute. "Think long and hard before you touch that curtain." Then he was gone.

One Mississippi. Two Mississippi. Three Mississippi. Four Mississippi.

16

"I know what happened. He called me. But I coulda figured it out the way you look."

It was four hours after Mike had bolted from the Emergency Department with his prescription. Two hours after Carl said something to Kensey about the ED being backed up like a toilet so put it into high gear so some of us have time to get lunch.

Now Manny was propped up in bed, drinking a can of Coke and working on a ham and cheese on soft white bread. His color was better — the nurses called it pasty — and he no longer winced when he rolled toward the little bedside table to deposit the can. Whenever Kensey came into the room he smiled. Except this time. He gave her a soft look that went along with what he said. "He pull that Billy the Kid crap with you?"

"Not the first time?"

"Used to do it in bars all the time. Thought it was cool."

Not counting Manny, no one knew about Mike's visit to the ED. Her note in the chart was just what Mike ordered: *The patient is a 43-year-old male who suffered a small laceration to his right thigh several days ago and now has a mild cellulitis. He is afebrile. There are no enlarged lymph nodes in the groin and the rest of his exam is essentially normal. Treatment: penicillin three times a day for ten days. Patient to return to ED if complications arise.* After finishing her note, Kensey spent forty-five minutes in the medical library doing research. Carl made the comment about being backed up like a toilet when she slipped back into the bullpen carrying an inch-thick folder of photocopies in her backpack. Now she knew what was going to happen to Mike. His spasms were going to spread and torture other parts of his body. He would likely develop *risus sardonicus*, the sarcastic smile. Minor stimuli would whip the facial muscles into a teeth-baring, shit-eating grin. Surely he would survive that, but there were worse things waiting for him.

"Do your friend a favor," Kensey said. "Get him back to the hospital. Otherwise he's going—"

"That's what he said you'd say, get him back to the hospital. Then he said you meant to shoot him up with all sorts a stuff, maybe truth serum or some shit like that."

"He's gonna die if he doesn't get treatment."

"He told the man the whole story, everything I said, trying to get himself off the shit list. For all I know his next assignment's me."

"He scared the crap out of me, you know that?"

"That reminds me," Manny whispered. "'Member that thing we were talking about yesterday?"

"What thing?"

He pouted and his cheeks flushed crimson. "I gotta drop a deuce and I can't."

"If you don't get out of bed all the fruit in that basket won't make you go."

"Give me a physic."

"A what?" She giggled.

"What my grandma used to call it. You know, a enema."

"You don't need an enema. Get out of bed and take a seat on the throne."

"With this thing hanging outta me? If nothing happens you order a physic."

"Can I ask you a question?"

When he didn't answer right away, Kensey knew he was running a list in his mind of things he didn't want to talk about. He looked at her out of the corner of his eye. "Should I turn up the TV?"

"I want to know what happens when you leave the hospital."

"Nothing. Just don't get rid of that little list you wrote." He paused for a moment and whispered, "It don't matter I believe you got one or not. Mike believes you got one. So does Sonny." Back to his regular voice: "They won't touch you, you don't go to the cops."

"I didn't mean me, Manny. I meant you."

Manny exhaled loudly. "That's all I been thinking about and it looks like rain. I made sure Sonny knows I named names so you're okay."

"You didn't have to tell me that."

"I'm a nice guy."

"You are."

"Good. Then I got a favor I been wanting to talk to you about."

Kensey shook her head. "No, please."

"Just listen. I know you already done me a big one." He put his index finger over his lips. "If Mike don't get me, Sonny's got guys just waiting in line. The second I'm better I gotta get outta town fast."

"What if I discharge you in the middle of the night?"

"They're gonna be watching my house. The second I show up." Manny held up his hand like it was a gun and moved his thumb forward and whispered, "Pow." He had Kensey's attention. Her eyes were wide, her mouth hung open like a Girl Scout hearing a ghost story. "So here's the deal. Suppose you went to my house and picked up my truck, parked it in the lot here so I can get in and go."

Kensey sat down in the straight-back chair. "You said they're watching it."

"Not yet. I'm still hooked up to this." He tapped the clear plastic tube running from his chest to the Pleur-evac. "Soon as it comes out, Sonny's got a guy there. Trust me."

Kensey curled her fingers around her ear, tucking her hair away. "Isn't there anyone else?"

"I got no one, 'cepting you." His voice sounded thick like he might cry. After Kensey blinked a few times he said, "It's over on the Northside. Two blocks from the church. I got the keys right here. Just think about it." He leaned over and opened the drawer on the bedside table. After jiggling a ring of keys he dropped them back into the drawer. "It's a Ford pickup, parked right in the driveway. Just get in and drive. We gotta move quick, before I get better."

"Where're you going to go?"

Manny smiled. "Two times you're a Good Samaritan."

"I didn't say I'm gonna do it."

"You wouldn't say, 'Where're you gonna go?' you weren't gonna do it. The answer is south. I'm going south, drive all night if I have to. Maybe get a job, put away some money. Somehow get back to Cuba. Start making sandwiches."

Kensey took a deep breath, ballooned her cheeks, and blew out slowly. "What if I did say no?"

"I don't make it outta my driveway. I been thinking 'bout it. I swear there's no way this can backfire."

Kensey checked her watch. "I'm late."

"One more thing. You told me you weren't there for the Seymour Rosen thing. I believe you. That's what I told Mike, she don't know nothing 'bout it. I know you, Kensey, the kind of person you are. You're feeling like maybe you shoulda done something and Seymour Rosen wouldn't have disappeared."

"So?"

"The thing with Alec Fortune, it's off. Mike called me, told me we gotta give back the money."

"You sure?"

"Yeah, I'm sure."

"Why stop now?"

"Look, you'n me got a balance and I'm not getting pissed or nothing but don't push it. Ain't no one touching him. That's all you need to know."

"But what if something happens to him?"

"I ain't lied to you yet and I won't start now."

Kensey nodded. "You should be going down for your X-ray soon." She walked quickly toward the door and pulled it open.

"What about tonight?"

"I'm busy."

"Tomorrow's good," he called, but she was already in the hallway.

17

"Now that says a lot about you," Kensey was saying as she pulled her front door closed and started down the three concrete steps. She was eyeing a midnight blue, frog-eyed Porsche 911 with a shadow of road dust around the tire wells.

Following Kensey down the walk, Alec straightened his light-colored topcoat— not that it was bunched up, but it gave him something to do while he chewed on what she meant. "I should've driven the truck," he said. He was wearing a tailored suit with a green shirt opened at the neck. No jewelry except for a watch with a leather strap. "I was trying to impress you."

"Was it a graduation gift?"

"How'd you know that?"

"What is it, a ninety-one?"

"Ninety."

Kensey turned briefly and grinned. "I guessed you're about ... thirty-five. So where'd you go to school?" She was at the car, bending over to check out the side panel on the passenger door.

"In Boston." Alec took in what she was wearing. A three-button jacket, tight around her breast, a short black skirt and low heels with thin straps that went around her ankles.

"Harvard, right? You should be more careful where you park."

"Why'd you say that?" Alec used the remote to open the doors and walked around to the driver's side.

"You've got a number of major dings in the door."

"No, about Harvard."

Kensey slipped into the seat effortlessly, a good eight inches lower than her Honda. "If you were B.U. you would've said, I went to B.U." She gave him a nice smile.

Silently, still digesting what Kensey said, Alec lowered himself into the driver's seat. He turned the key and the engine purred.

"So with the grit around the wheels you don't check the weather report before you take it out. And I bet you never park diagonally in two spaces."

The car eased away from the curb. He asked, "Is that a good thing?"

"I always hated that," she said.

Kensey admired his driving, the way he accelerated through turns and negotiated the narrow streets of Highland Park. Alec eased his foot down and the car responded instantly with a burst of acceleration. She felt herself press into the leather as they shot onto the Parkway and headed toward the city. In less than twenty minutes he pulled into the underground garage beneath Mellon Center, the second tallest building in Pittsburgh. He wound round and round down to the third level.

Wherever Kensey looked there was concrete, the fluorescent lighting showing how grimy everything was. They passed one massive gray column after another. The spaces next to the columns were tight and tricky to negotiate but worth the effort because one side of the car was protected. Alec found a narrow space in a corner with a sparkling new Lexus for a next-door neighbor. They rode the elevator up to the first floor.

Like most interns, dinner out for Kensey was usually a burger or salad at a bar. The Carlton was designed to impress. Colorful caricatures of athletes and politicos papered the walls in the wood-paneled bar. Waitstaff in black pants and stiff white shirts greeted Alec and Kensey with deferential nods. A quiet table in a cozy cubby was set with white linen, heavy flatware, and delicate wineglasses. Before they opened their napkins, a basket of fresh sourdough bread arrived.

Drinks were ordered: Alec a vodka martini, one olive, Kensey a glass of white wine. They made small talk waiting for the drinks. Finally, after the waiter had served the drinks and left them alone, Alec held his aloft and waited for Kensey to do the same. "There's a lot I want to say. One night is too short to say it all. Your courage or your beauty or your charm would have been reason enough to want to spend the evening with you. I'm very lucky. Cheers."

Kensey took a sip, then another. The waiter placed a large menu in front of her and she skimmed it quickly. "You got me here on a false pretense."

"Don't worry, this is just dinner. You'll be home before ten."

"There's no sushi on the menu," she said, then cocked her head to one side and raised an eyebrow.

"Touché," Alec said and nodded.

Before Kensey could smile at Alec, the waiter returned, this time placing a small plate of sushi in the middle of the table with two pairs of chopsticks. "Compliments of the chef," he said and went right back to the kitchen.

Kensey sensed he was resisting a smile. "So the whole thing was a setup," she said, using chopsticks to pick up a tightly packed barrel of rice topped with raw fish. "Sending me the yellowtail, the Porsche with the dirt around the wheels and the dings in the door, letting me stick my foot in my mouth."

"Ten bucks of sushi, an old Porsche. Whatever I've got to do."

Kensey snatched a second piece of sushi and gazed around the elegant restaurant. "This is nice. Thank you."

They talked some more, laughed at each other's stories, and ordered another round of drinks. Salads arrived. More talk, then dinner, prime rib for him with a dollop of horseradish, the mahi-mahi for her. Waiting for the crème brûlée to be torched in the kitchen, he said, "I read in the paper that cop's getting better."

"Thank you. I didn't know how to bring this up." Kensey worked her finger around the rim of her water glass. "He said something about you today."

Alec wiped his mouth with his napkin. "Am I going to need a Tums?"

"No, nothing bad." She held up her hand and waved him off. "He was told they called off doing anything to you."

"Why would they do that?"

"He won't tell me."

"This guy, Romero, had such a big mouth in the Emergency Department, now he shuts up?"

"Alec, ever hear the expression *scared shitless*? I can't get him to sit on the toilet because he's afraid if he does it means he's getting better and is going to be discharged and Sonny'll get him. Tomorrow he's going to need an enema."

Alec stroked his chin. "Does he have any idea we're having dinner?"

"Absolutely not." Her smile faded, her face serious. "I gave him my word I wouldn't contact you."

"And part of you feels guilty about breaking a promise to him."

"How'd you know?"

"Five minutes with you and I know."

Kensey took a long drink of water. "It makes no sense."

"Let's go to the police. Please."

"No. No police. We have this balance. He calls it *détente*. He promised me I'm safe as long as I don't go to them and I believe him."

"Don't you know he'll say anything he thinks you want to hear?"

Kensey stared into Alec's eyes. "Part of him is evil. I know that. But getting shot changed him for the better."

"I can insulate myself, Kensey. I can hire a dozen bodyguards. How long are you willing to look over your shoulder?"

Kensey leaned forward and whispered, "I'm trapped."

"And there's no way you can ask him who Sonny is?"

"I tried once."

"Say something like, 'Who *is* this guy, a cop?'"

"I don't think he's a cop." Kensey turned to see the waiter place a little custard cup in front of each of them. She waited for him to get out of earshot. "The balance is fragile. As much as I trust Manny ..."

Alec squinted at her.

"Him," she said quickly. "I meant to say *him*. As much as I trust *him*, he also scares me. All he has to do is mention to

Mike I'm asking too many questions and ... I don't want to even think about it."

"If we knew who Sonny was, we could devise a plan." Alec used his spoon to punch a hole through the caramelized sugar shell guarding the creamy custard. "Just think about it."

Ten minutes later Alec was tipping the girl in coat check and they were heading toward the elevator. Their shoulders brushed as they rounded the corner and when he caught her eye said, "If you think that was an accident..."

Kensey giggled and slipped her arm around his as they rode the elevator down to the garage. Alec's cell phone went off. He looked at the caller ID on the phone, then at his watch and said, "Sorry, it's my dad," then made a face to let Kensey know he really was sorry. He opened the phone. "Dad? Hello?" Snapping the phone shut, he said, "No reception." The elevator opened and he looked at his key ring with the black key bearing the Porsche logo. "Ride back up with me while I call back?"

"No, thank you," Kensey said. She put her hand out. "You trust me?"

"With my Porsche?" His voice went up like he was shocked.

"My boyfriend in college had one."

Alec put his hand on the elevator door to stop it from closing. "What, a nine- fourteen?"

"It's a Porsche."

"It's a toy."

"Go back up and take your call. Give me the key and I'll be waiting right here for you. You do trust me, don't you, risking my life for you and everything." His eyes left hers and dropped to her feet and the low heels with the straps. Picking up on this, Kensey raised her foot and turned it over so Alec could examine the length of her heel. "I won't get it caught on the clutch."

"Let it out slowly. It'll jump on you."

"I'll keep it under fifty in the garage."

"Funny." Alec was right next to Kensey but flipped the key in the air so she had to catch it.

"Maybe if it's not all scratched up you'll let me run it out of here." Stepping off the elevator she got a far-off look on her face and said, "Is the clutch on the left or the right?" Alec started to say something and reach for the door but Kensey had timed it perfectly. The door closed and he was headed back up toward ground level.

The first thing she did was pull out a compact and lipstick to do a quick touch-up. The little smile she performed to check her lips lasted long after she snapped the compact closed, fluffed her hair, and headed in the direction of the car.

Curling off the ramp from the upper levels was a heavy Cadillac, white with a gold-colored grill, easing toward her, headlights on, stopping every twenty feet to check out potential spaces that didn't seem to pass muster because the car kept creeping along. Kensey waited under a fluorescent light that flickered on and off and buzzed as if bees were trapped inside. The Caddy rolled by ever so slowly. Kensey could see the driver was a tiny gentleman with thick-framed black glasses big enough for snorkeling. Next to him was a bony woman with stiff blond hair and too much red lipstick.

The Cadillac crept toward the corner of the garage where the Porsche was parked. Kensey was hoping the Lexus was still guarding the passenger side when the Cadillac's turn signal started blinking. The car rolled to a complete stop before turning into the space where the Lexus had been. Kensey froze, watching the huge car lumber in a herky-jerky way as the driver kept trying to make last-minute adjustments.

Suddenly Kensey was walking quickly toward the Porsche, worrying that backing the car out might be more difficult than she anticipated.

The older gentleman sported a yellow hanky in the breast pocket of his blue blazer. He climbed out and admired the Porsche from several angles, leaving his lady friend in the Cadillac so he could study the German engineering. Then he circled around the rear of his car in shiny loafers and opened the passenger door. He looked quite noble helping her out, holding her hand in his while she stood up, then waited for her to hang her little purse from her shoulder before they started moving away from the car. Slowly they strolled toward Kensey, greeting her as she hurried by, anxious to see the bad news. Up close it was worse than she expected. The Cadillac was parked at a clumsy angle. With the concrete column guarding the other side of the Porsche, this was going to require some finesse. She looked back toward the elevator, the couple more than halfway there, then at the car. That's when a man stepped from behind the column and swiftly moved toward her. He was shorter than Kensey but thick, like he could swing a pickax half a day without breaking a sweat. He was wearing black work pants and a gray sweatshirt with a hood that was scrunched up behind his neck.

Her muscles froze, every one of them. She was unable to do anything but stare at this man as he approached, her breathing rapid, eyes dilated like black marbles. The only part of her that seemed to be functioning was her brain. She knew the older couple was probably still sauntering toward the elevator. But she couldn't make her mouth open, and the man was close enough to touch her when he raised his hand to show an old revolver with filthy adhesive tape wrapped thickly around the grip.

"Say a word and the hell with not messing you up." His voice was a hoarse whisper, coming out of a mouth full of brown teeth. He was near enough for Kensey to see his stubbly beard and the grease in his hair. Waving his weapon, he grabbed a thick handful of her jacket and tugged hard enough to snap her head back. She lost her balance and stumbled like she was going to fall, but his grip was strong. For a moment she dangled from his arm like a marionette. "Let's go," he whispered and yanked Kensey away from the Porsche, spun her around, and aimed her toward the back wall. Looping his arm around her neck, he pulled her close enough to let her feel the scratch of his beard on her cheek.

Shuffling sideways, tangoing between the bumpers and the concrete column, they made their way to a little corner the fluorescent lights ignored. Tucked away in the shadows, the man shoved Kensey against the wall and watched her tremble. He was standing in front of her, the tip of his gun pressing on the thick fabric between her breasts. Her hair was wild and his stink was in her nose.

"No cameras back here," he said.

"What do you want?"

"No one has to get hurt, you *capisce*?"

His eyes drifted down where she'd left the top button of her jacket open so a little wedge of flesh was exposed. Using the short barrel of his gun to ease the lapels of the jacket apart he squinted at a purple bruise. "What the hell's that?" he said and shook his head. "It ain't from me. You hear?" Now he turned his attention to her face. "Turn your head back and forth." Kensey looked one way, then the other. "You got any others?"

"Any other what?"

His neck twitched a couple of times but Kensey was too frightened to notice.

"Marks, goddamnit. What do you think?"

"On my hand." She brought her right hand into the man's view.

"Slowly," he said. "Don't do nothing fast," as she showed off where the nail had penetrated her palm. "Jesus, this ain't your week. That it?"

"Yeah."

"Put your hand down." He waited for her hand to drop out of view. "Now you remember, I didn't do neither of those."

"Okay." Her tongue shot out to lick her lips.

"Say it. Say I didn't do neither of those."

"You didn't do these."

"Good girl. We're gonna get along just fine."

Now Kensey realized he was moving his neck like there was a crick in it.

"What're you doing in a nice place like this?" He looked back at the elevator.

"I — I had dinner. That's all."

"Yeah, with who?"

"A friend. Just a friend."

"You're eating something hot, I'm out here with these fuckin' candy bars."

"Look, let me go. I swear I won't go to the police."

"You had steak, didn't you?"

"No, mahi-mahi."

He scrunched up his face. "What the hell's that?"

"Fish."

"Fish. Shit, they got steaks in there an inch thick and you got fish." He looked around. They were still alone. Leaning in close, he whispered, "You been a bad girl, broke the deal."

"All I did was tell him it's over and we had dinner. I swear."

"What's over?"

"That someone's gonna kill him."

"What the fuck. Keep it down." He turned his head — no sign of anyone behind them — then back toward Kensey. "I got six slugs in here, enough for anyone who gets curious. Now I gotta clean up the mess those dumb fuckin' cops made." His eyes wandered down to her chest. "Tell me about the one in the hospital."

Way off in the distance Kensey thought she could make out Alec standing in front of the elevators looking back and forth as if he was wondering where the hell she was with his Porsche.

The man's eyes were on her face again. "Hey, you deaf or something? What about the guy in the hospital?"

Now Alec was walking in their direction, checking his watch, head craning around this way and that, looking for her.

"All he asked was to go to confession for him. That's all." She spoke slowly and softly. "He told me not to go to the cops, and I didn't."

"Dumb fuckin' spic, telling you his shit. You got any idea how much they paid that motherfucker?"

Alec was behind his Porsche, slowly moving his head back and forth like a radar station.

"No."

"Like fifty K each time he pulled the trigger. Fifty ... fuckin' ... K. I know the last guy they're s'posed to hit's still walking around. And I don't give a fuck what he told you. Alls I want to know is how's he doing? Is he getting better?"

Kensey saw Alec stare directly at her, then he ducked down and disappeared.

"He was shot in the chest. You know that—"

"Too bad it missed his heart."

"It nicked it but collapsed his lung. He has a tube in his chest."

"So when's he getting out? Gimme a day, c'mon, c'mon." He rubbed the end of the barrel on the exposed flesh of her skin.

"You know Manny told me all about you."

"Fuck that. He don't know about me."

"He said if they ever screwed up there was another guy they'd send. Described what you look like. Said he was scared of you."

"Oh yeah?" He smiled, showing off those brown teeth. "He's still a dumb spic."

That's when Alec slipped out of the shadows and placed the barrel of his Glock against the man's head. In a quiet voice he said, "If you so much as move I'll shoot you through your head."

"It ain't even loaded. I swear. Put it against my head and squeeze one off. Jus' don't do nothing stupid, you know?" He lowered the revolver to his side. The man started to rotate his head.

Alec clamped his hand on the man's neck. "Keep your eyes straight ahead."

Feeling the gun leave her chest, Kensey moved sideways so the man was now staring at the wall.

"Didn't hurt her. She got a hickey on her chest and something on her hand. Ain't from me. Go ahead, ask her."

"He hurt you?"

"No, I'm fine." She touched her chest where the man's gun had been.

The man said, "You want me to drop the gun, mister? Just gimme the word."

"Just stand still." Alec reached down and twisted the weapon from the man's hand. "What's your name?"

"Berto."

"What the hell do you want?"

"Information. That's all. Wasn't doing nothing to nobody."

"Who sent you?"

"Call the cops you want. I got nothing else for you."

Alec kept the gun flush to Berto's head for half a minute. "Okay, Berto, let's make this simple. I count to five, either you start talking or I'll kill you. One." He pressed the gun harder, grinding it into his scalp. "Two ... three ..."

Tilting his head away from Alec's gun, he said, "Okay, okay. Guy by the name of Mike. Said if I hurt the broad he'd stick a gun up my ass and pull the trigger."

Alec let up on the gun so Berto could straighten his neck. "Is that Sonny?"

"Huh?" Berto started to rotate his head, so Alec reached around with his left hand and grabbed his chin to fix it in place.

"I said, don't fuckin' move."

Berto settled down. His breaths were coming louder now. "Mike, he's — he's a soldier. Sonny's the man."

"Last question." Alec eased his grip on Berto's neck, keeping the gun pinned to the back of his neck. "Who is Sonny?"

Kensey spotted it happening before Alec, Berto's hand sneaking inside his pants pocket. As he slowly worked it out she said, "Alec! He's got another gun."

Berto whipped out a stubby Smith and Wesson, small enough to hide in the palm of his hand, the kind women keep in their purse for protection. He drove an elbow backwards and caught Alec in the gut. *Bam!* There was the piercing report of gunfire that echoed off the concrete. Berto went down hard on his right side, his arm hidden somewhere under his torso. Kensey could see a growing puddle of blood under his shoulder.

Now Alec was poised above him, aiming the Glock with two hands, Berto's eyes looking somewhere in the direction of Alec's shoes.

"Where's his gun?" Alec said.

"Don't know. Alec! He's still breathing." Kensey voice was a loud whisper. "Oh God, he's gonna make it." She looked at Alec. "He'll come back. I just know it."

Alec saw that Kensey was crying. He said, "Let's give it a few seconds."

With a noisy grunt Berto rolled onto his back so his right arm was free. In the palm of his hand was his little black pistol.

Kensey said, "Alec," sharply, imploring him to do something right away.

Berto made a clumsy effort to aim his weapon but he couldn't keep the barrel from waving around. He looked up at Alec and opened his mouth to say something. He pulled the trigger and the gun went off with a little pop like a firecracker, the bullet missing Alec and Kensey.

Before the sound left their ears Alec squeezed off another round — *Bam!* — and caught Berto in the chest. Berto's arms went limp and he stopped moving.

Kensey knelt down.

"Don't touch him," Alec said and helped Kensey to her feet.

"Oh my God," she said.

Stowing the Glock under his jacket, he said, "You saw his gun. I didn't have a choice."

"I know," Kensey said and reached out for Alec's hand and looked down at Berto for the last time.

Their ears were still ringing but the garage was very quiet. Alec wrapped his arms around her and held her for more than a minute.

The last words spoken in that garage were Kensey's. "Get me out of here. Please."

18

When Alec emerged from the bedroom it was dark outside. He was wearing white drawstring pajama bottoms and finger-combing his thick hair. The house was middle-of-the-night quiet, the only light coming from the glowing numbers on the oven timer in the kitchen and the stack of stereo equipment in the great room.

That's where Kensey was sitting, alone, in a deep leather sofa shaped like an *L*, when Alec walked in. She looked quite petite in one of his crimson T-shirts with the word *Harvard* in white letters, her legs tucked beneath her, her hair looking better than his.

"So you couldn't sleep either," she said, then scooted over an inch or two so he would know to sit down next to her.

He squinted in her direction. "You want any lights?"

"Un-uh. I don't want the day to start."

"If I knew you were out here…" he said as he sank into the soft leather. "I mean, I was just lying in there looking at the ceiling. God, what a night. What time is it anyway?"

"Almost five."

"You sleep?"

She shook her head. "Tell me how I'm supposed to feel." Alec could see her wipe her eyes with the tips of her fingers.

"I'm a good Christian. I chose medicine for all the right reasons. But I don't feel anything about what happened. Like it was a movie I watched."

"If you kill a stray dog that's rabid you don't feel anything."

They were sitting next to each other, close enough to touch, talking back and forth, but looking straight ahead, not seeing the expression on each other's face. For a few moments they sat silently, not long enough to make it feel uncomfortable, each staring at a wall of squares and rectangles in a tight little group that Kensey figured had to be photographs.

"When I was in my first year at U. Mass. my mother showed up on campus one day," she said to break the silence. Looking in Alec's direction, she saw he was already staring at her. "I was walking back to the dorm with some friends and she was sitting on the steps crying. I thought she'd driven down to tell me my dad left her or something." Alec placed his hand on her shoulder and stroked it. "Two punks had stuck them up in a parking lot. My mother said they promised not to hurt them if they handed over their wallets. After they got the money, they made Mom and Dad kneel on the ground like the terrorists do in those goddamn videotapes. They told them to Mississippi-count to a hundred or they'd come back and kill them. So my dad goes, 'One Mississippi, two Mississippi,' and the punks turned around like it was all over. My mother swore she could see them start to walk away out of the corner of her eye." Alec heard her sniff back a tear. "Suddenly a gun went off and my dad got shot in the head."

"Oh, God."

"I don't know why they didn't touch her."

"They ever catch 'em?"

Kensey shook her head. "I never told anyone the whole story. I always leave out the part about them having to kneel down."

Alec pulled her closer.

She wiped her cheek with the back of her hand. "You want to turn on the TV?"

Alec dug between the cushions for the remote and a widescreen television slowly came to life. He found a local news station and they had to sit through a story about a high school senior who had been expelled for a hazing incident.

"After we left the garage last night, when we stopped at that church, did you light a candle or were you praying?"

"I went to confession, told the priest I took a man's life."

"You did?"

He nodded.

"You were in there a long time."

"At first he said nothing. I mean, it was dead silent for maybe a minute. I suppose he mostly hears people taking the Lord's name in vain and having impure thoughts. He had to think on it so long I was getting scared he snuck out and was calling the police."

"You told him you were saving a life?"

"No."

Kensey tilted her head to one side. The television was casting a bluish glow in the room. Her eyes were adjusting so she could make out a photograph of what she believed were grandparents. Next to it was one of a child standing in front of a Christmas tree holding up a new toy. Then photos of kids in rows, shortest to tallest. Maybe team pictures.

"Why not?"

"It's wrong to present your sins with an asterisk."

"Did the priest ask?"

"When he caught his breath. He said there must be a reason and I told him a little about it and he thought some more and told me to go home."

Kensey used a throw pillow to cover her bare legs. "When he first grabbed me I was so scared he had to hold me up with one hand." Kensey stared off toward the dark kitchen. Alec studied the way her forehead wrinkled as she was thinking. "You know what? He had horrible BO but his breath smelled like he just brushed his teeth. That's what I remember about him. His breath. Is that weird? When he got me up against the wall he said he wasn't going to hurt me if I told him what he wanted. I knew he was lying. It's what people say to keep you calm before they pull the trigger. Just like with my dad. But then..."

Something on the television caught her eye and she stopped talking. A reporter in a tie and windbreaker was standing at the entrance to the underground parking garage where the shooting had taken place. The scene shifted to footage inside the cement walls. Yellow police tape was strung between two columns. There was a chalk outline where they had left Berto on the concrete. The reporter was doing voice-over, saying the victim was named Roberto Comparino, that he was thirty-seven and from Scranton, and that he'd had lots of run-ins with the law, including some time in one of the state penitentiaries. Then the footage shifted to the dapper gentleman in the blazer and yellow hankie.

"Oh my God, I forgot about him," Kensey said. Never taking her eyes off the TV, she said, "Hold me, okay?"

Alec slipped closer to Kensey, put his arm around her shoulders, and pulled her toward him.

The gentleman was saying, "We got to the lot, me and the missus, around nine-thirty. I told the police the only person we saw was a girl getting into a car." He turned and pointed behind him.

Alec said, "He saw you?"

"For a second."

The scene shifted back to the reporter outside. He was saying maybe the shooting was drug-related and if anyone had any information they were to call the police. A phone number appeared on the bottom of the screen.

"Turn it off, okay?" she said.

The television went black and they were in darkness again.

While her eyes adjusted, she said, "About Berto. He pinned me against the wall and he spotted this bruise I have on my chest. He made a big deal saying he *didn't* give me the bruise and I better remember it."

"Then what?"

"I thought it was going to be about what Manny told me, you know, find out what I know. But all he wanted was a medical report."

"What'd you tell him?"

She shrugged. "I didn't know."

"The other cop, what's his name?"

"Mike. He's the one who gave me the bruise."

"Doesn't he come to visit his friend? All he's got to do is ask."

"Manny would never tell him. He's sure they want to know when they can kill him."

"That's what this was about?"

Kensey stared at him. "I think so. But that thing about my bruise? That's what I was thinking about before you came in. Maybe what he said was true, he wasn't going to hurt me."

"The second you told him what he wanted he would've pulled the trigger."

"I need to know."

"There's no way to know."

Kensey slipped from under his arm and pushed out of the sofa, taking long strides on thick carpet toward the kitchen.

"Where are you going?"

"He said it wasn't loaded."

"No way." Alec shot out of the sofa, in close pursuit. "No good'll come from that." Now the kitchen lights were on. They were on opposite sides of the counter, eyes focused tightly on Berto's revolver with *Colt* stamped on the barrel. It was next to a fancy chrome juicer. "I don't want to do this."

Using one finger, she nudged the weapon closer to him. "I need to know if Manny's been lying to me. I need to know if I can go into my house to take a shower and change my underwear."

Alec fumbled with the weapon before discovering how to release the cylinder. A two-second glance at the six chambers and he said, "Shit," and set the revolver back on the counter.

Without a moment's hesitation Kensey grabbed it and help it at eye level. She had an unobstructed view through all six chambers. Instantly she smiled, then looked across at Alec, her grin growing. He was no more than four feet away and Kensey could see he wasn't sharing the moment with her. For several seconds nothing was said, Kensey slowly returning the revolver to the counter, then gazing over at Alec. "I'm sorry. I shouldn't have insisted —"

"That's not what I meant."

"There was nothing else you could have done."

"You think I'm upset I killed him?"

Nodding, she said, "Yeah. I wish we had the other gun. No way would he have pulled it if it wasn't loaded."

"I'm not upset about that. Forget it," he said, his voice very soft, not at all angry. Alec tore a paper towel from a roll.

"Please tell me."

"Am I driving you straight to the hospital?"

She looked frustrated at the way he changed the subject. "No, I need to go home, change my clothes."

Lining his hands with the paper towel, Alec picked up the gun.

Something about the way his eyes refused to look at her made Kensey realize he was uncomfortable. "Alec, you were a hero last night, coming out of nowhere like you did. You put yourself in danger." She was talking faster and faster as she watched Alec wipe Berto's gun down. Her forehead was moist. Now she said, "All that matters is for the rest of my life I will remember seeing you across the parking lot and knowing ... and knowing I was okay with you there."

He smiled at her, using the towel to hold the gun while he got a ziplock plastic bag from one of the drawers and deposited it inside.

Finally she came around the counter and hugged him hard and he hugged her back.

Alec smoothed her hair and kissed her cheek. "What are you doing tonight?"

"I've got to run a quick errand. I could come over after. Do you cook?"

"I'll do something on the grill."

"Around nine?" Kensey gave him a quick kiss on the mouth, then another, this one longer, mouth open, tasting each other. "Maybe you'll drive me home so I can change my clothes." Then she scooted out of the room.

"Listen, I was wondering about something," he called out.

"What?" Kensey said from another room.

"Why don't you bring some stuff with you and stay here for a while."

Kensey appeared in the kitchen doorway with a smile. "Okay." Then she turned and vanished into the dark hallway behind her.

19

"So what's happening with the cop? Chest tube still in?" Susanne asked as they were walking toward the parking lot in Oakland after work. The weather was turning colder and she wore a light jacket with a scarf loosely wrapped around her neck. She was holding her hand out so she could examine her fingernails in the light of a street lamp as they passed beneath it. "Oh, God, look at these things."

"X-ray showed the tube was blocked and he was accumulating air. I removed the clamp. He wasn't upset."

"I hope he's enjoying the Health Center Hilton. Shall I have the concierge see about theater tickets?"

"He's terrified what will happen when he leaves."

"You have to put in a new tube?"

"No, I squirted in some streptokinase and it opened right up."

"That stuff's like Liquid-Plumr. So where is it I'm taking you?"

"I'm picking up a car."

"Whose car is it?"

"A friend's. I don't think you know him. The directions are simple."

"I'm supposed to get my nails done at eight."

Kensey glanced at her watch. "It's ten after now. You're gonna be late no matter what. And they look fine."

"They do not. Hurry," Susanne said, picking up the pace. She was holding out her hand, fingers splayed, waiting for the light from the next street lamp. "See, they're a mess."

Kensey gave a quick look. "It's too dark."

Their heels were clicking off the sidewalk as they headed onto an Oakland side street away from the bookstores and pizza joints. It was a residential street, two-story frame houses with wraparound porches long ago turned into apartments for grad students.

"A nurse said to me, 'Oh honey, you're never gonna catch a man with nails like that.' I called right away and made an appointment."

Kensey fell a step behind. The wind was blowing the branches of a big elm and making shadows dance around them. She slipped her backpack off her shoulder.

"What are you looking at?" Susanne's head went left, then right. "And what are you getting out of your backpack?"

Kensey was clutching the backpack by one of the straps, her other hand rooting inside one of the zippered compartments. "You know a girl can never be too careful."

Susanne took two steps back to Kensey. "What do you have in there, Mace or something?"

"It's nothing, forget it." Kensey started walking again, her hand lost inside the nylon compartment.

"They're following you, aren't they?" Susanne took three quick steps so she was right in front of Kensey. Placing her hands on Kensey's shoulders, she said, "Stop." Her head whipped left then right, searching out danger that might be hiding in the shadows.

"What about your nails, Susanne? They're a mess."

"Screw the nails. What do you have?" She grabbed the backpack and tugged it away from Kensey. Kensey's hand was empty as it left the compartment. Susanne dug right in. "Oh my God, you've got a gun. Where did you get this?"

"Shhhh. Ever since the other night I've been scared." She scanned up and down the block. Thatches of dense bushes. Cars parked everywhere. Empty trash cans waiting to be carried back to the house.

"That's it, you're staying at my place from now on." She handed the backpack to Kensey.

"Forget it. I'm just being paranoid." Zipping the nylon compartment, she slung the pack over her shoulder.

"No, you're not. They could be anywhere." Susanne's eyes were racing back and forth in their sockets, checking out the dark holes in the neighborhood. "You can have the bed."

"Susanne, I can't stay with you."

"Why not?"

Kensey started walking. "I'm staying with a friend."

Susanne quickly caught up and slipped her arm around Kensey's. Suddenly they were walking like girlfriends with nothing more to discuss than their sex lives. "Who, the sushi guy?"

"As a matter of fact, yes. Do you have to know everything?" They were going past a street lamp.

"You slept with him on the first date, didn't you?"

"Can we walk, please?" Again they moved through the darkness. "Thank you. And I swear I did not sleep with him. He knew I was scared so—"

"Wait a second. You told him? I thought no one's supposed to know."

They turned into a parking lot, kept going past Kensey's Honda, and slipped into Susanne's slick BMW.

"So ... where did you meet him?"

"The gym. His name's Alec."

Susanne turned the key. Dozens of dashboard lights came on to the sound of Mariah Carey blasting from the radio. She hit a button to silence it. "Alec. And you've had dinner with him exactly once and now you're living with him."

"In his guest bedroom."

"You are one lousy liar. I *knew* there was something different about you when I saw you this morning. How was he?" Susanne leaned on the steering wheel and stared at Kensey. When she didn't get an answer she said, "So where are we going to get Alec's car?"

"Northside."

They traveled the same route Kensey had taken on her way to St. John's, past the Heinz factory, climbing the steep hill. Susanne said, "What's his car doing up here?"

"I don't know, I think his secretary picked it up from the garage or something."

"So how'd he get home?"

"Susanne, the reason I asked you to drive me is I can ask you to trust me. So trust me. I know what I'm doing." Kensey leaned forward to read a street sign. "It's right here."

Susanne pulled over to the curb. "Where?" she asked, leaning over the steering wheel and peering out at the dark street. The two cars she could see were an old Chevy and a minivan with plastic over the driver's window.

Kensey hopped out of the car. "Thanks. See you tomorrow."

Before Kensey could close the door, Susanne said, "Wait a second," sounding worried.

Kensey picked up on Susanne's tone, but when she leaned inside the car said, "I really want you to meet Alec. Maybe this weekend."

"Don't close the door," Susanne said with authority.

"I'm fine," Kensey said with a breezy tone. "Go get your nails—"

"Kensey!" This time Susanne raised her voice. "I'm not leaving until you're safely in his car." She shifted the BMW into park.

"This has nothing to do with Detective Romero. I'm doing a favor for the guy I'm dating. That's all. Why're you trying to scare me?"

"You're carrying a gun."

"Alec got it for me. It's one of those things that makes you feel better if you've got it with you."

"But all I see is a horrible minivan."

"It's a few houses down, Susanne. I'm fine." She sounded sincere.

"Are you sure?"

"Yes." Now Kensey made her voice sound like she was getting irritated. "It's easier for you to turn around here."

"Call me while you're driving?"

"If that'll get you to the nail salon, I promise."

Kensey waited while Susanne engineered a U-turn and headed back down the hill before slipping her hand into the zippered compartment and gripping the gun. She headed down Burton Street, one street below Hemlock. The houses were small and bunched together. Several cars were parked on the street. Another one was up on cinder blocks in a front yard. Two dogs wandered across Burton and disappeared between some houses. There was the pleasant smell of wood burning in a fireplace. Walking on the low side she counted three brick houses before reaching a two-story white clapboard with a cord of wood stacked on the front porch. The house was dark and simple. A springy metal chair sat alone on the little patch of lawn at an angle that was good for looking up the hill toward St. John's. Kensey imagined Manny sitting out there on a hot summer night in his undershirt showing off his hairy shoulders, drinking a beer out of the can, rocking back and forth.

On the far side of the house was the driveway, two strips of concrete with grass in between.

Something touched the back of her leg. She jumped and let out a little yelp as she swung around. A scruffy dog was nosing around and she realized her hand was still in her bag. "This is ridiculous," she whispered and pulled out the gun she had lifted from Seymour Rosen's office. Moving to the street end of Manny's driveway, she noticed how dark it was between the two houses. A different dog poked its head out of the space between the houses and snuck past Kensey toward the street. Squinting down the driveway she could make out what looked like the front of a pickup.

Placing her backpack on the ground near the corner of the house, she plucked a penlight from a side compartment, wrapped her finger around the trigger of the Beretta, and took her first step down the grass walkway, slowly, her body at an angle so she was ready to turn and run if something happened. Turning on the tiny flashlight, the bulb emitted a brown beam that barely illuminated the ground beneath her feet. The air between the houses was rank with the smell of squatting dogs. Taking tiny steps, she moved several feet along the siding of Manny's house.

Something started growling, a low-pitched sound Kensey couldn't identify or locate. Her feet stopped shuffling. Right away she thought it was a dog, a big one. Maybe a rottweiler or a German shepherd, something meant to guard and intimidate, showing teeth, drool hanging from its jaw, waiting to be provoked. She raised the Beretta, trying to use a two-handed grip and maneuver the penlight at the same time. The penlight slipped from her fingers. It bounced off the concrete, then went to black.

The growl stopped and the air was quiet. From somewhere up the hill she could make out the happy sound of people singing. They would pause, wait fifteen or twenty seconds, then start over again. They were singing about Jesus, the same two or three lines over and over: *Jesus watches over us, never turns away.* Kensey turned so she was facing St John's.

Grrrrrrrrrrr. It was back. Right in front of her. Guttural.

The first week in the Emergency Department she had witnessed a young boy who had been attacked by a dog. He was in shock, straps of muscle hanging from his leg, tendons and arteries shredded beyond recognition, and there were marks in his femur where the teeth had dug in.

Now she was sidestepping back toward the street, arms crossed in front of her chest in case the dog was looking for something to grab, sliding against the clapboard of the house, moving slowly so the animal wouldn't mistake her retreat for anything aggressive, hoping for voices in the air singing about Jesus.

Not five feet in front of her a match burst into flame and the yellow glow lit up the face of a dark-skinned teenage boy. The growl stopped. "Whatcha doing?" he said in a singsongy way that made her think of a rap singer. He held the match out as the flame slowly moved toward his fingers. With a sharp wave of his hand the match went out and they were swallowed up by darkness.

"I'm here to pick up Detective Romero's truck for him."

Grrrrrrrrrrr.

Kensey was rendered motionless. She hadn't seen the dog but her hands went up even higher.

The growl stopped and the rapper voice replaced it. "Then why you packing?"

"Excuse me?"

"Look like some kind of a thirty-eight to me. Maybe a forty-five. That's a serious weapon, you just picking up the man's ride. Blow a motherfucker's head off."

"He gave me his keys."

"Why'd you ditch the backpack out front?"

"No reason."

"You did it case you need to get the hell outta here."

Grrrrrrrrrrr. This one low and mean.

Another match burst into flame. The boy held it out to light Kensey's face. "Don't be looking at the ground, sister. Mad Dog's right here, right in front of you," he said and snatched a cigarette from behind one ear and lit it. He dropped the match and it hit the ground and died. As he puffed the cigarette the yellow ember waxed and waned and showed off a face that couldn't have been more than fourteen or fifteen.

"Do you know Detective Romero?"

"Course I know the *po* - lice." Now he sounded gangsta. "The man told you 'bout me?"

In the glow from the ember he took a step toward her.

She took two back. "No, I swear."

"Man sends you on a errand and gives you his piece. Ain't like he's got a ride worth stealing."

"The gun's mine."

"Yeah, and I'm a honor student."

"He's in the hospital."

"I *know* the man's in the hospital. *Jee*-sus." His voice was louder now, knowing it would scare her. "Took a bullet's what he did. Been sweet as a virgin without the *po* - lice next door." He lit another match and saw the fear in her face.

Kensey thought it sounded forced, the way he kept saying '*po* – lice.' But he was still scaring her. "I'm taking care of him."

Mad Dog dropped the match and the gangsta cadence. "What're you, a nurse or something?"

"A doctor."

Mad Dog took a long drag and blew out a thin stream of smoke. He lit another match. It looked like he wanted to say something but didn't know how. "His wheels are back here." He began walking toward the back of the house. "You put him back together right, you hear me?" he said without turning around.

Lagging three steps behind, she said, "He's getting better."

They walked single file, Mad Dog growling once or twice like a sonar beacon. "Man owes me some folding money."

"Oh?" They'd reached the back of the house and in the dull light of the moon she could see the truck. She pulled out the cluster of keys Manny had given her.

"Said if I pass everything he'd give me fifty bucks. Three Cs and a D. You tell him that." He sounded proud, no longer a gangsta but a kid in the neighborhood.

"He may not be coming back."

Mad Dog swung around and gave Kensey a hard look. She said, "He may be leaving town."

"He didn't say nothin' 'bout me?"

"Look, I'm sure he wants you to have the money. My wallet's in my backpack—"

In the next second he took a quick step toward her and thrust his hands out like he was going to grab her.

Kensey recoiled, took a clumsy step backwards, and protected her face with her hands.

"Boo," he said, his hands out toward her, his fingers moving around like a child being scary on Halloween.

Kensey was breathing hard. When she noticed the gun was pointed nowhere in Mad Dog's direction she lowered it to her side. "You finished?"

"Don't want your money. Fuck you. And fuck Mr. *Po* - liceman too." He tossed his cigarette in Kensey's direction, turned and ghetto-walked into the darkness.

Kensey unlocked the pickup truck and climbed into the seat. Hanging from the rearview mirror was a set of rosary beads and a cross. Before she turned the key in the ignition she held the cross and thought about Manny and the boy.

20

The front doors of the Boot Slapper were painted black in the middle, blond wood on the top and bottom. From a distance they looked like the swinging doors on saloons in old westerns. Mike Dombroski pushed them open and stepped inside. He was wearing a three-quarter-length brown duster and a black cowboy hat with a gentle roll to the brim. Acting like he had all the time in the world, he stood there taking in the smoky room, giving a little nod to a couple of guys over at the pool table, touching the brim of his hat when a bosomy waitress in a fancy cowgirl shirt walked by. But Mike was out of breath. With the back of his hand he wiped a glaze of sweat from his forehead and smeared it on his pants.

People were moving to Toby Keith, playing loud enough to make you thirsty and horny at the same time. Mike moseyed across the room, the limp working to enhance the outlaw image, weaving slowly around the jukebox and little round tables in the direction of a long wooden bar that ran one whole side of the room. Mike looked exhausted, sacs under his eyes the size of saddlebags. The barkeeps, three of them, wore white shirts with string ties and black garters on their arms. A handmade sign above the bar read *No Guns In the Bar.*

Mike eased himself onto a stool, undid the buttons on his coat, and waited for one of the guys behind the bar to come over.

"Growing it back?"

Mike touched above his lip and felt the stubble. "Got any manure?"

The barkeep laughed. "You okay? You don't look so good."

"Nothing that a little bounce in the sack wouldn't fix."

"You're all sweaty. Hey, I got some Advil around here."

"Gimme four or five of 'em." Before the barkeep moved away Mike added, "And something to wash it down with."

"Shot'n a beer?"

"You ain't as stupid as you look." The barkeep laughed and Mike twirled himself around so he could check out the room. His hand went to his leg and began to massage his thigh. Toby had quieted down. Now it was Shania going on about feeling like a woman. This triggered two fat broads in tight jeans that made their legs look like sausages to start bopping to the music. One of them let out a war whoop.

"Here you go, Mike," the barkeep said. There was a frothy beer and a little shot glass waiting for Mike on the bar. He was holding some shiny brown pills between his fingers and dropped them into Mike's palm, then watched the cowboy toss them into the back of his mouth and flush them down with the whiskey. Mike banged the shot glass down on the bar hard enough to let people know he was there.

"Thanks, Doc," Mike said, acting as if he was feeling better already and started working on his brew. Just as he was placing the mug back on the bar, a pretty woman with long dark hair and breasts too big for her slender build snuck up from behind, whisked his cowboy hat off, and planted a big smooch on his cheek. Mike's leg kicked high and his arm shot out at the same time, knocking his glass of beer across the bar. He nearly toppled off his stool. Between the spasm and the pain he was rendered helpless long enough that everyone at the bar forgot about their whiskeys and gawked at him like he was a circus sideshow. When he was able to turn around he looked pissed.

"Whoa, cowboy, you're a little skittish."

Mike was breathing hard. His forehead was wet and his face flushed. Forcing a thin smile, he said, "Oh, Marnie. Jesus. You're liable to get hog-tied and spanked till morning sneaking up like that." He was still working to get air in and out of his lungs.

"Turn around so I can do it again," Marnie said, then raised a dainty eyebrow and smiled. When she saw what he was growing she giggled, "Hey, the tickler's coming back real nice," and leaned in for a quick kiss.

The barkeep was wiping up the spill as Mike was saying, "You want to get out of here?" He stood up, dropped some money on the bar, and headed toward the door with Marnie on his arm.

The fat broads in the tight jeans were getting into Shania, singing along, waving their fleshy arms over their heads, feeling slim and sexy as long as the song would last. One of them was gut-squeezed into a pink shirt with black stitching and shiny black buttons. She was bending over, hands on knees, wagging her big rear end in front of some sinewy dudes in plaid shirts sitting with their black shitkickers square on the floor. Now she turned around to face them, arching her back, shaking her chest, and putting on a good show.

As Shania was winding down, Mike and Marnie were passing behind the dancer when she spun around and bumped into him. His arm shot out just as it had at the bar and plunged into one of her breasts. This brought her audience to its feet. In about five seconds Mike was surrounded.

"Hey buddy, watch it," one of them said.

Another said, "Jesus Christ, look at him."

The pain was excruciating. It was everything he could do to keep from falling down. His teeth were bared and his back was in spasm so that he was leaning back like he was doing the limbo. Slowly his arm worked its way down to his side. Between gulps of air he managed to get out, "Forget it. She bumped in to me."

"You see what he did, Ernie?" the fat broad said to one of the guys.

"Ernie, take him outside," another said. "Teach the fucker some manners."

Ernie came back with, "You'n me, pal, right now, take a little walk."

Mike dug into his duster and pulled out some keys and handed them to Marnie. "Looks like me'n Bert are going get to know each other."

One of the guys said, "Ernie, you asshole. His name's Ernie."

Mike didn't look at him. He was saying to Marnie, "Bring the car around, this won't take long."

The whole group headed for the door, the fat broads, four guys in shitkickers, Mike and Marnie. Ernie shoved the swinging doors open so hard they banged off the stops and swung back fast enough to knock someone over if he wasn't paying attention. Mike said, "Go," to Marnie and she peeled away and headed around back.

The woman in the pink shirt who started the whole thing yelled good-bye and said she hoped Mike's friend was a nurse because he was gonna need one real bad when Ernie got through with him. Then she noticed the way Mike was walking. "Look at this guy, Ernie, check out the fake limp."

The guys in the shitkickers thought this was real funny. One of them hobbled along next to Mike, doing a pretty good imitation.

Ernie led Mike around the side where delivery trucks came in, behind a broken fence that hid a vile Dumpster. "All right pal, apologize to the lady or you're going ass-first in the Dumpster, then I'm gonna piss a six-pack on you."

Slowly, Mike worked the buttons on the duster and made Ernie wait, taking his time, watching Ernie standing there surrounded by his posse, arms out like a boxer. When Mike unfastened the last one he pushed the duster open like they do in westerns just before they draw their guns in a showdown. It looked as if he was going to take it off. Instead he turned slightly, his badge on his belt coming into view. Then he reached around back and whipped out his black service revolver.

Instantly Ernie and his friends backed up, putting their hands out in front of them, letting Mike know it was over. Ernie went, "Just like you said, Officer, forget it."

"Around these parts I'm the law."

Ernie said, "We don't want no trouble, sir."

"I could take you in and throw your ass in jail, Bert." He looked at the guy who corrected him in the bar. "You got something to say, pal?"

The guy shook his head.

Ernie said, "Look, I'm real sorry. It was just a misunderstanding. Lemme buy you a beer, maybe some wings."

"You and Miss Piggy, in the Dumpster."
"Oh, come on."
Mike racked the slide on his gun. "Get in the fuckin' Dumpster. Now. I get to five I pull the trigger. One. Two ..." Ernie and the girl in the pink shirt double-timed it into the Dumpster, Ernie helping her roll over the edge like a side of beef. "Now bend down, both of younz." Mike slammed the metal lid, tipped his hat to his little audience, and said, "Now if you'll excuse me, I gotta go get laid."

21

Daylight snuck through the drapes. Her hair was mussed in a delightful way, curling onto her cheeks and making her look like a frisky cabaret singer. Her fragrance filled his nostrils and reminded him of an English garden just after it rained. He knew he would remember this moment. That's how his brain was working, in syrupy superlatives he would laugh at if someone else said them. Now Kensey turned on her side away from him. He loved the way her hips swelled the sheets, enticing him even more. Ever so gently he eased the covers back, his fingers skiing the moguls of her spine in a southerly direction until they reached the soft basin of her lower back. Now they lingered, massaging softly, urging her awake.

She stirred.

He expanded his area of exploration and she moved into him and moaned softly.

"You awake?" Alec said. He glanced out the window. It looked like it was going to be a nice day.

Nothing.

He worked his hands lower and again she made a little sound that kept him going. After a leisurely interval he tried again, "Now are you awake?"

"Consider the snooze button hit, but don't stop winding the clock."

He smiled and snuggled his body next to hers. Kissing her neck, he slid his hand around the equator and traveled north until he cupped her breast. "What time do you have to be at work?"

"Whenever." Her voice had a dreamy quality, the way girls do in Broadway musicals when they've been kissed for the first time.

"It's after seven. I could make omelets."

"Whatever," she said and shifted her legs. "I haven't slept like this since ... mmm ... you know." Kensey scrunched the pillow and let out a sigh.

"That'll bring you back for more."

"I forgot what it feels like to be safe."

His lips brushed her shoulder.

She started to say something, then hesitated.

"What?" He smoothed her hair back.

"I was thinking maybe I could ask Manny about Sonny again."

"What if he lets Sonny know you're asking questions?"

Still buried in the pillow, she shook her head. "He wouldn't do that, not if I asked him not to."

Alec shifted his weight and rolled her onto her back so he could look her in the face. "This is why I said 'shit' when there were no bullets in the gun. Now you think you really can trust him. Believe me, the only thing on his mind is saving his own skin."

"You don't know him. Besides, I'm not saying he's going to tell me who Sonny is. But I trust him not to do anything to hurt me."

"He promised they were going to leave you alone. Look what happened in the garage."

"That doesn't make sense, I know."

"Maybe Sonny's panicking and wants to get medical information and take you out at the same time."

"Take me out?" Kensey laughed. "What is that, mobster talk?"

He whispered, "No."

"Oooooo, I like being your gun moll."

Alec rolled onto his back and stared at the ceiling. He spoke very softly. "It sounded less awful than saying he wanted to kill you."

"I know." She was smiling at him, sounding playful, rolling on her side, one leg slung over his, her fingers doing little pirouettes in the soft hairs on his chest. "Don't worry about it."

"When Manny leaves the hospital, Sonny'll do whatever he has coming. I don't really care." His eyes moved to hers. "You do, don't you?"

"Every day I'm taking care of him, talking with him, learning who he is."

"You didn't answer the question."

"I do care."

"If Sonny and Mike didn't exist and going to the police didn't put you in danger, would you?"

"This doctor-patient relationship is a special thing. I'd only go to the police to prevent a crime from occurring, not to report things in the past. It's not a whole lot different than your relationship with your priest."

"Then let's forget about who Sonny is."

"Don't make it sound like that. Trust me, I know plenty about doing the right thing." She propped her head on the pillow to get a better view of him. "Before I went to med school I was a nurse."

"Like your mom."

"Yep, I was a nurse in Hartford and I really liked it. I was taking care of a cancer patient who was end-stage and in the most horrific pain. All he did was roll around in the bed and cry. He couldn't eat. He didn't care if he peed himself. The only time I ever saw him sleep was when there was a medication error and he received a double dose of morphine." She stopped speaking and studied Alec's face, waiting for him to digest what she'd said. His eyebrow went up in anticipation and she continued. "It was my mistake. And when I told my patient he thanked me. Said it was the most sleep he'd had in three months." For the second time she paused.

"And?"

"Then he begged me to kill him."

"You did?"

"No. I was a good little nurse who went by the rules. I went to his oncologist, told him his patient wanted to die. The oncologist gave me a look and said they ought to throw the bastard in jail. He told me if I was a good Catholic I better not breathe those words again. Then I made a mistake. I told him about the medication error and how grateful the patient had been. I asked if we could at least raise his medication dosage so he could sleep."

"He fired you."

"Nope. There was a big nursing shortage. He made me write up an incident report about the medication error. I spent the next eight days watching my patient writhe in pain. The day after he died I quit and applied to med school."

"You've got moxie."

"If I *had* moxie I wouldn't have watched him for eight days."

■ ■ ■

"How's he doing?" Kensey said to the uniformed cop sitting outside Manny's door.

The cop looked up from the morning paper and smiled. "He's all about the bubbles, whatever that means."

Kensey laughed and pushed through the door. Manny was propped up on two pillows, watching television. The moment he saw Kensey in her pleated skirt and short white jacket, he gave a little thumbs-up and turned off the television. He shot her a nice white-teeth smile.

Kensey pulled out his set of keys and the parking ticket from the side pocket of her jacket and handed them over. "I wrote down where the truck is on the back. It's right near the elevator."

Manny flipped the ticket over and scanned the back. "You are a Good Samaritan. Now I owe you two. Hey, no trouble, right?"

"I got to meet Mad Dog."

Manny looked confused. "Mad Dog. Who the hell's that?"

"In between the houses, where your driveway runs? He's about fourteen, hangs out in the dark, growling like a rabid animal."

"Oh, that's Leonard. He lives next door. Used to be a nice kid. Since his daddy died he's going the wrong way."

"You owe him money."

"All right." Manny sounded excited. "Report cards were this week. What'd he get?"

"Three Cs and a D. I tried to pay him."

"He got pissed off, right?" Kensey nodded. "Don't worry 'bout it. C'mon, siddown, siddown, talk to me." When he leaned over to pull some magazines from the chair next to the bed, Kensey could see he was moving better.

"Uh-oh, sounds like you're setting me up for another favor."

"Who me?" He grinned. "Hey, lemme ask you something. 'Member you saw Mike in the ED? Well, he's getting worse. Called me this morning, said he had some kind of spasm or seizure last night. He wants you to give him something for it."

"Tell him he needs to be in the hospital."

"What's he got?"

"Tetanus."

"Tetanus? Jesus Christ, I thought that was like polio or something, you know, extinct."

"Just tell him."

"Okay, okay."

"Now it's my turn for a favor."

"Name it."

"I want you to tell me who Sonny is."

"Sonny." He let out a low whistle like he wasn't expecting that. His hand swiped at the bristles on his face.

"You know I trust you, but I'm worried what will happen when you're down in Florida."

"I told you I made everything right. No one's gonna touch you. I made sure they know you wrote everything down. You have my word, Kensey."

"I hate looking over my shoulder. I took down the shower curtain. Every closet's wide open. I put the mattress right on the floor."

"I don't know who he is. All's I know is the name." He crossed himself. "The truth."

"You told me that story about meeting him in a bar."

"I'm any lower on the totem pole, I'm underground. I met him once, like I tol' you, in a bar. It was dark and he had on a baseball cap. I wouldn't even recognize him. After that all he wanted to do was deal with Mike."

"Can you ask him?"

"Mike? You crazy? No fuckin' way." He looked at Kensey, saw the look on her face. "Sorry."

"It's okay." She rubbed her forehead like she'd just developed a headache.

"I gotta worry about what Sonny'n Mike're gonna do when I get outta here. And I'm worrying about you all the time. But no matter how much I'm worrying about you, I ain't gonna find out who Sonny is."

"Forget it." She stood and put her stethoscope in her ears.

He could tell she was pissed the way she said *forget it*. "Hey, I never got to tell you about my sister."

"I'm already late," she said, readying her stethoscope. She was looking away from him as she nestled the stethoscope in the thick fur of his chest.

"No, you'll want to hear this. I never told this to nobody."

Kensey pulled the stethoscope from her head.

"Will you sit down? Please?"

She sat down in the straight-back chair and crossed her arms in front of her chest, the stethoscope dangling from one hand into her lap.

"When we were coming over here from Cuba, remember I tol' you?" Kensey nodded. "I was like seven. We were on this boat no bigger'n thirty or forty feet. It was a old fishing boat, belonged to my uncle. All we had was some jugs of water and some brown rice and candy bars. They were Snickers. I used to love Snickers. Anyway, it was him and my aunt and my mama and Nina. That was her name, Nina. She was three and I was in charge of her. So my uncle lashed this rope around her waist like a leash and I was s'posed to watch her. Every once in a while there were these dolphins swimming by and Nina loved different kinds of fish so I put her up on the side of the boat. I was holding the rope good and tight so no way something could happen, but my uncle started screaming that she was gonna fall in. Then he hit me." Manny pointed below his right eye. "Right here, knocked me down. So he tied the rope to my ankle real tight. My foot was all purple and everything but I was scared of my uncle so I didn't say nothing."

Kensey's mouth was open a bit and her hands were folded in her lap.

Manny continued. "That night, everyone was jus' sleeping on the deck, bunching up rags and old clothes to get comfortable. Nina was right next to me all curled up. Mama told me I was a good boy." He licked his lips and swallowed hard. "When it was morning Nina was gone. The rope was still around my ankle, but Nina was gone." He had tears in his eyes.

"I'm sorry."

"I swear, you ain't going over the side of the boat."

"I believe you." She put on her stethoscope and listened to Manny's chest. "You sound good, Manny. I'll stop by later, maybe clamp the tube again."

"Make sure you come 'cause I got one other thing to talk with you about."

"I knew you were leading up to something." She scowled at him in a friendly way.

"The story was because I wanted to tell you, not to get something outta you."

The door opened and Dr. Taggert strode into the room in a crisp, white coat, the bouncy black tubing of his stethoscope arcing out of his side pocket. He was wearing half glasses and carrying a metal chart that he flipped through as he said, "So, Detective, how are you today?"

"Pretty good, Doc. I feel like I'm in good hands with Dr. Shaw here."

Dr. Taggert looked and seemed surprised to see Kensey in the room. "Doctor," he said with a little nod.

"Good morning, Sir."

"And how's our patient?" Dr. Taggert went back to the chart, flipping the pages, reading bits and pieces of the medical record.

"His chest tube was blocked yesterday. I flushed the tube with streptokinase and it opened up in less than an hour."

"Yes, yes, I see you used streptokinase. You try to open it with a catheter first?"

"No, Sir. The X-ray looked as if the fluid might be loculated. Streptokinase seemed like the treatment of choice."

"The treatment of choice," he whispered without looking up. Snapping the chart shut he handed it off to Kensey. "Make certain your note reflects the fact the fluid was loculated. I don't see any mention of it."

"I'll take care of it."

Dr. Taggert said to Manny, "Well, then, I think everything's under control." Back to Kensey: "Dr. Shaw, if you're finished here I'd like to have a word with you."

"I was just saying good-bye." To Manny: "See you later, Detective."

Kensey opened the door and held it for Dr. Taggert, who was already moving toward it.

"Yo, Dr. Taggert," Manny said the way a street-smart would talk to a beat cop.

Dr. Taggert turned toward Manny, saw him pushed up on his elbows, needing a shave, the sheet not covering his hairy chest, the adhesive tape around his chest tube looking grimy. "Yes, Detective."

"That it?"

"I'm sorry," his voice crisply professional, letting Manny know he didn't have time for bullshit. "Is there a problem?"

"You're my doc, right?"

"Dr. Shaw and I work together. But I'm your attending, if that's what you mean."

"That means you get paid, she don't."

He frowned and peered over glasses. "I suppose one could look at it that way."

"Then how come every day you come in here asking me how things're going and never once use that thing?" He was looking at Dr. Taggert's stethoscope.

Dr. Taggert didn't miss a beat. His voice was silky when he said, "Excuse me for just a minute, Detective. I'll be right back."

Dr. Taggert gave Kensey a look that hurried her out the door. The two moved down the hall together, far enough from the uniformed cop so he wouldn't know what they were saying. Dr. Taggert said, "Last time someone spoke to me like that I divorced her."

"He's under a lot of stress."

"Get back in there and explain the workings of an academic hospital."

"I sure will."

"If he's not out of here in forty-eight hours I'm not going to be happy."

"Yes, sir."

He turned to walk away, then spun around toward her. "There's a Detective Hennessey who wants to interview you at police headquarters. You have any idea what that's about?"

"He's investigating Detective Romero's shooting. Probably about that."

"What do you know about the shooting?"

"Nothing."

"Well, be quick about it. The ED's short-staffed without you."

22

Manny's phone started ringing when Kensey and Taggert were halfway down the hallway. On the TV one of the perky morning talk-show hosts was trying her hand cooking the way they do in Japanese steak houses, using a knife to cut up shrimp as quickly as possible and doing acrobatic moves when plating the food. He let it ring while he watched her screw things up, but she seemed to be having a pretty good time. Finally he dialed the volume down, still smiling as he grabbed the phone from its cradle. "Hello?" He sounded distracted. "Hey, Mike, how's it going?" Now there was some life to his voice. "Yeah, just talked to her, told her about the seizures just like you wanted.... Jesus Christ, what the fuck difference it make? Spasms, seizures ... who the hell knows the difference? Anyway, she said you should come back to the ED because you need treated." Now raising his voice, he said, "'Cause you got tetanus, idiot." He stopped speaking and listened intently, shaking his head a couple times, waiting for a break in the conversation. Finally: "How the hell should I know that's another name for it? Okay, okay, try this. Can you open it all the way, like you're eating a giant hoagie? ... Okay, so don't go ballistic, maybe she don't know what she's talking about. That's why she wants you to come to the ED so she can figure out what the hell's wrong with you. ... No, Mike, that ain't the way it is. She's not *angling* to do nothing to you. ... 'Cause I trust her, that's why. I been talking with her and I know what she's about.... Fuck you," he said, jabbing his finger in the air to make the point. "I know she ain't interested in me.... You know what? You're an asshole. And I don't see her as a piece a' ass. ... For the second time, fuck you." Manny dropped the phone into its cradle and turned up the television. Al Roker was doing something silly but Manny wasn't laughing.

■ ■ ■

Down on the first floor, Detective Hennessey was waiting in the bullpen, off by himself on one of the little chairs with wheels, reading the sports section of the *Post-Gazette* laid out on the desk in front of him. He didn't see her at first, not until one of the nurses said something to him and he hopped up and spun around and headed toward Kensey. "How are you?" he said as he held out a hand to indicate she should walk toward the sliding doors. He was in a nice brown suit with a red-and-blue striped tie. If Kensey didn't know he was a cop, she never would have guessed. Maybe he could be an attorney or a stockbroker.

"Wait a second. Where're we going?" Kensey stopped to let an orderly wheel a man on a gurney past them.

"To the station. I need to show you something."

"About Manny Romero?"

"As a matter of fact, no."

Kensey shrugged and followed the detective through the doors. Outside it was sunny, the two of them having to squint in the brightness. "I'm parked right over there," Frank said, pointing to a white Buick Skylark, unmarked, waiting in one of the spaces reserved for ambulances.

"Do I sit in the front or back?"

Frank smiled, enjoying the joke, showing he was a good sport. Then he hustled around to the passenger side, opened the front door, and held it for her.

He reminded her to buckle up and they were underway, crawling through Oakland traffic. When she realized the trip wasn't going to be quick, Kensey said, "I was in enough trouble with Taggert without you going to him."

"What kind of trouble?"

"That's not the point." They rode silently for half a block, Kensey staring out the front window, looking at the Pitt undergrads crossing Fifth Avenue with their backpacks, sensing Frank's head turned toward her. Without looking his way, she said, "I missed the diagnosis with Detective Romero. You know that. He almost died because of me."

Frank switched lanes. "I wasn't trying to get you in trouble," he said, gunning it through an orange light. "Last time in the ED?" Now he was weaving in and out of traffic, chatting as if they were cruising a quiet country road. "When I brought you that muffin? I got the sense you were real uncomfortable being alone with me."

"Give me a break."

"You seemed to be announcing to the nursing staff where you were going so I would know that they knew exactly who you were going to be with. I figured if Dr. Taggert knew, maybe you'd feel more comfortable." He looked at Kensey. "Sorry if I did the wrong thing."

They rode in silence the rest of the way, the whole trip taking about fifteen minutes. The parking lot in front of the station was full so Frank slipped into a space across the street in the McDonald's. "Egg McMuffin? Coffee?"

"I'm fine."

They crossed the street. Coming out of the station were Sapphire and B.J. in full regalia, little leather skirts, spikey heels, big loopy earrings. Sapphire thrust her arm out to closeline B.J. into stopping at the same time she was saying, "Look who's here." When they got closer she called out, "Hey, it's Kelly."

In his quiet way Frank said to them, "Girls, please," and placed a hand on Kensey's back so he could escort her safely up the steps.

"Ex - *cuse* me," Sapphire said, one hand on her hip, some hooker attitude in her voice. "The girl happens to be a personal friend of me'n B.J.'s so don't be rushing her up the steps like we're gonna jump her or something."

Kensey stopped. So did Frank. "Nice to see you again," Kensey said with a thin smile.

Frank gave Kensey a look that said, You know these two?

Now the four of them were standing in a little group, uniformed cops giving them a wide berth as they left the building, peeking out the corner of their eyes and reminding themselves to ask Frank what the hell that was about.

"Hey, Kelly, the hooker bench? Wide open, baby, feel free to stretch out and carve your initials in it."

B.J. was looking up at the sky, scrunching her forehead. "Kelly? It's not Kelly, is it? Don't tell me ..." A smile lit up her face. Her teeth were wildly crooked. "It's Kensey. I knew it."

"Duh," Sapphire said and banged her fist off her forehead. "Short for *Ma*-Kensey. I ain't so stupid as I look. So you here to see Adkins or what?"

"No, I'm talking with Detective Hennessey."

"Oooooo, he is a cutie," Sapphire said and leaned back to check out Frank's rear end. "Mmm, I wouldn't mind some of him." To B.J. she said, "Hear that, Beej? Kensey got herself one helluva keeper." Back to Kensey: "All *we* ever get is some grab-ass cop who locks eyes on my tits whole time we're in the car."

"That's enough, girls," Frank said.

Sapphire said to Kensey, "Have to go to court next week. 'Member last time? Goddamn, that was something, all hell breaking loose." Her voiced went up an octave. "They kicked us out." To Sapphire: "All because a' this one."

"Good-bye, girls," his voice firm. Frank moved up the concrete steps with Kensey following. As he was reaching the front door …

"Yo, Kensey." Kensey did an about-face and looked at Sapphire shielding her eyes from the sun with her hand. Her nails were some shade of turquoise and long enough they had to be fake. "'Member last time you asked about Adkins? Did he have a nickname or something? Well I axed around and the answer is, he don't. Jus' Cap'n Adkins." Sapphire and B.J. waved and strutted toward the street.

As they walked through the door, Frank said, "You're not going to tell me about that are you?"

After they were inside, walking past the empty hooker bench and the desks with uniformed cops typing reports, interviewing suspects, drinking coffee, and reading the paper, Kensey heard someone yell out, "Hey, anyone seen Dombroski?" And before anyone could answer, Frank sort of glanced her way. He looked for some kind of reaction. Anything. A hesitation in her step, a furtive look around. None of that. She marched along and when someone else called out, "He left fifteen minutes ago," Frank wondered if she was holding her breath. Or if her cheeks looked flushed. He couldn't tell for sure. All he knew was her hair was shiny and there was that mole on her cheek....

"So what do you want to show me?" she asked when they were nearing the coffee machine.

Frank didn't seem to hear her.

This time louder: "Detective, what do you want to show me?"

"Oh, in the back, some video."

Kensey swallowed hard and her hand went to her face. If Frank had been looking at that moment, he would have seen her fingers shaking. He led her through a thick metal door, past half-a-dozen cells, three on each side of the hall, most of them empty, Kensey doing her best to stare straight ahead. As far from the front door as they could walk was a small square room with a table and two wooden chairs that didn't sit flat on the floor. A black metal trash can was overflowing with the remains of too many meals from across the street. Over in a corner was a metal cart holding a Panasonic television and videocassette recorder.

"Have a seat. I've got to check something. I'm getting some coffee — you want some?"

"Cream and sugar."

Frank disappeared, the door closing with a thud and she was alone in the room. It smelled like cigarettes and body odor. She turned around to see if one of the walls was a mirror. All four were cinder block with the paint starting to peel. She crossed her legs and uncrossed them. It seemed her hands had a life of their own, folding and unfolding, twitching, misbehaving. It wasn't more than five minutes that Frank was gone but Kensey would've sworn under oath it was longer.

Finally the door opened and Frank came in with two cups of coffee, a bottle of water, and a black videocassette.

"What were you checking?"

Frank hesitated for just a second. "Excuse me?"

"You said — right before you left the room — that you needed to check something."

"I was getting the tape."

"You were checking out the girls from outside."

"I was getting the tape and using the rest room."

"When you said you went to Taggert so I would feel comfortable, I almost thought you were being sensitive."

"I was. Cream and sugar," Frank said and set one of the cups in front of her. He breathed deeply. "I've got to go over some videotape with you." He slipped the cassette into the recorder, rolled the metal cart up to the table, and turned on the television. He sat next to Kensey, holding the remote control in his hand, and aimed it at the VCR. Tiny LED lights came on. Kensey heard a whirring as an image appeared on the screen.

It was a black-and-white picture of an escalator, looking down from above, that looked more like a still photograph than a moving video.

When nothing happened Kensey asked, "What's this about?"

"This is security video in the lobby of Mellon Center." After several seconds two women stepped on the escalator and slowly glided up toward the camera. They were chatting and clutching shopping bags. When they got to the top they stepped onto the polished floor, took half-a-dozen steps, and walked out of view.

"Now take a look at this guy," Frank said.

The camera showed a man in a dark hooded sweatshirt step on the escalator. He was eating something, staring straight ahead, his neck twitching away like it had a crick that needed to be popped into place by a chiropractor. Nearing the top, he shoved the last bite in his mouth and dropped a shiny wrapper on the floor. He looked around as if he weren't sure which way to go, then headed off to his right and out of camera range.

Frank was staring at Kensey as he stopped the video and backed it up until the man was stepping off the escalator and dropping the wrapper. That's when he froze the picture.

Kensey could feel her heart speed up and her cheeks get warm.

When Kensey didn't say anything, Frank went, "His name's Roberto Comparino. Went by the name of Berto. You recognize him?"

Dutifully, Kensey leaned forward and studied the screen. In her mind she was counting, one Mississippi, two Mississippi, three Mississippi. All the way up to ten. Slowly she shook her head. "No, don't think so."

"You sure?"

"I'm sure."

"He lives in Scranton. Thirty-six years old. Divorced. Father of three. Two girls, Maria and Mary Alice. One son, six years old, Berto Junior, lives with their mother."

Kensey shrugged her shoulders.

"You were going to say something."

"No, I'm good." She sipped some coffee. It tasted bitter and she made a face.

Frank nodded toward the television. "Peppermint Pattie."

"What?"

"That's what he was eating. A Peppermint Pattie. One of the homicide guys found the wrapper, three more down in the garage. He musta had a thing for 'em." He watched Kensey take a deep breath as if she needed fresh air. "You okay?" Frank hurried to open the water.

Kensey reached for the bottle, a few drops of water spilling on the way to her mouth. She took a sip, then another, finally downing a third of the bottle. "Thanks."

"So," he said, waiting for her to look him in the eye, "You ever hear of this guy?"

Kensey didn't look back at the Panasonic. "I told you, no."

"Okay if we keep going?" Kensey nodded, Frank wondering if her silence meant something. "There's more." Frank started the video again. The picture briefly continued with a view of the escalator. Without warning the image flickered and switched to a picture of a wide hallway. "To save time I put together the highlights." The hallway was empty, no movement from the camera. They watched in silence until Berto sauntered into view. The camera was shooting from above and off to the side so Kensey couldn't get much of a view of his face. She could see his neck twitching away. Absently his hand slipped into a side pocket and pulled out a second Peppermint Pattie. Without looking at his fingers, he unwrapped the candy and took a bite. "He's got some sweet tooth," Frank said while Berto checked his watch, then leaned back on his heels and stared at the wall. "Where he's standing, they've got some artwork. You can't see it, some modern stuff. Looks like he's wasting time. Now watch."

A woman walked between Berto and the artwork. She had large breasts and a tight skirt. Berto turned to gape at her as she walked away so that you could see his face, straight on, an image they could use for his mug shot. Frank used the remote to freeze the picture. "That help?"

Kensey could see most of his face, the stubbly beard, his thick eyebrows, the palooka nose, those deep-set eyes. Not lingering over the image for more than a second, she turned toward Frank. "No. Who is this guy?"

"He's a punk. Been arrested seventeen times. Armed robbery, attempted murder. Came an awful long way just to get shot to death in the garage."

Kensey's tongue parted her lips and wetted them. "Was he taken to the ED?"

Frank shook his head. "Un-uh." He sounded surprised by the question. "Went right to the morgue." Frank peered at the television, squinting his eyes a bit. But Kensey felt his eyes on her even if it was in his peripheral vision.

Her breathing was measured, hands folded into one another in her lap. A couple times her tongue parted her lips to keep them moist. Other than that she was frozen. She focused her attention on the power button of the Panasonic.

"This guy's a nothing. No one would notice if he dropped dead. Almost like he's disposable. Most cops with a creep like this? They spend ten minutes with the eyewitnesses and call it a night. I don't do that."

Frank turned his gaze on her. He looked at her neck and could pick up the pulse in her carotid. He knew she was rattled.

"So," he said. No words had been spoken for almost a minute. "You notice his neck?"

"I did."

"What's that about?"

"He could be nervous. Maybe he's got Tourette's.

"Tourette's?"

"It's a neurological condition characterized by tics."

"That reminds me. Guy on the force's been having some kind of tics. He's sitting at his desk the other day, talking on the phone. Someone bumps into his desk, his leg kicks out like he's a placekicker or something. Ever hear of anything like that?"

"Could be a lot of things. Maybe he should see a doctor."

"Tourette's, maybe? What do you think?"

"Someone bumped into him?"

"No, his *desk*. He was just sitting there."

"Maybe they startled him."

Frank sat up suddenly and opened his mouth wide. "That's startled." He slid his chair back from the table. It made a chalk-on-blackboard squeak. His leg kicked out, Rockettes-style. "This caught my attention."

"How long's it been happening?"

"I don't know. A couple days, maybe more."

"Maybe your friend had an injury to his leg."

"He's not a friend." Frank paused, giving it time to sink in. "Just a guy I know. As a matter of fact, he did hurt himself. You're pretty sharp." He stroked the side of his cheek. "What'd he tell me? Oh yeah, fell down in his basement and cut his leg. He didn't think it was much of a big deal."

"What'd he cut it on?"

"A nail or something."

"If you develop spasms after a cut on your leg the first thing I'd wonder about is tetanus."

"Tetanus! In my whole life I never heard of someone getting tetanus."

"Tell him he needs to see a doctor."

Frank nodded. "Maybe I'll do that." He picked up the remote control and pressed the play button. While Berto was checking out the woman's ass for several seconds, he popped another Peppermint Pattie into his mouth, checked his watch, and strolled out of view. Again, a momentary flicker and the scene shifted, this time to the basement of the garage. The lighting wasn't nearly as good. A series of wide shadows crossed horizontally. Cars were parked nose-in on both sides. Berto appeared and was walking away from the camera. Only the back of his head and sweatshirt were in the field of view but it was Berto, taking ten steps, checking his watch, looking left, then right, finally ducking between two cars and exiting stage right.

The scene flickered. "We're jumping ahead here." Frank used the remote control to fast-forward more than a minute. Automobiles whizzed by like they were stock cars on a tight track. Finally a big white Cadillac zoomed through the field of vision. When its brake lights came on Frank hit play.

A woman in a short jacket stepped into the shot so that she too was photographed from behind. She had short hair and was slowly walking away from the camera. When she was nearly out of view, she stopped, evidently noticing something off-camera.

Frank readied the remote, aiming it at the black videocassette recorder, his index finger poised over the pause button.

The woman waited several seconds, took a single step forward, hesitating as she turned slightly....

Pause.

Part of the side of her face could be seen. Kensey swallowed and reached for the bottle of water. She took two swigs and wiped her mouth with the back of her hand.

"The second I saw this," Frank said, "I wondered if it was you."

Already Kensey's head was shaking back and forth. "I've never been in that building."

"You sure?"

"Yeah. I don't even have a jacket like that. You can check my closet."

Frank leaned close to the TV. "I believe you. It almost looks like she has a mole on her cheek just like you do."

"It's not me."

Frank hit play. The woman took half-a-dozen steps, angled off to the right, then slipped out of view. The screen was filled with a still scene of cars and concrete.

"This woman might have witnessed a murder."

Kensey did not respond.

The older gentleman with the hankie and his date strolled toward the camera and leisurely moved out of camera range. Frank stopped the video. "Unfortunately, some of the cops here act first when it comes to obstruction of the administration of law and ask questions later."

Kensey swallowed. "Are you accusing me of something?"

"I'm not one of those cops, Kensey. I just want you to know people get arrested for withholding information, that's all."

Kensey stood. "If there's nothing else, Detective, I've got to get back to work." She headed for the door.

"Unfortunately, the resolution's not good enough to pull off a license plate. There's only a little more—"

But Kensey was striding toward the door. A sharp yank on the handle and she was gone.

Frank Hennessey sat by himself and sipped his coffee. He aimed the remote control and played the VCR. The video image flickered. It continued along without anything happening while Frank had time to take half- a-dozen breaths.

Off to the right and far away there was a bright burst of light, as if someone took a flash photograph. Twenty seconds later there was another. He sipped his coffee, placed the cup on the table, reached for the remote, and aimed it. Reentering from the right was the same woman, her head now turned sharply toward her left. She took several steps into view, turned away from the camera, put both hands to her mouth, and appeared to be staring at something in horror that the camera could not see. Again, Frank froze the image. He was staring at that mole on her right cheek, thinking about Kensey and smelling the last whiff of her perfume. This went on almost a minute before Frank hit the eject button.

Before he bolted from the room he pulled the videocassette from the machine, used his thumb and forefinger to snag enough of the videotape so he could start pulling it out of the cassette. It took less than a minute, the pile of shiny brown spaghetti growing on his lap. Before it became unmanageable, he heaped it on the table. Finding a white bag adorned with golden arches in the trash can, he stuffed the whole mess into it and dropped it back with the rest of the garbage.

23

Alec started the sauce when he arrived home. Onions and garlic in a sauté pan with oil. Then a can of tomato sauce, another of plum tomatoes. A teaspoon of sugar. Basil and parsley. Two mashed anchovies and he resisted the urge to doctor it up any more. The recipe was his mother's, written on a greasy three-by-five card in her peculiar little scrawl. He baked a dozen meatballs, then plopped them into the sauce. Finally he prepared the eggplant, cutting it into slices, dredging them in an egg bath and bread crumbs, and then deep-frying until they were just this side of crispy.

By the time Kensey rang the bell he'd assembled eggplant parmigiana with a layer of sliced meatballs and had it bubbling in the oven.

"Smells like Little Italy in here," Kensey said when he opened the door and handed her a glass of wine. In one hand she had a green garbage bag. Plopping it on the floor, she leaned in for a kiss. Before they sat down in the living room, she demanded two more and a hug, and she breathed him in.

"Something happened today," she said on the couch. Her legs were folded beneath her. They were sitting close enough to kiss if the mood moved them. She could smell his aftershave. She glanced around at the surroundings, the photograph wall, the masculine furnishings. The bottle of red wine on the counter reminded her to take a sip. "Remember the police officer I told you about who was investigating the shooting?" Alec nodded. "He was waiting for me today. He made me go down to the station."

Alec leaned forward to place his glass on the table. Kensey saw the muscles in his jaw tighten. His hand was shaking and the wine sloshed around in his glass as if he were drunk. "Why the hell would he do that?" There was a tone to his voice that was new to Kensey. An edge, an element of fear or anger, she couldn't decide which. But he was different, that's all she could tell for sure, and that surprised her.

"I'll get to that."

"No," he said, "Tell me now." His chest was heaving as he breathed. "Jesus Christ, did you tell anyone?"

Kensey gave him a hard stare. He could hear her breathing. Gently and deliberately, she placed her glass on the table. The front door was across the room and next to the kitchen. She stood and started walking.

"Wait a second, what's going on?" When she ignored the question and kept beelining toward the door, he pushed himself up. "Kensey, where're you going?"

She was bending over to grab the garbage bag, refusing to look back at him. He moved quickly across the room. Her hand grabbed the knob. Almost immediately his hand was on top of hers. But gently. She tugged the door open and he said, "One minute, Kensey. I know I just said something wrong. Just give me a minute."

She stood there, hand on polished brass, focusing on the street and the boxwood hedges. "Go ahead." She spoke crisply, no anger that he could pick up.

"I'm sorry. I know you wouldn't say anything. That was a stupid, insensitive thing I just said."

She turned toward him, eyes shiny wet. "You're goddamned right it was."

"Kensey, we've both been through something horrible. I don't know if I'm always going to react the right way."

"You saved my life. And if you think I would do anything ... *anything* ... to put you at risk—"

He placed his arms on her shoulders and kissed her.

"I'm gonna make mistakes. That just popped out of my mouth." He kissed her again.

"Now will you let me tell you what happened?"

Alec nodded. Kensey closed the door, dropped the green garbage bag back on the floor, and returned to the couch. Before sitting down he snatched his glass from the table and downed it in three swallows.

"He showed me a security video, the guy coming into the building."

"Who? Berto?"

"Yeah. And let's not call him that. Please. It's creepy, you know, like we know him."

"Sorry."

"It was like a dream. He's riding the escalator, eating a Peppermint Pattie, gawking at some woman with huge breasts."

"Was the cop watching you to see if you were surprised?"

"How'd you know that? And he made a point of telling me about the guy's children, like if I knew him personally I would open up. Then he froze his face on the screen and asked me if I had ever seen him."

"What'd you do?"

"I went like this." Kensey leaned forward, squinted, and shook her head back and forth.

"Can I apologize again?"

"Just give me a kiss." She leaned in close and tasted him.

"We okay?"

"Yes." Another kiss. "So, then there's video of him in the garage, ducking between the cars." She was silent for several seconds. Her voice was very quiet when she said, "And there's some video of me."

"Where?"

"In the garage." Quickly she added, "Don't worry. There's nothing of us together. Or you. When you were sneaking up you must've gone off to the side out of camera range."

"What could you see?"

"Just a brief shot of my face."

"So he knows you were there."

She shook her head. "I don't think so. The lighting was awful. When I was waiting for this Cadillac to go by, the lights on the ceiling were acting up."

"Okay," Alec said, sounding the way Kensey imagined him doing during one of his board meetings. In control. "First thing tomorrow morning you see my attorney."

"No. I told you, he wasn't sure who it was. The woman had short hair and," Kensey touched her mole, "a little mole. It could've been a lot of women. He wouldn't have let me walk out of there if he was sure."

"He have *any* more pictures of you?"

She shook her head. "In that bag over there is the outfit I wore just in case the detective wants to check my closet."

Alec smiled. "God, you're good."

"Alec, I swore to you the other night I would take this to my grave. And nothing's changed. But the whole time I was sitting in that little room drinking that crappy coffee, I was thinking maybe we should have gone to the cops that night. I mean, we could have told them he was trying to mug me."

Alec pulled away and gently placed his hands on Kensey's shoulders. "Listen to me. Even if we convinced the cops it was a mugging that got out of control, Detective Romero and Sonny would know different. And maybe with all the publicity, that other cop, Mike, maybe he'd pay you a visit." He squeezed her shoulders, not enough to hurt but enough to let Kensey know he was upset. "I swear it was the right call. I'm not wrong about this." He walked over to the kitchen and came back with the bottle of wine. As he neared the sofa he held the bottle aloft.

"Please," she said and held up her glass.

Alec filled their glasses, expertly twisting the bottle before pulling it away to prevent a drip. "So," he said after he settled back down on the sofa, "where do we go from here?"

"I imagine Manny — Detective Romero — will be discharged from the hospital in the next two, three days."

"Good. I can't wait for him to get out of your life."

"Don't worry. He's going south and says he'll never come back. After that, I imagine things will feel back to normal."

Alec waited, held his glass between two hands as if he had something weighty to say. "You ask Detective Romero what he knows about Sonny?"

Kensey nodded. "Says he met him once, in a bar. Sonny talked to him and Mike. Before they knew it, they were on the payroll. After that Mike was the go-between."

"You believe him?"

Kensey sipped her wine and let some time go by. "No. He's a cop. He would have checked the guy out. Don't get me wrong. When he says he fixed it so I'm safe, I believe him. Manny'd never hurt me, but he wouldn't rat out someone either. He knows who Sonny is."

"I'd like it if you stayed with me until the detective is long gone."

"Let's see how well you cook Italian."

■ ■ ■

"The doc ain't gonna surprise me walking in or anything?" Mike was standing inside the door, leaning back, using his shoulder blades to push it closed.

"She left a half hour ago. Said you gotta get medical help."

"The fuck does she know." Mike opened and closed his mouth like he was miming someone screaming, doing it a bunch of times. "Bullshit I got lockjaw."

"She ain't sneaky."

Mike gimped across the room, holding his thigh with one hand. He was getting worse. Manny could see him sweating, his light blue shirt sticking to him. He sat in the straight-back chair, not backwards as he usually did. Right away he bent over to one side so he could fish a can of Skoal from his pocket. "Look, I can't stay long. Just wanted to see how you're doing."

"Pretty good."

"When're you getting out?"

"What's the big deal when I'm getting out? Jesus. You have to say it every time you walk in?"

"It's what you say when you visit someone in the hospital. Just want to know how you're doing."

"Maybe a week."

"That long, huh?" Mike packed a pinch between his gum and cheek. The can still opened, he held it out. Manny waved him off.

"I go home, do some packing, then I'm outta here."

"Let me know, I can give you a lift."

Manny used the remote control to turn the volume on the television louder. "You didn't say nothing more to Sonny did you?"

"Fuck no." Mike worked his tongue around the tobacco. "Sonny finds out you're gone he's gonna come after me for the address."

"Come with me. Like we talked about."

Mike shrugged. "You leaving town and all, how come you ain't said nothing 'bout the money?"

"Half of it's mine."

"I don't gotta be telling you this ain't the time to divvy it up."

"Listen, we're partners, right? 'Partners' means half is mine."

"I know what 'pardners' means. I'm just not sure we're fifty-fifty."

Manny pushed himself up on an elbow. "I said to myself yesterday this was a conversation we're gonna have." His eyes went wide. "Fuck you. We're fifty-fifty from the get-go and you know it."

"We ain't at the beginning no more. You wanna hear some numbers?"

"Start with five hunnerd large."

"Give or take."

"No, it's five hunnerd," Manny said. "No give. No take. Just like you said in the car before Cheap Charlie's."

"Done. We got five hundred between the two of us." Mike held up a finger. "One. I did Seymour Rosen by my lonesome." He popped a second finger to join the first one. "Two. Alec Fortune we got paid for but got pulled off. I ain't the one fucked up Charlie Hawk."

"There was no goddamn way to know there was another shooter."

"He put a bullet in you, he didn't open your mouth."

"We went through that already, why I did it, so let's not go through it again."

"Someone wants to be a religious nut and all that crap, I don't have a problem. But explain me why it ain't a sacrilege a guy does the shit you been doing?"

"You'd be a better person you had some faith."

"Before this happened you're spouting off 'bout religion all the time. Since you been in here, you keeping the faith, baby?"

"I pray every day. I pray for you too." Manny's fingers dug around in the matted hairs of his chest and unearthed his cross. He kissed it. "Anyway, I figure I'm good for my half of the money."

"Okay, okay, so let's say you get two-fifty."

"Good."

"I did Seymour Rosen."

"You said that already."

"I figure I get your take for that. That's fifty."

Manny sighed. "Fine, so two hunnerd."

"Whoa." Mike pulled back on imaginary reins. "Sonny wants back for Mr. Fortune."

"You're gonna nickel-and-dime me down to nothing."

"That's why it ain't the time to divvy up the money."

Manny eased back in the bed. His eyes searched the ceiling. "Forget it. I don't need it where I'm going."

"For all I know, one a' Sonny's guys is watching me."

"What's that mean?"

"I'm looking over my shoulder is what it means."

Manny rolled on his side toward Mike. Quietly he said, "Something happen?"

Mike stroked his stubbly mustache. "Nah, nothing specific. Just a gut feeling."

"I'm telling you, come with me."

"Just so there's no misunderstanding, anything happens, I take care of number one."

"What's that s'posed to mean?"

"Wasn't for the doc poking her nose into things—"

"I tol' you she's off limits." Manny pointed a thick finger at Mike.

"No, Sonny said she's off limits 'cause of that list. I don't take orders from you. It turns out Sonny's coming after me? his word ain't worth shit anymore. By the way, I checked her out. Hangs with a chick's got this real curly hair. Maybe I go talk with her some time, wrap her up like a burrito, find out where the fuckin' list is."

"Kensey gave me her word."

"The doc's a liability. The fact that you trust her makes you a liability."

Manny slammed his fist into the mattress. "Anything happens to you's my fault, not hers. You come after me you got a problem."

"Don't think I won't." They stared at each other. "Hey, I gotta go." Mike pushed up and turned toward the door.

"Yo, Mike. This didn't go right. Come back tomorrow. I'll get her to give me something for your spasms."
Mike turned around. "Oh yeah?"
"What time?"
"After my shift. 'Bout seven." He headed toward the door and pulled it open. "You'n me are pardners. I know. Six months from now only thing you'll remember is her body and she won't remember that much about you." He walked into the hallway.

24

Frank Hennessey cruised into the Riverside Garden Apartments. Ten AM and the gravel lot was mostly empty. Not one of the cars was worth looking at, Fords and Chevys, older models with crooked tailpipes and rusty pockmarks. Four red-brick buildings were arranged in rows of two, laundry flapping on the line out back and busted tricycles in front. Frank was wearing a tweed blazer, no tie. He headed for Building 3. Out front two toddlers were chasing after a basketball. No one was watching them.

The lobby was small and dark. No furniture, an empty pizza box on the floor and flyers for a Chinese restaurant on the wall. Hallways headed left and right. A handwritten sign with the words *odd* and *even* and arrows pointing left and right sent him to the left and toward 107. Passing several doorways, he caught snippets of game shows and talk shows.

He knocked on the door and waited. Music was playing on the other side, rap music with a heavy beat. He couldn't make out the words even when he stood still and turned with his head sideways so his ear pointed at the door.

He knocked again, this time harder. From inside, a woman's voice said, "Yo, is that the door?"

Another woman's voice answered that she didn't hear nothing.

He knocked a third time, five raps hard enough to hurt his knuckles. One of the voices said, "I'm naked, get the door."

After the sound of footsteps, the music stopped. Frank waited. The music started again, more rap, this time a different artist. At last the door opened to the limits of the chain. "What?" a woman's voice said.

It was dark on the inside. Frank couldn't see who was peering out at him, just an eye blinking through the narrow opening. He said, "Uh, is Mary Patterson here?"

"Mary Patterson." She sounded surprised. "Who wants to know?"

The smell of marijuana leaked into the hallway. "I'm Frank Hennessey. Is Mary home?"

"Wait." The door closed and the woman hollered, "Mary." She waited. "Mary, some boy's here to see you, dressed up nice." The way she said "Mary" with a high-pitched girly voice sounded like she was making fun of Mary and Frank at the same time.

Another woman said, "Who is it?"

"It's Frank, your date."

Frank stood in the hallway at ease, hands behind his back, staring at the pine door. Across the hall one of the neighbors opened her door and stared at him.

"Why the hell're you calling me that?" Mary said on the other side of the door. She didn't sound angry. More confused. Finally, the door opened two or three inches, the chain still doing its job. A bloodshot eye checked him out. Before either of them could say a word the door pushed closed and Frank could hear Mary whisper in a way he was supposed to hear,

"Quick, put the drugs an' shit away. It's the *po - lice*." Feet with heavy shoes clunked off bare floors but Frank thought it sounded like someone jogging in place right next to the door, the sound not changing in volume one little bit.

Frank picked up on the sound of the chain being undone. The door pulled opened halfway and Sapphire stood there in a pink fluffy bathrobe with her long hair pinned back in a thick ponytail. "Why, Detective," she said in a breathless voice. "No drugs or shit here." Affecting a seductive pose, she opened the door the rest of the way.

Frank wondered if she knew she was doing Marlene Dietrich. He hesitated for just a second.

"Detective, are you coming," she said and drew the word out to make it sound dirty, "or going?"

"Just wanted to ask you a question."

"You look scared, Detective, like a virgin. I only bite after I get paid." She ran her tongue around her lips.

Frank took several steps into the apartment. It was shadowy, the only light from an expensive-looking television in the corner with the sound too low to hear. A sofa and a kitchen chair were arranged in front of it. Now the smell of marijuana was thick.

"What the hell're you looking at?" Sapphire said behind him, sounding pissed off. Frank swung around rapidly. The door across the hallway slammed shut. Sapphire gave her own door a dainty little push. It closed quietly. "Now that's better, Detective."

"The other day—"

"You shoulda seen the look on your face when I said hi to Kensey."

"I'm sure I looked surprised."

"That whole thing 'bout the hooker bench? That was for you, baby."

He could feel his cheeks glowing. "You mentioned something about Captain Adkins and a nickname."

"And what did I mean by that?" It was obvious she liked how this was going.

"Yeah."

"Don't think I didn't catch you putting your hand on her back like you were gonna protect her from me'n Beej. I know you got the hots for her."

"That's not true."

"I seen the way you looked at her."

"You're wrong."

"Then you just here as a cop?"

"Yes. Tell me about the captain's nickname."

"Why didn't you ask her yourself?" Frank opened his mouth to say something. Sapphire wouldn't let him. "Lemme guess. You either asked Kensey and she wouldn't tell you or you didn't have the balls. Unzip so I can see."

"I'm worried about her. She's in trouble. Now what about that nickname?"

"She still over the medical center?"

"Am I wasting my time?"

"Talking to a girl like me ain't never a waste of time." She waited a beat. Then: "What kind of trouble?"

"So is that where you met her, at the medical center?"

"Un-uh." Sapphire dug in the pocket of her pink robe and came out with a crooked cigarette with rolled ends. She lit it, took a long drag, and slowly let out her breath. "Met her on the hooker bench. You want a hit of this?"

"I'm good."

"Jamaican."

"So how *do* you know her?"

"What kind of trouble she's in?"

"Look, all I want to know is about that nickname."

"This like an interrogation? You ask the questions and I don't."

"That's right."

Sapphire held the joint between two fingers like it was a Virginia Slim, placed her hand on hip, and said, "Listen to me, Mr. *Po* - lice Officer."

"Maybe I should go."

"Time for you to be quiet, Frank. It's my turn. Don't you be giving me that crap 'bout Kensey being in trouble and you here to help. You need something from her and when you get it you'll forget about her. That's the way cops are." She pointed a finger with a big ruby ring at him. "Chick don't go out the window in the *po* - lice station, the cops not fucking with her."

"What are you talking about?"

"Me'n B.J. saw the whole thing. She's on her way to talk with Captain Adkins, the next thing you know she hightails it up the stairs like she seen a ghost. Never came back down. Now, less you got other bidness with me, I gotta mow the lawn down at the Y and hit the street." She took a puff of the joint and walked past Frank and into the dark of the hallway, a wispy trail of smoke behind her.

■ ■ ■

Manny was sitting in the chair, a white sheet around his waist, Turkish-towel style, his feet bare on the linoleum floor. The

Pleur-evac was silent, a clamp compressing the chest tube that snaked its way to the foot of his bed. The television was on but he was angled toward the door, fixating on it, the remote control loosely in his hand.

The door opened and Kensey smiled at him. Right away the volume was raised to camouflage levels. "Come in quick," he said, "We gotta talk." He reached out and patted his bed, the sheets and pillowcases looking crisp. "The nurse just made it up."

"Reversal of roles."

"I guess so," he said in a hurry. "Look, I need to ask you a favor. Last one ever."

"That's three."

"Good things come in threes. Father, Son, Holy Spirit."

Sitting on the very edge of the bed, Kensey frowned. "What?"

Manny smiled. "You look pretty. You always look pretty."

Several feet above their heads the television went to a newsbreak about the Children's Hospital of Pittsburgh. Businessmen in dark suits and white hard hats were gathered around a skinny little kid who was digging the first shovel of soil from the site of the new hospital. After a round of applause the story continued, a reporter interviewing some of the businessmen about the fund-raising campaign.

Kensey and Manny were unaware of the excavation, Kensey saying "Enough."

A familiar voice filled the room. Alec Fortune was chatting informally with the reporter.

Kensey's gaze drifted up toward the TV. Manny saw this and followed close behind. For less than a second Alec's face filled the screen, a triumphant grin on his face.

Neither Kensey nor Manny uttered a word, silence filling the void until another face filled the screen and the reporter was asking someone else a question.

"Enough?" Manny's voice repeating the last thing he'd heard her say, his eyes on Kensey's face as she gawked at the television.

"What?" She realized he was staring at her and smiled uncomfortably.

"You said 'enough.'"

"I did? Oh, yeah. Enough with the you-look-pretty stuff."

"No, I mean it."

The way he was scrutinizing her face made her wonder if he knew what was going on with Alec.

"You look like you've been on vacation or something. Rested."

"All right, Manny. Tell me what you want," she said, sounding like an older sister onto her brother's bullshit.

"No, really. I told you in the ED you were pretty. I 'member that. You look like you're — I don't know — in love."

Kensey didn't have an answer for this one. She blinked several times and looked up at the TV. Some shiny new cars were being shown.

"You got a boyfriend or something?"

"I don't know."

"What's he like?"

Facing him, she placed one hand over the other in the shape of a T, the way football coaches do to stop the clock. "Too personal."

"Hey, c'mon, what kind of guy gets a sharp girl like you?"

Kensey smiled. "That's one of the nicest things anyone's ever said to me. You better ask your favor 'cause right now I'm buttered up."

He leaned toward her and dropped his voice. "Me'n Mike got paid a lot of money. Maybe half a million dollars."

"All from Sonny?"

"Yeah. Like I tol' you, Mike was the go-between. Sonny paid him and he kept the money in his house in a safe. Just so you know, I don't want the money. Okay?" He waited for Kensey to nod. "Not a cent. You know I'm not the same guy I was a week ago. Anyway, yesterday me'n Mike got to talking about the money. All Mike's doing is wheeling and dealing. Long story short, he ain't gonna give none of it to me."

"If you don't want the money—"

"The sister at the church? I want her to get it."

"So is that why you wanted your car? You're going to steal it?"

"No way. As soon as I get out of here I'm on the fastest road south." He looked at Kensey, gave her time to think about it. When she looked at him with big eyes he said, "Like I said in the ED, you look like a Good Samaritan."

Kensey raised her voice. "You want *me* to break into Mike's house?"

"Shhhh." He quickly glanced at the door, then back at her. Quietly: "Are you crazy?"

"There's a key hid under the mat in the back of the house. He's got a wall safe in the kitchen, back of where he keeps the cereal. Combination's twelve, seventeen, thirty-two. The whole thing'll fit in one a' those green garbage bags."

"And what if he shows up—"

"He won't."

"How can you be sure?"

Manny leaned back and grinned. He looked as though he was having a good time.

"What're you smiling at?"

"You always tip your hand."

"About what?"

"You're asking questions."

"What's wrong with asking how you're sure?"

"You don't ask a question like that you're not thinking of doing it."

"It's just a question. Don't attach any meaning to it."

"No way. This is B and E, and you know it. Right away you're thinking how it's gonna work instead of why you're not gonna do it. I been a cop long enough to know when somebody's brain kicks into high gear."

"Can we talk about something else?"

"I swear to you, Mike won't be a problem."

"Manny," she said in a way to let him know to shut up and listen. "They're serious about knowing when you're getting out of here."

"Who? Sonny?"

She nodded. "A guy named Berto tried to scare it out of me."

"The guy killed in the garage?"

"I tell you what happened, it's just between us?"

"Same as what I tell you."

Kensey went through the story, ending with how her 'friend' came to the rescue.

"I bet it was your boyfriend."

This surprised Kensey enough that she held her hands out to the side, palms up. "That's the part of the story you're interested in?"

"The other part, it don't change things much. Yesterday? Mike asked me the same damn thing. I wanna be sure I'm heading south on Seventy before anyone realizes I'm gone."

"So I can discharge you whenever?"

"What's your boyfriend, some kind a' cop?"

"No."

"He carries a gun."

She shook her head. "He surprised Berto and took the gun away from him."

"What'd you tell him, he was mugging you?"

Her mouth went dry. "Yes."

"You hang onto this guy. I'm serious."

"Tell me how you know Mike won't show up."

Manny gave a toothy smile. "He's coming here tonight around seven."

"Tonight? I can't do it tonight, I have—"

"Time's running out." Manny glanced down at the silent Pleur-evac. "This thing could be out in a day or so. Besides, you don't want to be thinking about it, getting yourself all worked up. He's coming 'cause I promised him I'd get a salve for his leg from you." Manny opened the drawer on the little bedside table and pulled out a half-used tube of Neosporin. "Nurses squirt this around the chest tube. I figured I'd hand it to him. While he's here we'll shoot the shit. Even if he doesn't stay it takes more'n twenty minutes to get to his house from here. I figure you call here couple minutes after seven. I say something like 'No, this's room seven-twenty-four, Mr. Covington's next door, you better call the nurses' station.' You'll know he's sitting right in that chair."

"Should I wear surgical gloves?"

"That's a good idea."

"What if someone sees me going in?"

"Seven o'clock it's pretty dark. He's got all sorts of trees'n bushes on the side. Drive by the house a couple minutes early, make sure it's just like I tol' you before you walk up."

"So how do I figure out your half of the money without wasting time?"

"That's why you need one a' those big green garbage bags. Give the sister the whole thing."

"Oh, Manny, I don't know."

"Hey," he said. "Twelve, seventeen, thirty-two. The key's under the mat."

25

"Vodka martini, Ketel One, and—" Alec arched an eyebrow toward Kensey, caught her eye and said, "A glass of white wine?"

The waitress nodded. Before she could move, Kensey said, "Better make mine a Diet Coke."

With a deferential smile the waitress headed for the long wooden bar running the length of the narrow restaurant.

"Are you on call?" Alec glanced around Tessaro's, a cozy little grill not far from Kensey's rental in Highland Park. The place was starting to fill up. Soon it would be three deep at the bar waiting for tables. He eyed the specials on a blackboard above her head.

"No, I've got to go back to the hospital and do my discharge dictations. Otherwise they withhold our paychecks. Don't worry, I'll be ready for a nightcap before bed."

"They've got lamb chops. That might be good."

Glancing toward the back of the restaurant she could look into the kitchen through a picture window. One of the cooks was dropping a thick burger on the grill.

"You okay?" Slipping her hand in his, he gave it a little squeeze.

The drinks arrived. Kensey gazed at him and smiled weakly. "Fine."

"Here, give me your other hand, it's jumping all over the place."

Briefly they did the two-handed-lovers thing across the small table. Pretty soon she giggled and lowered her eyes to the drinks and said, "Unless they're bringing straws," and wriggled free of his grasp. Every time the door opened a blast of autumn air whipped across the table and they had to grab the little cocktail napkins to keep them from flying away. Tonight she kept her dark maroon jacket buttoned, the collar up. She sipped her Diet Coke. "It's one of those days I'll be happy when it's over."

"I know you well enough to know something's bothering you."

"Manny Romero's going to be discharged soon."

He sipped his drink and savored the vodka and what she'd just said. "So what's the bad news?"

"Medically, it's terrific. Soon as he walks out of the hospital, they're going to be waiting for him."

Alec took his time, glancing left and right, before asking, "You told him about Berto?"

"No. He knows it's a race to get out of town before someone shoots him. He made me sneak him a pair of scrubs 'cause his clothes were ruined. And he wants me to discharge him without anyone knowing."

"You're too emotionally involved."

"It's not that I like him." She took a drink, knowing the way she said it sounded defensive. "It's just that … I understand him. You know *The Sopranos*? He's like Tony. A killer we love because we know him."

"Manny Romero is not Tony Soprano. Maybe we should order."

"No matter how bad you are, you've got some good inside. You know what Manny said to me?"

"What."

"He wishes he could give all the money Sonny's paid him to charity."

Alec sipped his drink. "He's working you."

She pulled back and frowned. "Why would he *work* me?"

"Because you know enough to put him in jail for about a hundred years. Because you're a variable he can't predict."

"He's not working me."

"He's such a good person he won't tell you who Sonny is."

"If you knew him you'd understand it's the way he's constructed. He wouldn't rat out anybody."

Alec, his hand on the table, pointed a finger at her. "You be careful around this guy. He's clouding your judgment."

"What I'd like him to do is go to jail. But that's not going to happen."

"So, when's he out of our lives?"

"Three, four days, max. Now we can order."

Alec leaned over the table and grabbed the finger of a surgical glove that was poking out of Kensey's side pocket. It released with a snap. "In case you have to do surgery on the way home?" He chuckled.

Kensey snatched the glove back, then threw in a seductive smile. "Hey, nosy, how do you know it's not for later?"

They both laughed and something must have caught Alec's eye because he abruptly turned his head to the left and then back toward Kensey. "Oh, my God. My dad just walked in."

"Where?"

Standing inside the door was a silver-haired gentleman, perfect posture, handsome in a camel's hair topcoat with a Burberry scarf around his neck. He was alone.

Pushing back from the table, Alec whispered, "I didn't tell him any of the stuff about Sonny. He'd go crazy." He took a single stride away from the table, turned around, and said to Kensey, "Or you." Before she could react, he was across the narrow room, greeting his father with a big hug. Kensey studied the two in conversation, Alec pointing toward her one time as if he were talking about her. As the senior Mr. Fortune unwound his scarf from his neck he rolled his eyes at Alec and shook his head as if he'd heard enough.

Finally the two men approached the table and Kensey thought she was getting a glimpse of the future. The senior Fortune was a good-looking man with a thick shock of hair and an eye for fashion. He looked sharp in a brown blazer over a powder blue shirt and silk rep tie. Kensey stood as Alec placed a hand on his father's back and said, "Pop, say hi to Kensey Shaw. Kensey, my dad."

After the how-do-you-dos the three of them sat around the table, the senior Mr. Fortune quickly catching the eye of a passing waitress and calling out, "Chivas, neat." Then he placed his elbows on the table and turned toward Kensey with an expression on his face that made her think what he was about to say was important. "So Kensey Shaw, you must be something special for my son to dash across the room to warn me to be on my best behavior."

"Dad, please."

He glanced back at his son. "I didn't even have my coat off—" The waitress placed a small glass of scotch in front of him, he thanked her, took a generous swig, looked like he was enjoying the moment, and continued where he'd left off. "He says to me, 'Pop, don't embarrass me. And no funny stuff.'" He winked at Kensey so Alec wouldn't see.

"Alec speaks very highly of you."

Mr. Fortune looked back at Alec. "She's a good liar. I like that." He drained his glass.

"No, it's true," Kensey said with a smile.

Mr. Fortune placed his hand on her forearm in a nice way. In a soft voice he said, "I'm teasing. But I can't remember Alec—" He looked at his son, his hand not moving from its perch on Kensey. "Okay I call you Alec? Or are we formal tonight, Alexander?"

Alec chuckled, "Alec is fine."

Mr. Fortune said to Kensey, "He had one nickname, you know."

Alec leaned forward. "Dad," he said sharply and squirmed in his seat.

The elder Fortune continued: "Stinky." He laughed and brought his glass to his lips but it was empty. Holding it up in the air, he signaled the waitress.

"Pop, didn't you say you were meeting some people?"

Mr. Fortune looked around the room and nodded to a small group standing at the door. "Next time I see you I'll tell you why we called him Stinky." Patting Kensey's arm, he said, "Nice to meet you, dear." He pushed up from the table, squeezed his son's shoulder, and said, "Give me a call tomorrow. I've got an idea we can run with." In a loud voice he greeted his friends as the waitress handed him a fresh drink and strode away from the table.

Quietly Alec said, "You can't choose your relatives," and slapped a silly grin on his face to emphasize the point. Draining his glass and holding it aloft the same way his dad had, he said, "So tell me about those gloves."

"I thought we'd play doctor." She shot him a mischievous smile.

"Anything else in there?" Alec made a playful grab for her pocket. "Hey, what's that?" he asked and fingered something through the fabric of the jacket.

"Now you've ruined it." She pulled out a little penlight that had a pharmaceutical logo on the side. "A drug rep gave it to me today, but if it's not a surprise it's no good." She stuffed the glove and penlight back into her pocket.

"What time are you coming over?"

"Nine."

"Nine," he said, sounding whiny. "Manny gets to see you more than I do."

"But you get to see more of me." She checked her watch. "What about those lamb chops?"

■ ■ ■

The house was on a quiet street, a two-story clapboard with a tiny porch in front, a driveway off to the side, and three or four sturdy pine trees protecting the other. Kensey cruised by slowly. No lights were on, but the other houses on the block were lit up. She liked how thick the pines were. Motoring down the block, she made the turn and rolled to a stop.

It was just before seven. Pushing a single button on her cell phone, she waited several seconds before a voice picked up.

"Hello."

"Is this Mr. Covington?"

"You're a few minutes early. You seen the house yet?"

"Yeah, it reminds me of yours, the porch and everything."

"I got mine first. Hey, I don't want to be on the phone when he gets here. Call me back."

The line went dead. Kensey checked her watch, decided to give it ten minutes, and dialed Alec's number. She told him she was down in medical records signing charts and playing with the little penlight. He said he was sorry for coming on so strong about Manny and she said, No, she appreciated his concern. Then he wondered exactly what she'd planned for him with the surgical gloves and the penlight and Kensey acted like her battery was going dead and cut him off in mid-sentence. The last thing he said was something about how she really should tell him because he couldn't even concentrate on the television.

Now it was ten after seven. Dialing the phone, she took a deep breath.

"Hello."

"Is this Mr. Covington?"

"No, Covington is in seven-twenty-two. You better call the nurses' station." Manny didn't say anything for several seconds, mumbled "No problem," and hung up.

Kensey got out of the car and headed down the street. She walked slowly. When she reached Mike's house she twirled around, experiencing a vertiginous view of his neighborhood. The street was empty. Turning toward the house, she took determined strides across the lawn and ducked between two pines and into the gloom of the thick branches. Now the footing was difficult with the darkness and exposed roots and she tread slowly.

Kensey snapped on the surgical gloves and moved to the back of the house.

The driveway wound around the house on the opposite side and ended in a gravel oval off the back porch. Her breathing sounded wheezy and she noticed how dry her mouth was. There were enough trees and shrubs to offer privacy, but she was starting to sweat even though she could see her breath coming out in little puffs of white.

The doormat was black rubber, torn at one corner. She grabbed it, turned it over, and snatched the key.

Mike Dombroski's back door was painted white except for an area below the knob where it was almost black. Three parallel strip windows offered a limited view of a dark kitchen. Beyond it was a living room in shades of black and gray. Before Kensey turned the key in the lock she checked her watch. Seventeen minutes after seven. No matter what, she promised herself, she'd be out of the house before seven-thirty.

The lock was stiff. She had to grab the knob with one hand while turning the key with the other and jiggle it, but the door wouldn't budge. That's when she took a step back, reared up, and kicked the door below the knob. It swung open wildly and banged off the counter. Kensey stood there with her hands over her mouth for half a minute before she could go on.

Stepping across the threshold, she closed the door until it touched the jamb. Although the penlight was new, it did a terrible job illuminating the kitchen, a spot of yellow light so small it had to be moved around so she could identify objects a little bit at a time. The sink was stacked with dishes. An oval table with two chairs had a jacket slung on the back of one. The counters were mostly empty except for a six-pack of beer and two bags of chips. The acidic smell of sauerkraut lingered from a previous meal.

Looking through to the living room she could make out a television set and some easy chairs but didn't explore further. One by one she opened cabinets until she found the one with the cereal. The last item she pulled from her pocket was a folded green garbage bag. Flipping it on the counter, she placed the penlight in her mouth and bit down on the metal clip to keep it lit. She began removing the boxes and lining them up on the counter. Frosted Flakes. Honey Nut Cheerios. Trix. As the cabinet emptied, the round knob of the safe was exposed.

A box of Cap'n Crunch was in her hand when she heard a loud click and the living room was suddenly filled with light. She dropped the box. It opened and cereal scattered over the floor. Kensey was unable to move, her mouth gaped open and her hands held in front of her as if she were still holding the box. At least a minute went by, Kensey holding the position like she was made of wax. The only thing still working was her eyes. They focused on the door to the living room and searched for shadows that moved.

The house was still.

After a while her muscles began to feel sore and she realized she was drooling around the penlight. She took a single step toward the living room and waited. Another step. Then another. One more and she was standing in the doorway peering a little deeper into Mike Dombroski's world. A single lamp was lit, on the street side of a brown-fabric recliner. Kensey could see where it was plugged into the wall by way of a black plastic box with a dial. A timer.

Now her shirt was sticking to her. She crossed the living room, stepping over newspapers and magazines and a pair of socks and turned off the lamp. The darkness was welcome. It felt safe. Briefly, she worked the penlight around the room. An old sofa was pushed against one wall. A blue aluminum baseball bat leaned in the corner with a cap balanced on top. Not far from the front door was a closet, twin louvered doors that pulled open from the middle. The floor was dark wood, nearly black, the only covering a dirty rectangular rug in the middle of the room.

Kensey returned to the kitchen and used her foot to gather the cereal in a pile.

She checked her watch. Seven-twenty-one. She moved the penlight to her mouth, grabbed the garbage bag, worked it back and forth between her fingers to separate the two sides, and was ready to pop it open with a snap of her wrists when she heard a footstep crunch on the gravel drive.

Her muscles moved all at once. By the time the garbage bag touched the floor she was halfway to the living room, around the corner, fumbling for the sofa with one hand while moving toward the closet. The doors were cheap pine. Kensey jumped inside and as she pulled the door behind her, something wedged under it so that it closed almost all the way before getting stuck.

The doorbell rang. Then it was quiet. It rang a second time. A third.

Kensey could peek out the narrow opening into the dark living room. Someone was standing on the front porch, cupping his hands against the window and leaning close to look inside. The figure moved away.

The doorbell rang again. A minute of silence followed. Kensey could hear the metallic sound of a key working the lock. The door opened and someone stepped into the room.

Kensey was crouched down, one knee on the floor. The crack between the doors was big enough for one eye.

The person clicked on a big flashlight and did a quick scan of the room. Chair, television, sofa, socks on the floor. "Fuckin' pig," a man's voice said, thick like he had a two-pack-a-day habit. Kensey could make out his shape, short and powerful. He was wearing a tight T-shirt and baggy cargo pants. His chest tapered at the waist and when the light bounced back off the television she spotted a long rattail starting at his neck and running nearly a foot down his back. Satisfied with the way the living room looked, he said to himself, "Come out, come out wherever you are." He placed the flashlight on the floor so the beam shot up to the ceiling and picked up the recliner and placed it in the middle of the room, facing away from the closet. Finally he took a seat, flashlight in hand, aiming it first toward the front door, then toward the kitchen. With little effort he could sit in the chair and keep an eye on both doors.

The man pushed out of the chair and headed into the kitchen. From the other room Kensey could hear the crunch of the cereal beneath his feet. He said, "What the fuck," loud, like he was disgusted. It was quiet after that until he came back into the living room with some beers. He reached behind his back and slipped a large handgun from a holster, plopped himself into the recliner, pushed back so the footrest snapped out, and propped up his legs comfortably. He popped a beer. "To Mike," he said, holding the beer out as if making a toast, took a thirsty mouthful, set the gun in his lap, and reached down to the floor and turned the flashlight off.

For the next half hour Kensey heard him chugging beers, crushing the cans and bouncing them off the wall. Sometime after the third one his breathing eased into a relaxed cadence and Kensey wondered if he was falling asleep. He moaned, shifted his weight in the chair, and went back to his easy respirations, drawing air in with a rattle and exhaling silently.

Kensey's leg was starting cramp. She shifted her position and was beginning the process of stretching her hamstring —

Creak. It was the sound of a squeaky floorboard, loud enough to wake the man.

She sucked in her breath and froze every muscle in her body. All she could hear was the steady sound of the man breathing. He was still asleep. Several seconds went by and now her leg was really hurting. She massaged it but the pain was getting worse. Moving very slowly, Kensey leaned forward to shift her weight to her arms so she could extend her leg —

Creak. The same sound, this time louder.

Kensey stopped thinking about her leg and was totally focused on the man in the chair. She was making too much noise. Any second she expected him to push out of the chair and yank the closet door open. Kensey peered out of her hiding place but couldn't see him stirring. More time went by. She wasn't going to move again no matter how badly her leg throbbed.

Creak. This time Kensey realized she wasn't the one making the floorboards squeak.

A silent figure slipped between Kensey's closet and the recliner. In dark silhouette he crept across the room with a limp. He was holding something in his right hand. When he was behind the chair he racked the slide of a pistol as he spoke. "I want you to place the gun on the floor. Don't drop it." Kensey recognized Mike's voice.

The man in the recliner startled. "Huh?"

"I've got a forty-four. The bullet'll go right through the chair and then through you."

The man shifted his weight. Then there was the sound of a metal object being deposited on the floor. Mike limped over to the wall and a light in the ceiling came on. He turned and moved back to the recliner, leveling a large handgun at the back of the man's head.

The man shot his hands into the air. "Hey, don't do nothing to me, man."

"Who the fuck're you?"

"The name's Jimmy."

"Okay, Jimmy, you have exactly one chance to get out of here alive."

"You're the boss, man. Just tell me how to get home."

"Any time you move, go slow."

Jimmy nodded.

"Now," Mike said, "see that rug? Stretch out on it."

Keeping his hands in the air, Jimmy knelt on the rug and slowly eased himself down on his back. Mike limped over to the recliner and pushed it off the rug. Kensey could see Jimmy's head craning around to watch every move Mike made.

"Not the long way, you idiot. The short way."

Jimmy pivoted around so that he was in the middle of the rectangular carpet, the fabric running from his shoulders to his ankles.

"Slide to your left." Mike kept an eye on what Jimmy was doing. "That's it, keep going. More … more. Stop."

Kensey could see Jimmy lying on one edge of the carpet, Seymour Rosen style.

"Reach down with your left hand, grab the rug real tight.... Tight! Not like a fuckin' pussy. That's better. Now roll to your right."

Jimmy rolled over and dragged the carpet around him. As soon as Jimmy's back was to Mike he gave him a shove with his fancy cowboy boot and winced in pain. Jimmy spun quickly, rolling over two more times. After he was mummified, Mike placed his gun on the recliner and retrieved the baseball bat from the corner. He was moving with considerable effort; each step full of pain. Placing the cap on his head, he resumed his position standing above Jimmy, taking some swings as if he was on deck.

"Gimme your full name."

"Jimmy Giordina. Back in Scranton they call me Jimmy G."

"What the fuck is it with Scranton?"

"What's the big deal?"

"Who called you?"

"Like you'n me don't know."

"You know a guy name of Comparino?"

"Who, Berto?" He saw Mike nod. "You don't wanna be calling him for no job or anything."

"Why's that?"

"He's a poser. He ain't nothing."

Mike placed his boot on Jimmy's chest. "And you are?"

"I ain't never done time. Berto gets caught lifting a pack a' gum."

"You turned off the fuckin' lamp, asshole. Why don't you put a sign outside says you're waiting for me in the dark."

"What?"

"Don't play loose with me. You're a dumb fuck. Now who sent you?"

"C'mon man, don't make me say it."

"Lemme just turn the truth machine on." Mike swung the bat and caught Jimmy where his hips were wrapped in the rug.

Jimmy screamed. "Okay, okay," he hollered. Now he was talking quickly. "Sonny. It was Sonny sent me to get the money.

That's all. I wasn't gonna hurt you. No way. Sonny said just poke the gun in your ribs and take back what you owe him."

"Your gun loaded?"

"Who carries an empty gun?" Jimmy sounded out of breath.

"Maybe Sonny said get the money and then kill me."

"No way, man. All's Sonny said was get the money. Nothing 'bout putting a bullet in you."

"So where'd you'n Sonny meet?"

"A bar in Scranton. Said a guy like me could make some serious dough working for him. And I wasn't s'posed to kill you."

"That ain't the way Sonny works." Mike walked toward the kitchen. "Grease your tongue you wanna see the sun come up."

Mike disappeared into the kitchen, the light went on, and both Kensey and Jimmy heard him call out, "Hey, you make a mess you clean it up." Jimmy began struggling, trying to roll over, wiggling his feet and knocking his head around.

After a short while Mike was back in the doorway and watched Jimmy hassle inside the carpet. "Hey, knock it off." Jimmy glared at him. "Twelve, seventeen, thirty-two. That's the combination in case somebody asks."

"Shit. What're you telling me that for?" Jimmy went spastic, thrashing his shoulders and head about, but not loosening the carpet one bit.

Mike laughed at him and went back into the kitchen. Other than Jimmy's raspy breathing it was quiet. This time when Mike wobbled back into the doorway he was holding packets of cash in both hands. "I bet you thought there was two-fifty or so here." He shook his head. "You're lucky. It's all here. Five hundred eighty." Kensey followed Mike all the way back into the kitchen. He called out, "I used some to buy the Vette." Then Kensey heard the sound of the refrigerator door being slammed, a beer was popped open, and Mike hobbled back into the room. As he went over to the lamp and reached under the shade to turn it on, he said, "No one's robbing Dodge City so long as I'm marshal." Mike eased himself down on the recliner as if he was afraid his leg would hurt, the beer in one hand, the blue bat in the other, and placed his feet on Jimmy like he was an ottoman.

"C'mon, man, I told you the truth. Sonny wants his money's all." He struggled and raised his voice. "Now let me go, goddamnit."

Mike picked up Jimmy's flashlight. "So what'd you do to get in?"

"I picked the lock."

"Then what, you're looking round for the safe and you dropped the cereal when the light went on?"

"Man, I just sat here, had a couple beers. I didn't drop no cereal and I don't know nothing 'bout a safe."

Mike one-handed the bat into Jimmy's side with a dull thump. Jimmy screamed. "What'd Sonny tell you to do?" Jimmy was whimpering. "Now, or the next one's to your head."

"Okay, okay." Jimmy's voice was shaking. "Sonny said get the money'n take you out. There, I said it. Then I'm s'posed to wait for your buddy to get out of the hospital and take care a' him too, get whatever money's he's got. That's it, on my mother's grave."

"Wasn't for the girl putting her nose where it don't belong—"

"What?" Jimmy sounded confused.

"I jus' gotta be takin' care of number one, that's all. And you, Mr. G., ain't part of the future." Mike stood and wielded the baseball bat above his head. As he took a step forward and started to bring it down, Kensey closed her eyes.

26

The phone rang two minutes after Susanne arrived home. She was wearing stiff new jeans with big cuffs that swished when she walked and a yellow T-shirt that was way more expensive than it looked. Standing at the little chrome mirror near the front door she let it ring, waiting for the machine to pick it up.

For as long as she could remember, her head had been covered with an unruly mop of red hair her mother insisted was her best feature. But she hated it. And tonight she was smiling at someone she didn't know, a woman with auburn hair streaked with wisps of blond that flowed to her shoulders without a single curlicue. Shaking her head, Susanne giggled at the way every strand fell back into place when she stopped. Her fingers luxuriated in the silkiness. The heck with the phone. It was probably her mother wanting to know how her hair looked. With a quarter-turn to the side, Susanne teased herself with a flirtatious look she might give someone in a bar who asked for her number.

Finally the machine picked up on the seventh ring. Instantly Susanne swung into a perky duet with her recorded voice, telling whomever it was that she was out and about and please leave a message. Then there was that piercing beep and a man's voice said, "Uh, hello?" Then silence. Silence that went on long enough to make Susanne turn away from the mirror and give the phone on the kitchen counter a long, hard look. "Dr. Smerdell, this is Detective Frank Hennessey with the Pittsburgh Police. I'm investigating a recent homicide. If you're home, please pick up. I wonder if this might be a good time to stop by and talk."

Before he stopped speaking Susanne was hurrying toward the kitchen, reaching for the cordless phone, fumbling with the button and trying to get it up to her ear all at the same time. "Hello."

"Dr. Smerdell?"

"Is Kensey okay?"

"She's fine." His voice reassuring. And confident. "But that's why I wanted to speak with you."

She looked at her watch. "You mean tonight? It's after ten."

"I know it's late.... I could stop by now or I could meet you at the station tomorrow morning. Either way. I'm sure Kensey's mentioned me."

"I heard about you. This has to do with Kensey?"

"And the investigation."

"Does she know you're calling me?"

"Uhhh..." He sounded confused. More silence followed and by his tone Susanne wondered if he was thinking he didn't want Kensey to know he was contacting her. "I don't want her to think I'm going behind her back. Maybe it'd be better if you didn't tell her what this was about."

"It's not anything bad, is it?"

"No, no. Cross my heart, it's nothing bad."

"I guess it's okay. You need directions?"

"You're over on Highland, three-thirty-two."

"Third house from the corner." After hanging up the phone she headed upstairs and kicked off her shoes, then slipped on a pair of light blue fuzzy slippers. A minute later she was back downstairs, passing time on the living room sofa, the cordless phone in her hand, one of her fancy throw pillows in her lap. She was staring at a repeat of *Friends* on her little Sony television. Twice she tried to phone Kensey but never got past the fourth number. When the bell rang she startled and fixed her eyes on the front door, then back at the pretty friends munching muffins in their comfy coffee shop.

Next came a knock, a loud one. She tossed the pillow aside like a Frisbee and moved toward the door.

"Who is it?" she called out six feet away.

"Frank Hennessey, we just spoke." He had a friendly way of speaking.

"Just making sure."

"You feel more comfortable seeing my badge?"

"I guess." And she reached for the gray curtain that guarded the skinny window next to the door.

The little door on the mail slot squeaked open. Detective Hennessey's voice on the other side of the door said, "Coming through," in a neighborly way, like it was no bother at all. Susanne received his black leather wallet with the gold detective's shield inside. It was embossed with the words *City of Pittsburgh* and heavier than she expected. Susanne pushed aside the drape on the side window. Liking what she saw, she opened the door.

The first thing Susanne noticed was the real friendly grin on his face. Once his eyes focused, he gave her a funny look like he wasn't sure who she was. "Dr. Smerdell?"

"That's me," she said and smiled at him as she touched her hair lightly with her fingers, making sure it wasn't caught on her ear.

"Sorry, I heard you had curly hair."

"I decided it was time for a change."

"Looks nice." He put a smile back on his face, standing on the front stoop in a brown corduroy sport coat with leather buttons and a light blue denim shirt with a wide tie that knotted poorly at the neck. He put out his hand palm up. Susanne stepped forward and placed her hand in his as if she had accepted his invitation to dance the minuet. While they shook hands the detective said, "I need that back," motioning with his head to the black wallet in her other hand. That got Susanne giggling nervously and she returned his shield and let go of his hand. She noticed her hand was moist.

On the spot Susanne agreed with Kensey. He was cute. And he was wearing cologne that smelled very masculine. She especially liked the way his hair rolled over his collar in back and curled up. "Call me Susanne. You want to come in?" she asked and took a step to the side so he had a view into her living room. As the detective crossed the threshold she was saying, "You said this was about Kensey?"

"I heard you're her best friend."

"We can talk in here," and she pointed to the sofa and easy chair. He was taller than she was by nearly six inches. She checked out his broad shoulders and as he turned to step into the living room, Susanne caught her reflection in the mirror and fluffed her hair once or twice.

When she looked back at the detective she noticed he was favoring his right leg, throwing it out each time he took a step. Then she watched him survey the room, admiring the photograph of her family on the coffee table. As he glanced at the television Susanne raced over and flicked off the picture. "I thought it was the news. Can I —uh ... get you something to drink, Detective?"

"Frank."

"Frank." She smiled.

He wiped his hand over his brow. "I been feeling sweaty all day. How 'bout a cool one?"

Susanne moved toward the kitchen, did a quick about face, and said, "I.C. Light or Zima."

"I'll go for the brew." He shot her a little wink that put a smile on her face and sent her to the refrigerator.

Calling out from the living room, he said, "In a bottle's fine. Hey, you got any Advil or something stronger?"

"Your leg?"

"I think I tore a muscle or something playing racquetball."

She returned with the beer and a bottle of Advil and handed him the beer. While he upended it and took a pull, she opened the blue-and-white bottle and shook nearly a dozen little pills into his open hand.

"Oops," she said and before she could scoop any of them back he threw them into his mouth, said "cheers," and scarfed them down them with a hit of beer. "Frank," Susanne said, "you don't know what you're doing to your liver. You should never take more than—"

"Thanks."

"—three." Susanne shook her head. "It's hard to stop being a doctor."

"Same with being a cop." He eased himself into the easy chair. "You not having anything?"

"I'll never stay awake." Susanne settled on the sofa, the detective not more than five feet away, her legs tucked under her, his legs crossed, and she noticed he was wearing thick-soled work shoes with the tie and jacket. "So ..." she said.

"You know all about Detective Romero."

Susanne nodded. "A little."

He swallowed some beer, held out the bottle to look at it, and winced.

"You don't like light beer. I've got some wine."

"That's okay. Look," he said, leaning forward, his elbows on his knees, getting down to it. "I'm worried about Kensey."

"Me too."

"Then we got to talk about some stuff. Manny Romero?" He waited for Susanne to nod. "He's getting out soon. At least that's what Kensey told me."

"We discussed him on rounds yesterday. His air leak's pretty much stopped."

"So what's that mean exactly?" He leaned back in his chair.

She watched the detective massage his leg, not the way you do with a charley horse, but gently as if too much pressure would make it worse. "That means she'll pull his chest tube. After that he's on his way."

"When?"

"A couple days."

"Two?"

"I don't know. You better ask Kensey."

"Like I said, I know she's your best friend. I don't know why she's playing her cards so close to her chest. She's hiding something."

"She's scared, that's all."

"I figure she don't like me much."

Susanne nibbled on her cuticle.

He shook his head and said, "You don't have to say nothing if you don't want."

"No, it's just that I don't know. Since she's got a boyfriend I don't see her as much."

"Let's go back to that night everything happened—"

"You mean at the church?"

"No, after. Kensey couldn't go home. Manny's partner, that Mike Dombroski, was waiting for her. She told you, right?"

"You know that?"

"Yeah."

"Then why isn't he arrested?"

"Your friend, that's why. Look, the department's totally corrupt. All sorts a' dirty cops. Christ, she barely trusts me, said if I say word one to the captain she'd deny everything. Besides, Kensey said she worked out some sort a' deal."

Susanne's eyes open wide. "A deal?"

"You don't know about that?"

"Un-uh."

"You know what went down at the church."

"You mean that cop trying to kill her?"

"Yeah." He swallowed some beer. "You know why?"

Susanne reached for the throw pillow and pulled it onto her lap.

The detective said, "Look, I didn't come over here to make you feel uncomfortable or nothing."

"No, it's just that I don't want to say something and have Kensey get mad."

"Mike Dombroski heard her in the confessional, telling the priest about the murders he and Romero committed."

She leaned forward. "That's right."

"She told you that night, when she came over here."

Susanne nodded. "Please don't say anything to her."

"Let me ask you something, Susanne. If that cop wanted her dead at the church 'cause she knows something she shouldn't know, why the hell's she still walking around?"

He watched her tug at the collar of her T-shirt. "I don't know. That's why I've been so worried about her."

"I know that you know. Kensey told me."

"I *don't* know."

"Kensey won't go to the cops so long as Manny keeps Mike off her ass."

"Really?"

"You didn't know that?" His fingers stroked his upper lip. It looked to Susanne like he was growing a nice mustache.

"No."

"Then why do you think she wrote that note?"

"What note?"

"The one she gave you for safekeeping." He sat forward and winced, putting his hand on his thigh as if he was experiencing a jolt of pain. "Just in case. Everything Manny told her in the ER was there."

Susanne looked over at the front door, then back at the detective. Her breathing had quickened.

"If you give me the note, I'll bust both their asses."

"She was pretty shook up when she got here but I swear I don't remember anything about a note."

"Listen to me. If you'n me don't do something to stop him, he's gonna kill her."

"I swear I don't know anything about a—"

"Okay, fine." Suddenly his tone was different. He sounded as if he was trying to contain himself from getting pissed off.

Susanne picked the phone up from the sofa. "Let me call Kensey and ask her where it is."

"No," he said, his voice loud enough to make her freeze. "I wanted to do this the nice way."

"What do you mean?"

"I meant we coulda had a good time together. Now I need the truth."

"But I told you the truth."

He looked down at the floor. "You just got wall-to-wall in this place or you got any rugs?"

27

"No matter what, promise you're not gonna get mad," Kensey said, coming through the front door like a gust of wind. She threw her arms around Alec's neck and hugged him hard. "God, I needed that." It was ten minutes after ten, Alec in a pullover sweater and holding reading glasses in one hand, Kensey wearing her maroon jacket.

"I'd never get—" He caught a whiff of her neck. "Whoa," he said, pulling away. "What *is* that?"

Kensey lifted her maroon jacket to her nose and sniffed. "Some baseball jersey in a closet that absolutely reeked." She kissed him. "I've got a story. No, a great story." She broke away and headed for the living room, taking big steps, bouncing off her feet. "First I need a drink."

Alec chuckled. "It's like you're on speed. What the heck's going on? I've never seen you like this." He walked over to the bar and removed two bottles. "The usual?"

"The usual. I like that." While Alec went to work on the kitchen counter she dropped onto the sofa and leaned back into the luxurious leather. "The usual," she said, almost to herself. "It sounds like we're an official couple. Anyway, for the first time I feel like this whole mess's gonna disappear very soon. Maybe tonight."

"Which mess?" Alec was moving toward the couch with two glasses, his vodka and her white wine.

Kensey reached out for the glass, a delicate piece of handblown crystal, held it up, and declared, "To you not getting angry with what I'm going to tell you," and took three noisy gulps.

"Okay, okay, enough." He sat on the edge of the sofa, angled toward her.

She shifted her body so she could look him in the eye.

"You remember Manny's partner, Mike?"

"You had a nightmare about him last night. I forgot to tell you."

"Well, I don't think he's ever going to bother me again."

"What?" He brought the vodka to his lips without looking at it.

"I broke into his house several hours ago."

"Are you crazy? What the hell did you do that for?"

Kensey went through the story. Sparing no details, she described how she had watched Mike work Jimmy over, and finally, when Mike was finished with him, how he had wielded the bat over his head.

"You watched this?"

"One hit man working over another doesn't affect me the same way it would have ten days ago. Jimmy wasn't there just to get the money. Mike got him to admit that he was brought into town to kill him. Manny too."

"So Mike's still alive?"

"Barely. He has *risus sardonicus*."

"Risus what?"

Kensey clenched her teeth together and bared them like a rabid dog, twisting her face into the most hideous grin. "It's the sarcastic smile. Mike was standing there ready to swing the bat down on Jimmy's head. It was obvious Mike was going to kill him. I closed my eyes so I didn't have to watch. Then Jimmy let out this unbelievable scream. When I opened my eyes, I saw Mike collapse on the floor. His whole body went into spasm. I got a great look at his face and saw his expression. *Risus sardonicus.*"

"What's it mean? He's crazy?"

"He's got tetanus. He's going to be dead very soon, even if he gets treatment."

"Then what happened?"

"It took Mike ten minutes to recover. He was on the floor in the fetal position. He moaned and got all sweaty. Tetanus is unbelievably painful."

"What happened to the guy in the rug?"

"Jimmy didn't know what to do. He watched the whole thing. When it looks like Mike is coming out of it he starts asking him if he's okay. You know, trying to sound like he's concerned. Mike says don't worry about it, he's just got spasms. Jimmy says maybe he should drive Mike to the hospital. Mike says no f-ing way, he doesn't have lockjaw and he says, Watch. Mike opens and closes his mouth and does it pretty well, but I could tell it was hurting him to do it."

"What was Jimmy doing?"

"He has no idea what Mike's doing opening and closing his mouth. And just like that they start talking. Mike says, 'So what's he worth?' Jimmy says something like, what who's worth? Mike goes, Manny. And Jimmy says, 'Oh, five thousand.'"

Alec said, "That's all?"

"That's what Mike said. 'That's all? Five Gs?' Sounding real surprised. Now he asks Jimmy what he's getting paid to kill him. Jimmy says, 'Five thousand ... for the both of you.' And Mike goes, 'Five thousand, Jesus Christ,' like his feelings are hurt." Her wineglass was empty. "Can I have some more?" She handed the empty glass to Alec.

He went over to the kitchen where the bottles of Ketel One and white wine stood side by side on the counter. "Keep going," he said as he refilled his glass first, drained it in three swallows, refilled it, and poured the wine for Kensey.

"Somehow, Jimmy got Mike to tell him how much he and Manny got paid."

"How much?" Alec was back on the couch.

"More than half a million. Jimmy acts real impressed and the whole time I can see it's working. Mike's gonna go easy on him. Then Mike says, 'Hey, asshole, you supposed to call Sonny after you kill me?' Jimmy says sure, you always call after a job. And Mike says that gives him a good idea. He says maybe he'll pay Jimmy twenty thousand to take out Sonny. Jimmy thinks that's a pretty good idea. They start shooting the breeze. Mike gets himself back in the Barcalounger, Jimmy's still rolled up in the rug, but they're talking like they're drinking buddies.

"Jimmy tells Mike about how he always wanted to have kids but he has a low sperm count. And Mike says he wished he had a problem like that 'cause he's knocked up three girls and they all had to get abortions. Anyway, this goes on about ten minutes. Finally, Mike says, 'Hey, how 'bout a beer?' Jimmy says, 'You bet,' and Mike limps off to the kitchen. Jimmy raises his voice so they can keep talking even though they're in different rooms. 'This sure is a weird way to meet somebody.' The refrigerator slams shut and Mike comes back into the room looking pissed. I mean, he looks like he's possessed.

He goes, 'There's only one left, where the f are my beers?' Jimmy admits he had two of them waiting for Mike. Instantly, Mike grabs the bat off the floor and ends it with one swing."

"What?" Alec's mouth was dry. He worked his tongue against the roof of his mouth and tried again. "What happened next?"

"Mike went into the kitchen and made a sandwich, came back, and turned on the TV. He took one bite and spit it out. Then he watches some sports show with his feet propped up on Jimmy's body while he drinks the last beer. When he's done he takes a shower, puts on a sport coat and tie as if he's going to work. He's barely able to drag the body out through the kitchen. When I heard him drive off I came out of the closet."

"And got the hell out of there, I hope."

Kensey sipped her wine, holding the glass with both hands. "After I opened the safe and took all the money."

"You robbed him?"

"Yep. Every penny." Kensey sat up straight and beamed.

"And the money, it's in your car?"

"No, I went over to St. John's and gave it to the sister. In case anyone asks her I—" now Kensey dropped her voice an octave, "disguised my voice."

"Does Manny know what happened?"

"I'll tell him tomorrow. Right now I need a shower."

"Maybe you're in shock."

"No, I'm pumped." She leaned toward him and threw her arms around his neck.

"You know I was thinking ... maybe it's time you and I got away. A weekend with no stress."

Kensey pulled away slightly so she could go nose to nose with him. "Sounds great."

"When I was a kid my family bought a house up in Ligonier. It's absolutely my favorite place in the world. How about if we slip away Friday night, drive up there, light a fire, get out those rubber gloves and that little flashlight …"

Kensey giggled. "Let's go now. Friday seems such a long way off."

"It's in two days. And you need a shower."

■ ■ ■

Kensey went straight up to the seventh floor the next morning. She could hear the television out in the hallway when she was saying good morning to the uniformed cop.

Manny had a scowl waiting for her when she pushed through the door. He didn't say a word until the door closed all the way. "No matter what, goddamnit, you call after a job. No … Matter … What. You hear me? Especially after what I heard happened." Sitting in his straight-backed chair, bare-chested, the chest tube spanning the distance from the chair to the foot of his bed, he was working hard to breathe, his skin sucking in under his collarbone with each breath.

She stood with her back toward the door, not bothering to take off her red coat with the toggle buttons. "Are you okay?"

"No, I am not okay, been up most of the night wondering where the hell you were."

"You're out of breath."

"I'm just pissed, that's all."

"Take some deep breaths."

Manny pulled air in and out, doing it three or four times before his breathing slowed.

"There," Kensey said. "That's better."

"Mike called me, told me he'd taken care of some punk named Jimmy, tried to take the money." He pointed a thick finger in her direction. "It's a good thing I told you do a drive-by just to make sure." He took a deep breath. "What, were the lights on?"

"Manny, slow down. The house was dark."

"So how'd you know?"

"The guy, Jimmy, he showed up *after* I was inside."

"Goddamn, I knew it went wrong."

"I'm sorry."

He nodded as though he heard her but was still pissed. "So you beat it outta there?"

"Not exactly."

"Mike told me every cent was in the safe."

"I was there. In a closet."

Manny's fingers shot up to his neck and located his cross.

"He called you after he killed Jimmy and drank a beer and watched TV."

Manny kissed his cross. "Thank God you're okay."

"I saw his disease. The next few days are gonna be ugly."

"You heard what he said about the money."

"Yeah, soon as you get out of the hospital the two of you are gonna get together to divvy it up."

"He wants to get me alone, that's all."

"After he dragged Jimmy out to the car and left all the lights on, I opened the safe and emptied it."

"You did?"

"And I delivered it to the sister just like you asked."

Manny sat there without speaking. He lowered the sound on the television. "I was really pissed at you last night for not calling."

Kensey sat quietly. Finally: "You think you'll be ready to get out of here in two or three days?"

"I still get out of breath."

Kensey knelt down and used her stethoscope to listen to his chest.

He said, "You know the cop sits out there? Not the guy there now. Rick. Does eleven to seven. He's been hitting on one of the nurses. The redhead with the knockers? Two of 'em disappear sometime around two."

Kensey said, "Take a deep breath."

Manny pulled in a lungful and coughed it out. "Damn, that hurts." He watched Kensey move the stethoscope around. "You heard what I said?"

"It hurts when you cough."

"Not that."

"Yes, I heard. And I know what you're planning to do." She stood. "Then what? No more détente?"

"All that was, was a way to get things started between you'n me."

"You said something about as long as you're in here."

"Fuck you, you don't trust me. I thought we had something better'n détente."

"Don't say that. I do trust you."

Looking her up and down he said, "Hey, I never seen you wearing your coat before."

"Oh, that reminds me," and her hand dug in one of the big side pockets.

Then he said, "He's gonna come after you, you gotta know that."

"Who, Mike?" Now Kensey sounded out of breath. Her empty hand pulled free of the pocket. "He told you that?"

"In so many words. Your friend too, one with the curly hair. What's her name?"

"What does he know about her?"

"He's sure she knows."

"When's this gonna happen?"

"You told her, didn't you?"

"Yes. When's this gonna happen?"

"Soon as I get outta here."

"How do you know?" Kensey lowered herself to the edge of the bed and crossed her arms so it looked like she was hugging herself.

"I know how the guy thinks. I seen him plan a job. He won't do nothing till I'm gone 'cause he knows I'd go postal."

Kensey wiped her eyes.

"C'mon, I didn't tell you this to make you cry." Manny grabbed a box of Kleenex from the bedside table and handed it to her.

"I felt so good last night. Now I can't breathe." She wiped her nose.

"Look at me." He waited for her eyes. "I've sat in the car with him hundreds of times. I know him like I know myself. He carries a gun but I never know him to shoot anybody. He rolls them up..."

"In a rug. I have one of those rugs. It was my grandmother's."

"He roll Seymour Rosen up in a carpet?"

She nodded.

"The other thing about Mike, he won't do a job during the day, no matter what."

"So maybe now it's time to go to the cops."

"You do that Sonny'll be after you hard."

"Susanne. Her name's Susanne Smerdell and she's got one of those rugs in her bedroom."

"You shouldn't of told her."

"I swear she won't say a word."

"But you swore to me you didn't tell anyone."

Kensey sat up a bit straighter. "I had to go someplace that first night. Mike drove by my house."

"And what about your boyfriend?"

"You know that he knows."

"Tell me he's a cop."

"No." She waited a second before saying, "Tell me who Sonny is."

"Maybe your friend's a public figure, someone I heard of."

"We're not playing twenty questions. I won't tell you and that's that."

"He's someone obvious, ain't he? It'll come to me and I'll go, 'Damn, I shoulda seen that.'"

"Manny, tell me what to do."

"Nothing's gonna happen till I get released. Find a reason to keep me here a little longer and get over to your house and pack some things so you don't have to go back for a week."

"You mean like go now?" Kensey looked at her watch.

"I mean like go now."

28

Kensey was streaming down the hallway on the seventh floor, the side pocket of her red coat bouncing off her hip with each stride, something heavy inside of it.

Stepping off the elevator was Dr. Taggert, a gaggle of third-year medical students in tow. Everyone was wearing a white coat, the students short ones that looked like cheap sports jackets, Dr. Taggert a three-quarter-length one with his name stitched in blue over one breast. They were heading toward the nurses' station in no big hurry, Dr. Taggert holding court, evidently in the middle of an amusing anecdote because the students were jockeying for position to hear what he was saying.

Kensey nodded briefly as she hurried to catch the elevator.

"Dr. Shaw," Dr. Taggert said, his head tipped down so he could look over his half-glasses. He stopped and the students quickly assembled in a semicircle behind him.

Kensey slammed on the brakes and spun around. "Sir." The elevator doors closed behind her.

"You seem to be in a hurry."

"Just late for the ED."

Dr. Taggert pushed back the sleeve of his coat and peered at his watch. "I have seven minutes of."

"I thought it was later."

"No. Seven minutes till the hour. Please join us. So, how's our friend?"

"Cranky. Up in a chair. His lungs are improving."

To the students Dr. Taggert said, "Thirty-seven-year-old patient, an undercover cop, came in a week ago with a gunshot wound to the chest." To Kensey he asked, "Thirty-eight caliber?" Getting a confirmatory nod he continued, "Carl Daley — some of you know him — tapped fifty cc's of blood from around his heart. Now we're dealing with a persistent pneumothorax." The students nodded knowingly. Turning back toward Kensey he asked, "Did you have a chance to look at the detective's chest X-ray from yesterday?"

"There's minimal air leak. I'm going to leave the tube cross-clamped, repeat a chest X-ray first thing tomorrow, see if there's any further accumulation of air. Maybe I can pull the tube tomorrow, get him home in the next day or so."

"You're not comfortable pulling the chest tube today?"

"No. I went over the film with the radiologist."

A female student named Kathy, hair pulled back severely enough to make it look like she was using Botox, asked, "Dr. Taggert, isn't this an unusual course for a pneumothorax?"

"Good question."

Kathy beamed.

Right away the other students were rolling their eyes, recognizing Kathy had asked '*isn't* this' rather than '*is* this' an unusual course for a pneumothorax. A subtle point to be sure, but it was obvious she already knew the answer and was asking the question to showcase her understanding.

One of medical students coughed and uttered, "asshole," but it was hard to tell for sure what he said. If Dr. Taggert picked up on the drama he didn't let on. He said, "Dr. Shaw, the students have their noon conference today. I'd like you to look up and report on the incidence of prolonged air leak in pneumothorax." He turned to the eager faces and said, "Okay, we've got a half hour before Morning Report. Who's got the next case?" Immediately Kathy thrust a chart toward him and launched into a memorized monologue about a patient who had been admitted during the night with a gastrointestinal bleed. Dr. Taggert began skimming the pages as she blathered on.

"Sir?" Kensey hadn't moved.

Kathy stopped speaking and checked her watch. Dr. Taggert didn't budge. It looked as if he was still engrossed in the patient's chart, but his eyes shifted to peer at Kensey over the rim of his glasses. His brow was furrowed. He waited.

"Six to eight percent."

"Excuse me?" Dr. Taggert said. Silently he closed the chart and slipped it under his arm.

Kathy noticed this and sent a glare Kensey's way.

"Six to eight percent of air leaks can be prolonged more than a week."

"Better check your source before the conference. The incidence is much lower."

"The general-surgery textbooks do quote one percent."

Kathy was shifting from one foot to the other as if she had to go to the bathroom.

In an even voice Dr. Taggert said, "Go on."

Instantly Kathy was ready with, "His hematocrit was twenty-seven and we typed and cross-matched—"

Dr. Taggert whipped off his glasses and scowled at her. "Not you, dear."

Now the rest of the medical students were smiling, but it wasn't clear whether they were happy their colleague wasn't able to present her case or they sensed an even bigger confrontation was about to happen.

Kensey said, "That's if all cases of pneumothorax are lumped together."

Dr. Taggert set a serious stare on her, not saying a word but setting the stage for a stinger. Finally, he said, "How do you propose we determine incidence?" He was waiting for her to stumble.

"A retrospective study by Keenan in the *American Journal of Cardiothoracic Surgery* addressed that. He suggested a separate category for penetrating wounds to the chest. The incidence goes up dramatically depending on the size of the projectile causing the injury. With gunshot wounds it's six to eight percent."

Kensey studied Dr. Taggert's face for a sign of what was to follow. He always had the last word. One-upmanship was fair game with your peers, never with one's superior.

Kensey watched the little muscles around his eyes tighten. She knew her heart was accelerating. Absently her hand slipped into the pocket of her red coat and she grasped the tight little brick she'd picked up in Mike Dombroski's closet. Everything came back in a rush. The sweaty softball jersey draped around her neck. Smelly sneakers on the floor. And a blue Nike bag with a big yellow swoop under her left knee. Spending more than an hour with it, she got to know the bag pretty well. It was made of thin nylon, empty, except for a single pack of new fifties held tightly with a paper strap. Right now she was holding five thousand dollars in her hand.

"Dr. Shaw. Have you given any thought about how you handled the situation in the ED when Detective Romero was admitted?"

"I've spent hours replaying it in my mind."

"Would you handle it differently next time?"

"I wouldn't have tapped his chest."

"What?" The metal chart tumbled to the floor as he took a tiny step toward Kensey. The medical students must have noticed this because they took a step back, giving the two a little space. No one dared to retrieve the chart.

"Detective Romero understood the gravity of the situation. In my estimation he made a lucid and reasonable request not to have further treatment. I should have respected that."

"Like hell you should. How can you possibly determine he was lucid in the schizophrenic environment of the ED?"

"By listening to what he said to me."

"What could he possibly have said that emboldened you to make such a decision?" The veins in his neck were standing out like vines on a tree trunk.

"He spoke confidentially. I'm bound to respect that."

Dr. Taggert ran his fingers through his silver hair. "That's a shaky argument." He straightened his arm to reveal his watch and glance at it. "Pulling the patient-confidentiality excuse … never again."

"Yes, sir."

Dr. Taggert took several steps toward the elevator and punched the button. "But I believe every intern deserves one get-out-of-jail-free pass. You just burned yours."

"I understand."

"I trust you'll have Detective Romero on his way home in the next forty-eight hours."

"Yessir."

The elevator opened and Dr. Taggert held the door. "See you at noon conference, Dr. Shaw."

"Sir." Kensey did a 180 and headed away from the elevators, toward the uniformed cop.

"Dr. Shaw, it's two minutes before the hour. Aren't they expecting you in the Emergency Department?"

Kensey turned and walked backwards. "I forgot to give Detective Romero something. I'll just be a second."

■ ■ ■

"Hey," Manny said, checking out the tight brick of fifties in his big mitt, "No way you're the type to hold back on the sister." His mouth curled into a suspicious grin.

"I almost forgot to give it to you," she said. "I found it in his closet."

"Oh yeah?" He sniffed the money.

"In a Nike gym bag."

"Blue one with the big yella swoop?"

"Yep. I figured if it wasn't in the safe, it's not part of—"

His lips tightly together, he shook his head. "Unfortunately, it ain't Mike's. It's part of Sonny's dough. He must've forgotten it." Manny ran his thumb along the edge, riffling the bills. It sounded like he was shuffling cards.

"How can you tell for sure?"

"Banks don't do it this way. With fifties I never seen it add up to five Gs. They wrap twenty or forty. There's a hundred bills here. That's the way Sonny does it."

"Oh." She eased down in the straight-back chair next to the bed.

Manny glimpsed over at the clock. "Hey, it's after seven. You better get marching, you gonna pack and be back here before someone notices."

"You want me to take it to the sister?"

While he considered this he rubbed his cheek. "I don't know." His nails scratched on his thick beard. "You think I should grow a full beard?"

"What?" she said and it caught her off guard for a moment. "No. I never really liked them. Too scratchy."

He rubbed his cheek some more. "Maybe if I'm going for a fresh start."

"That's why I thought you needed travel money, you know, you heading straight out of town."

He looked at the door, the way he always did when he had something important to say. In a quiet voice: "I been giving some serious thought to that."

"You're staying? What about Sonny?"

"Hey — no names. And I ain't staying. I figure there's a little business I got to take care of." Manny held up the brick of fifties. "Too many loose ends, you know? I don't like leaving with stuff hanging."

"I know what you're talking about: Mike."

He gave her a friendly smile. "You'n me got one goddamn good détente going. Why make it more complicated? I tell you what I'm gonna do, you got more to worry about. And you don't want to worry about shit you don't have to." He wrapped the money in a paper napkin from his nightstand and shoved it in the back of his drawer.

"Then why'd you say anything?"

"'Cause I'm so comfortable with you I sometimes forget. Now get outta here and be careful. Something happens to you then I maybe gotta hang around a few more days and that's just enough time for one a' Sonny's guys to find me."

■ ■ ■

Eight minutes later Kensey arrived in the Emergency Department. A trickle of patients was trudging through the automatic doors while the security guard was directing foot traffic. Physicians and nurses were zipping in and out of rooms.

Kensey spotted Helen in the bullpen and made up a story about leaving the stove on and having to shut it off. She weaved around a fat woman in a wheelchair, waited while two paramedics pushed a stretcher through the automatic doors, and walked into the morning sunshine.

A yellow taxi was just pulling into one of the ambulance bays. The back door opened and Sapphire stepped out in impossibly pink capris and four-inch stiletto heels. Immediately she spotted Kensey and gave her a big wave and hello. She pulled out a huge roll of money from her tiny purse, peeled off three bills, and leaned into the cab. She cooed to the driver, "Wait a moment, sugar, this won't take long as I thought." Then strutting toward Kensey, Sapphire went, "How you doing, girlfriend?"

"I'm okay. What're you doing here? Are you sick?"

"Me? No. Something I gotta tell you."

Kensey squinted in the bright sun. "Oh, yeah?" A police car cruised into an empty bay and two uniformed officers stepped out.

"Hey, don't sound like that, girl. Like my mama said, it's always better to know."

"Know what?"

One of the uniforms gave Sapphire the eye as he walked past. She fluttered her fake lashes at him. "Honey, you looking to party?" The uniform kept going, acting as if he hadn't heard her, marching toward the automatic doors. "Hey, I'm talking to you. I did your partner, last week. Maybe you want some." When the automatic doors opened and the officers were gone, she said, "That detective you were with the other day?"

"Hennessey."

"Yeah, Hennessey. He came to see me. Tracked me all the way the other side of the Liberty Tubes, asking questions 'bout you. How do we know each other, that sorta shit. But what's really burning him is what's up with the captain's nickname. 'Member I said he don't have a nickname out front of the *po* - lice station?" She waited for Kensey to nod. "You didn't see it but his eyes got so big it made me say, 'This ain't over,' to B.J. after you went inside. *That's* why he drove all the way out to see me. Captain Adkins's nickname. Is that weird or what?"

"So what'd you tell him?"

"Tell him?" She reached out and touched Kensey's arm like they were old friends. "I told him nothing. Shit, I don't know you can trust that guy."

"That's all he wanted?"

Sapphire pulled some hair from her face that was sticking to her lipstick. "Yep. What is it with that nickname anyway?"

"I don't know. Someone mentioned he might have a nickname. That's all."

"Listen to me, girlfriend. Hennessey was on a fishing trip's all. He don't know nothing."

Kensey looked back at the emergency entrance, then at Sapphire. "Thanks."

"Now I'm gonna tell you something else. Once in a while I toss a cop a freebie. Never hurts to know someone. One a' my guys said Hennessey is Internal Affairs. You know what that means?"

Kensey nodded.

"Unless you dating the guy, why the hell's IAD paying so much attention to Dr. Kensey Shaw?" Sapphire fished in her little purse for a cigarette and a purple lighter.

"I'm not sure."

"You know he s'posed to be checking out dirty cops. Not you." She lit the smoke and took a long drag. "Like why'd he bring you down the station in the first place?"

"Just to look at some surveillance tapes. He thought I might know somebody who witnessed a crime." Kensey felt as though she was hearing her own voice on a tape recorder. It sounded high-pitched, fake.

"Unless you're mixed up in something—" Holding her cigarette between two fingers in front of her mouth, Sapphire took a step back. She checked out Kensey wearing her backpack slung over one shoulder and red toggle coat right out of Talbots. "And, girl, I seriously doubt you are. I'd be real fuckin' careful what I said around him or any other cop. Look, I gotta go." Sapphire ducked into the cab and tapped on the driver's headrest two times. She waved bye to Kensey as the cab backed up.

Kensey hopped in her car and drove to Highland Park. Traffic was heavy. It took twenty minutes. She was thinking about Frank Hennessey when she turned onto Bryant and kept going right past her little white clapboard and all the way around the block. She recognized every car in front of every house. Fords and Chevys. Subarus and Hondas. Completing the 360, her next-door neighbor, a fat woman named Maria, was finishing a walk with her cocker spaniel and heading home. Kensey pulled up right in front of her house, waved to Maria, wished her good morning, and started up the walk.

She was moving purposefully, reviewing in her mind all the things she needed to pack. Clothes. Toiletries. A photograph of her mom and dad. That was it, all she needed to camp out at Alec's for the next week or so. She strode up the walk, key in hand, plunged it into the lock, opened the door, stepped into the foyer, and threw the door closed as she slipped the backpack off her shoulder and was heading for the stairs ...

The sharp pop of gunfire, a single shot, came from the living room. It echoed in her head so many times that she couldn't tell how many shots had been fired. She stumbled to the floor. Quickly she curled into a little ball and covered her face with her hands and waited. For several seconds the house was quiet; the only thing she could hear was the wild pulse in her head.

A moan came from the living room. It sounded like a foghorn off in the distance, a man's voice, low and rumbling. After a while the moans were replaced with the desperate sound of someone drowning in his own secretions.

Her face shiny with perspiration, Kensey dragged her backpack as she scampered across the front hall and away from the living room into her little dining room and around the cheap rectangular wooden table with four matching chairs. She ended up in a back corner where she hunkered down. Never pulling her eyes from the living room, her fingers tore at her backpack and she plunged her hand into the zippered compartment, whipping out the Beretta. Holding it with two hands, Kensey aimed it toward the living room. From where she was, all she could see through the forest of wooden legs was the side of the television set and the armrest of her sofa. The tip of the barrel moved in an endless circle. She looked down at the bare wooden floor beneath her, touched it lightly with one hand, whispered, "Oh, my God," and tightened her grip on the Beretta. Time went by. The gurgling continued, less frequent now, every five or ten seconds. It was an awful sound.

Now her arms were getting tired. The tip of the barrel was making bigger circles. More time went by. Finally, she said, "I know who you are." Her voice was soft, maybe too soft for anyone to hear. "Dombroski?" This time, louder.

A gurgle and a wheeze and something that sounded like "Help" but Kensey couldn't tell if her ears were playing tricks on her brain. She waited some more. The tip of the gun was no longer leveled to shoot someone in the chest. It was aimed to shoot off somebody's kneecaps. And the circle was growing bigger. Her small catalogue house from Sears was quiet. The gurgling had stopped.

Her hair was matted to one side of her head, her sweater dappled with dust. Grasping the gun in one hand, she pushed up to a standing.

"Can you hear me? I've got a gun," she said, taking her first step toward the living room. "What'd you do with my grandmother's rug?" She had two hands on the gun, TV-cop style, right hand around the grip, left around the right. It was a tedious process inching her way toward the living room. Only ten steps but it took several minutes.

The living room shades were drawn. Mike Dombroski was sitting in her corduroy recliner in the middle of the room, the chair eased all the way back, his legs up on the little footrest as if he had been watching television, blood soaking the right side of his denim shirt and pooling in his lap. His head was turned to the side, away from Kensey. If she studied him closely she could make out the rise and fall of his chest. "You hear me?" He didn't move. A blue aluminum baseball bat was resting against the chair.

Next to the recliner was a small wooden coffee table. Her textbook on internal medicine was lying open in the middle of the table. On the floor next to the chair were two beer cans, crushed in the middle.

In Mike's right hand was a gun with a very long barrel, coated in blood so that Kensey couldn't tell what color it was.

Kensey sniffed the air as she stepped into the room, smelled the blood, moved around Mike slowly, never lowering her weapon. "Where're your fancy boots?"

Mike bobbed his head slightly. He wheezed out, "There's no fuckin' note."

"What're you talking about?"

"That *day-tant* thing. You made it up."

Mike's eyes drifted to the side, so he was looking at the back wall of the living room.

"Hey, was that for me?" Along the back wall was a blue and rose Oriental rug, rolled up in a sloppy spiral, sitting on top of the cheap carpet that came with the house. "It was my grandmother's. Then it was in our dining room. I used to play Barbies on it. When my mom got wall-to-wall she kept it rolled up in the garage. Said it was for me when I got my first place." Mike let out a grunt. "Every time I looked at it this week I thought about Seymour Rosen."

Mike's eyes moved in their sockets to focus on Kensey. His face was dripping with sweat, his color ashen.

Kensey raised her gun, showing it to him. "You left this on the floor when you carried him out."

Mike's lips moved, but nothing came out.

"And I was in your closet when you killed Jimmy last night."

Mike's eyes closed and slowly opened.

"Twelve. Seventeen. Thirty-two. Five hundred eighty-six thousand dollars. You said five-eighty but it was eighty-six. I counted it before I gave it to Sister at St. John's."

"Fuck you." His speech was slurred.

"I bet you didn't know there was a pack of fifties in the Nike bag. You want me to call an ambulance?"

His eyes opened and focused on her. They were tired. Finally he nodded, two times.

"Tell me who Sonny is."

In slow motion his head went back and forth.

There was a cordless phone on the end table by the sofa. Kensey snatched it and dialed. "Hello," she said, "This is Kensey Shaw, may I speak with Alec Fortune?"

His hand started to twitch and his eyes opened wide as he tried to move his weapon.

Kensey made eye contact with Mike. "He knows. I went to him the next day. You never would have got near him." Then she said into the phone, "Alec, it's me. ... Mike Dombroski was waiting for me when I got home. I must have startled him when I closed the door and he shot himself in the chest."

Mike was shaking his head back and forth, coming back to life. He raised the gun several inches. Before it could pose a risk he dropped it back in his lap.

Mike heard Kensey say, "He's dead," into the phone. He coughed out a glob of bloody mucous. He was breathing hard, wheezing and choking, trying to speak. His skin was turning the color of the sky before it rains.

Kensey listened before saying, "Just leave him?" Then she listened some more, finally saying, "I've got all that.... No, I'm fine, I feel ... great. I'll go back to the hospital and I'll meet you here around seven. Whatever you say, Alec. ... Me too."

She punched a button on the phone, replaced it on the coffee table, and sat on the sofa facing him. "Manny said you'd come but not until after he got out of the hospital. He said you only did jobs at night."

Mike opened his eyes and curled his lips into a hint of a smile. He whispered, "You think you got it figured out." Some blood trickled from his nose. His breathing became labored. Finally he managed to say, "Sonny's still gonna kill you."

"I tried to tell you, you've got tetanus, Mike."

His eyes looked at her. He was barely breathing.

"I'm going to sit here until you take your last breath."

Mike's eyelids drifted shut. His chest stopped moving and his head slowly eased to one side.

Kensey reached for Mike's neck and felt for his carotid pulse.

She lowered her gun and looked around the room, then picked up the textbook from the table. Before closing it she saw that Mike had been reading the section on tetanus. Replacing the text in the bookcase, she picked up the beer cans and dropped them into a small wastebasket.

Suddenly she screamed and glared in Mike's direction. "How do you know there's no note?" She snatched the blue aluminum baseball bat. "Goddamn you." She swung hard, stepping into it and catching Mike square in the upper chest.

Then she dropped the bat, grabbed her black Beretta, and sprinted for the door.

■ ■ ■

Kensey had to smash the window in the kitchen door with the butt of the Beretta when no one answered the bell. Not ready to venture inside, she called out, "Hello? Anybody home?" When there was no answer, she curled her finger around the trigger and stepped onto the blue-and-white-sheet linoleum. The kitchen was cold and tidy, nothing going on except the blinking light on the answering machine. Pushing the button, she activated a chirpy voice: *"Hi, it's Mom. I can't wait to hear how your hair looks. Give me a call. Bye."*

A cursory glance around the dining room revealed only a butcher-block table with a beat-up set of cane-back chairs. She went back through the kitchen and into the living room.

In the middle of the carpet was a fancy throw pillow. Not far away was an empty bottle of I.C. Light and a blue fuzzy slipper.

"Susanne," Kensey called out, loud enough to remind her how frightened she was. When there was no answer, she slowly crept up the carpeted stairs holding her weapon out in front, arms straight, aiming just below her line of sight.

At the top of the stairs was the bathroom. A Nordstrom towel with a lavish blue monogram sat in a heap under the sink. Yellow urine stains speckled the white toilet seat.

"Oh, God," she said under her breath.

Finally, the bedroom. Now Kensey moved more slowly, her shoulder brushing along the wall as she made her way down the short, carpeted hallway. Waiting a few seconds before daring a look, she stepped into Susanne's bedroom.

The first thing she saw — the only thing she saw — looked like a fat palm tree on its side with a spray of auburn and blond fronds spewing from the top.

Kensey gagged and the back of her mouth filled with the contents of her stomach. Susanne's body had been mummified, the tan backing of a rug the only part visible from where Kensey was standing.

The room reeked of perspiration. And urine.

Kensey took in the rest of the room. The drawer of the bedside table had been dumped on the bed. Clothes from the closet were strewn everywhere and the mattress had been flipped on its side against the wall.

Tiptoeing her way across the room, Kensey knelt down next to Susanne. She brushed the hair from her face.

Susanne shuddered and made a sound like water sloshing through a drain.

Kensey recoiled, catching herself before she fell backwards. "It's me, Susanne. Kensey." Right away her hands worked feverishly to unwind the carpet.

Susanne's eyes seemed unable to focus, rolling around in her head as if she were experiencing vertigo. Briefly, she stared at Kensey's face as she finished her first revolution. "Is he still here?"

Kensey spun her a second time, then a third. When she was done Susanne was on the edge of the dark blue rug, her yellow shirt slick with sweat. The crotch of her jeans was two shades darker than the rest of her pants.

"He's dead."

Susanne whipped her head back and forth. "Where? Where is he?"

"He's at my place. In the Barcalounger."

Susanne began to sob. "Now you're going to call the cops, aren't you? Tell me, tell me you're not gonna do something stupid."

"I can't."

"Do you have any idea what I've been through?" She started to cry.

"He hurt you, didn't he?"

"He was going to." She pushed up to a sitting position, legs splayed out in front. A quick tug on the front of her shirt separated it from her skin. "He went out to his car and got a baseball bat. I was so scared he was gonna kill me."

Kensey wrapped Susanne in her arms. "Thank God you're okay."

"When he came back he dropped the bat and he undid his belt." Susanne sniffed back some tears. "Then he slid his pants all the way down. I thought he was gonna make me give him ... you know."

"Oh my God."

"No." Her voice got stronger. She was calming down. "He had this bandage on his thigh and when he ripped it off, his leg looked all infected and he said, 'You're a doctor, is this tetanus?'"

"What'd you say?"

"I told him I didn't know. Then he kept asking me for a note. I didn't know what he was talking about. He said if I didn't give it to him he was going to break my ribs. All of a sudden his whole body went into a contortion and he passed out on the floor right next to me. I must've fallen asleep or something 'cause when I woke up he was gone. Did you hide a note here?"

"There isn't one. Can you get up?"

"I think so." Kensey was helping Susanne up when she looked down at her crotch and said, "Oh my God, I peed my pants. Kensey, I can't take this anymore."

"It's almost over. Manny's going home soon."

"This is ridiculous, you protecting these killers."

"I know it is."

"I want you to do something for me."

"Anything."

"Tell Taggert I had to go home. Make up something. Call me when it's really over." She took a weak step toward the door.

"Aren't you going to change your pants?"

"Not till I get home."

Kensey heard the front door open, then close. Then the BMW squealed away from the curb. Before she went back to her house, she straightened up the bedroom, threw the towel in the hamper, and wiped down the toilet.

29

It was nearly dark when Alec rang the doorbell. Standing on the little square of concrete that served as Kensey's front porch, he could hear the evening news, one of those cute little stories they run at the end of the broadcast to ease you down from the war in Iraq. He noticed the shades were drawn on the windows to his left. Looking the other way, he could make out a table and chair set, but there weren't any lights on, just the wash of light from the front hall.

Wearing an old pair of jeans and a sweatshirt, Kensey was quick with the door. Her hair was wet and shiny. Right away she smiled at the sight of Alec in black workout clothes, a Pirates cap pulled down low on his eyes. She hugged him hard, breathing the last wisps of his aftershave, too happy to be in his arms to notice the smudge of dirt on his cheek or the filth under his nails.

"I thought you'd never get here." She pushed the door closed until it clicked and noticed Alec was hanging back as far from the living room as he could get without backing into the dining room.

Alec was leaning to one side, trying to steal a look at the body. The room was mostly dark. All he could see was the blue and rose Oriental rug lying exactly where Mike had dumped it on the dull gray carpet, the blue light from the television dancing on it. "The TV's in there?"

Kensey nodded.

"That's where he is, in there, right?" Jerking his head toward the living room, sounding mixed up.

"I didn't touch him, like you said on the phone."

He wrinkled his brow. Kensey picked up on it right away.

"I had a weird day. I tried everything. First I was upstairs reading. I couldn't concentrate. Then I cleaned the kitchen. Then the bathroom, which I hate. I couldn't get him out of my mind."

"So you sat in there?"

A quick nod. "And watched TV. Soap operas. The cooking channel. I felt like a fly drawn to a flame. I couldn't be in other parts of the house with him in the living room."

"That's weird."

"Thank you."

"I would have been as far away as possible." A second glance toward the living room and he said, "We might as well get started. It's going to be a long night."

"Before we go in there..." She paused and by the tone of her voice had something important to say. "This morning on the phone? I lied to you."

"You killed him." It came out quickly, like it was on the tip of his tongue waiting to jump out. "I figured maybe you did, but I wasn't gonna say anything."

"No, it's not that. He shot himself, just like I told you. The thing is..." she hesitated, unsure if she should continue. Finally: "He wasn't dead when I called you."

"What? He was alive?" He made no effort to hide his shock.

"Barely. He could hardly breathe. I was afraid if you knew he was alive you might get upset."

Alec scratched the back of his neck while he was thinking about this. He reached out for Kensey and pulled her in close. After several seconds he said, "Is there another reason?"

Kensey looked up at him with wet eyes, not saying anything right away. By the time she mumbled, "No, no other reason," enough time had gone by that she'd sent up a red flag that maybe there was something else.

But Alec knew to let it go. "You ready?"

"For the first time in a week I feel free. Like a huge weight's been lifted off my shoulders. Let's do it."

Kensey held out her hand, showing him the way. "You've never been here before."

"I was thinking about that on the way over. I'm supposed to say, *Nice place you got here*."

Kensey giggled nervously. They took several steps to the threshold of the living room. Mike was lost in the shadows, the television now turned away from him so Kensey could watch it from the sofa. She reached into the living room and ran her hand up the inside wall. "It's pretty gruesome."

The lights went on the same time the thick smell of dried blood hit their noses.

"So that's him." Alec took the scene in, Kensey staring at his face, noticing the smudge of dirt for the first time.

Mike was in the recliner in the exact position he had been when Kensey checked his pulse, work boots up on the rest, toes pointing out, head to one side, chin on his chest, eyes three-quarters closed. His shirt looked stiff with dried blood. There was no way to tell it used to be a nice shirt.

Some time slipped by before Alec said, "So where's the gun?"

They were still in the front hall, their feet not yet touching the carpet. Kensey noticed he was breathing hard. "Your face is all dirty."

Alec's hand shot up and rubbed his cheek.

"Wrong one," she said, licking her fingers and reaching out to rub the other one clean.

"I had to use a pick to break up the ground. It was hardpan. Took me an hour and a half."

"What were you digging?" she asked just as the answer hit her and she went, "Oh ... I was wondering what we were going to do with him. Where?"

"Armstrong County, about forty-five minutes from here. Some woods where I went hunting one time. A lot of deer. Not a lot of houses. So where's his gun?"

"Right there in his lap."

"We bury it with him. If someone ever finds him it'll confuse the hell out of 'em, shooting himself in the chest at point-blank range."

"Manny said he never used it on a job."

"What about the church?"

"I guess he meant on a job he planned out. Always found something to wrap them up in. Then it was easy to kill 'em."

Alec glanced around the room. His eyes settled on the blue and rose Oriental rug. "Waiting for you, huh?" His eyes moved to Kensey, looking for a nod. When he got one: "You didn't touch anything, did you?"

"I felt for a pulse in his neck." They both looked down at the blue bat on the floor with blood all over the sweet spot. "I wiped it down."

Alec squinted at the body. "So tell me again why this happened."

"In the later stages of tetanus practically anything can set off an involuntary muscle spasm. He was lying there waiting for me. I came home early and slammed the door. That startled him, his fingers seized up and pulled the trigger."

"So what're we gonna wrap him in, the rug?"

"It belonged to my grandmother. She'd understand."

A commercial with boppy music was playing on the television. If either of them noticed it was still turned on, you couldn't tell.

Alec shifted his gaze toward the front windows. "Were the curtains closed when you got here?"

"I should have noticed coming up the walk. I never close them."

Deep breathing like a free diver before a descent, he said, "Let's get to work."

They donned surgical gloves. Working together they unrolled the rug next to the recliner. Using green garbage bags, they began to line the faded blue and rose pattern of the rug. In a casual way Kensey said, "There *was* another reason."

Alec looked up at her. "For what?" He made it sound as though he'd forgotten their conversation in the front hall.

"Why I said he was dead when he wasn't. I wanted him to die knowing I went to you and told you everything. That I beat him a long time ago."

Alec let a bag slip from his fingers and fold over on itself when it landed on the carpet. "What did he say?"

"Nothing. He tried to lift his gun but was too weak."

Alec's eyes went to Mike for a second, then back to Kensey. "It's creepy talking in front of him." Alec bent down and picked up the garbage bag. "Let's get him out of our lives."

"Alec, I was set up."

"What do you mean *set up*?" Alec kept working, making sure the bags were straight.

"This morning Manny said Mike was coming after me. That nothing was going to happen till after he left the hospital. He told me to pack up what I needed as soon as possible and not worry because Mike never did a job during the day, only at night." Kensey brushed some hair from her face with the back of her gloved hand. "I've been worrying about it all day."

"You know too much."

"I put myself on the line for him. On some primal level I thought we connected."

"You didn't call him or anything, did you?"

"No, I never went back to the hospital. I called in sick, said I had a fever. What would I say anyway?"

"Good. First thing tomorrow go in there like nothing happened. Walk in the way you normally do. The moment he sees you you'll know. Look at his eyes, his body language. Watch his breathing. You'll know."

"And if I can't tell?"

"Don't say a word. The less people know the better."

They were standing on opposite sides of the Oriental rug, both staring at Mike, knowing the hard part was about to begin. Kensey picked up the remote control for the television from the sofa, Alec thinking it would be nice not to listen to the Daily Double when they were hefting a dead body. Instead the sound went louder, filling the room with questions about

Egypt, foods that start with the letter Z, and rhyming words. She turned and said, "That's better. You ready?"

"I'll get him under the arms, you grab his legs."

When they were in position Alec counted one, two, three. Kensey grunted and together they heaved Mike out of the recliner and deposited him on the Oriental rug with a thud. He was horribly askew, in one of those random poses shown by chalk outlines on police shows, arms pointing in opposite directions, as if he was fleeing the scene of the crime.

The green garbage bags were slippery so it was easy to straighten him out and arrange him at one end of the rug, his length running the width of the carpet, just like Kensey had witnessed twice in the last week, except his head wasn't extending beyond the fringe. Alec flipped one end of the carpet over Mike's torso. Using his foot he began to roll him up.

"God, look at the chair," Kensey said.

The corduroy was sticky with dark blood.

Alec turned to Kensey. "I rented a steam cleaner. It's in my truck. Before we go we'll get the blood out, then I'll drop it off at the Salvation Army in the morning." He finished rolling Mike in the rug.

"The truth machine."

Alec raised his eyebrows and wrinkled his forehead.

"That's what he called it when he rolled Jimmy up. The guy couldn't move and Mike whacked him with that bat until he was telling him everything he wanted to know."

"The only thing I don't like about this is getting him from the house to the car."

Kensey went over to the window and pushed a curtain aside to peer out. "It's dark."

Alec said, "We should wait. I'll get the steam cleaner, then we can watch something other than *Jeopardy!* We see anyone outside, *Hi, how you doing, just moving a rug to a friend's house, come meet my friend Alec.* Okay?"

More than two hours later, the Barcalounger looked better than the day it arrived in Pittsburgh. The rolled-up rug with Mike in the middle was in the front hall. They'd washed their hands, eaten salami and American cheese sandwiches and had beers sitting on the sofa, watching a reality show that tried to gross-out contestants by making them touch disgusting things. The irony hit them at the same time. They looked at one another and laughed in an uncomfortable way.

Soon they were at the front door, the steam cleaner already in the pickup, Alec squatting with his hands under the thicker part of the Oriental rug where Mike's shoulders were, ready to hoist it.

He waited on his haunches for Kensey to squat down. When she did: "Lift with your legs, not your back," and they grunted in unison and hefted the body. Alec reached out and opened the front door, stepped outside, and looked left and right. "We're good." They lugged the rug like they were carrying a canoe stuffed with gear and stepped into the night.

"God, the air smells good," Kensey said and they carefully trekked down the three concrete steps, Alec leading the way with the thicker end, Kensey five feet behind, struggling with the end of the rug where his ankles were. She could see the pickup in dark silhouette. "I think I'll need a drink when we're finished."

"We can stop some place on the way home."

"And maybe some pizza. That would taste great." She almost sounded giddy. "And let's sleep here tonight. I want to sleep in my own bed with you."

Alec shot her a toothy grin. "I like the way you sound." Before Kensey could say anything—

"Kensey, is that you?"

"Oh, hi, Mrs. Polan," Kensey speaking between heavy breaths to a stout figure coming toward them with a nervous little dog. She and Alec were almost at the truck, not slowing down.

"You moving?"

"No. Just loaning a rug to a friend."

"Oh, yeah?" Mrs. Polan said, getting closer, the dog pulling at its leash in the direction of the rug.

"And looking for someone to take a nice Barcalounger off her hands." Alec nodded toward the house.

Now Mrs. Polan was looking back at the front door, wide open with yellow light spilling out on the front stoop. She tugged on the leash so her dog wouldn't get in the way. "Is this the one with the fancy car?"

"This is Alec."

"I saw you getting into a two-seater the other night. What was that, one of those little Subarus?"

Alec and Kensey were at the pickup, Alec hugging his end with one hand while he worked the latch to lower the back.

"No, a Porsche." He smiled back at Mrs. Polan.

"Fancy-schmancy."

"Mrs. Polan lives two doors down." Then to Mrs. Polan: "I'm loaning the carpet to a girlfriend who can't fit it in her car."

"A Porsche *and* a pickup. What're you, a doctor?"

"Just a businessman."

Mrs. Polan, hair up in a swirly scarf, was moving in close with her little dog. "It's so late. What is that, an Oriental? I see the fringe."

Alec looked at Kensey. "Didn't I say that to you?" He turned to Mrs. Polan. "They should give her more time off so she can do things like move carpet when it's light out, don't you think?"

"Yes, they should." Mrs. Polan was on the curb, squinting behind round glasses. "What is that, six-by-nine? It looks bigger."

Alec stood next to the back of the truck, Kensey swinging in a wide arc, stepping off the curb so the rug was lined up to go in straight.

Mrs. Polan gazed back at the house. "So what about the chair?" The little dog was pulling toward Kensey's little square of lawn, ready to do her business.

Alec and Kensey were sliding the rug forward, Kensey walking toward the pickup's bed. Getting it in halfway was quick work, then it got difficult. Alec had to hop up on the bed and pull it while Kensey pushed.

"So what about the chair?" Mrs. Polan said a second time.

In order to close up the back, Alec had to lift the ankle end up while Kensey slammed the hatch. The spiral end-cut of the Oriental rug was a foot in the air. Kensey checked to make sure Mike's boots weren't sticking out.

"Just a Barcalounger," Kensey said.

Her arm outstretched as the little dog squatted, Mrs. Polan tried to sound casual when she said, "And you want to get rid of it? Maybe I could take a look at it sometime."

Alec said, "How 'bout right now? You like it, we'll move it for you tonight."

"It's wet," Kensey said quickly.

Alec shook his head. "It's just damp. We steam-cleaned it. You know, maybe get a couple bucks for it."

"Oh," Mrs. Polan said, sounding disappointed, letting the little dog drag her down the sidewalk.

"Not for you. Kensey'd be happy for you to have it." Alec slipped his arm around Kensey.

"Great," she said, looking back at the carpet in the dark pickup. "I betcha that carpet's nice."

"You want to see the chair now?" Kensey and Alec started toward the house.

Mrs. Polan gave the leash a hard tug. "What color is it anyway?"

30

Frank Hennessey was waiting for Kensey in the waiting room off the ED, the one with the red vinyl chairs where they had talked the night Manny Romero was shot. A mother with a fussy baby was sitting across from him, the mother spending more time eyeing Frank than her sick infant. Two men with enormous guts commandeered the couches. Next to Frank, a man was balancing a yellow hard hat on one knee and a black lunch pail on the other.

Every time the sliding glass doors *whooshed* open, Frank popped out of his seat and stepped to the doorway to take a look. When he was not jumping up at the sound of the door, he was skimming the *Post-Gazette*, specifically the sports section, folded into a neat little rectangle.

Whoosh. Frank hopped up, took three steps to the door, and leaned out. Kensey walked in, slipping off her coat that covered a dark plaid skirt hemmed just below her knees and a knit sweater. She was moving quickly toward the bullpen. Frank tossed the newspaper onto his plastic chair, snatched a brown paper bag that was on the empty seat beside him, and took off after Kensey. "Dr. Shaw?"

Kensey spun around and kept on walking, backwards, taking two or three steps before easing to a stop and giving him a second look. He was wearing a suit and tie but the top button of his shirt was undone. When he got closer Kensey was ready with, "You and I need to talk," sounding as if she'd arranged the meeting rather than the other way around.

Frank nodded as he said, "Works for me," and watched Kensey's eyes lower to take in the brown paper bag he was carrying.

Standing in the busy walkway, the *whoosh* of the doors signaled the arrival of more patients. Someone was retching in one of the exam rooms. Kensey said to Frank, "If that's breakfast, I already ate." Definitively. End of discussion. Then she turned to face the bullpen.

Frank looked a bit sheepish, even foolish, holding the crinkly brown bag in his hand, like a school kid bringing a sack lunch on the day they were having a pizza party.

Carl Daley was busy on the phone, a leg up on the counter, leaning back in his chair, scratching his scalp with his ballpoint pen in the closed position. Depositing her red coat on the desk, she called out, "I'll be a minute." He gave her a little wave, telling her it was okay with him, and Kensey marched away from the bullpen, past Frank and back toward the lounge. He followed two steps behind, then three, Kensey moving fast, too much in a hurry to notice Frank tossing the brown paper bag in the trash, taking long strides past exam rooms, the storage room, two giggly nursing students coming back from a smoke, giving them a little nod as she whizzed by. Around the corner and Kensey was reaching for the heavy door of the lounge, pulling it hard, slipping inside and letting it go right away so Frank had to quickstep and grab it.

A sleepy resident in blue scrubs and white clogs was stretched out on the couch reading the newspaper. He looked up to see Kensey standing above him. "Hey, Kensey, turn on the TV if you want."

"It's getting busy out front."

Looking at the clock in the wall, the resident said, "Carl's got four minutes to play God," then realized someone else was in the room. He sat up in a hurry, thinking it might be Carl, saw Frank standing there in a suit with his square jaw, and mumbled "Excuse me," and hurried from the room.

Now they were alone, Frank and Kensey standing several feet apart to face each other. Morning light snuck through an opening in the curtains. It sliced across the room and lit up a pizza box on the floor.

"I'm going first," Kensey said, arms crossed, standing firm in the middle of the room, stethoscope around her neck like a scarf.

"Okay," Frank said, his hand searching for his tie, his face pink, a hint of moisture on his forehead.

"You're IAD, right?"

"Is something wrong?"

"You're goddamn right something's wrong. Right now I want to know: Am I a suspect?"

"No. As you said, I'm IAD. I don't investigate civilians."

"Then why're you asking around about a silly conversation I had a week ago about a stupid nickname?" She crossed her arms.

Frank's lips tightened. "Oh, her."

"Sapphire."

Frank pushed the newspapers aside so he could sit on the sofa. "Actually, her name's Mary Harding, from Harrisburg. How do you even know someone like that?" He was trying to sound conversational, anything but confrontational.

"I work in the busiest ED in the city. All types are welcome."

He let out a breath, almost a sigh, letting Kensey know this was off the subject. "Last week Mary was arrested for solicitation. Fourth time in three months. While she was waiting for a prelim she caused a near-riot in the station right in front of Captain Adkins."

"If that has something — anything — to do with me, I'll eat one of those muffins."

"They were bagels."

Kensey looked at Frank's empty hands. "Whatever."

"You remember the station, those big wooden benches lined up in rows like a bus terminal?"

"I saw them when I looked at those surveillance tapes."

"Well one of 'em — the second to last one — that's the one the girls want to sit on whenever they get busted. Make a big deal if anybody sits on it except hookers." He waited for her to take in what he'd said, watching her hand squeeze into her own bicep. "You know where I'm going with this?"

Kensey eyed a clock on the wall, avoiding his gaze. "I know you're going past seven, which makes me officially late."

"Cause before all hell broke loose the arresting officer spotted a young woman on the hooker bench who wasn't a hooker. Looked out of place talking to a couple of the regulars. This girl was clean-cut, short brown hair, nice clothes, real pretty. No feather boa or stilettos." Kensey swallowed hard and Frank saw it.

"Is this going to be like that time with those surveillance tapes?"

He shook his head. "I promise."

Kensey wondered if he was going to ask her to come down to the station to have the arresting officer check her out.

"Anyway, after Mary pulled her little stunt, wrapping the feather boa around the neck of the desk sergeant just so she could take a pee, the young woman was gone. Flat-out disappeared. The thing is, the arresting officer happened to be closest to the front door when everything happened. They locked down the station for more'n five minutes. The arresting officer swears no one came in or out."

"How'd she get out of there?"

"She went out the second-floor window."

"So what's that have to do with Detective Romero?" Before he could say another word, Kensey added, "Or me?"

"That was the morning *after* Manny got shot. Like nine hours later. Mary told me it was you."

Now Kensey's hands were shaking. She wiped a tear from her eye. "If I'm not a suspect, why don't you leave me alone?"

"I can't stop worrying about you."

"Trust me, I'm fine."

The heavy door opened just wide enough for someone in scrubs to see something was going on inside. The door closed and whoever it was called out, "Sorry."

"Over and over I'm asking myself, What spooked you in a police station? Did you hear something?"

"Maybe whoever it was, was in the bathroom and by the time she came out the lockdown was over and the officer didn't notice her leave."

"Can I tell you what I think happened? You went into the station to report a crime and the guy you were gonna report turned out to be a cop."

"If that's true, Detective, whoever that girl was should be scared to death there might be other dirty cops, shouldn't she?"

"Mike Dombroski."

"Is that the cop who spooked the girl?"

He nodded. "You ever run into him visiting Detective Romero?"

"Un-uh."

"Detective Dombroski didn't show up for work yesterday." He watched her swallow, picked up on the way she blinked, the wrinkles in her forehead, how she tucked her hair behind an ear. Her tongue wet her lips and her cheeks went tight. He spoke softly when he said, "Are you okay, Kensey?"

"I'm fine."

"Hey, why don't you sit down."

Now they were both seated, Frank on the sofa, Kensey in one of the easy chairs.

She swallowed. "What's this have to do with me?"

"Seventeen years on the force. Not once did Mike fail to show up without calling in. I went over to his house, his car was gone. An officer located it in Highland Park. The twenty-*two*-hundred section of Bryant."

"You know where I live?"

"Twenty-one-twenty."

Kensey stood. "I've gotta get to work."

"For reasons I do not understand you are enmeshed with Detective Romero way beyond the scope of the doctor-patient relationship." He tugged at the neck of his shirt.

"Are we done?"

"Almost. Remember when I asked you about a buddy of mine on the force with some strange spasms?"

"I told you he should see a doctor."

"It was Dombroski. And I told him what you said. Last time I saw him he was limping around, all sweaty like he had a fever. So when he didn't show for work — before we found his car — I wondered did he end up in the hospital. I got out the phone book and started calling around. You know what I found? First call, he was here in the Emergency Room end of last week. Right here." He watched Kensey breathing faster now, as if she were taking a brisk walk.

Now he reached into his side pocket and pulled out a folded sheet of paper. "Got this from Medical Records before you got here." Opening it, he read, "Michael Dombroski. Chief complaint: limp. Says he signed in to see you right here." Folding the photocopy he said, "Oh, I imagine Mike'll turn up. He's quite the ladies' man. Probably shacked up in the next block and lost track of time."

Kensey started toward the door. "Detective Romero will be discharged in three or four days. After that I don't expect we'll need to see each other again."

"Three or four? I heard it was sooner."

"Who told you that?"

"Dr. Taggert."

"No. It's three or four." She opened the door and walked out.

■ ■ ■

After splashing water on her face and dodging Carl Daley in the bullpen, she stood outside Manny Romero's door, the uniformed cop still sitting in his ass-pinching little chair, ignoring the sports section in his lap, wondering why Kensey was standing there with her hand on the doorknob as if she was scared to death to go inside. The cop opened his mouth and was about to ask if she was all right —

In one swift move she opened the door and slipped inside.

Manny was not in the bed or the chair. As usual, the television was on, this time *The Today Show*, one of the guests showing off her legs, laughing like she was having the best time in the world. The fruit basket was gone now, the windowsill empty. The sound of running water came from the bathroom. The door was opened and Kensey could peek through the little space between the door and jamb to see Manny's hairy back hunched over the little sink. He was shaving, a skimpy white hospital towel wrapped around his waist. Sidestepping to her right until she was standing in the middle of the room, she studied him working the disposable razor where his beard drew up to meet the mustache, being careful not to cut himself. He stretched his skin tight with one hand, leaned toward the mirror, and squinted. Kensey said nothing, taking it in, not realizing Manny was free at last from the leash he had worn for a week, his gold cross hanging down almost where the steam was rising from the sink.

Kensey concentrated on Manny, watching his hands, how confident they were, sliding that razor over the same patch of skin, three swipes in the up direction. Whatever Matt Lauer was saying couldn't compete with what she was watching. She was focused on the sound of the water rushing into the sink, watching Manny dip the razor into the water and shake it off before it went back to his face.

Matt threw it to commercial. A noisy jingle filled the room. The razor now touched Manny's face, the right side this time, dragging it north, his eyes drifting from the mirror toward his room where the music was playing. He spotted her, arms across her chest, stethoscope around her neck, and he turned his head quickly and went, "Ouch," and made a face as a little drop of blood appeared on his cheek. "Damn." He turned and snapped off a square of toilet paper and tore off a corner. There were lines of white shaving cream on his face. "What are you, watching me?" He winked.

Kensey could see the clean square of bandage where the chest tube had been. "Didn't want to startle you."

"Don't worry, you didn't." He dabbed the toilet paper on the spot of blood and it stayed in place, turning red in the center like a bull's-eye. "What's going on? Didn't think you were coming."

"Sorry, I was running late." She smiled, trying to make it sound casual.

He looked back in the mirror. "I guess I'm done. These disposables stink." He grabbed a white hand towel and wiped the remains of shaving cream from his face. He looked in the mirror, first at his face, then let his eyes travel to take in Kensey. The dab of toilet paper was doing its job. "So you want to tell me what's going on?"

"Getting ready to send you home soon."

"I mean yesterday. How come that other doctor — some Indian fella I never seen before — pulled my tube? I thought you were gonna do that."

"I was sick. So if your lungs sound okay—"

He leaned forward. Squinting. Being observant. "You know you don't look right. Maybe you're not ready to come back."

"I'm fine."

"What's wrong, Kensey?"

"Nothing."

Wearing the white towel and nothing else, Manny moved past her. He smelled like menthol. And soap. "It don't take me long to get to know somebody. I'm pretty good at sizing people up. And right now, something's up."

Kensey licked her lip.

"There." He pointed at her face. "You just licked your lip. I noticed you do that sometimes like when you're nervous."

"I was just saying if your lungs sound okay maybe you could go home. No one needs to know it's today—"

"Not today, okay? Tomorrow. I got some stuff to do when I get out, I need to rest up."

"You look pretty good."

"Tomorrow." This he said firmly.

"I don't know. Dr. Taggert's been on my case to get you out of here."

He sat on the edge of the bed, his belly hanging over the top of the towel, taking one or two heavy breaths, looking at Kensey. "Now that we got that settled, what's making you look like that?" He grabbed an apple from his bedside table, wrapped a fresh Kleenex around it, and began polishing the skin.

"When I got home yesterday, Mike was there."

Manny snapped his head around to look at her. "Last night?"

"No. Middle of the day. Right after I left you. He had my grandmother's Oriental rug waiting for me."

"Shit." He sat there, eyes fixed on Kensey, Kensey watching his Adam's apple bob up and down like it was made of something springy. "So what'd he want?"

"He's dead."

Manny's hands stopped polishing the apple. "Good thing I told you where to find the safety."

"I didn't kill him."

"Huh?"

"He was reading one of my textbooks. Had the page opened to the chapter on tetanus."

Manny motioned with his hand for Kensey to hurry up with the story.

"One of the things you get with tetanus is you get very jittery."

"Spasms. He told me about 'em. What's this got to do with him being dead?"

"When I closed the door, the sound made him go into a spasm and he shot himself."

Kensey was standing in the middle of the room, her eyes on Manny sitting on the bed.

He sat quietly for a while, chewing on what she'd said. "You called the cops they woulda been here by now."

"I wouldn't do that."

"Where is he?"

"I don't want you to ask me that."

"Middle of the day, huh?"

"Yep," she said, now sounding to Manny like he should be reading between the lines.

"So why don't you sit down?"

"I'm not staying that long. It's twenty of eight."

"You didn't even use that yet." He jerked his head toward the stethoscope around her neck.

"Fine." While Kensey placed the stethoscope in her ears she could see he was thinking. Before she got close enough to touch it to his chest, Manny said, "Wait a second," the skin around his deep-set eyes tight.

Kensey popped the soft rubber earpieces from her canals. Manny said, "So what just happened here?"

"You mean about you going home?"

"Un-uh, sister. Something to do with Mike showing up your house."

Kensey ignored this, readying the stethoscope a second time. "I've got to listen to you, then get down to emergency."

"Not yet, I said." He waved her off, pushing himself to a standing, tightening the towel around his waist, then pacing the room in his bare feet. "Now I know why you don't look so good." His face looked angry.

"I told you I'm fine."

"You ain't sick. You don't trust me."

"That's not true."

"Oh, yeah?" he said, like he was looking for a fight. "A girl walks into somebody's room and doesn't see him, she goes, 'Hello? Hello?'" His voice with a singsong quality. "'Specially when you hear water running in the john and maybe he's on the can or something." He tramped toward the bathroom as if retracing the steps in a crime, turning to Kensey and catching her eye. "You snuck in and laid a trap for me."

"I did not."

"Yes, you did. So when I cut myself, what'd that tell you? That I was *surprised* to see you?"

"You did seem surprised."

"Like you wouldn't be. I'm all alone in the john, look out in the room and next thing there's someone standing there, spying on me."

"I wasn't spying on you."

"What were you doing?"

"Waiting for you."

"Un-uh. You come into a room, you go 'Hello.' You don't watch someone doing his private business."

The door opened and a candy striper with a mouthful of braces stepped inside. Manny glared at her.

Kensey took the opportunity to meander to the far side of the room, her back to the window, the stethoscope squeezed tightly in her restless hands.

Holding up a sheet of paper, an envelope, and a pen the teenager said, "You wanted these." Manny held out his hand. The girl hurried across the room, an uncomfortable grin on her face, handed the items to him, then scurried back into the hallway.

He waited for the door to close all the way before saying, "Fuck you, you think I'd do that to you." Bringing his gold cross to his lips, he kissed it right away.

Manny remained by the door to the bathroom, Kensey eclipsing the bright light of the sun, a halo of light around her body.

"Don't you talk to me like that."

"I'll talk the way you deserve, Kensey. From the beginning we always been straight with each other. You think I set you up. Goddamn! I shared secrets with you. Dirty secrets that'll probably get me killed." He tossed the writing instruments onto the floor. "I trusted you."

"Then it's just a coincidence that Mike was there in the middle of the day, the same day you told me that it couldn't happen."

"If those things never happened they never woulda invented the word *coincidence*."

"It's a coincidence that almost got me killed." She was crying.

"Fuck you. There, I said it again."

"Would you please sit down on the bed."

"So we done now, huh?" He sat down on the edge of the bed.

Kensey placed the stethoscope in her ears, approached Manny, and listened to his chest. He knew the routine, not saying a word, pulling breaths in slowly, coordinating with Kensey moving the scope around his hairy chest, one inspiration and expiration every time the stethoscope landed.

Manny put his hand on her arm, as he would at a funeral for someone who needed comfort. "I wanted you dead it woulda happened already. I know that story about writing everything down was bullshit first time I heard it. But I made goddamn sure Mike believed it."

Kensey headed toward the door. Over her shoulder she said, "I'll see you tomorrow."

Manny was quick with, "What, you're not coming back?" As if this visit was no different than the others.

"Since you're not going home today, I'll see you in the morning."

"Kensey, hold on."

She was at the door, half-turned around. "I've got to go. I'm late."

"This wasn't s'posed to go like this. I saved you the last pear."

31

Kensey was stretched out on Alec's big leather sofa, her stocking feet on the edge of the coffee table, a glass of wine balanced on her thigh. Her eyes were nowhere in particular, focused somewhere on the wall of photographs behind the silent television. If Alec had to guess, he would have said she was looking at the shot of him holding a giant lobster above his head. He couldn't be sure, standing where he was in the kitchen in front of the refrigerator, crewneck sweater over cuffed khakis, smiling at everything he saw.

Sliding a bottle of Ketel One from the freezer, then pouring it into a wide-mouthed glass, he said, "So what'll it be, Chinese?" Loud enough so she would hear.

Not focusing her eyes, Kensey said, "That's fine." She brought the glass of wine to her lips, holding it there so she could whiff its bouquet if she had the mind to, but not taking a sip.

"That's fine, 'I'm in the mood for Chinese,' or that's fine, 'I don't care what we eat, I'm just gonna stare at the wall?'"

"Huh?" She peered over at him, the glass of wine not moving an inch.

"Kensey, do you want me to order Chinese food for dinner or do you have another suggestion?" He rolled his eyes playfully.

"Chinese. I could always go for dumplings."

"Just so you know, when you're ready to tell me what happened today...."

"Nothing happened." Kensey's gaze flitted around the room.

With a knowing chuckle, Alec turned to the freezer and replaced the bottle of vodka. "Okay, now that I have a portion of your attention, how 'bout we get some noodles, Sichuan string beans, a scallion pancake or two?" He took note of the way Kensey was sitting on the sofa. All of a sudden her shoulders shrugged in an uncomfortable way while her index finger skated the rim of her wineglass. "Maybe it was something that happened with Manny Romero."

She looked at him with eyes that looked like they wanted to cry. "Just like you said, I went into his room this morning."

"You want to tell me?"

"He was shaving. First time he was anywhere except his bed or the chair." There was a break as if she was finding the right words. "I stood there — maybe a minute or two — waiting for him to see me. The TV was on so he didn't hear me come in. He's got this mustache-beard combination so he was being very careful shaving around it. When he spotted me he gave himself quite a nick, had to use a little piece of toilet paper to stop the bleeding."

"What's the first thing he said?"

"'Ouch.' Then he said something like, What're you doing, watching me?"

"Was he shocked to see you?" Alec sipped his vodka as he stood at the kitchen counter.

"I'm not sure. He didn't gasp like he was seeing a ghost. I mean, don't guys cut themselves all the time?"

Alec considered this. "So ... if it was no big deal what happened and you're convinced he didn't set you up for Mike, you would have heard me the first time I asked if you wanted Chinese."

"I was looking at that picture with the lobster. The ones at the Cape aren't that big."

"It was Maine." Alec waited for Kensey to say something. When she didn't he said, "Something else happened."

Pulling her feet from the coffee table, she shifted her body toward the kitchen. "He figured the whole thing out."

"What thing?"

"Why I was there."

"Not unless you told him about Mike." This he said quietly, his voice not giving away how he was feeling.

She looked down at her wine.

"I told you it wasn't a good idea."

"He didn't seem upset that Mike was dead."

"What did he say about ... you?"

"He said ... I'm not the type to sneak into somebody's room and spy on 'em in the bathroom. The only reason I could be doing it was to see his reaction."

"He get pissed?"

"A little. Mostly he was hurt." Kensey took a sip of wine.

Alec joined her on the couch, placing his glass on the table in front of him. "So after all that, any chance it was a setup?"

"No."

"Well, now we know." Alec reached out to stroke Kensey's hair. "What about you, Kensey? You okay?"

She turned her head and kissed Alec's hand. "I'm fine."

"I bet he looks better than you do. How's he doing, anyway?"

"Last night, when we were burying Mike? The on-call resident pulled his chest tube."

Alec sat up and smiled. "Finally. You kicked him out?"

"I should have. He's fine. He insisted he had to rest up for something."

Alec reached out for his vodka. Before he took a sip he said, "So he can make a clean getaway."

"Of course."

"So when's this all over, tomorrow?"

"All day he was telling the nurses the day *after* tomorrow. So many people heard about it I bet he's hoping Sonny'll find out. Even the cop outside his door thinks it's in two days."

"But it's not."

"He wants out tomorrow. And he wants it quiet."

"You gonna miss him?"

"Things are just swirling around in my head."

"Maybe we should talk about it."

Kensey took a long swallow of wine. "If Manny hadn't confessed to me that night, I wouldn't have gone to that church and Father Flaherty would be alive."

"But I'd be dead."

"Exactly. That's why I'm so goddamn confused about my feelings for Manny."

"He tell you where he's going when he gets out?" Alec picked up the remote control and zapped the television to life. The local news was just beginning.

"He's terrified of Sonny. He won't even go home to pick up his truck."

A voice on the television said something about a missing police officer. Instantly the two aimed themselves toward the television to see one of the reporters interviewing Captain Adkins as he was leaving the station, the captain in a dark overcoat, walking to his car, clearly unhappy being ambushed in the parking lot. Captain Adkins was saying, "Detective Dombroski has been under tremendous stress since his partner got shot." Kensey and Alec leaned forward at the same time and watched the scene shift to daylight footage of a narrow street lined with trees and tidy lawns, a city tow truck pulling away from the curb with a beat-up sedan up on two wheels. The reporter, now in voice-over, described how Mike had not reported for work and that his car was discovered abandoned in Highland Park on Bryant Street. Then there was a shot of his official academy photograph, Mike looking young and serious in his new uniform. He was staring down the camera, hair close-cropped and showing a tightly trimmed mustache. On the bottom of the screen was a phone number to call if you had information about his whereabouts.

Kensey said, "I didn't see any car that looked like that."

Now the studio anchor put on a concerned face and asked the street reporter how Detective Romero was doing.

Kensey's eye still on the television, she timed what she was saying so she would hear what they had to say about Manny: "Must've been in the next block."

The reporter looked cold, standing in the middle of the dark parking lot, clutching the microphone with gloved hands. Behind her Captain Adkins was easing his Crown Victoria into the street. "Good news. We just learned Detective Romero will be discharged the day after tomorrow. No word yet on when he'll be returning to work."

Alec whispered, "As long as it wasn't on your street." Pulling his eyes from the TV, he said to Kensey, "Sonny's got to know it now. Day *after* tomorrow." Alec stood. "Another?" He held out his glass.

Kensey handed her wineglass to Alec.

As he headed back toward the kitchen he said over his shoulder, "Let me guess. You're going to discharge him tomorrow night."

"I picked up his truck and parked it in the lot next to the hospital."

Five strides and he was on the other side of the coffee table, looking down at Kensey. "I would have thought that's something you would have told me."

"Please don't use that tone. I didn't tell you 'cause I knew you'd get mad."

"I'm not mad."

"Look in the mirror."

Alec said, "Sorry." He forced himself to take a deep, cleansing breath. "It's just that sometimes you scare the hell out of me with the things you do."

"He's driving straight out of town."

"Goddamn, I don't trust him one bit." He headed back toward the kitchen.

"He's reformed." Kensey glared at Alec, but all she saw was the back of his shirt as he entered the kitchen. "Near-death experiences change people. Don't you know that? I wish you could have met him."

"You know something? I never even saw a picture of him on TV."

"Just before I left at the end of the day I went back to examine him. I was feeling guilty about the whole thing and wanted to, you know—"

"Apologize?" Alec was opening the freezer, getting out the Ketel One.

"No ... make things right." Kensey grinned as she said, "The first thing he said when I walked into the room was, 'Hey, I know you wouldn't spy on me when I was in the john.' Like he'd given it some thought and realized he was crazy for thinking it."

"So what'd you do?"

"I said it was no big deal. Then he lies down on the bed so I can listen to his chest. Two seconds later he taps me on the shoulder and winks at me. *Then* he says, 'So who put you up to it?' He's pretty smart."

Holding the Ketel One in his hand, he stood in the entrance to the kitchen. "What'd you say?"

"Don't worry. I laughed it off."

Alec snatched a cordless phone from the counter. As he punched numbers he repeated, "Scallion pancake, string beans, and some noodles."

"Steamed dumplings. Don't forget." She watched Alec hold the phone next to his ear. "When I was leaving he gave me this huge hug."

"Like he's got the hots for you?"

"No, like when my mom dropped me off at Y camp and wasn't going to see me for two weeks. That kind."

Alec spoke into the phone, "Good evening, this is Alec Fortune." Kensey noticed his voice was different. It had a happy, confident sound to it. "I'd like to place an order..."

■ ■ ■

Ten minutes later Kensey was alone. She was coming out of Alec's kitchen, her glass three-quarters full, the bottle of chardonnay halfway down. She wandered over to the wall of photographs, sipping the wine and lingering over pictures of Alec as a boy with his family. It surprised her how much Alec looked like his father. The two of them deep-sea fishing together, playing golf, and wearing Harvard shirts at a tailgate party.

The end of the news droned on in the background. The sports and weather were being reported in tight little segments. The wine was delicious and she was allowing the glow to work.

Kensey was thinking about Manny, starting to form the plan for tomorrow. Instead of sending him home at night, what if she went to the hospital early— say, six AM— and discharged him when it was still dark? That would work even better. My God, he'd be in West Virginia before anyone would know. Wait a second. What about the uniformed cop? He'd be there. And he'd report it to Captain Adkins.

A door squeaked, then closed. Kensey's head snapped away from the photographs. Standing absolutely stone-still, her breath locked inside her lungs, she glanced toward the front door. It was heavy and paneled and rose up almost as high as the ten-foot ceiling. From across the room she could tell it was not the front door she had heard. That would make a louder noise when it closed. Her eyes drifted toward the kitchen. The bottle of wine was on the counter, the fancy corkscrew close by. The only color in the open kitchen was a wire bowl brimming with clementines. Kensey waited. Someone on the television was predicting the Steelers would go fourteen and two, thirteen and three at the worst. She swiped some hair from her face and felt the wetness on her forehead. Calling out, "Alec, you back with the Chinese?" her voice breezy and casual but the expression on her face showed she was faking it. After a bit, she continued with, "I'll set the table or are we going to eat in front of the TV? I think *Lost* is on tonight." She took several soft steps toward the coffee table, grabbed the remote to silence the television, then stood rigidly still and shut her eyes.

All of a sudden the house seemed to be teeming with sounds. Warm air was rumbling through the system of ducts. Cold wind rattled the maple trees in the yard. A car with a bad muffler drove by. And the hum of the big Sub-Zero refrigerator sounded as if the compressor might be dying.

"Alec?" She heard her voice growing higher pitched. More time went by, maybe thirty seconds; it was hard to tell. "Alec, why aren't you answering me?" This time, fear crept into her voice. Her eyes returned to the front door and immediately strode toward it, depositing her wineglass on the kitchen counter as she passed by. Pulling the heavy door opened, she had a clear view of the dark street over the tightly trimmed box hedges. It would have been reassuring to see someone walking a dog or getting out of a car. She would have waved and called out a greeting. Just to know she wasn't alone.

The street was barren. Parked directly in front was her little Honda. All she had to do was run down the walk and take off.

Venturing onto the front porch, her feet felt the cold through her socks. A low ironwork fence surrounded the porch. Kensey grabbed it and watched the wind trying to shake the last leaves from the trees.

Quietly, so no one could possibly hear, she whispered, "This is ridiculous." Then she stepped inside, carefully leaving the door opened just a crack, just in case.

The wind whistled into the house. Taking measured steps past the kitchen, Kensey ventured toward the rear of the house, away from the bedrooms. Before heading down the carpeted hallway her fingers located a switch that turned on a ceiling lamp. Alec's wood-paneled office was on the left. A single window looked out on the empty driveway. Built-in bookshelves lined one wall. The cozy room was empty.

Several steps down the hall, she reached the laundry room. Kensey eased the door all the way open to see a side-by-side washer and dryer, a sloppy heap of whites on the dryer.

Three steps away was a closed door. Gingerly, she worked the handle. Locked. She called Alec's name. Nothing.

At the end of the hallway was the back door, heavy pine with three narrow panes of fancy cut glass arranged at 45-degree angles in the top half. The little button in the brass knob was tucked into its locked position. An outdoor flood lighted a large brick patio studded with tables and chairs. The wind gusted and a cluster of leaves played tag then quickly scattered from view. Kensey grabbed the handle and shook the door. It was closed tightly in the jamb. She opened it. The hinge let out a squeak. Two times she opened and closed it, concentrating on the noise. It sounded the same. Perhaps. Kensey's eyes darted around. She scanned the patio. It was surrounded by leafy bushes and ornamental trees. Little mushroom lights dotted the perimeter, casting circles of light that blended into one another on the brick.

Pushing the door closed, Kensey headed back toward the lights of the kitchen. She was striding faster now, wondering if she was being silly but deciding to check the other side of the house where the bedrooms were. Maybe she should get her gun. Zipping past the locked door, then the laundry room, three more steps and she passed Alec's wood-paneled office —

That's when he grabbed her from behind, right out of the darkness of Alec's office no more than a heartbeat after she went by. He moved so quickly she didn't have time to react. A flash of blue was all her brain registered before she felt one hand slap over her mouth at the same instant his other arm wrapped around her trunk and squeezed hard enough to accordion the air out of her lungs. His grip on her mouth was strong. Even if she wanted to turn her head to get a look at his face there was no way.

"Don't fuck with me," was all he said as he dragged her backwards into Alec's office. Right away he moved her to the window so he could look out on the driveway. Kensey's face was angled away from the window toward the built-in bookshelves filled with bestsellers and reference books. "I heard him say something about Chinese. Where'd he go, Emperor's Palace?" His arms were bare, the thick hairs irritating her neck enough to make her want to scratch.

Her eyes were out of control in her head, racing in every direction. Screaming into his fleshy hand, she was hardly able to make a peep.

He unwrapped his arm from her trunk and quickly placed the barrel of a gun to her neck. "Listen up, I ain't gonna kill you, you settle down and stop hollering. I wanted you dead it woulda happened already."

Kensey's mind froze on the words he chose. Shoved into that little corner of Alec's study Kensey knew who it was with his hand clamped over her mouth. The voice. The whiff of menthol. And the dense thicket of hair on his arm.

Every goddamn word he ever said to her took on new meaning. She was the loose end. Maybe Alec was too. And how the hell did he find out about Alec?

They waited at the window for several minutes, Manny silent, Kensey breathing through the fingers of his hand, the metallic taste of blood in her mouth, Manny using the floor-length curtains for cover.

And they waited some more, Manny focused, not once drifting his eyes from the driveway, Kensey forced to stare at the dark spines of Alec's books.

Keeping his hand over her mouth, he pulled the gun from her neck. "Try something and I get rough."

Kensey felt his hand worm its way between his chest and her back, then up toward the back of her neck. He pulled away from her for several seconds, his hand moving back and forth as if searching for something. Kensey realized what he was doing. Looking for his cross so he could kiss it.

A second later the hollow sound of a cast-iron frying pan smacking Manny in the head broke the silence. A noise came from his mouth, a single grunt as his life force was knocked sideways. At the same time, Manny released his grip from Kensey's mouth and she inhaled fresh air into her lungs. Slowly he melted to the floor. He was wearing blue surgical scrubs. The way he ended up on his back, one leg curled under the other, gun on the floor, head turned awkwardly to one side, made Kensey cover her mouth with her hand.

Alec said, "Is this—"

Just then Manny started to move. Alec bent over and whacked him on the head a second time. Kensey shrieked, "Stop it. Stop it!"

"That's him, right?" Without waiting for confirmation, he said, "I don't care what you say, this asshole's never getting up." He stood poised with the frying pan above his head as if it was a flyswatter and he was waiting for an insect to land.

Kensey bent down and touched the side of Manny's neck. "Don't worry, his pulse is thready."

Alec thought she sounded angry. "He was gonna kill you. He was gonna kill us."

"I know." Her voice distant. Still kneeling next to Manny she said, "You can put that down. He's not getting up."

Alec squinted at Manny's chest. Every few seconds he took a breath. "You okay?" Alec asked, dropping the heavy pan on the floor. He snatched the gun from the floor, then helped Kensey up and took her in his arms. The two stood very close, Alec rubbing her back, Kensey crying into his shoulder, the room otherwise quiet.

When she pulled away and said, "I'm okay," Alec kissed her. "You were right all along."

He flipped on the lights. Alec took a step to the side and got a good look at Manny's face. "God, I pictured him looking meaner."

"He fooled me."

"I thought he wasn't supposed to get out till tomorrow."

"He must've snuck out." The she added, "He told me he had some unfinished business."

"Why didn't you say something?"

"I didn't think it had anything to do with me."

Gently he stroked her hair. Manny did not move. Every third breath or so he made a grunt that sounded like a snore. Alec said, "I've got some duct tape down in the basement. We'll need something to wrap him in." He stepped back and held Manny's gun out. "You okay to hold this on him?"

Kensey nodded and wrapped her hand around the thick grip.

Alec took several steps toward the hallway before changing his mind and returning to see Kensey holding the weapon sideways, eyeballing it closely. "You okay?"

She nodded.

Alec said, "There's no rush."

"No," Kensey said quickly, "let's get it over with."

"Let me check to see if the safety's off."

Without looking at the weapon she said, "I don't see the red dot."

Alec gently took the weapon from Kensey, flipped it on its side, and worked the safety with his thumb. "How'd you know about the red dot?" Handing it back to her he said, "Be careful." Then he left.

Alone with Manny, Kensey slid the safety on and placed the gun on the desk. She knelt down close enough to touch him. He was breathing slowly, as if in a deep sleep. But something was out of place. Was it the scrubs? And his hair looked different, totally slicked down with shiny pomade. Maybe that was it. Manny Romero looked like someone who worked at the Medical Center.

No. His neck was naked.

From a distant part of the house came Alec's voice. "You okay?"

Kensey called out she was fine. She searched behind the drapes, then in the corner where the bookshelves started. Nothing. She studied his breathing. It was getting noisier, as if he was slipping into a deeper sleep.

After a quick glance toward the door she slipped her hand under Manny's shoulder and rolled him several inches to the side. There was not a drop of blood on the carpet.

"What are you doing?" Alec was in the doorway, a thick roll of gray duct tape in his hand.

"I was looking for his cross. I thought it might've come off when he fell. He never took it off."

"Is he alive?"

Manny's mouth was half open and the tip of his tongue was oozing out. "See his tongue hanging out like that. It's called the Q sign. Means he's really out of it."

"When's it gonna happen?"

"Soon. Alec?"

"What?"

She turned toward the desk. "The safety was on."

"It doesn't matter."

Manny let out a snore. Kensey and Alec looked down to see his skin turning ashen.

Kensey said, "It means something."

"I know what you're thinking and you're wrong. He was here for business. Not to scare us."

"If he was planning to kill me why was the safety on?"

"A guy like him, a pro, one flick of his thumb and it's off."

"I guess."

"Kensey ... you're his unfinished business."

"He never looked at me or said my name. Not once."

"You want to believe he's a great guy, go ahead." Alec's voice was louder now, making a point. "But he's a killer and if you weren't here his next stop would've been your house."

"How'd you sneak up on him anyway?"

"The front door was open. I saw it from the street. It seemed like maybe something was wrong so I parked next door. I could hear him talking from the kitchen."

With a loud *rrrrrrrip*, Alec yanked a length of tape from the roll and knelt down next to Manny.

"What're you gonna do with that?"

"Put it over his mouth."

"It'll kill him," Kensey said.

"He's dying."

"Listen to me, I despise what he stands for and how he deceived me. I wish he was dead. But I don't want you to kill him."

"He's got to die right here, right now, then this whole thing's over. Pretty soon Sonny forgets it ever happened."

"Then I want to wait with him."

Manny's chest heaved and he took a noisy breath. Bloody mucous hung from one of his nostrils and it moved in and out with his breathing.

"I'm okay with that. But I'm securing his hands and feet, just in case."

The roll of duct tape was on the floor. "Let me do it, Alec. Please. You hold his hands." Alec held Manny's hands together like he was praying. Kensey pulled off some tape, wrapped it around his wrists, then wound the roll around and around until she was satisfied they were secure. The process was repeated for his feet.

"Let's leave him alone," he said and began to lead her from the room. "We'll wait in the living room."

"No," she said. "I'm staying."

At that moment an awful choking sound came from Manny's mouth, his tongue getting in the way of the air moving in and out. His chest was heaving and suddenly his arms were wrestling with the tape.

After three deep guttural sounds, Manny stopped moving, his chest at peace.

Without hesitation Kensey dropped to his side, took his pulse at the side of his neck, and placed her ear next to his mouth. She shook him. "C'mon Manny, breathe," she said in a loud voice. She shook him again.

"Kensey, it's over."

She looked up at Alec. He could see tears coming down her cheeks. He watched helplessly as Kensey leaned over Manny and began CPR, forcing her breath into his mouth, then compressing his chest half-a-dozen times, another breath followed by more compressions. Again she said, "Manny, breathe," in a loud voice but Alec could hear a quality that signaled she knew it was over. Another thirty seconds of breathing for him and compressing his heart and she gave up.

"Where the hell is his cross?" She looked up at Alec.

"I don't know. I'm sorry."

"We cover him up with a sheet. A nice one. Bury him in it. The way he would want."

"Anything you say."

"One more thing."

"Just tell me."

"I want to do the digging."

32

Riding the hospital elevator up to seven the next morning, all Kensey could think about was what had happened after Manny stopped breathing. Alec had placed another glass of wine in her hand and told her to drink up, she was that upset.

Alec was sitting close to her, his hand around her shoulders, fingers gently stroking her neck the way her mother had done on those concrete steps outside her dormitory. After some time went by and the wine was working he said, "First thing you do tomorrow morning is go up to his room, walk in like you do every day, stand in there maybe ten seconds, then come back to the nurses' station and say something like, 'Hey, where's Detective Romero?' But you gotta sound confused. It's important."

Turning to look him dead in the eye she said, "Goddamnit, not now, Alec, okay?" She tasted vomit in the back of her throat.

But now, in the elevator, she was thinking it was a pretty smart thing to do, especially because they couldn't find his car keys or his truck in the dark and maybe Hennessey would show up asking questions.

The shiny elevator doors opened. Kensey stepped off and moved down the hallway, not looking into the nurses' station, trying to walk the exact way she did every morning going from the elevator to Manny's room. Everything was working the way she hoped it would until she bumped into an old man on a stretcher and had to apologize and wait with him until the orderly came and wheeled him away.

The little chair the uniformed cop sat in to guard Manny was right where it always was, empty this morning, a copy of yesterday's *Post-Gazette* folded underneath beside an empty container of coffee. Not looking back toward the nurses' station, Kensey pushed the door open, stepped inside, saw the unmade bed and the empty windowsill except for a single pear right in the middle. Three empty Coke cans rested on a stack of magazines on the bedside table. For a long second she thought about crying. She went into the bathroom, spotted his toothbrush, and reached out to touch his razor.

Back in the room she opened the drawer on the bedside table. Mostly it was empty, just some napkins and a pack of gum and —

The door opened. A nurse with short hair and a pimply nose leaned into the room. "Didn't anyone call you?"

Before Kensey had a chance to say, Why, what happened? the nurse opened the door all the way and slipped inside. "He signed himself out last night, just after you left. The cop who sits outside at night, Eddie? Says he went to the bathroom and Detective Romero was gone when he got back. I'm sorry."

"No one saw him?"

The nurse shook her head. "He left an envelope with your name on it, leaning against that pear." The nurse looked at the windowsill. "I've got it out at the nurses' station."

Kensey snatched the pear before she followed the nurse into the hallway, listening to her say, "Poor Eddie. I came on at eleven and he was still checking the hospital up and down. Around midnight he had to get on the phone and explain to someone how he had horrible diarrhea and must have been in the bathroom when the detective snuck out. After he hung up the phone he walked out without saying a word. I thought he was gonna cry. He just waited for the elevator, never looked at us for one second."

The envelope was taped to the front of Manny's chart. It was a long white one, thick at the bottom, hinting there was more than just a letter inside. On the front it said *Dr. Shaw* in block letters. Kensey slipped into a chair on the far side of the station, away from the unit clerk and the nurses having their morning coffee. She read the letter.

Dear Kensey,

I know I should have told you I was leaving but you would only worry. Remember that day we saw you know who on the TV wearing a hardhat for the children's hospital? Well for a second I thought you knew who he was. I bet he's the big news today. Everything makes sense don't it? <u>No unfinished business</u>.

Manny Rodriquez Romero

P.S. I had this cross when I was eleven. Maybe someday you and me will see each other again. I hope.

Kensey placed the letter on the desk. She poured Manny's cross and chain from the envelope into her hand and wrapped her fingers around it.

"You don't have to show it to me if you don't want." Frank Hennessey was pulling up a chair and helping himself to a seat. Kensey could smell his aftershave. It smelled nice, not perfumy like you get at a drugstore. The detective looked around, nodded at one of the nurses, then let his eyes settle on Kensey.

She noticed he didn't have anything to eat with him. "Before you ask, Detective, I don't have any idea where he went."

"Did you have any idea he was planning to escape?"

Kensey shook her head. "Of course not. What he did, leaving against medical advice? It's not against the law, you know."

"I know. But he was the focus of an active investigation."

"Tell me something. Do you know for sure what he did?"

"Detectives Romero and Dombroski had been partners in a squad car until four years ago. That's when they went undercover. His partner was always too razzmatazz for me." Frank gave a dismissive wave of his hand. "Anyway, these undercover guys get into situations the brass doesn't even want to know about. Sometimes their investigations put them in the same room with piles of money. So what if there's a thousand bucks missing when they close the case. It's hard to prove and nobody goes looking for it. But with these two it happened more than it should have. The shooting at Cheap Charlie's that brought him here? Not even the captain had a clue they were investigating someone there. Too many things about the story didn't feel right. That's why I got involved."

"And when he sneaks out at night ..."

"You gotta wonder."

Kensey slipped the gold cross into the side pocket of her white coat. Detective Hennessey watched her hand emerge empty. "Well, I didn't know."

"What happened to your hand?"

Bringing her hand up for a nonchalant glance, Kensey smiled. "It's nothing. Just a blister."

"Let me see." Frank reached out and his hand hung in the air between them for one, two, three seconds. It was getting close to the point where he would have to pull it back empty if she didn't do something.

Kensey placed her hand, palm up, in his. Grasping her hand gently, he examined her palm like a fortune-teller reading the future. Centered almost perfectly between the base of her thumb and pinky was a quarter-sized open blister, the base red and raw. Frank examined it closely. "This is going to get infected."

"I'm fine. Really," she said, her hand still nestled comfortably in his.

Catching the eye of one of the nurses, Frank said, "Do you have some Neosporin and a Band-Aid?"

The nurse hopped right out of her seat and before Kensey could offer much of a protest the items were delivered to Frank.

As he opened the yellow packet of Neosporin and squeezed a wiggly worm of antibiotic goo onto her wound, he said, "You doing manual labor when you're not saving lives?"

"*Nooooo.*" She drew out the word in a friendly sort of way, as if there might be an amusing anecdote how she got such an awful sore.

Fixing the Band-Aid to her skin and gently tamping the middle down to spread the medicine, he asked, "Does it hurt?"

"No, I'm fine." Her eyes lifted to his face. Frank was looking at her. "Thanks." She smiled uneasily. "I guess I should take my hand back."

"Oh." He sounded embarrassed and quickly released his grip. "So," Frank said, buying some time while he considered his words, "I don't know if you noticed, but I was talking with one of the nurses when you stepped off the elevator."

Kensey shook her head.

"If you walked into Detective Romero's room thinking he was there and he wasn't, I would've thought you'd be back out before the door closed wondering where the heck he was."

"I looked in the bathroom. That's all. I was heading to the door when one of the nurses—"

"It just seemed like you were in there a long time." Frank placed his hands on his knees like he was going to stand up. "Well … something tells me we're not going to be hearing from either one of them again."

"I guess the same for you and me."

"I'll call it progress you're not smiling when you said that."

That made her smile. She cocked her head to the side and for a second she looked like she was enjoying the moment. "Look, Detective, he told me as soon as he got out of here he was heading south and was going to keep going until he couldn't go farther."

"That cross he wore, I know it was special to him. He give it to you?"

"Yes." Kensey swallowed hard.

"All this time you were hating me, I was thinking more about protecting you than making an arrest."

"I didn't hate you."

"Yes, you did." In a whisper he asked, "Did Dombroski have seizures?"

"I don't know."

"C'mon. We're in the locker room."

Kensey rubbed her forehead. "From what you told me it was tetanus."

Frank thought about this. He leaned closer toward Kensey and she didn't pull away. "Like maybe if he cut himself on a rusty nail over at the church?"

"That's exactly how something like that could happen."

"Is that why he came to see you in the Emergency Department?"

"Please."

Frank nodded. "Last thing, something I thought you'd want to know. Before I came here, I went over to Detective Romero's place. You know, look around. I ran into a kid named Mad Dog catching a smoke between the houses."

Kensey's eyes widened.

Frank caught her pupils dilating, quickly adding, "No way you'd know a kid like that, just a punk who lived next door. Anyway, I asked him did he see Detective Romero last night. You know what he said?" He watched Kensey shake her head. "Last night his doorbell rings and there's Detective Romero putting a crisp fifty in his hand."

"Oh my God," she said.

"Something about staying in school."

"What a nice story."

"That's nothing." Frank waited for Kensey to wipe something from her eye. "Then the kid said Manny handed his mother five thousand bucks, said it was so he could go to college."

"Then what?" Kensey's voice was thick.

"Then he drove off into the night, never even went into his own house."

Kensey blinked some more, right before a tear escaped and trickled down her cheek, making its way toward her little mole. Frank reached out and wiped it away.

The nurse with the short hair approached, stopping far enough away to show she realized she was intruding on a private conversation. "Excuse me, Kensey, but they're calling from emergency, wondering where you are."

"Tell them..." She had to pause to clear her voice. Giving it a second try she said, "Tell them I'll be right there." Now turning to Frank she said, "Thank you for telling me that ... Frank. I mean it." Then she pushed out of her chair and hurried toward the elevator.

"Kensey," Frank called. "Don't forget your letter." It was still on the counter where she'd left it.

Kensey retreated, snatched the note, said, "See you, Frank," and quickly tri-folded it as she stepped on the elevator.

33

They were eating sushi on little plates in the room with the big television, a bottle of champagne on the coffee table, Kensey still working on her first glass, Alec on his third. Next to the bottle was Manny's gold cross, the chain coiled up in a little pile like a gilded snake. Neither of them was paying attention to the local news, a series of commercials running between segments.

All this while Alec was saying, "There wasn't a note or anything?"

Kensey said, "No, just the cross in a white envelope. My name was on the front."

"That's weird."

She said, "What?" right away, as if she'd been waiting for him to say it.

"Manny taking the time to get an envelope and leave you his cross without a note or anything."

"Oh." Kensey popped a piece of pink salmon into her mouth.

"Oh." He imitated the way she said it. "You sound surprised." Alec looked casual in jeans and a white rugby shirt.

Kensey had come directly from the hospital, her bag dropped on the sofa next to her, not yet in stocking feet. "I didn't know what you meant."

"You didn't think that was weird? The cross in the envelope."

"I guess."

"Not because of the note."

"No." Kensey sipped her champagne, glancing at something on the television. "Oh my God." She moved to the front of the cushion.

At the bottom of the screen were the words *Officer's Car Found*, and the scene was of a wooded area, the headlights from half-a-dozen cop cars illuminating a heavy-duty tow truck driving away with a beat-up pickup truck. Immediately the camera shifted to a female street reporter in a ski parka with the news logo over her breast. She was describing how the truck belonged to Detective Manny Romero, who had left the Medical Center against medical advice sometime yesterday. Behind the reporter several cops were climbing into their cars and pulling away.

The reporter was saying that the pickup was discovered on Overhill Road, a private road off —

"Shit. That's right behind here." Alec got up on his knees and turned around on the cushion so he could put his face up against the big picture window that looked out over his backyard. Instantly he was leaving an oval of condensation with his breath. "You can see the headlights through the woods. My God, he came through the backyard."

"We never drove back there …." Kensey's voice drifted into silence. Just then Frank Hennessey walked behind the reporter on the television, looking like one of those fancy TV detectives in a stylish topcoat. Briefly the reporter turned toward Frank as if she had a question to ask him, but he kept moving until he was off-camera.

Alec was staring at Kensey, aware her jaw was hanging open. If her champagne flute weren't on its way to empty she would be spilling it all over the carpet. "Is that the guy? Hennessey?" Still on his knees, he placed his hands on Kensey's shoulders and massaged gently.

Kensey held her breath. "That's him."

"You're not worried, are you?"

She shook her head. "Oh, that feels good."

Alec could feel the muscles in her neck soften as he increased the pressure. After awhile he said, "So what if he comes here. We don't have anything to hide. There wasn't a single drop of blood. I vacuumed the hell out of the carpet today. He must have picked the lock 'cause there's no sign of him breaking in. At worst they'd figure he came by and left without getting inside. Hell, I'd invite him in."

Kensey turned suddenly and said, "That's not a good idea. Please don't do that."

"Okay, I won't," he said softly. "I promise." He eased her head down so she was looking into her lap. With his hands on her shoulders he was using his thumbs to knead the muscles running up the back of her neck. "You know this is over, Kensey. No one can hurt us." When Kensey didn't respond, Alec said, "Why *did* you think it was weird with the cross?"

"If he was planning to kill me why bother with the cross?"

"Okay, maybe he was just after me. What difference does it make now?"

"Why would he come after you?"

"To shut me up."

"If he knew he had to shut you up, then he knew I would be here. He didn't say one word to me."

"So why did he come?"

Kensey looked up at him. "I don't know."

Alec stopped massaging and sat next to her. "You don't think he felt an obligation to finish the job he was hired for in the first place?"

"Not on your life," she said strongly enough that Alec would know not to challenge.

"What if it wasn't his idea?"

"Sonny?"

"Exactly. What if Sonny got to Manny before he left the hospital?"

"You mean like the cop who was guarding him, or Captain Adkins."

"Or Hennessey. Says all is forgiven if he kills me."

Shaking her head, she said, "What happened to him in the hospital transformed him."

"No way to know."

"I guess."

While Alec poured some champagne into her glass he said, "So, we're going to the country tomorrow, right?"

"Absolutely." Kensey smiled.

"My dad may be up there with us, do a little hunting."

"Separate bedrooms?"

"I'm a big boy."

"Good. I liked your dad."

Alec got up and headed past the kitchen toward the back door. "I got a little surprise for you," he called over his shoulder.

Kensey rolled her eyes. She could hear the squeak of the back door opening and then closing. It reminded her of Manny and she reached out for the gold cross and clasped it in her hand.

The phone rang. Kensey craned her neck to look out the picture window. She could see Alec leaning into the tiny backseat of his Porsche. Putting down her flute and hustling to the kitchen, she grabbed the cordless on the fourth ring.

"Hello?" she said in a voice that announced she was answering someone else's phone. Tentative. At the same time she was leaning over the counter to look down the hallway to see if Alec had made it back inside. Listening for no more than a second or two, she suddenly snapped to attention and whipped her head around. "Excuse me?" She nearly let the phone slip out of her fingers.

She managed to keep the phone to her ear a few moments longer, one hand on her forehead. "It's Kensey," she said, then was silent, waiting for the other person to speak. Finally: "Oh, I didn't know anyone ever called him that." Turning toward the back hallway she saw Alec coming through the door, clothing box in hand, the word *Orvis* inscribed on the cardboard in green letters. He had a wide smile on his face.

"Who is it?" he whispered, coming into the kitchen. He placed the box on the counter.

"He's here now," Kensey said into the phone, then holding out the phone to him, whispered, "It's your dad."

Alec took the phone and immediately said, "Hey, Dad," but it looked as if he was eyeballing Kensey as she stumbled out of the kitchen into the great room and over to the big leather sofa. Almost immediately she tried to get absorbed in whatever was on the television.

In the kitchen Alec was saying, "Don't worry about it." Kensey was looking devastated, like a person who had just found out her loved one wasn't going to make it. Then Alec said, "Anyway, we're going up when Kensey's finished with her shift at the hospital. I got her that jacket from Orvis. I think she'll like it."

When the conversation was over, Alec placed the phone on the counter and scrutinized her. She was sitting on the edge of the sofa, hands gripping the cushion like a runner in the starting blocks. "My dad and those nicknames, I warned him. He's excited to see you." He opened a clear plastic box on the counter, popped a piece of sushi into his mouth, and carried the opened box into where Kensey was sitting.

"I've got two more pieces of yellowtail and three salmon. The tuna's better, don't you think?" He said this as he crossed the room, the top of the container bouncing gently each time he took a step.

Kensey was staring at the television. Or the wall. Or nowhere at all. Slowly, she rotated her head back and forth.

Alec responded: "No? I'll keep it out. Maybe you'll change your mind. They're no good the next day." He sat down, Kensey not reacting, hands together on her lap Catholic-schoolgirl style, posture perfect, ramrod-straight, eyes intent on the wall of photographs. "Which one are you looking at?"

Kensey did not answer or move.

Alec could see she was trembling. He reached for his drink and took a swallow. Holding the delicate flute in front of him so he could admire it he said, "I should give up vodka for this." Then, looking at Kensey: "Too bad we don't have something to celebrate every day, you know?" He was seeing Kensey in profile, jaw tensed, upper lip curled, eyes refusing to blink. Now focusing his attention on the wall of photographs, he said, "You looking at that one in the corner?" He was referring to a beautifully framed blowup of Alec in between his dad and one of the Pittsburgh Steelers with a big 58 on his jersey.

"That's Jack Lambert. Remember him? Meanest sonofabitch you ever saw play the game. My dad knew someone who knew him. One night he came over to play cards with my dad and his buddies. I came down the stairs with Dad's Steelers jersey and Jack put it on so we could take the picture. See? It's way too tight. Afterwards, he did all sorts of funny muscleman poses and ballet twirls." Alec took a swig of the champagne, smiling at the way it tasted. "What a guy."

Kensey had not budged for several minutes now.

Alec placed his hand on her back and rubbed gently. Her shoulders went up as if she had gotten a sudden chill. "Hey, look, I'm sorry you're so upset. He's a bit of a silly old goat. I told you that. That's why I tried to warn him not to embarrass me with nicknames that are a thousand years old."

Kensey wriggled her back. "Don't."

"I thought you liked that."

Kensey still had not looked at him.

"One time I was on a blind date and ran into him in a restaurant just like you and I did the other night. I must've been about twenty-five. He told the girl all the men in the family have big penises." While he enjoyed a chuckle and a bit of champagne Kensey turned to stare at him. Her eyes were red. "Hey, you okay?" Now she turned away. "God, he had a million nicknames for me. For a while he was calling me Pigsty. I never made my bed. Then I was Romeo in the seventh grade 'cause I had a girlfriend who was a year older. Of course Alexander whenever I got in trouble. I guess that's not a nickname. He practically never called me Alec."

Not looking his way she asked, "What's your dad's first name?" Her voice was soft, the way people talk at funerals.

"Alec. Same as mine. I thought you knew that." His eyes squinted just a bit as if he was confused by the question.

"No. You always referred to him as your dad."

"That's what he is to me. Dad. Actually, the original name of the business was Alec Fortune and Company. After I moved back to Pittsburgh I joined him and worked my way up from salesman. When I made it to VP he wanted to change the name of the company to Alec Fortune and Son, but everyone started making jokes that it would be confusing, you know, the *N* and the *Y* missing like it was a typo."

Kensey sniffed in like she was holding back tears.

"Listen to me, Kensey. It's going to be okay. Nothing's different between you'n me. We just have to talk some things out."

"I never could figure why that guy didn't have bullets in his gun."

"What guy?" Alec sounding warm and syrupy.

"In the garage. I thought you were so brave." She wiped her eyes.

"So many times I wanted to tell you, I swear. Once we talk, it's going to make sense. I swear. Let me get you a Kleenex."

Tears were running down her cheeks. Alec wiped one away with his hand. "Don't bother. I got one here." Pulling her bag on to her lap, she rummaged through it. "Shit."

"Wait," he said and hurried into the kitchen. As he returned with a box of tissues, he saw Kensey standing between the sofa and the coffee table.

"Don't come any closer." Now she showed the Beretta.

His arms shot out, palms toward her. "Whoa, we're on the same team, Kensey."

"You were using me the whole time."

"Not true. I fell in love with you the first day I met you. You were so courageous and vulnerable at the same time. And your little mole. My God, I wanted to put my arms around you."

"Shut up … shut the hell up."

"Okay, that's fine, whatever you say. You've got the gun."

Kensey and Alec were standing eight feet apart, staring at each other. Finally Kensey said, "Sit on the sofa. Go real slow."

Taking his first step, he said, "I'm going slow. Slow is the way I'm going. So what happens now? How the heck're we gonna sit down and talk this whole thing out you holding a gun on me?"

"I know why Seymour Rosen was on the list. Why was your dad?"

Alec eased himself onto the sofa. Before he said another word he chugged the rest of his champagne. "It's a business decision, pure and simple. He owns every goddamn share of stock in our corporation and pays himself a million dollars a year. But he hasn't set foot in the office since the day I took over. He's bleeding us to death." He held his hand up as if she was about to interrupt and needed to be silenced. "I know, I know, you think it sounds greedy. But hear me out. My father is no saint. Remember those companies I told you about? The ones that went belly-up and we took over so we could fix 'em up. Well, guess what. Dear old Dad worked the books on those companies, making it look like they were going bankrupt. My approach is faster."

"Shut up. I've got to think."

"Call the cops. Go ahead. Hey, got the red dot showing?"

In an instant she flipped the gun on its side and scanned it quickly. "Yep. I can't do the safety with my thumb like the pros. I need two hands."

"Do you really think you could shoot someone?"

"Last night I would have squeezed the trigger if I thought Manny was about to hurt you. This isn't going to be a problem."

"Okay, do it. No more talk. Just cross that line in the sand and squeeze one off. Before you go wipe down everything. Don't forget the bathroom, kitchen. Christ, you better hire a cleaning crew. With Romero's car four hundred yards from here it won't take long for some enterprising cop to knock on your door and want to talk with you."

Kensey pivoted slightly and squeezed off a round in the direction of the television, putting a bullet in the right upper corner. The screen immediately went dark.

"Now you owe me eight thousand bucks."

At that moment Frank Hennessey appeared from the hallway leading to the bedrooms. His topcoat was unbuttoned. Underneath he was wearing a suit with a red tie.

The first thing Kensey did was look over at Alec on the sofa. He had a big grin on his face and was in the process of crossing his legs in a casual way.

Taking two steps back so she could keep an eye on both of them, Kensey said, "Goddamn you," to Frank.

"Hey," he said. "I'm on your side."

She was moving the gun back and forth, covering both of them. "Give me one reason why I should believe you."

"My gun's holstered."

"Pull it out and shoot him."

"There's no reason to shoot anyone. And if you pull the trigger, I'll arrest you."

"Look, if you're not involved in this thing, get the hell out of here."

"Hey, Detective," Alec said. "Why don't you arrest *her* before she shoots me?"

"Shut up," Kensey said. Then to Frank: "What are you doing here, anyway?"

"I was taking the same walk Manny Romero took last night."

"I mean in the house."

"Through the window I saw you with the gun. Manny came here last night, didn't he?"

"Yes," Kensey said. "It didn't make sense until now."

Frank eyed Alec. "Why'd he come?"

Kensey said, "To kill his boss."

Alec said, "Fuck you."

Nodding his head toward Alec, Frank said, "That's why you were in his room so long, making it look like a surprise."

"I knew and I didn't know."

"How about if I call this in. That make you believe me?"

"No."

"I will arrest you."

"I heard you." She glanced at him. "You don't know what I've been through."

"I'm listening." Frank took a step toward her.

"Stay where you are, Frank. Don't make me kill him."

"Why?"

"The only two people who know what the hell happened are dead. And I have no idea where we buried them." Then to Alec: "You know what the worst thing is? Your dad's going to find out what you were going to do to him. And I don't believe the crap about him running a scam."

"Detective, I'm getting up and you better protect me."

Frank said to Alec, "Stay put, sir," but Alec was scooching forward on the cushion, shifting his weight to his legs — *Bang*. The Beretta sounded. Alec shot backwards into the sofa as his shirt grew crimson with blood.

Kensey lowered the weapon. "The end." She said it loud. Then turning to Frank, she added, "You can pull your gun and shoot me or arrest me. I don't care."

Epilogue

Kensey arrived early at the restaurant, ordered a glass of wine, and kept an eye on the door. The last two days had been wild. Seven hours at the police station. And then there were the reporters. Dozens of them. *The Today Show* came to interview her. Her mother would be there first thing in the morning. Just the thought of going through everything that had happened another time exhausted her. Having to talk about how Frank happened by the window and realized Alec was holding a gun on her. Then Frank somehow snuck in through one of the bedroom windows and surprised Alec, wrestling the Beretta away from him and eventually shooting him with it when he grabbed a Glock that was hidden under the sofa.

And Frank confirmed every word she said. Except for the part about being a hero.

Now the door opened and Kensey was smiling as Frank came across the restaurant, dressed casually, a grin out to here. She sprung from her chair and met him halfway. She gave him a hug and right then and there he held her cheeks and kissed her for the first time.

Author Biography

Jim Tucker was raised in Elkins Park, Pennsylvania. After studying mechanical and civil engineering at Tufts University in Boston he attended Columbia University College of Physicians and Surgeons in New York City.

He completed his internship and residency in pediatrics at The Children's Hospital of Pittsburgh and has been in private practice ever since.

Jim has pursued a life-long interest in magic. Years ago he co-owned a restaurant called Hog Island Hoagies in Pittsburgh that specialized in Philadelphia-style hoagies and cheese steaks – a money pit that served great food. He has run the New York City Marathon twice. Now Jim's an avid golfer and plays platform tennis during the winter. For the past 5 years he has taken up glassblowing.

His wife, Kim, is also a pediatrician. They have three sons and one grandson.

Jim has also written the Jack Merlin series, **Abra Cadaver, Hocus Corpus** and **Tragic Wand**. All are available on Kindle as well as in paperback through Amazon.

Made in the USA
Middletown, DE
17 November 2022